Rivertown Heroes

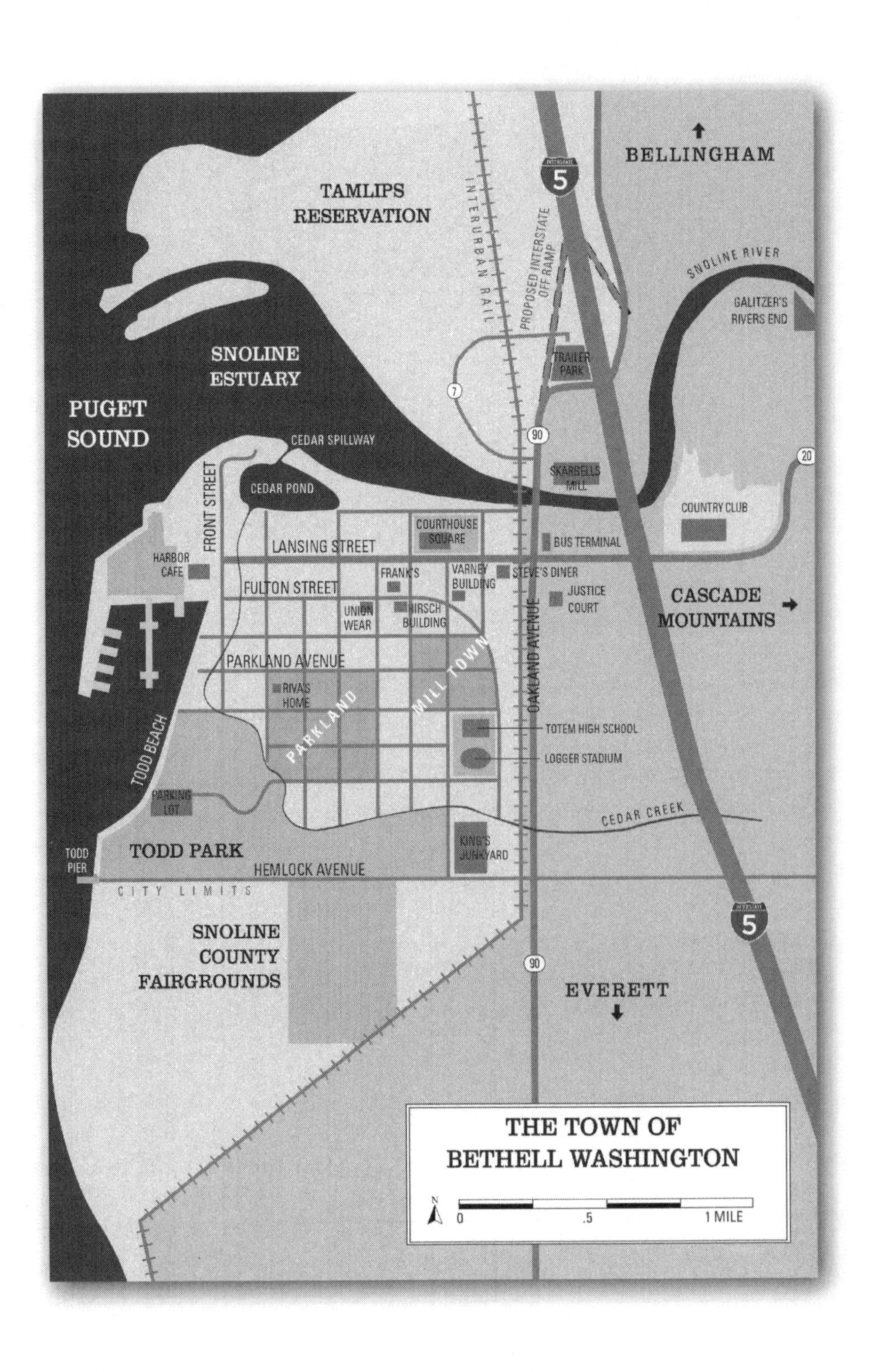
BELLINGHAM
TAMLIPS RESERVATION
INTERURBAN RAIL
INTERSTATE 5
PROPOSED INTERSTATE OFF RAMP
SNOLINE RIVER
GALITZER'S RIVERS END
SNOLINE ESTUARY
TRAILER PARK
7
PUGET SOUND
90
CEDAR SPILLWAY
20
SKARBELLS MILL
CEDAR POND
FRONT STREET
COUNTRY CLUB
COURTHOUSE SQUARE
LANSING STREET
BUS TERMINAL
HARBOR CAFE
FRANK'S
VARNEY BUILDING
STEVE'S DINER
FULTON STREET
JUSTICE COURT
UNION WEAR
KIRSCH BUILDING
CASCADE MOUNTAINS
PARKLAND AVENUE
MILL TOWN
OAKLAND AVENUE
RIVAS HOME
PARKLAND
TOTEM HIGH SCHOOL
TODD BEACH
LOGGER STADIUM
PARKING LOT
CEDAR CREEK
TODD PARK
KING'S JUNKYARD
TODD PIER
HEMLOCK AVENUE
CITY LIMITS
SNOLINE COUNTY FAIRGROUNDS
5
90
EVERETT
THE TOWN OF BETHELL WASHINGTON
N
0
.5
1 MILE

Rivertown Heroes

A NOVEL

* * *

Mike Cohen

ISBN-13: 9781532879258
ISBN-10: 1532879253
Library of Congress Control Number: 2016906720
CreateSpace Independent Publishing Platform
North Charleston, South Carolina

Contents

Prologue

* * *

I CAN CONJURE UP MY hometown Bethell, Washington, by shutting my eyes and imagining I am a child again, settling my rear on a swing seat—the swing set in Bethell's Todd Park, a green forest jewel on rushing Cedar Creek. I can feel the rough wooden slats of the seat under my thighs as I clutch the iron chains hanging from the frame. I am restless, yearning to see Bethell from the sky in the moments before the summer sun sets.

I urge myself up into the air with breathless grunts, arms driving at the chain links, legs stretching straight in front. As the pull of gravity propels me faster, I become an airborne piston veering upward, a leg-powered engine, panting with anticipation for that moment of weightlessness at the pinnacle.

The speed forces wind into my mouth. I bend and stretch, and I go yet faster and rise higher. Dogs chase me, but as I bend and pull, bend and pull, I fly above them all.

My pendular arc expands. I raise myself upright on the seat, as if it were a viewing platform. Below me is the township of Bethell. Cedar Creek guides summer waters over a spillway, down into the Snoline River estuary and out into salty Puget Sound. While I pump away, perhaps five thousand souls—Bethell citizens, men, women, and children—prepare for evening meals in the waning slanted light.

I can also see the filigreed light poles up and down Lansing Street. They lead to Courthouse Square near Oakland Avenue. There, one block south on Fulton Street, sits the Hirsch Building, constructed long ago by my grandfather,

Zayde Albert. The old red bricks, trimmed by yellowing and chipped terra-cotta, are illuminated above the cement sidewalk.

To the south of Fulton Street is Parkland, my neighborhood. I am transported there, past the tree-lined streets, up the house steps, and inside, into my first bedroom, a dormered nook with wallpaper covered with frogs, muskrats, and moles. My window peers out on our laurel hedge below and the alleyway beyond. From my window I can see across Bethell, all the way back to Todd Park, thus completing on a spectral summer night a fabric of memory and light woven into and through me like the blood vessels of my own body.

From above the elms and firs of Todd Park, I see them: my family and our friends, all there on the hot end of an August Sunday. The park hums with families and parties like ours, but not like ours.

Our family—my father and mother, Leon and Pearl Hirsch; my older brother, Ritchie; and my unmarried aunt, Riva Hirsch—has traveled here together in our Packard, windows down in the heat. Our companions' autos arrive at the same time. As always, we all park in the southwest corner of the dusty parking lot and unpack. Each time, we carry our gear to a particular clump of fir trees with picnic tables assembled around a stone fireplace near the children's playground.

The families who accompany my Hirsch relatives each Sunday are the Raskins, the Ashers, the Galitzers, the Guthmans, and sometimes the Kings. All immigrant Jewish families, each with a unique saga of origin, travail, and arrival in this summer paradise on the banks of Puget Sound in the Eden-like estuary of the Snoline River, its royal trees and soft animal cries a welcoming and comforting presence, like the amen at the end of a prayer.

I know each person in our group as a kind of relative. I have been instructed to call the adults in our group by the title "Auntie" or "Uncle," although my only real kin among them is my auntie, Riva Hirsch. We bear a certain connection to one another that I unconsciously grasp and appreciate. There is a trust among us on these Sundays in the park, a common way of manner and of speech. There is an acceptance, a safety that is ours exclusively. In this company we are not different, and we are safe.

As little as I am, I know that World War II is over. My father, whom I had known only as a photo of a soldier who went away, now has become real and has returned home to Bethell. My mother looks at my father with eyes I have not seen before. Even in the park with the other families close by, my parents hug each other in a different way than they hug me.

We children play in the sun under our parents' watchful eyes. My mother delivers cautionary directives as I race away.

"Nathan," she admonishes, "slow down. Be careful on the playground." Knowing that she keeps an eye on me, I experience an incalculable joy; spontaneous laughter pours out of me. I jump and whoop with the pleasure of being near my mother.

The women are wearing rhinestone-trimmed sunglasses and cotton sundresses in shades of lemon and raspberry. Their pump shoes of straw and painted toenails step softly on the cut grass.

My father and my so-called uncles play catch with intensity, my older brother, Ritchie, with them. Stripped down to their ribbed undershirts, the men wear their pleated workday pants, some held up by suspenders. All have hats, some felt, some straw. The brims shroud their faces in the bright light, but I can still recognize each from afar, their darkened brows; strong, prominent noses; and wary, deep-set eyes. The cigarettes and cigars clenched in their teeth glow and smoke as baseballs whoosh in the air and pop into gloves. They are home now from the four corners of the earth, no more rifles to clean, no more uniforms to iron, no more shoes to shine.

Coals burn orange in fireplaces made of smooth river rock. Freshly made hamburgers—my mother calls them *ku kletin*—and Hebrew National wieners are laid out on wax paper, plump and crimson, waiting for the barbecue coals to burst into flames.

Wooden picnic tables—one for children, one for adults—have been covered with red-and-white checkered tablecloths and then smothered with plates mounded with white-bread buns, coleslaw, Jell-O salad molds, mason jars of homemade dill pickles, and containers of French's mustard and Heinz ketchup. A feast for summer's kings.

We boys are clad only in shorts and tennis shoes. We scamper about shouting. Our skin is summer freckled and nut-brown. Arlene Asher is the only girl with us, but she is as lively as the boys. She races about in a dress made of the same calico as that of her mother, Claire.

In a pack we frenetically leap from playground apparatus to apparatus. We whip about the merry-go-round, shoving the platform faster and faster, suddenly jumping on and precipitously leaping off. Then we thrust the carousel around again for more dizzying speed. We catapult ourselves straight up on the teeter-totters and then abruptly drop to the ground with a bump. We buzz like insects. The sun energizes us.

Wobbly from the exertion, I drop to the soft, cool grass. As I lie on the park lawn, my legs grow longer. My chest swells with each breath. If my cotton T-shirt were still on my body, I would burst through the thin fabric. As I lie there, the trees throw their cool shadiness across the playground. The sun curves toward the horizon. Broad maple and oak leaves darken. The Douglas firs—black, inscrutable sentinels—stand guard. The sound of their shaking is all I can hear.

The smoke from the coals rises, and the smell of frying meats magnetically draws me back to the picnic tables and our circle of kinfolk. We look the same as all of the other families gathering in Todd Park. Across the field and around each fire pit, I see the same hatted men, the same sundressed mothers, the same children frolicking on swings, teeter-totters, and merry-go-rounds, the same smells from identical river-stone fireplaces with hamburgers and hot dogs grilling. I see no foreign faces, hear no foreign voices. The only sound is the wind in the trees, the same trees sheltering all of us in a singular American summer.

From a baseball diamond on the other side of the field, the crack of a bat striking a ball jerks my head skyward, and I see a rocket rise from afar. It arches toward my uncles, who are playing catch with my father and my brother. There is a game across the field, and someone has hit a home run. The ball hits the earth, running on its own engine, rolling toward our circle.

In silence the men watch the ball slow to a stop. Across the faraway field, the players there watch it progress as well but make no movement to retrieve it. They too have become silent and separate.

The ball stops, white on the green lawn, and for a time no one moves. Then Ritchie runs over and grabs it up, takes three giant steps, and hurls it like a man toward the players on the other side of the park. A fellow in a red baseball cap catches it and yells back, "Thanks."

Ritchie's eyes are on fire. He is breathless. "Let's take 'em on!" he shouts, but no one moves. "Come on. Let's make our own team."

My father waves Ritchie off.

"Whaddya talking about?" my dad, Leon, says, chewing on his cigar. "Don't be crazy. We're not taking anyone on. Don't talk nutty. Now let's have a little pepper. Don't just stand there holding the ball. Throw it, goddamn it."

Ritchie picks up our ball and makes a reluctant throw, his face etched with disappointment. My uncles and my father go back to their own game of catch. They stand there in their own part of the field, safe and separate, waiting for my mother and my aunties, both real and pretend, to call us to eat. The interlude with the rest of Bethell is at an end. We are together, uninterrupted but alone too, not quite ready to be part of the others around us.

This is the Bethell where I grew up. It is the Bethell that I know. This is the place that I once called home.

Book 1
Washington, DC

* * *

CHAPTER 1

The Hand in the Glove

* * *

"CAN YOU BELIEVE THAT STORY he just told, Mr. Hirsch?"

Reverend Arthur Cook has sat sphinxlike for two days of court, barely nodding to me from the time we enter the courtroom in the morning to the slam of Judge Sirica's hammer at the end of the day. Suddenly the reverend is talking to me, his lawyer, Nathan Hirsch, in a hushed tone of astonishment. His mouth is sagging open with amazement after Horace Parker, the witness and victim, finishes his testimony intended to put the reverend in jail.

I look incredulous too. For the first time in this proceeding, I am not distracted by Reverend Cook's disdain for me. If you can believe Horace Parker, tiny Reverend Cook, who is no more than the height of a Shetland pony, viciously attacked Mr. Parker, a black mountain of a man, a decorated ex-military policeman, and a uniformed government security guard. Horace has piously sworn Reverend Cook slashed him repeatedly and unrepentantly with an open-blade razor, the kind used by barbers in the '30s. Horace Parker has just rolled up his sleeves and shown the jury three knife slashes crisscrossing the back of his forearm, which is the size of a Virginia ham.

And all over a woman—Mrs. Parker, or "the missus," as Horace has just described his wife. Yesterday the jury met the weeping missus who, when sworn to testify, had no intention of confessing any greater sin than being a good churchgoer and, much to the prosecutor's dismay, refused to acknowledge that she saw the altercation between her husband and the reverend.

No question that the missus is Horace's match—she's oversize in every way. All hips and breasts swaddled in burgundy crepe, she appears to outweigh the reverend even if he were sopping wet. As nervous as this case has left me, I find myself drifting off, trying to understand taste and sex.

Reverend Cook is a reserved man, one who was a force in the civil rights movement a decade ago. Now the same Reverend Cook, who claimed inspiration from Gandhi, looks shocked at the suggestion that he and not Horace Parker was the aggressor. But that is what Officer Parker has just said. He has testified that he caught the reverend kissing the missus and that the reverend pulled out an old-fashioned straightedge and sliced the officer's arm in three places. Since nobody was there with a candle, the tale of the fight between the two men is a liar's contest.

I nod to Reverend Cook in agreement and take the time to look around the courtroom, hoping against hope that Shira Loeb has taken some time off from her clerking job at the court of appeals next door to give me a little moral support in Judge Sirica's courtroom. No luck, however. Though Shira and I have lived together since graduating from law school, she is nowhere in sight. I sigh, thinking Shira is probably grinding away in a cramped courthouse library carrel on the judicial record of some convicted defendant who may have had a lawyer no better than me.

My boss, Lynn Reilly, is also not in attendance, by design and plan conceived with and approved by the reverend. Nonetheless, he has sent Hulda Pollak, his massive secretary, to "help" me.

Hulda is an outspoken legal secretary, a dangerous old pro, and no friend of mine. She sits in the first row of visitor benches behind the barristers' tables, and no one has chosen to sit next to her. Who would? Glistening, as the Virginians refer to sweating, Hulda radiates heat, the smell of West Virginia grit, and District of Columbia contempt for everyone and everything legal.

Hulda is a spy. One screw-up by me that she reports back to her boss and mine, and I am undone.

Judge Sirica, who is presiding over this trial, is also not on my side. Not one smile bends his lips. They say he was a boxer. This is surprising, for he is a tiny wizened guy with nasty crow-like eyes. He peers at me only infrequently, but when he does, his eyes reflect at best boredom and at worst thinly veiled contempt.

I guess I can understand why his mind might be elsewhere. While he is down in this courtroom, he must be thinking of the Watergate grand jury upstairs that he supervises, the jurors there looking to indict half or more of President Nixon's White House team and perhaps President Nixon himself. And the *Washington Post* says Judge Sirica is a Republican. Watergate must stick in his craw.

Yesterday I saw the Watergate jurors being led like sheep past our courtroom, their "JUROR" tags dangling on chains around their necks, their faces grim. They were heading to lunch, but if you considered the serious looks in their eyes, they could have been heading to a hanging.

If I think too much about how the reverend feels about me, intermixed with Judge Sirica's indifference or contempt (I cannot tell which)—not to mention the distraction of Watergate—I will not be able to do my job. I can remember the coaching of my older brother, Ritchie, an intense athlete and competitor. Ritchie would be hammering away at me.

"Stay in the game. Focus."

I try my best, with eyes unblinking, jaw set, a modest grimace on my lips, tongue lingering in the corner of my mouth. If he were here with me, Ritchie would say that being the reverend's lawyer is no different from standing at the plate with a baseball bat on my shoulder, waiting for the next pitch.

On the witness stand, in his green museum-guard uniform, Horace Parker looks comfortable, his righteousness spreading over the jury like his girth spreading over the lip of the witness chair. He looks as if he could crush the reverend just by sitting on him.

"And they think I wasn't frightened by that figure filling up my doorway?" the reverend whispers to me. For the first time in this courtroom, the reverend angles toward me so that our knees touch, and no one can see us, much less hear us, as we talk. Reverend Cook's left eyelid perpetually droops as he whispers to me, giving him a skeptical view of me as his lawyer. This is as it should be, since he had wanted my boss, Lynn Reilly, and not me sitting next to him in court.

"In all sense and manner, Reverend," Lynn Reilly had said, pushing his thinning hair off his forehead as we sat in his DuPont Circle office, "you want the jury to see a novice representing you, an innocent face. With a smart noggin, to be sure. Because with all your character, your excellent reputation, your imposing presence, and your brilliance as a preacher, Reverend, you win on the strength of your telling of this sad episode and not on a stale recounting of the case by some counsel of lesser skill than you. No disrespect, Mr. Hirsch."

I nodded—no offense taken—but in fact my face reddened, and I gripped the chair. Now I was the counsel of lesser skill, hardly the kind of endorsement I wanted from my boss.

Lynn Reilly always speaks crisply, with a slight Maryland drawl through his buck teeth.

"Now, Mr. Hirsch here, he'll take care of the details. The jury will be on his side, the young lawyer trying to do his best. The jurors will have lowered expectations. You, Reverend, and no one else, will thrill and engage the jury with your declaration of the falsehood of Mr. Parker's story. I can assure you that the jury would be disappointed if they could not carry your words and your image into their deliberations at the case's end."

I could see the logic in my boss's strategy. This case was lock, stock, and barrel about the reverend. The jury would either believe he was innocent, a man who defended himself against an enraged husband, or find him guilty, an adulterer who failed to tell them the truth.

I was to be the fellow who simply announced that the reverend had arrived. I'd introduce him to the jury, giving him the opportunity to thunder out the truth of his innocence.

Lynn Reilly, the latest of my mentors, was always respectful. It was part of his power of persuasion. But selling me to the reverend had been an uphill battle even for Lynn Reilly, the master of the District of Columbia criminal courts. Reverend Cook's sagging eyelid told the tale, that droopy eye staring a message at me: "You mean I'm gonna have to let some white boy do a man's job?"

I prayed that my eyes did not affirm the reverend's assessment; I silently pursed my lips with seriousness to keep from an involuntary blink or two. Alas, in one flinch, I feared he had me. But I judged the reverend too swiftly.

"Mr. Reilly, you want me to put faith into your view." The reverend always speaks with a slow, deliberate musical cadence, the hallmark of his ministry. "You claim I need your guidance, your fine hand, with your representative, so to speak, doing the legwork. Well, that's fine, sir. Now you give me your hand."

I watched as the reverend reached over to grasp Lynn Reilly's hand in expectation of their bond. His requirement of commitment was unmistakable.

"I will take your Mr. Hirsch—your glove, as it were—into court with me," he says, "but I will expect you to place your hand, this hand that I now hold in mine; I expect your hand inside that glove, if you see my point. And knowing that, I'll walk into that courtroom having had the benefit of your defense. Do I have your hand in this, sir?"

The reverend had nailed me down to a T. A puppet. It must have showed that there was plenty of room for my boss's hand to push and pull me about as the protection of the reverend might demand. I realized it too. I had been emptied by the death of my older brother, Ritchie, whose life had been taken from him in a Southeast Asian rice paddy.

The thought of a world without Ritchie left me hollow and spent. He had been so vital and assured. I could see Ritchie pitching with inexhaustible velocity at the top of the ninth, watch him in full stride with a football tucked in his right arm as he stiff-armed with his left some fool who had attempted the impossible task of dragging him down alone in midfield. I could watch Ritchie's hijinks with Phil and Gene, his adoring pals, clowning around the Zesto Drive-In on a twilit summer night.

And I could hear Ritchie moaning and thrashing about as he made love to a naked girl in his hideaway crawl space above the family garage, a cave padded with old military-surplus wool blankets, unaware that he was being spied on by me, his envious thirteen-year-old brother. Ritchie was my compass, and I believe with a lawyer's conviction that I lost him forever because of what I put in motion. My loss, my doing.

Two hours before the reverend meets with us at the end of the court day, I relate to Lynn Reilly the effectiveness of Officer Parker's direct examination, panting by the end. The specter of cross-examining the monstrous Mr. Parker has left my skin clammy.

My boss knows I am anxious; he has assured me that my cross-examination is simply to introduce the reverend's testimony. The hand always directs the glove.

"I told you it would be a slam dunk." My boss smiles at me, all buck teeth and thinning blond hair. His grin astonishes me.

"What do you mean?" I say. "The jury's not going to care who started it. I can tell, Mr. Reilly. The jurors seemed to like Parker."

"Please, Mr. Hirsch. Nobody likes a bully. You just need to show how superhuman he is. Show the difference between the two of them. That will show that the reverend could not have frightened Officer Parker. On the other hand, the sheer size of Mrs. Parker's hubby scared Reverend Cook out of his wits. And believe me, the reverend will say he was terrified. That's all the jury will need to know to find the motive of self-defense."

I must look dubious, because Lynn Reilly pats me on the shoulder. "Don't worry about the reverend. He'll do fine. After all, if the jury thinks he's a liar, he is the one who will be doing the time. Just get the good officer Parker to fess up to being as fearless as he is, and you'll have set up the reverend to do what reverends do best: leave 'em spellbound."

* * *

I arrive at the courtroom early in the morning and take the calming step of setting up my note cards for the cross-examination of Officer Parker. As I flip the cards, my mind begins to drift. My hold on DC has always felt fragile; while this place has served me as a temporary moorage, the opposing currents of my small-town family world seem to draw me back. Even as the courtroom begins to stir, I sense with resignation that those currents have yet again washed in my past.

When I close my eyes, familiar faces and whispers surround me. They are a presence from the home I left—Bethell, on the shores of Puget Sound in Washington State. I find myself involuntarily sighing; it is my permanent phantom jury, ready as always to adjust my successes downward and judge my blunders as fatal. Their shuffling feet, the clasping of hands in surprise, their grunts, and the critical muttering make my shoulders slump as I try unsuccessfully to shut out their spectral sounds. Among them are my Hirsch family relatives, our Bethell neighbors, my teachers and classmates, and even the myriad of local shopkeepers I have known my whole life. The living among them mingle easily with the dead, casting cocked eyes from the front row on the events I experience.

This sensation of my private Bethell jury is not new to me. When I try to shut it out, the jury ebbs and then materializes, releasing its verdicts into the air around me, accompanied by the patter of Northwest rain on roofs and the slap of tidal waves on rocky beaches, the sounds, smells, places, and people from whom I have long tried to separate.

I awaken with a start. The courtroom is filling with functionaries, bailiffs, marshals, clerks, and assistant DAs. They raise dust motes as they open briefcases, fold newspapers, brush chair seats, and tuck coats behind them, all reaching assigned positions in the court before Judge Sirica appears. None, not even the reverend, have any idea that there will be two juries in the box watching me cross-examine Officer Parker. One self-appointed, one selected by Judge Sirica. I am not sure which will matter more.

Horace Parker again assumes the stand, as comfortable as if he were sitting in a movie theater. I rise and approach the bar. Lynn Reilly has painstakingly drilled me on the questions I will ask.

"Mr. Parker, can I call you 'Officer'?" I ask and take a deep breath. Mrs. Jefferson, the last juror in the front row, maternally crinkles her face at me. "You're doing fine, son," her smile says, and I am momentarily heartened.

Willie Smith, the assistant DA, just smirks. The day before, during the break, when we stood in the men's room stall to stall, Willie said out loud to anyone who could hear, "I am kicking your butt." Zipping myself quickly in retreat, I thought he was right.

I am sure that as far as Willie is concerned, my examination will go right along with his direct examination establishing Officer Parker's legitimacy and decency. A security guard. A man to be honored and respected. Someone who would not lie about who attacked whom.

"Now, Officer Parker, you told the jury you served in the military before your present job in the National Gallery."

"I did." Officer Parker sits straighter, if that is possible.

"You were a military policeman, I believe."

"Yep."

"And served with distinction?"

A nod and a "yup."

"Any awards?"

"A number of ribbons." Horace Parker tries to look humble, but he is pleased pink to be able to talk in detail about his achievements. He has a remarkable record.

"What were they for?"

"Oh, there was a stockade breakout in Korea," he says.

"Pretty serious, Officer?"

"Oh yes." Officer Parker laughs with a rumble of menace. "We had prisoners running around like escaped mice. Seven of 'em."

"Did you personally catch any?"

"Got 'em all," Horace answers with satisfaction.

"You got them all?" I appear suitably impressed. I stroll over toward the jury box, just as Lynn Reilly instructed me.

"That way, once the witness is going with you," my boss explained to me, "you have him facing the jury as he's talking to you. Then, when the high point in your examination arrives, you have the jurors looking right into his face."

Lynn Reilly is like a football coach. He calls the plays. I execute them. It's working just as he indicated it would. The jury is looking at Horace Parker.

"How exactly did you accomplish the capture, Officer?"

"I was at the door." Horace grins, his mouth cavernous. I imagine him downing a double cheeseburger in one bite. "They had to get by me to get out."

"Seven prisoners," I marvel. "What did you do to subdue that number of men?"

"I kinda used the first one as a club to knock the others out. It was like bowling." The memory makes him laugh again. I look at one of the women in the jury. Horace's laughing about his exploits at bashing people is starting to wear thin. Oblivious to sounding like a braggart, Horace loves the chance to tell his story. By now the jury must feel that this man is a force of nature—and not always a nice one.

"Officer Parker," I inquire, "are you trained in the martial arts?"

"Yessir. Judo and jujitsu." Horace's answer snaps like a salute.

"Have you kept it up?"

"Every week. Yessir."

Willie Smith, the prosecutor, looks up. He has realized that his victim just described himself to the jury as a one-man army.

"So, if I may," I ask, "back to the jailbreak in Korea. Anybody armed?"

He recites, "The usual: jail shivs, sharpened spoons. And one smuggled gun."

"And the commendation you received declares that you disarmed an entire jail wing."

"That's what it says all right." Horace shifts his weight in the witness chair, as if to put another bad guy to rest. The jurors have to be thinking how it was impossible for this man to have let the little reverend pull a razor on him.

"All the knives?" I question.

"Yessir." There's Horace's salute again.

"Were there any big guys?"

Another rumbling laugh. "Not as big as me."

"But good size?"

Horace nods.

Now, just as Lynn Reilly had forecast, the jury has all of the facts about this formidable fighting machine. The step is for me to bring Horace's reputation home to Washington, DC.

Some of the jurors are shifting around with nervousness. I hope they're getting worried that Officer Parker might jump over the ledge of the jury box and pounce on them next. But maybe they are just tired of me dragging this out. I have no idea which it is.

"You must be proud of the commendation," I note with respect.

"It helped get my job with the gallery," Horace concedes.

"And you were given an award at your church as well, were you not?"

"Yessir. The Harmony Baptist Church gave me a plaque at a Sunday service."

"And so everybody knew about your physical feats?"

"I suspect so," Horace answers. I can see he's getting a little uneasy about where this is going.

"Now, Officer Parker," I ask, "have there ever been any acts of violence in your neighborhood? Anybody ever robbed and assaulted?"

"Yessir. All the time. We don't get the police help we need."

I acknowledge that it's a problem by nodding my head in agreement. Horace Parker lives in a tough neighborhood.

"Officer, have you ever been robbed on the street?"

Horace laughs spontaneously. There is that booming self-confident rumble again. It is like the starting of a diesel engine with a nasty exhaust.

"Nobody that dumb gonna take me on." He grins.

"I can surely see that." I grin back. "So that experience of yours in the service—you taking out seven men—that experience was well known, then?"

That question seems to yank the prosecutor, Willie Smith, straight out of his chair. He is positively shouting out his objection.

"Only admissible if he knows your honor." Willie is agitated by Horace Parker now telling the jury that people in his neighborhood might be afraid of him. But Horace answers without waiting.

"Yessir. I think so."

"Wasn't it Reverend Cook's church where your military exploits were announced to the community?"

"Hmmm," Officer Parker says. It's all that he can say.

I marvel at Lynn Reilly's insight. "Trust me, Mr. Hirsch," Lynn had intoned, the light from his desk lamp shining into his intense face. "Mr. Parker will hobble the prosecutor's case if he acknowledges that even the reverend might have been afraid of him."

Lynn Reilly, the puppeteer, again was on target.

"So, Officer Parker," I say, "if I can summarize, you are well known as one of the strongest men in your neighborhood, so that no one tangles with you, yes?"

"If you say so," Parker mumbles. He looks at me, and because of where I am standing, the jury can see his eyebrows knitted in anger. I wouldn't want to run into Horace in an alley after that look. Nor would the jurors. Even Horace knows he is not much of a victim anymore.

And now my penultimate question, rehearsed and rehearsed with Lynn Reilly and Reverend Cook late into the night: "Mr. Parker, could I ask you to look at Reverend Cook?"

At this question the reverend rises slowly, with great dignity, as planned, his five-foot-four frame a fraction of the size of the massive Horace Parker. I can see the eyes of two of the jury members darting back and forth, measuring the tiny alleged assailant and his gigantic judo-trained victim.

"Officer," I ask innocently, "would you say the prisoner in the Korean stockade that you picked up to knock over the other six escapees was bigger or smaller than Reverend Cook?"

My sympathetic juror, Mrs. Jefferson, openly smiles. There are giggles in the courtroom. Judge Sirica cements my cross by slamming his gavel and calling for quiet.

"You've made your point, Mr. Hirsch," the judge cautions. "Move on." But there is respect in his tone.

The jury hears his respect too. Afterward, the reverend's stem-winder testimony drives home the last nail in the coffin of the prosecutor's case. After they have returned to the jury room from a lunch at a nearby restaurant on the government's tab, the jury acquits the reverend in ten minutes.

The reverend shakes hands with the jury members, and some applaud. As we leave I turn back to the empty courtroom. I think I hear the phantom Bethell jury whispering among themselves, yet again not satisfied with my performance.

The accolades back in the office after Reverend Cook's acquittal are meant to feel like a reward for my auspicious beginning and for Lynn Reilly's success. The reverend lifts both of our hands in the air as a sign of victory. Trays of paper cups filled with cheap champagne circulate, and all staff and lawyers grab them as a toast is offered. But the cross on Horace Parker and the reverend's acquittal that followed were not my doing. I served only as the glove that delivered the blow while the hand inside, aiming the glove, was the great Lynn Reilly.

Actually I may have fooled one young comely secretary, Deirdre Neil, who works for Reilly's partner, Aaron Sugarman. Deirdre is short and dark and has never taken notice of me in any way. Now she has crossed the foyer with her right hand extended and a cup of champagne in her left.

"Well, imagine that. Your first trial, Nathan," she says, grasping my hand with worshipful closeness. "A defense verdict."

"Call me Nate," I say.

"Then Nate," Deirdre teases, "what will you do to protect your perfect record?" Her smile suggests she would like to be part of my success today. Or maybe I am so relieved to be at the end of an ordeal that my eyes can soak up a pretty girl standing next to me and read into her words more than is there.

"Well," she says, her white teeth gleaming, "here's to you. A personal toast." She has refilled her cup and moves her bare arm to let our paper cups bang together, but, being paper, they spill on my shoes. Deirdre leans into me to avoid being splashed. I smell in her perfume a jangle of jungle fruits, flowers, and desire.

"Dear me," she says, "I've made a mess." But she stays close, her breast shoved a bit too intimately into my side. Just an office flirtation, I say to myself. We separate, grinning, and move away to speak to others, as if it is no more than that.

Reilly and Sugarman's other associate is Alfred Gibbons, my senior by three years. He tips his cup of champagne toward me, but his eyes cancel any element of congratulation. If I were him, I would resent that the most junior member of the team got the nod to represent the reverend. Perhaps he knows that every word of the cross-examination came from our boss, that each measured hesitation between my questions had been choreographed by Lynn Reilly.

Alfred is prematurely balding. He sidles over to me with a crooked smile for everybody else in the room, as if he were an undercover cop with a secret assignment. The hubbub in the room is fueled by the champagne. Albert hooks my arm and gestures at our boss.

"Isn't that just like him, chinning with Reverend Cook. Look at him over there, playing you. Now that the case is over, he's the reverend's hero. Why? Because that's where the referrals will come from, and that's what Reilly wants. And believe me, Cook wants Reilly to be his hero. It makes him a big shot to be represented by a hotshot and not by a trainee."

Alfred smiles that bogus smile in my face and whispers to me, "You know he told the reverend and everybody else who asked that he wrote your opening statement and closing argument verbatim."

Alfred's voice hisses with pretended resentment on my behalf. I, the trainee, just nod, feeling that Lynn Reilly has already flunked me. If I told Alfred that *verbatim* was a falsehood, that in fact Lynn Reilly simply gave me cue cards, I would look stupid and petty. Since my sole spontaneous role at trial was to open the courtroom door for my client on our way in and on our way out, why would Lynn Reilly do more than simply use me?

When the reverend finally takes his leave and the lawyers return to their desks, the March sun is setting. I retreat to my windowless cubicle around the corner from the celebration in the foyer. Outside, the secretaries continue to prattle away rather than to go back to work. The mail on my desk that accumulated during trial is all rubbish. I throw it in the trash, loosen my tie, turn off the desk lamp, and sit in the dark, ruminating. I hear only the squeaking of my chair as I rock back and forth.

I admit to myself that there is plenty of room in the glove for Lynn Reilly's hand. Without me, the terrible events that drove Ritchie out of my family would not have occurred. This is why Lynn Reilly's total management of me feels somehow fitting, more like a recognition of my vacuous condition and less like a verdict. It is who I am.

I recall the message from Reverend Cook, as insightful a man as I have met, that he whispered to me following the jury's acquittal: "Thank your lucky stars, Mr. Hirsch, that you have Mr. Reilly to guide you. Just pray that he keeps his faith in you."

Lynn Reilly has hardly encouraged others to have faith in me. Hulda Pollock, Lynn's legal secretary, said but one thing to me on our return from the courthouse: "Where's the cab receipt for you and the reverend?"

"I forgot to ask for one," I stammered. "Too excited, I guess."

"Too excited to get a receipt, eh?" She snorted. "Then you pay for the cab." Hulda, who had sat through the whole trial, simply turned on her heel and stomped away, muttering in that indecipherable West Virginia dialect of hers. In her eyes I have flunked law-office management 101. Having typed Lynn Reilly's cues for my use at trial, and having listened to me deliver each, Hulda couldn't care less about my courtroom performance.

You have to be careful what you want, I think. I begged Reilly and Sugarman for the opportunity to prove myself and now sense I do not fit in the role I coveted. Perhaps I never will. Every tactic Lynn Reilly prepared me to carry out could have been performed by someone else. If Alfred is right, it is only a matter of time until my boss decides, notwithstanding my eminent skill as a mimic, I am also eminently replaceable. Do I wait for Lynn Reilly to put me out on the street, or do I strike out on my own? I smell the title—LAW OFFICES OF NATHAN HIRSCH—and I then I think, Who am I kidding?

I comfort myself with the thought that at least the jury liked me, that I still possess the power to make a terrific initial impression. It is the very least a first-rate mimic should be able to pull off.

Spontaneously I reach for the phone to place a long-distance call to Bethell, my hometown, using the office charge code. Uncle Harry King always told me to call him if I needed to. And I needed to now.

Harry King, himself a lawyer, has been my mentor, my teacher, and my counselor from my childhood, through my bar mitzvah, all the way to my acceptance to law school, in which he played a role. Although he is not my biological kin, Harry has always seemed to carry with him a safety net for others and served as the bedrock support of my late father, my entire family, and, for that matter, all those I grew up with in Bethell. For my entire life, I have revered and imitated Uncle Harry, and for his part, I always drew his affection. While my need for his singular approval might be childish, I can no more escape my need for it than shed my skin.

I dial the operator and ask her to dial collect to Harry King's home number, the only one I know. The phone rings forever. Then: "Who the hell is it?"

The operator asks if the contact will accept the call.

"OK, OK." I hear a smoke-soaked voice rumble like "Old Man River."

"Uncle Harry," I say, "I got some news, great news."

"Nathan, it's the middle of the day. Are you crazy? Do you know how much daytime long distance costs?"

"I know," I say, "but you told me to call if it was important."

I blurt out the whole Reverend Cook story like a little kid.

"Uncle Harry, I got him off. I won my first case." I prattle into the phone, making much of it up as I go, forgetting about the role Lynn Reilly has played. It is all about me.

Harry stops me in the middle. "OK. OK. I can only take so much. What time is it, anyway?"

"Quit making such a deal about the time," I say. "It's five in the afternoon here."

"But the cost, you *schmendrick*, you idiot. This is going to bankrupt either you or me. Now that you're such a big *macher*, big shot, I think I'll send you the bill. Besides, for you to win the case, it musta been a slam dunk. Anybody crazy enough to hire you has got to have an incompetency defense."

I am used to Harry's bluster. I hear the metallic smack of his cigar lighter and imagine the *fomph* when the tip of his latest Cuban clasped between his fleshy lips lights up.

"So?" He exhales. "So really? You walked him, eh? Great job, Nathan. Just don't let it go to your head. They don't charge the innocent, so don't forget. The next time you get a plea deal. Remember, it's just as easy for those jury people to fall in love with Mr. Law-and-Order Big-Shot Prosecutor."

Harry is winding up the call.

"Now let me go back to work, will you? And again, mazel tov. Somebody's going to have to earn a fortune to pay for this call. I've got to hang up before I have to file bankruptcy."

The phone click leaves a pang of loss. Harry's voice echoes in my memory. It is as if my sole supporter has evaporated. Even over the telephone, the cigar scent seems to stick to my clothes. I long to smell Harry's dense, almost smotheringly vegetative exhaled smoke.

I notice that a card was slid under my door while I was chattering at Harry. I stretch down and pick it up off the floor. The card's scent reminds me of jungle fruits, flowers, and desire. I read the message inside.

"I've swiped a bottle of the bubbly from the office stash, and my roommate is out for the evening. Maybe I can make up for spilling my toast. I'm at 2517 22nd St., Apt. 5F. Don't disappoint me and let the champagne go to waste. Your admirer, Deirdre."

In all probability Shira is hunkered in her spot in the court of appeals library. She will not be home for hours, maybe not at all.

I pick up Deirdre's card and put its fragrance to my nose. I fold it, exposing the address, and slip it into my suit-coat pocket. I choose to leave my briefcase in the office, and as I close the door behind me, my excitement rises.

I could use a night with someone who thinks I am worthy of a toast.

CHAPTER 2

The Treasure

* * *

IN THE MORNING, IN THE apartment I share with Shira Loeb, my head feels about to split open. Too much champagne the night before.

I stumble to the kitchenette, seize a coffee cup, dig about for some Alka-Seltzer, extract two tablets, and throw them in the mug. The sizzle, spray, and pop give me some relief.

I look around for dirty dishes, a pile of discarded clothing, or some other sign that Shira has been here, but there is not a dish on the counter or any female garb carelessly strewn about. It has been days, well before the Cook trial began, since I have seen her momentarily abandon the court of appeals library stacks and her alcove there.

I swallow the bubbling swill in the coffee cup and consider what I will say to Deirdre when I arrive at work. The swirling fizz reveals a tawdry side to last night in Deirdre's bedroom. As we lie there naked, the two of us joined by a thin sheen of sweat, I see that one of her false eyelash sets has detached and lies undetected on her bedspread. I wonder about the consequence of unbalanced eyelids.

It is remarkable how clear my head has become after the fact, despite the champagne. Perhaps in the course of our collision—hardly lovemaking—I have come to my senses. I ponder whether it is universal for males to separate so quickly as they deflate. I ask myself, where have I lodged my lost jockey shorts, which were shucked with Deirdre's tugging assistance? I think as I retrieve a pair from the thrash of sheets that I should check the brand and size to determine whether they were mine.

I imagine seeing my brother standing there in the shadows, approving my nighttime antics with a girl in her underpants and naked from the waist up: "I told you it would be cool. And remember, it doesn't matter." Laughter falls from his lips.

With Deirdre asleep I experience a relentless rhythm of distance, her one-window bedroom seeping loneliness. Her bedding carries the scent of detergent while another memory—Bethell's countryside smell—pushes all others away, fills my nostrils with air infused with the sawdust from the Skarbell Mill and with winds flavored by the briny shoreline that at low tide crackles with dry seaweed.

Here in DC the humid air reeks like an imperfectly cleaned Dumpster, a warm astringent finished with a smear of forgotten rotten fruit.

My cleared head in Deirdre's bed questions the safety of my strange nighttime surroundings. Traveling backward in time from this place, there have been too many close scrapes that pop up: smoking dope but avoiding detection under my parents' noses; getting drunk on Olympia Beer in Bobbie Raskin's backyard potting shed; chasing country girls in Everett, Washington; drive-ins after away football games; and luring one of the local honeys with the promise of moonshine-quality booze and a once-in-a-lifetime orgy with two crazy Jew boys from little Bethell up Highway 90.

Then it gets darker. Tripping over drunks in the alley behind the family jewelry store while throwing out garbage. Some are sour-smelling loggers, others Tamlips tribal members too drunk to find the road to the reservation, stains in their pants like Rorschach tests, stains that look like bogus road maps leading to nowhere.

Is this where it ends, in someone's apartment at three in the morning, head full of unrelated memories, rushing good-byes through blunted lips, fearing bad breath? Deirdre must be the sole Reilly and Sugarman office denizen who does not know I'm just a windup doll, a Lynn Reilly stand-in. I cringe to think how foolish she will feel when the watercooler gossip catches up to tell her that last night she slept with a pretend trial lawyer, a facsimile of the real thing.

I suspect I will just stop at her desk in front of Aaron Sugarman's office on the way in and greet her with a good morning, as if the two of us were simply working for the same boss, I forgiving her for picking me up, mistaking me to be a hot prospect for success, me forgiven for sleeping with her under false pretenses.

I try Shira's phone again before leaving our apartment, but she does not answer. She has no idea of my victory in the Cook case. The phone in her office takes no messages.

In all respects Shira appears to feel that we have no obligation to each other than to share the rent, a point of view that, after last night at Deirdre's, I seem to have also affirmed.

* * *

At Reilly and Sugarman, the receptionist, Janice, greets me with mock surprise.

"I would have thought they'd give you the day off," she jokes.

"No rest for the wicked," I quip and hurry to my office. I avoid Deirdre, who is down the hall at the copy machine.

I find some Pepto-Bismol lozenges in my desk that I chew down, wondering if Lynn Reilly will want to postmortem the Cook trial with me. Then I think, Why? We won. He coached every move for me. It worked. What is left to say?

Hulda enters my office, and without a word she plops a pile of papers into my in-box. On top is a carefully folded article from the local page of the *Washington Post*, a weekly column titled "People to Watch."

Hulda would be the first to tell you she is not my secretary but deigns to deliver my mail. Probably she culled the *Post* article that sits like a crown on the mail of the day. The column contains a blurb about the Cook case:

"This week, newcomer to the criminal defense bar Nathan Hirsch walked the Reverend Arthur Cook safely past a government indictment in federal court. Hirsch is the latest addition to the stable of talent employed by the redoubtable Lynn Reilly, who grew up in the shadow of Pimlico. It is too early to tell, but with Mr. Hirsch in the Reilly paddock, the stable may be full."

The adulatory tone in the piece that sneaks through the flippant horse-race metaphors unnerves me. My boss and I both know I am no race horse. By now he may be regretting his decision not to try the Cook case himself and personally reap the compliments.

And if Hulda has shown that article to me, it is also on the way to my boss's desk. I am seized with a wild notion to sneak in and remove it before Lynn Reilly has a chance to go through his mail. He might not be flattered that he made the decision to add me to his stable after all.

* * *

I wanted Lynn Reilly to hire me from the first moment I saw him at the law center. He had real-world skills beyond celebrity. Throughout the center's learned bookish halls, all declared him to be a peerless lawyer. He unceasingly participated as a law-center lecturer, judicial-panelist mentor, and fund-raiser. He inspired paroxysms of praise from all quarters.

Even condescending, remote old Dean Gaghan in his wrinkled stale suits, a burning cigarette snared in his mouth's corner as he strode unimpeded through the law-center halls, an ancient barrister from an earlier century—even this perpetually glum man who had no use for his new students positively lit up and beamed as he greeted my future boss as a law-center guest. It was as if, suddenly humbled, Dean Gaghan were presenting Lynn Reilly to the law center's first-year students as his superior.

"A treasure," Dean Gaghan warbled, grinning like a drunk, admonishing us to hang on Lynn's every word, as he intended to do himself, bobbling a bit at the microphone, almost hitting it with his bald pate, bowing and scraping in the presence of the law center's treasure, whose words of greeting and well-wishing were traditional and simple and, like an appetizer, simply teased my palate.

The shared history of Lynn Reilly was that after a hardscrabble Baltimore Catholic upbringing, he attended the law center on scholarship and won every student debate contest imaginable. Then he followed his brilliant five-year career as an assistant US attorney in Baltimore, where he cracked a huge corruption case that took down the governor. After that Lynn started on his own as a criminal defense attorney in Washington, DC, and became widely regarded as the next Edward Bennett Williams, defeating the government in headline-winning case after case.

The treasure dressed like a businessperson. Of average height, he had a high, intelligent forehead and combed his hair in a flounce from one side over the top, to hide a balding spot. As for Lynn's bucktoothed grin, which he undoubtedly could now afford to fix, those big teeth, I learned, were his trademark. Sticking out that way, they did make him look boyish in the courtroom—innocent, charming, gracious, and nonthreatening, an almost friendly presence. The social page of the *Washington Post* had carried a picture of his entire family at a fund-raiser picnic: a plain, brown-haired wife and four boys ranging from infancy to eight, all with the trademark Reilly buck teeth. You could see why juries loved him.

But not my classmate, Charlie Hogan, an ex-marine back from service in Vietnam. Charlie had little patience for pretense and palace heroes.

"Why make such a fuss over the guy?" he cryptically observed. "I heard he just got lucky. So he won a mock trial here, a moot court there at the law center. So the profs loved him. Big deal."

But it occurred to me that I might be able to repeat the Treasure's path to success with his help in the flesh. I knew that he would be judging one of the first-year mock-court competitions. I cajoled a second-year student doing the scheduling to add me to the list to appear before the panel on which Lynn Reilly was a judge. This was not hard, since most first-year students viewed Lynn with supernatural awe and fear, believing they might melt under the fierce Reilly questioning as they stood there. And, thus demolished by the Treasure, their careers would be gone before they had even begun.

The law-center student courtroom known as McDivitt Hall, named after a wealthy donor, was half lecture amphitheater and half courtroom. Its indirect lighting illuminated a rounded heaven of ceiling into which fading legal echoes tried to escape. Paneled walls of acoustical tiles and walnut darkened the room into a dense chamber towered over by the judge's long, ominous bench. The hall seemed formidable, solemn, and dangerous.

The hallways outside McDivitt Hall were lined with glass display cases filled with trophies—tarnished punch bowls, behind which were suspended candid photos of aggressively grinning boys in suits, their teeth bared like wolves'. These students were the winners of the school's cherished moot court events, and the punch bowls were the trophies carved with the names of successful generations of contestants. In the center I saw the photo of young Lynn Reilly, bucktoothed and with a full head of hair, grasping a punch bowl handle like a sword hilt, holding it high in the air. A performance for combatants to copy.

My territory.

The stage in the McDivitt was the advocate's podium, a cockpit hunkered between tables for the opposing advocates. An aluminum microphone coiled up from its front like the head of a metallic snake about to strike anyone who uttered a false word.

Two large electric eyes also faced the speaker. One blinked green when the contestant was to begin, and one halted the speaker with a blast of crimson. In between the blinking lights, questions poured from the judge's bench, relentlessly wearing down any unprepared contestant. Standing there in a moot court event and placing one's hands on each side was akin to jumping on a bucking bronco. You could be thrown off.

After watching older students clutching the bucking bronco as they flung legal lightning bolts at one another, I crept into an empty McDivitt, stepping up to the half-darkened podium.

Standing there in the dim light, facing an empty judicial bench, I began to comprehend the burden of an advocate: a loss of words, dampness springing out on my forehead, and a growing heat on the back of my neck, as if I were being watched. I could hear my Bethell jury murmuring in the shadows. I felt paralyzed and wrenched my hands free. No one was there. My unnerved moment had passed unobserved, and thus I could retreat safely back to being a mimic trainee, a Lynn Reilly look-alike.

Less than a month later I was standing again at the podium, pointing in the air, gesturing as I argued the mock appeal I had connived to get before the judges, including Lynn Reilly. My Bethell jury lurked there too, judging the outcome.

All contestants and judges received a two-page statement of facts, pale words on two skimpy sheets that formed the immutable universe of the contest. They revealed that my client, a Mr. Albert Jones, had been convicted of a vicious and violent murder. At his trial the government had used as evidence a pair of muddy shoes the police had seized from Mr. Jones's home without a search warrant. The fact sheet stated the deadly truth: the mud on the shoes matched footprints found at the bloody and muddy murder scene. The shoes were the same size as those Mr. Jones wore when he was arrested.

I found myself grasping the McDivitt podium, arguing that the warrantless search of Jones's home had been unreasonable and thus unconstitutional. I felt the flow of my words to be utter gibberish. A desperate fear rose in me that the unseen audience seated behind me would believe it to be gibberish as well. "But Jones was a murderer," my Bethell jury whispered to one another.

I was tethered to the fact sheet like a goat tied to a post. I argued round and round in a circle, bleating aloud. My rotation was finally interrupted by Lynn Reilly, who must have been getting dizzy.

He smiled. "Mr. Hirsch, you concede that Mr. Jones's guilt was apparent from the admissible evidence?"

I stalled. "Well, I don't know if I would say apparent."

"Would you say the evidence conceded to be admissible supported the conviction?"

"One could say that," I grudgingly admitted.

"Well, then," Lynn said, "let me ask. Was that evidence of guilt strong?"

"Yes."

"Perhaps overwhelming?"

"Possibly."

"And the central evidence of guilt unchallenged at trial?"

"Only the seizure of the shoes and their admission as evidence was challenged." That damned fact sheet, I thought.

"Then I ask you: why is a new trial necessary, since no other objection to evidence has been made and when the weight of the admissible evidence is, by your own statements, overwhelming?"

There it was. Lynn had all but obtained my concession that the police officer's sins were meaningless because the untainted evidence of guilt on the accursed fact sheet was crushing and overwhelming. My client was utterly guilty. I thought I heard my Bethell jury's soft snickers before they evaporated into the McDivitt's vaulted ceiling.

The podium's light uncorked a red glow on my face, insisting my time was up. I retreated to counsel table and collapsed into my chair in shame. Lynn had pressed me down with his questions like a relentless hammer driving a nail into soft wood. My failed Lynn Reilly look-alike strategy reddened my face like a sunburn.

Then out of nowhere came an unexpected compliment.

Lynn smiled at me. "Mr. Hirsch, you must have done a great deal of debate before your law school career. I congratulate your courage in holding on to your argument. I could have done no better with your facts."

I flushed with pleasure. In that moment I wanted to be him. I wanted to dress like him: button-down, three-piece, Ivy League. I wanted to be in his low-temperature skin and feel that thatch of hair—in his case blond and thinning—droop across my brow. I wanted to possess those piano-player fingers so I could gesture about the courtroom, my digits slightly bent with righteous conviction.

My longing energized me to rush forward as Lynn was packing his case at the judge's bench. In a burst of words, I asked if he would mind at some time reviewing my moot court brief.

He could only say no. But instead he gave me his card and told me to call his secretary for a time.

A week later I found myself at the door of a Dupont Circle brownstone row house. At the top of the stairs, next to the door, a brass plate bore the number 1425, and the engraved name REILLY AND SUGARMAN, ATTORNEYS AT LAW stood at metallic attention. I clutched my moot court brief in my hand. I did not even have a notebook or briefcase.

"How was my brief?" I asked as I was seated in Lynn Reilly's first-floor office, surrounded by papers piled like pillars in a Greek temple of antiquity.

"I wouldn't have a clue. Never read it."

My face fell. Lynn grinned at me.

"I love doing the judging in the McDivitt, but here I don't handle the briefs. My partner, Mr. Sugarman, heads that department."

I was crestfallen. I assumed the judges were versed in our writing.

Lynn took another tack. "What are you doing this summer, Mr. Hirsch? It took moxie for you to come here. We can always use someone with a little moxie."

I couldn't believe what I'd heard. Lynn Reilly was one of the most celebrated criminal defense lawyers in the District of Columbia, and I heard him offer me a summer job.

CHAPTER 3

Trial by Ballet

* * *

As I play with the *Washington Post* article and weigh calling Uncle Harry King in Bethell, my desk phone rings.

It is Charlie Hogan, my law-center classmate, now an assistant in the US attorney's office. "I'm surprised they're letting you answer calls anymore." Charlie's voice is measured, laconic. "I just assumed you would be overwhelmed, protecting the innocent."

"You would be surprised," I say. Charlie isn't too wrong. My phone has rung repeatedly; since the verdict, black residents who have been recently indicted by the DC grand jury seem for the moment to be clamoring for "lawyer Nathan Hirsch" to defend them.

"Over in our office, Willie Smith claims it was the reverend's sermon that did him in, not you," Charlie says. I hear him exhaling cigarette smoke. "Watch your backside."

Charlie treats me as if I were his younger brother. He takes seriously that Ritchie was a marine who died in Southeast Asia. His loyalty to me is familial and greater than his duty as an assistant US attorney to law and order.

"The truth is Lynn Reilly won this one," I say. "I get the best supporting award for following directions."

"All the same"—Charlie's voice is serious—"Smith feels you jobbed him. He's looking for a takedown."

* * *

In law school Charlie Hogan wore his hair in a military crew cut, as if he were still a marine. He wanted nothing more than to be a prosecutor. He was skeptical of Lynn Reilly's reputation for never having lost a trial.

But Charlie had never seen Lynn at work. I insisted Charlie go with me to hear his annual lecture at the center on courtroom methods.

"Even if the government is on the side of the angels and the defense is evil," I said, "Lynn Reilly is worth an hour of your time." As I talked I jammed down a tuna sandwich from the center's cafeteria.

"Nobody wins them all," Charlie said as we cleared off our trays. "He probably cherry-picks cases. Solid government's case, no Lynn Reilly. That's hardly heroic, buddy boy." But Charlie agreed to hear the lecture anyway.

Lynn was standing there as we walked into the sloping lecture amphitheater, making eye contact with each student coming through the door, giving each a slight greeting. He nodded to me, then turned to the next student.

Some students took their seats and munched their lunches. Some chatted by the door.

Without introduction Lynn began to talk. "You see, a trial is like ballet. There is a grace, a moment, and only a moment, when the jury wants to have the truth revealed by a particular witness. In that moment you have their attention because they expect you to illuminate the evidence, to expose the truth."

Lynn waved his long, thin fingers as he slowly said *iLOOMinate*, rhyming the central syllable with *broom*. The room had grown silent.

He looked at the front row and smiled.

"It is all reflected in your comfort with the facts. You don't need to be all worked up to get the jury's attention. Proof of facts is common sense, after all. If you look at it from the juror's standpoint, he ignores any evidence that comes in easy, that isn't the subject of a battle. He wakes up at the smell of a fight." Lynn stuck out his jaw and made fists like a John Sullivan-era boxer. Everybody laughed.

"If you can figure out a dispute about one fact and you can stage a fight, you can win a trial. The key is evaluating the facts objectively. You can't believe in the romance."

Lynn drew a heart on the board with white chalk. His fingers remained dusty.

"Do you know what the romance is?" he asked. "It's the story the client brings to you on a platter, as if you are the one deciding the case, as if you are the judge and jury. The client thinks he is hiring you to judge the facts. But the simple truth is your judgment one way or the other won't be helpful at all. Not a bit."

Lynn drew a red crisscross on top of his blackboard heart. "If you as the lawyer buy into the romance, you won't investigate the facts yourself. You'll just listen to your client's tale of woe. If you do that, the trial will be a revelation to you, a mystery you will not be able to fathom. And the prosecutor will convict your client as sure as summer heat in this town. You will have no chance. None. The romance of your client's story will always break your heart. That's why it's a romance."

Lynn picked up an eraser and wiped the board clean. Then he drew a circle and wrote, "One good fight."

"Instead, if you find out everything there is in the case on your own, I guarantee you'll spot where the facts get fuzzy, where there is an opportunity to wage that one good fight and win by persuading everyone in the courtroom that you know what happened. And if the jury believes you're truthful, they will listen to you when you signal them that they should pay attention. That's the choreography part of the ballet."

Lynn walked about the podium like a lion tamer in the center ring.

"You see, the line between guilt and innocence under law is as sharp as a knife. For instance, a man who shoots another is innocent of murder if provoked with a deadly force and placed in fear for his life, yes? But who has to prove the presence or absence of provocation? It is a matter of the burden of proof and the burden of going forward."

He paused and took a breath.

"It's the prosecutor's burden, the constitutional burden on the state, to prove no provocation. To prove the absence of a defense." Lynn spoke these words as if he were reciting from the Bible.

"Now, the prosecutor will duck the burden if you let him, but in every case the defense has the opportunity to persuade the judge of the right to demand that the state prove the entire case, including the absence of a defense, the absence of provocation."

The room was pin-drop still. Prove the absence of defense. Cars on Fifth Street muddled and grumbled toward the Capitol. Lynn Reilly's voice was soprano but soft. The listeners in the back row leaned forward to hear him.

"When you conclude in your own mind that the prosecutor has overlooked his burden and that there is one key fact, one element of the crime he cannot prove beyond a reasonable doubt, you have discovered the opportunity for your client to walk out of the courtroom a free man."

Lynn wrote on the board the words "one doubt." You could hear pens scribbling now throughout the room.

"That's all," he said. He faced the room, his eyes roving the faces of the students, stopping here and there, connecting. Now Lynn began to speak again, his voice testimonial. "The prosecutor is entitled to no latitude, no doubt. But your client is entitled to a doubt. That's the heart of our system. And the isolation of that doubt and its presentation to the jury, that is the core of the ballet.

"In each case, each time you start a new trial, you will have to teach the jury and judge to trust your version of the burden and the facts given that burden, and not to trust the prosecutor's assumptions or his analysis. That is the job you will have.

"So when you advise a client to either plead guilty or to go to trial, you must know all there is to know about what happened, who has the burden of proof and the burden of going forward, and what the critical facts will be for the defense. You have to decide when to get the jury's attention with a fight, and you must know the ballet of the fight so you can look at those jurors and know you and they are thinking about the facts in the same way."

Lynn wasn't smiling anymore. His eyes swept each row, his voice board flat. "When you can do this, you can win."

After classes were over for the day, late in the afternoon, I hailed a yellow cab to take me to work at my boss's law firm of Reilly and Sugarman, in the neighborhood known as Foggy Bottom. The cabby wore a Senators baseball cap and shades. His neck bubbled with sweat.

"Lawyer, huh?" he said with unsparing disbelief.

"Nope. Just a law clerk."

I tried to digest the heart of what my boss had said at the law center. "One good fight." That was the heart of it. If you knew all of the facts, you could choose just one good fight and win in court.

Reilly and Sugarman offered no relief from the late-fall temperature. The law office could have doubled as an oven in which hot air simply was circulated by fans, typewriters, and fast-moving bodies oblivious to the temperature.

From the hall I could see Lynn Reilly leaning over a secretary's desk peering through a raft of papers, his tie loose, his sleeves rolled up. He was reading through little glasses propped on the promontory of his nose.

Lynn glanced toward me, a blank stare. I panicked. Then he focused, grabbed a piece of previously typed-on paper, scribbled a note, and thrust it at me. His words were almost unreadable. It looked like a name: Rolando LaPlante.

"Mr. Hirsch. Nathan," he said slowly, plainly. "I want you to do me a favor, if you would. Go to Mr. LaPlante. Tell him you represent Jeffrey Moore."

I must have been too stiff, paralyzed by the heat and by being addressed as Mr. Hirsch.

Lynn repeated, "Tell him you represent Mr. Moore."

This time I nodded and croaked, "OK."

"Good," he said, having my attention. "Ask him if he knew Mr. Moore and if so whether he saw Mr. Moore on Wednesday, December twenty-third, 1967. If you're not too busy."

Then Lynn Reilly went off to his office, straightening his tie.

His secretary, who appeared to be wearing a wig, turned to me and grinned.

"Come over here, sonny boy," she said. "You gonna work for me on this one. And it's Hulda. Hulda Pollak. Now, Jeffrey Moore is charged with conspiracy to sell cocaine. Rolando LaPlante lives in the north section of town." She took away the paper Lynn had given me and wrote a house number on it.

"Lynn gave you your little question to ask. Don't forget it. Just call me with LaPlante's answer, yes or no. Call me from a phone booth. You have our number, right?" Hulda's upper lip was strewn with a display of perspiration.

I looked with despair at the address. It was on upper Fourteenth Street, a destitute neighborhood that never saw a white face unless it was inside a car going no slower than thirty miles an hour.

At the law-center orientation sessions less than a year earlier, the faculty had made no bones about it. Never go to North DC, they warned. Bad place. Too dangerous.

I looked for a way of asking about the assignment. "Isn't that a pretty tough place for a…" I wasn't sure how to say *white boy*.

Hulda chortled with glee. "You betcha. Be back before dark. Anyway, we'll be able to identify your body. They don't eat people up there, just slit a throat or two." She looked at me hard. "You too scared, sonny boy?"

She said it in a mean way, a dare. I took the bait.

"No, I'm not too scared. But what do I do when I talk to Rolando LaPlante? Do I need a tape recorder? Am I supposed to get him to sign a statement?"

"Not this time." Hulda had a country accent halfway between an Appalachian miner and a Chesapeake Bay crabber. "Just make the call. Take a cab. And bring back the receipt, please."

I was to learn that *sonny boy* was the term Hulda used for all short-termers whose names she said she couldn't waste time remembering because they were going to be gone soon.

The address Hulda had given me was in as poor a neighborhood as I had heard. Every day the *Post* and the *Tribune* were filled with stories of murders and assaults in North DC. The cabby confirmed it.

"Why is a boy like you goin' up there?" He shook his head mournfully.

I thought maybe I'd get lucky, and LaPlante just wouldn't be around.

The block where Rolando LaPlante was supposed to live was treeless and filled with row houses radiating the heat of a late-fall day. They leaned together to avoid falling down. Bricks were missing here and there. Windows were shuttered, and doors were barred and sometimes covered with sheets of plywood. The street-level windows that were uncovered revealed unpainted interior walls.

"What do I have pay you to stick around?" I asked the cab driver.

"You don't have enough money," he said as he threw a piece of paper at me out of the window, and then he drove off. I picked up the paper. It was my receipt and the only evidence as to how I had arrived in this place.

I was on my own.

Across the street a bunch of young black kids in shorts were playing. I stood there in the wrenching heat, looking about for a minute as I tried to calm down. The waves of heat rippled in the street. I took my jacket off and put it over my arm.

On the corner was a small store with a pay phone outside. You'll be OK, I said to myself. Besides, your witness probably isn't around.

I went up to the house and rang the doorbell. An unshaven man smoking a cigarette opened the door. He wore an Italian T-shirt exposing muscular arms. I guessed the man stood three inches taller and weighed fifty pounds more than I did. I could smell his body odor.

"Who the fuck are you?" The smoke he blew in my face carried with it the stench of beer.

"Hi." My voice squeaked. "I'm looking for Rolando LaPlante."

The man just stared past me at the street and blew more smoke. I knew I had no business being there.

"And what do you want with him?"

I took this as a statement that he was Rolando. I repeated my directions. "I represent Jeffrey Moore. I need to know if you met with Mr. Moore on Wednesday, December twenty-third, 1967." My voice was a tremolo of uncertainty.

He leaned against the doorframe, frowning. "So. You rep-RESENT some mean Jeffrey motherfucker Moore. Issat so, huh?" He spit out the words, his head bobbing as he spoke. The children across the street had stopped playing and were watching the drama.

"Lemme tell you, Mr. I rep-RESENT. I don't even know any Jeffrey motherfucker Moore. How the hell could I have talked to somebody I don't even know? Now get the fuck out of here." He slammed the door.

I was alive but had failed. I walked to the little corner grocery store, with shaking hands put a quarter in the pay phone, and called Hulda. I told her the cabby had refused to stay. Hulda chortled at my distress.

"Now, you just stay put by that little ol' store, sonny boy, and I'm sending a cab to come and get you. And sonny boy, be sure to remember the receipt."

I gasped, then remembered that piece of paper dropped from the cabbie's window. I had forgotten I picked it up and placed it in my pocket. I thanked God that at least I had the receipt safe. If I failed Hulda's admonition to get the cabbie's receipt and the next one as well, she would rub my inexperience in my face until the skin peeled off.

The cab took over an hour. Crossing DC late in the afternoon was impossible. I arrived at the office at six thinking it was time to go home. The hot air fans, electric typewriters, and secretaries all chattered away as if it were nine in the morning.

Hulda glared at me and then gave me a typed document. An affidavit from me, Nathan Hirsch. It stated that on June 21, 1968, I had spoken to a man who responded to the name Rolando LaPlante, and in response to the question I uttered, he denied he met with Jeffrey Moore on Wednesday, December 23, 1967. The affidavit also announced that attached to it were the two cab receipts that framed the time of my visit with Rolando LaPlante. That's why Hulda insisted on the receipts, I thought.

"OK, sonny?" she said.

I responded that the document was accurate, but I could not figure out why this mattered in the least. Hulda produced a pen, which she stuck into my hand, and told me to sign. After I scratched my name across the signature line, she notarized my signature and hollered, "Lynn, we got the affidavit."

Lynn Reilly stuck his head out of the door, walked to Hulda's desk, and read my affidavit with a toothy grin.

"I'm sorry," I stammered, "he just wouldn't admit to the meeting, Mr. Reilly."

"Of course he didn't. You did just fine. Just fine."

"Why is it so important?"

"Let me see if I can explain it. You see, Mr. Moore is not a big fish, but the government claims he has some business associates who are. They were all charged together with conspiracy. Mr. LaPlante is supposed to connect him to the conspiracy. Now he says that on a key date, they didn't speak, and he didn't even know Mr. Moore."

Lynn looked me in the eye.

"A week from Thursday, maybe Friday—I'll let you know—you'll come to court in a dark suit and be prepared to say what's in this affidavit."

"A witness?" I gasped. "I've never testified."

"Maybe this will be the first time," he said, "but only if Mr. LaPlante denies the contents of your affidavit here."

I looked puzzled.

Lynn grinned. "Mr. LaPlante just gave the jury a reason to doubt the truth of the prosecutor's case and a reason to believe me when I say they have failed to prove Mr. Moore guilty beyond a reasonable doubt."

I didn't get it at all.

"Mr. LaPlante is the government's only witness connecting Jeffrey Moore to the conspiracy. And Mr. LaPlante is going to contradict himself about a meeting with Mr. Moore on December twenty-third, 1967. He either didn't tell you the truth or won't tell the truth in the trial. If the jury doesn't believe him, they will have a basis for reasonable doubt."

I remembered the words of Lynn Reilly's lecture earlier that day: "When you conclude in your own mind that the prosecutor has overlooked his burden and that there is one key fact, one element of the crime he cannot prove beyond a reasonable doubt, you have discovered the opportunity for your client to walk out of the courtroom a free man."

* * *

After the first day of Jeffrey Moore's trial, Lynn called me into his office. "Nathan," he said, using his peculiar convention in which an urgent directive was phrased like a polite request, "could you please arrive in Judge Otto's courtroom at exactly nine thirty tomorrow morning?"

I must have looked distressed, because my boss laughed.

"Now, Nathan, I suspect your presence in the courtroom alone will be enough," he said. "I may ask you to stand up, but that will be the extent of your performance. But be on time, please."

At 8:45 a.m. the next day, dressed in my only suit and afraid to be late, I arrived early at the federal court by cab. The day was a roaster. The combination of heavy humidity and my sleepless anxiety the night before left me feeling like a flu victim. Even without the swelter and nerves, entering a federal courtroom reminded me of being a specimen on a slide.

I pulled on the large brass knob of the leather-padded door leading to Judge Otto's art-deco-era courtroom. At first it stuck, but then it popped free with a grunt and swung open, and I self-consciously peered inside.

Lynn Reilly's directive had made my arrival seem pivotal, as if the entire courtroom would be waiting for my nine-thirty appearance, but the twelve rows of wooden pews were all but empty, as was the jury box. The warm courtroom possessed the musty smell of an empty shipping crate.

Judge Otto sat on his high bench surrounded below the dais by his bailiff, a court clerk, and a stenographer armed to the teeth with a tape recorder and transcriber. The judge's hangdog jowls made him look as if he were in a perpetual yawn.

The lawyers occupied the two walnut counsel tables: the defense to the left side and the government attorneys and FBI agents to the right. US marshals stood in the rear, their polyester coats lumpishly covering their shoulder holsters.

Lynn and his bow-tied partner, Aaron Sugarman, sat at the defense counsel's table with a young black man in conservative clothes. He looked like a banker with an modest Afro. That must be Jeffrey Moore, I thought. I had never seen him in the office.

No one spoke above a whisper in the vast room, but even the flipping of papers or the snapping of a paper clip sent sound waves echoing about the two-story-high chamber. A spotlight bulb in the ceiling was burned out. I wondered how the janitors would get all the way up to replace it.

Lynn was arguing a point of law to the judge. He stood at the podium, his hands, for the most part, resting on its walnut sides. Only periodically would he slightly raise his right hand. It seemed as if that hand were floating on its own, an independent agent fluttering in agreement with the point Lynn was making.

"Your Honor, we object to the government calling Mr. Rolando LaPlante, because they know his oral testimony must contradict his written sworn statement, given to the FBI at a time closer to the date of the charge and thus a more accurate recollection of the facts than his testimony in court today, which will be at least false and possibly perjurious." Lynn's argument was rhythmic and measured. His tone reflected certainty without histrionics or theatricality.

He had a point. It was a felony to lie in sworn statements given to the FBI. These written statements, filled out on FBI Form 302, thus called 302s, were used to make sure of the content of a witness's trial testimony in federal court. The defense received the 302s only immediately before the witness's testimony.

The judge leaned forward toward the assistant US attorney, who sat to the right of the podium.

"Mr. Smith, do you disagree with Mr. Reilly's assertion that the witness plans to testify to facts contrary to his sworn written statement?" The judge asked his question a soft, raspy voice.

The assistant, a tall dark-haired man, rose and rapidly stated a predictable answer: "Mr. LaPlante may have been confused when he signed the sworn statement during the investigation, but in any event, a witness's credibility is a question for the jury, Your Honor. They can weigh Mr. LaPlante's testimony, which, as Mr. Reilly knows, is what a jury does."

"Your Honor," Lynn answered softly, "I do agree with one point counsel has made. One might doubt the entire case if indeed they believe Mr. LaPlante is untruthful. More important, however, I have asked why the government, in the search for the truth, should be allowed to proffer as truthful a witness who, they now concede, will swear differently as to material facts. Should the government be allowed to place before a jury a witness who was untruthful even to its own agents? Why should we all not have a doubt as a matter of law in such a case?"

Judge Otto spoke with solemnity. "I am permitting the prosecutor to call Mr. LaPlante. I appreciate Mr. Reilly's objection, but I am persuaded that the better course is to let the jury form its own opinion. However, Mr. Smith, since the government does not dispute that the witness will testify differently from his sworn statement, Mr. Reilly will be given broad discretion in bringing out this matter to the jury. Motion to exclude denied. Bring in the jury."

The courtroom leaped into action. Marshals rose and crossed the room. The bailiff smoothly retreated to the jury door. I could hear him say to someone that court was ready to begin. Chairs scraped the floor. Coats shuffled onto grunting, slow-walking jurors.

I looked about the seats behind the government's table. I recognized Rolando LaPlante. Unlike at our meeting, he was freshly shaven, and under his black suit now he displayed a stylish white shirt with long collar points and a thick tie. He seemed comfortable as the assistant US attorney rose to speak.

"With the court's permission, the government will call Mr. Rolando LaPlante to the stand."

I listened to LaPlante's testimony for some ringing moment when the jurors would gasp, but there was none. At the end the assistant US attorney simply stopped and said, "I have no further questions. Your witness."

Lynn Reilly took one piece of paper with him to the podium. He looked directly at Rolando.

"Sir," he said, "please recall that today you testified regarding your meeting with Jeffrey Moore on Tuesday, December twenty-third, 1967."

Lynn's voice was not the melodious baritone you would expect of an orator, but high pitched, almost squeaky. Yet he used his voice musically, like a flute hitting all the notes, and when he wished he added humor at the end of a line with a lilt.

Rolando nodded.

"Yet your own written statement made to the government is silent about that meeting, is it not?"

"It is," said Rolando, "but I can explain."

"Yes, sir," Lynn said. "Now, on Wednesday of last week you spoke with Nathan Hirsch, a young law student who came to your home, did you not?"

LaPlante hesitated. "No. I didn't, I think. I am not sure," he stammered.

"Mr. Hirsch is in the courtroom, Your Honor. May I request that he stand?"

"Go ahead, Mr. Reilly."

I felt the color rise in my face. I was about to be a witness. Lynn had not prepared me.

"Mr. LaPlante, do you recognize Mr. Hirsch?"

"I'm not sure," said LaPlante. "Yes, I think so."

"Now, I have Mr. Hirsch's affidavit here, Mr. LaPlante. With the court's permission, I would have this affidavit marked as defense exhibit eleven." The judge nodded.

Lynn handed the document to Mr. Smith, the assistant US attorney.

"This is your copy, counsel." Lynn moved slowly, never ceasing to stare at Mr. LaPlante as he walked to the clerk's dock below the judge and handed the original to the clerk, who handed it to the judge.

"Now, Mr. Hirsch asked you if you were Rolando LaPlante, did he not?"

"Yes, I think so."

"And then you asked him what he wanted, correct?"

"Something like that."

"And then he asked you, sir, whether or not you had met Jeffrey Moore on December twenty-third, 1967, did he not?"

"If that's what he says."

"And was your answer to Mr. Hirsch, Mr. LaPlante, the same as your sworn written statement to the government, in which you made no disclosure about such a meeting, or was it the same as your testimony in court that you gave a few minutes ago?"

"I told the truth here."

"Mr. LaPlante, in which of your sworn statements did you duplicate your statement to Mr. Hirsch? Your sworn court testimony or your sworn pretrial statement?"

"I told him I never met with Moore because I wanted to get rid of him."

"So then, Mr. LaPlante, your statement to Mr. Hirsch was the same as your sworn statement before you became a witness in court, is that not correct?"

"That statement was not true," LaPlante blurted out. He clearly wanted to protect his courtroom performance. I watched a woman in the jury box fan her face with disgust.

"I didn't tell the truth in that statement, but I told the truth here." Rolando was visibly sweating. It may have been the contradiction in his testimony that made him perspire or perhaps only the heat of the day outside. I suspected that jury would deem it to be the latter and not the former.

"So you lied to Mr. Hirsch and lied to the officers who took your statement, is that correct?"

"And I'm telling the truth now," Rolando stated. His tone was defiant and a bit too loud.

"Mr. LaPlante, you would be the first to admit that reasonable people might disagree with that last statement."

"I don't care one way or the other. I never lie in court."

"But otherwise anything goes, it seems. Thank you, Mr. LaPlante."

At the break Lynn said to me in a whisper, "Fine job, Nathan, fine job. It went better than I thought, but I'm afraid you'll have to leave the courtroom."

"I really want to hear your closing, Mr. Reilly," I said.

"The jury will do better with Mr. LaPlante's lies and a memory of you, not your presence. We can talk about it later." He smiled with those protruding teeth. "Besides, the prosecutor may want to put you on the stand. You might not like that experience." I must have paled.

I waited in Lynn's office for the defense team to come back from Judge Otto's court. I slipped into my boss's chair and fiddled with the papers on his desk. I leaned back and put my feet up just as the door popped open and Lynn strode in, tie loose and face worn. Aaron Sugarman was close behind, bow tie twitching happily above his Adam's apple, his bearded face flushed and a smile a mile wide on his lips.

Lynn didn't even notice me as I slid off his chair. He just collapsed on one corner of his yellow couch and kicked off his shoes.

"Bourbon," he shouted. Hulda came in from nowhere with a glass filled no more than one inch with a caramel-colored liquid and no ice. Lynn swallowed and hollered, "Whoeet. Brown it up." He all but threw the empty glass to Hulda.

I knew they were ebullient; I wanted to be part of their excitement.

"What happened?" I asked.

Aaron Sugarman smiled. "Jury back in a half an hour. Not guilty."

"Where's Jeffrey, our client?"

"We never celebrate with clients like Jeffrey," Aaron said. "There's too much bad blood between him and the FBI. They'd tail us, tap us, bug us, film us. Who needs it?"

I was shocked. "But he was acquitted."

Breathless, Lynn joined in. "They never forget, Nathan m'boy, never. You let your guard down, some lifer gumshoe you just embarrassed, why, he'll put you on the cooker. Smash you like a walnut under a hammer. Jeffrey had a tail the minute he left the courthouse. We have a Fourth Amendment to the Constitution because the government doesn't always play it straight. Most agents will steal evidence out of a man's home and afterward get a search warrant if they think they can get away with it. Well, they can't. You old enough to drink? Hulda, another round. Let's hear it for Mr. Rolando LaPlante."

That night I looked in my bathroom mirror. I attempted to imitate Lynn Reilly's sweeping eyes, unblinking, clear, and prophetic. I held up my fingers in the mirror, trying to make them bend like Lynn's bent during argument. My eyes, my fingers, imitated my model's presence in court.

In the light of the bathroom, I achieved a semblance of the real thing, but I feared that was the best I could do. I suspected I would always be a mere imitator of the real thing.

CHAPTER 4

Uncle Harry King of the MOTs

* * *

THE QUEASY FEAR OF BEING permanently damaged by alcohol reels about me in my cubicle. All echoes of yesterday's celebration and success from the Cook case have evaporated. I sit restlessly and attempt to retrieve my focus. New pleadings in a criminal case my boss has assigned to me sit on my desk, but the words refuse to be readable.

I rummage around inside my desk drawer. My fingers hunger to find a mint, a candy, something I can place in my mouth to erase the coating of discomfort on my tongue. I try to breathe deeply now, but the thump in my chest fails to respond and slow down. Some agitation in me has joined forces with my hangover. The reappearance of the Bethell jury during the Cook trial should not have unnerved me, but it did. Ritchie, what was I supposed to learn, I think, as if my brother's ghost could answer.

I was afraid of Horace Parker, but Lynn Reilly was not. My boss—not I—saw that Horace was a Goliath easily taken down with a slingshot. Lynn saw Horace's weakness; I sensed nothing. I am not like Lynn Reilly. I am not like you, Ritchie; I am not a natural.

Perhaps I was spoiled by the small-town adulation I received in tiny Bethell. Standing out among the rural kids there—perhaps feeling like a big fish in a small pond—conditioned me. Perhaps my jury is telling me that in the District of Columbia, the legal pond of ponds, I will always be a minnow.

I long for some reassurance but from whom? Shira? Hardly. I am spiraling inside, dizzy from more than drink. Perhaps I should spend the money and again call Uncle Harry King in Bethell. I could read him the *Washington Post* article. His approval would settle me like a therapeutic dose.

Then I stop. Who am I kidding? Uncle Harry would debunk the entire newspaper. He would call the writer names. I would feel worse, more toxic, from Harry's ridicule than from the ringing in my head left by Deirdre's purloined champagne.

The phone lies in its cradle, daring me to risk being taken apart by Harry's acerbic tongue. I stare at it but do not budge. Harry speaks to me without the assistance of telephones, poles, and wires.

* * *

Even when I went home to Bethell during law school breaks, Uncle Harry would never meet with me in his office. Instead I would get this kind of call: "Nathan, kiddo, see me at Loggers Stadium. I got a problem you can help me with. But first I want you to see something. There's this kid playing this afternoon. Name is Thorquist, Thorgard, Thorsomething. Got big forearms just like Popeye. Or maybe Thor." He would hoot at his own joke, voice deep and clustered.

"Kid could be the second coming of Mantle if he would just stop swinging his bat at every ball, or his *schvanz* at every *hubba*." More hooting from Harry.

Or, "Nathan, meet me at Steve's Diner. Somebody wants a mortgage, and I'm gonna help 'em. They teach you how to do the paperwork for collateral at that fancy law school?"

Collateral was a big deal for Uncle Harry. Though he was licensed to practice law, he also was a licensed bail bondsman, a notary public, and a real estate broker. All of that allowed Uncle Harry to receive money or property as the middleman, whether it was a business deal, a lawsuit, or the process in a criminal case of getting his client out of jail.

"Your uncle Harry is a wheeler-dealer, no question about that," my dad once said. "But he is our wheeler-dealer."

Even in the 1970s, Harry still had an incredible shock of black hair for a man in his fifties, a fleshy face, a thick ridge of eyebrows, and sagging eyelids over eyes that were mountain-lake blue and just as cold. He had a mushy way of talking, a deep voice like a throat needing to be cleared, almost hoarse.

Uncle Harry had never married and occasionally escorted my spinster aunt Riva to the social events put on in Bethell. Harry was no more my relative than any of the handful of Jewish men and women in Bethell who were not members of the Hirsch family. Calling Harry "Uncle" was reassuring to me; I always had looked to him as being somehow special.

My view of Harry was shared by the other five Jewish families in Bethell, who among themselves somewhat cryptically referred to one another collectively as "members of the tribe," or MOTs, pronounced "em-oh-tees." In fact you could count the Jews living in Snoline County on the fingers of two hands.

Among the MOTs there were spats, quarrels, jealousies, even feuds, but despite these all-too-human relationships, I think my parents and each of my so-called uncles and aunties drew a certain comfort from this connection, given that other memberships weren't so welcoming or available.

Even in Bethell and Snoline County, with a population well under twenty thousand, the lumber mill families had formed the Snoline Country Club around a golf course built in the '20s. Someone had promptly limited members to Christians, as if any other religion might pollute the holy enterprise of golf. This token of exclusion stuck in the craw of the Hirsch family and increased the interdependence of the MOTs on one another.

With the unspoken division not far from anyone's mind, it probably felt natural that Harry stepped in as the MOTs' leader. His deep, leathery voice could speak with an elaborate vocabulary like the formally educated lawyer he was or roar with the raucous words of a hand on the floor of the Skarbell Mill. He bragged that in trying a jury trial, he could sound earthy, as if he had just cut down a stand of trees or pulled in a net full of salmon.

"King salmon," he crowed, "the biggest, fattest, and tastiest. And named for my family." This was Harry's way of saying he belonged in Bethell, country club membership or no country club membership.

For a while in the 1950s, Uncle Harry had taught beginning Hebrew to the little gaggle of MOT kids. Each week the class would meet at the home of one of the class members, always in the kitchen.

My class was made up of Hannah and Arlene Asher, whose parents, Oscar and Claire, owned a furniture store in Bethell. Bobby Raskin was there; his dad was the math teacher at the local vocational-technical school. Also attending were the Galitzer twins, Ralph and Roger, whose dad, Frank, had a men's Western-wear emporium near my family's Fulton Jewelry in the Hirsch Building.

Finally, in addition to my brother, the class included the Guthman boys, Alvin and Robert, who were dark and silent. Everybody talked about Mr. Guthman and his wife, Ilsa, who were World War II refugees and had been admitted into the United States only because of Uncle Harry's sponsorship. He arranged for Mr. Guthman to be hired as a bookkeeper at Skarbell's, Bethell's only remaining lumber mill.

Before our Hebrew class on Sunday, Harry would smoke a cigar, and the smell of tobacco vapor clung to him. When he breathed, the scent of burned fall foliage ricocheted through the kitchen classroom.

Hebrew classes consisted of our memorizing the sounds of the Hebrew letters from sheets on which the letters were printed in huge fonts. Then Harry would also write the words on a small blackboard he carried with him, and we would repeat the words letter by letter, first in unison with Harry, then alone. The meaning of these Hebrew words never, ever came up. *Kaa vod atta. Tuuh feel ah. Ley oh lahm voh ed.*

In unison we boomed the sounds out the windows of our study house each Sunday morning. I wondered what the gentile neighbors thought when they heard our meaningless chanting.

After an hour or so, Uncle Harry would abruptly stop us and bring out a bag of fresh bagels, some with jam and cream cheese, some with onions and smoked salmon. We would wash down the bagels with giant glasses of thick chocolate milk. Where he found those bagels every Sunday morning, I haven't a clue; the closest Jewish bakery I knew of was Brenner Brothers, over two hours away in Seattle.

Harry called us the Bethell Hebrew Scholars, and the name stuck.

"Where are the scholars meeting this week?" I would ask my dad, hungry for bagels and cream cheese. I didn't think of us as belonging to Bethell. I thought of us as Harry's Hebrew Scholars.

Sadly, Harry stopped teaching when I was seven, and our little group then moved on to Mr. Guthman as our new teacher. Mr. Guthman's eyebrows were knitted in a perpetual frown. He terrified everybody with his disapproving German-accented English. His statements sounded like criminal indictments:

"You didn't study," he would say, then put on black-framed glasses, which swelled his eyes to a primitive ferociousness. "I can tell. You simply didn't study." He would then rise, walk over to the next student, and stand there towering above the victim, thrusting down a new sheet of unpronounceable Hebrew letters into the poor victim's face and commanding in that flat guttural style, "Now you read."

But nothing would come out. Mr. Guthman froze everyone's tongues, including those of Alvin and Robert, his own sons, who also went mute when it was their turn. Our inability to demonstrate progress in pronouncing this tangled aggregation of Hebrew letters enraged Mr. Guthman, and he would rail at us for laziness.

During Mr. Guthman's short tenure as our Hebrew teacher, the food stopped flowing, the little band of students quit cooperating, and the class disbanded. When the Ashers pulled Hannah and Arlene out, our class was doomed, and frankly I was relieved.

The Hebrew lessons reemerged in a different format when I turned ten. My dad informed me that Uncle Harry would tutor me to read Hebrew for my bar mitzvah. Harry secured the student version of a portion taken from the Torah, the first five books of the Old Testament. This one small bit, called a *par'sha*, was the one that was read in synagogues the world over on the Sabbath closest to the date of a boy's thirteenth birthday.

Uncle Harry wrote on the inside flap in my training book, "To Nathan, from Harry King."

"This here book is yours, my boy," Harry said to me as we started my training, this time just the two of us in my kitchen. "For the rest of your life, you'll never forget what you are learning."

Harry worked with me for three years to memorize the sounds of the entire Hebrew text, interspersing the readings with a reintroduction of fresh bagels, cream cheese, smoked salmon, and chocolate milk that refreshed me, as in the past. It worked perfectly.

Kaa vod atta. Tuuh feel ah. Ley oh lahm voh ed.

When I was thirteen, my bar mitzvah took place in the Bethell VFW hall, which any Bethell family could rent for special occasions. I was surrounded by my family, the Galitzers, Ashers, Raskins, Kings, and Guthmans as well as my dad's pals from the local chapters of the Shriners and the VFW lodge. The Shriners felt it was appropriate to wear their red felt fezzes, thus looking like visiting Turkish potentates. The vets dressed in semi-uniforms of white shirts, black pants, black spit-shined shoes, and black overseas army caps, an aging army of overweight sport fishermen.

From a perch on the VFW stage between two huge unfurled flags—Old Glory and the Washington State green banner—my knees knocking, my hands sweaty, I screeched out the Hebrew paragraphs from a huge book that substituted for a parchment Torah scroll, the real deal used at big-city bar mitzvahs.

I droned away in Hebrew's singsong traditional style, just as Uncle Harry had trained me, taking great comfort in the fact that not one soul in the room had any idea whether what I uttered was correct or mishmash. Either way, my parents sat there with glistening eyes. The vets and the Shriners clapped at the end. It seemed that George Washington himself, his face in the middle of that state flag, was also listening and sighed with relief when I finished chanting Hebrew phrases backward on a sunny Saturday morning.

Afterward Harry smoked two cigars, crowing to anyone who would listen that like him, someday I would be a lawyer or, even better, a rabbi, and I would teach the next generation of Bethell bar mitzvah students just as he had taught me.

"If I ever have a son, I want him to be like Nathan," he said, his arm draped around my shoulders and his paw clutching his cigar and its glowing ash.

I had no idea why he should be proud of my mumblings. I simply concluded that the cloud of malodorous cigar smoke Harry inhaled daily caused him to permanently hallucinate.

I applied to law school with Harry as my model, and so it made sense that I asked him as a legal practitioner to endorse me. When I called Uncle Harry to ask for a letter of recommendation, I offered to go by his office.

Instead he countered with a growl, "No need for that. Write whatever you want, and I'll stop off at your folks'. Touch it up, maybe. But make it good. If I have to rewrite it, I'll eat your ma and pa out of house and home."

Harry's willingness to use my words as if they were his was a scary proposition. In preparation for his scrutiny, I composed, recomposed, and rewrote the expressions I imagined someone else might write to describe me.

After three full days of typed fabrications, exaggerations, irrelevancies, embarrassed head scratchings, and paper crumplings, I finally came up with a one-page single-spaced letter for Harry to edit. I was too humiliated to have my mother type it, so I hunted and pecked the final draft with critical care. That took another day.

Harry came to our house and clutched my draft with his big hands, reading it with lightning speed. He chuckled over some of my phrases, which he repeated out loud, muttering, "such bullshit" as he frowned over his crummy tortoiseshell reading glasses.

I blushed as Uncle Harry looked at me. The presumption of describing myself through Harry's eyes caused my scalp to sweat.

"Got a pencil?" Harry said. He made some cursory changes here and there, but I could see he had failed to amend the text much, really nothing of substance, and began to hand the draft to me, then pulled it back.

"Pearl!" Harry hollered. "I need ya to type something." My mother came out at his bellowing.

"What about another draft of this letter?" Harry said.

"I'll type it," I said.

"Naw, let your mom do it for me. OK, Pearl?"

"Fine, not a problem," Mom said. "And while you wait, Harry, some coffee?" Then she called to the next room, "Leon, come in here and get Harry some coffee, will you? The man's helping our son get into law school."

I heard the grumbling in the back of the house near the kitchen. My dad emerged, his shirt askew from his pants. He held his newspaper in one hand and Harry's coffee in the other.

I got the idea that Uncle Harry wanted Pearl to see what he was doing for her darling son. My dad Leon couldn't have cared less and retreated to his newspaper, his face buried in the business section.

But Pearl was another story. After she had typed the letter on high-quality onionskin paper and brought it to Harry for his signature, her face was beaming from the praise Harry had heaped on me.

Clearly Harry had gotten the approval he had wanted from Pearl, and I had his endorsement accompanying my application. Looking back at the process, I realized I had never once set foot in Uncle Harry's office.

I expected that sometime Harry would ask me to practice law with him. Of course my answer would be "no," but the honor that would flow from the invitation was something I wanted. It was, in a sense, like an insurance policy.

* * *

Uncle Harry's parents had founded the first auto-wrecking yard in Bethell. It was car wrecks that put them on the map, especially after World War II. In fact when I started driving, my first car was a 1952 Dodge that Dad bought from Dale King, Harry's brother, who ran the business.

Harry's dad, Zalmon (Zolly), and Harry's brother, Dale (real name Mendel), had filled the yard with junked autos from the '20s and '30s. During the war, when all new parts flowed exclusively to the military, Dale made a small fortune keeping the local repair shops supplied with recycled parts harvested from the wrecks in the yard.

Dale had also attracted a new group of customers. Local car clubs, known as hot-rodders, mostly populated by Bethell's mill hands, sprang up after the war. The clubs had their own jackets and badges. They would take the carcass of some crashed jalopy and rebuild the motor with odds and ends from wrecks of a more recent vintage. They hung out with their girlfriends at old garages and barns that served as shops and clubhouses, rebuilding their "rods" and drinking beer.

Clubs from as far as two counties away bought salvage parts from the Kings' junkyard. The local rebuilt autos were somewhere between the roaring stripped-down speedsters racing at county fairgrounds and the crafted and painted California beauties that were featured in car magazines. The rods were coveted by every local kid, whether born on a farm, in a lumber camp, or in Bethell's neighborhoods.

Harry told me at Steve's Diner over a cup of coffee that when he had come back to practice law in Bethell, Dale had sent to him "all those screwball racers who were in a jam, grease under their fingernails, grease in their hair. Who could tell the difference, hair oil or lube oil? Smells the same."

The club members would get loaded at their shops, pack up their cars, roar through town with their mufflers off, and head out to Route 7 and drag race into the night on a deserted strip of road on the Tamlips Indian Reservation.

"Saturday night was a war zone in Bethell between the county sheriffs and the clubs, lemme tell ya." Harry pointed his cigar at me. "When racing and drinking got them crosswise with the law, who bailed 'em out? You got it. Me."

These rod owners became Harry's first "multiples."

"Listen up," he said to me. "You'd starve to death around here if all you did was get the fees offa' local drunks. So I have a bail bondsman's license too. No sense sending somebody to Everett for a bail bond. I post for 'em at the same time I appear for them in court and get them out of the hoosegow on the spot. Nobody complains about not sleeping overnight in John Law's back bedroom."

Harry exhaled cigar smoke.

"When the sheriffs put a hot-rodder in jail, I get 'em to work on time the next day, and they give me their souped-up cars, or sometimes their homes, as collateral that they're going to show up in court like they were told."

"But then they go to jail, right?" I asked.

"Naw. I got a deal with the prosecutor all ready to go, so if they don't show, it's warrant time—you know, arrest. But when they do show, everybody's so happy they clap 'em on the back, say, "Good boy, now don't do that again," suspend a three-day jail sentence, and give 'em a little poke-in-the-ass fine. Very popular."

Harry was also prepared to loan his clients enough cash so that in one stroke, they could pay their fines to the court, pay Harry his legal fee, and pay the premium for a bail bond. Harry brought notes or IOUs with collateral papers right to the courtroom or jailhouse for his clients to sign on the spot.

Actually my dad informed me that Harry borrowed cash from our business, Fulton Jewelry, so he could make loans to his clients on the nights of their arrests. In that way Harry had the ready cash to handle the maximum number of arrests and bail bonds over any given weekend.

I asked my dad about the ethics of this arrangement.

"Ethics?" my dad snorted. "Go ask any of those guys whether they put any money aside for a rainy day. Can they post bail? Hell no. Now they need some dough. OK, so Harry's there with some money from his brother, maybe some from the Hirsches. For our trouble Harry charges a little more than the going interest rate at the bank, not a lot, and we split it equally. Hell, lotsa times his clients don't pay off. Then what? There's lotsa risk in it for what is really a public service. No cheering, believe me. Nobody's saying thanks."

When a hot-rodder did not appear on his court date or defaulted on his loans, Harry would turn the collateral—the title documents, commonly known as pinks—over to Dale, who would repossess the car and auction it off to his cronies.

Sometimes the bail for multiple offenders was so high, Harry required mortgages on his clients' homes in Mill Town to secure their return to court. And when they failed to pay off the loans, Harry foreclosed on the houses and rented them back to his clients, always offering to transfer back their titles when they paid him in full.

"A man's home is his castle," Harry would say, holding his cigar philosophically in the air, "so sooner or later they find a rich uncle, or somebody dies and leaves 'em an inheritance. They bring the cash to me, settle up, and their Mill Town castle is theirs again."

I meant to ask Harry if he collected rent in the meantime, but I felt I would be prying into business that was not mine. While there did not seem to be anything illegal about this practice, I was uncomfortable that some of the kids in my classes in Bethell's schools were living in homes Harry had taken from their families.

Harry's family name, King, was a corruption of the old-world moniker the family had brought from Russia. To Harry's father, his name implied royalty:

Zalmon Ben David, or Zalmon, son of David. David had been a king, and "king" in Hebrew was *Melech*. So Harry's father changed his name to Zolly Melech. Later he just used Zolly King. King. It seemed so American.

The junkyard had a sign with "KING'S AUTO PARTS" painted in green and trimmed in black accents, in a wooden yoke above the cyclone-and-wood fence. The junkyard sat on the Lynch farm, on Hemlock Avenue close to the little grocery store and the county fairground, which Zolly had purchased fifty years before.

Actually Dale named old man Lynch manager of the wrecking yard. Old man Lynch was a retired railroad engineer who lived next to the yard in a two-room ramshackle structure that once had housed his family. He stayed drunk most of the time, and we neighborhood kids would hide and giggle, watching him weave and stumble into the Hemlock grocery, where we went for candy.

On one occasion old man Lynch was unable to make it to the bathroom inside, and, leaning against the porch, he unzipped his workman's suit and relieved himself with the hydraulic force of a field horse. It looked as if old man Lynch had unreeled a brown garden hose from his trousers.

I was astounded at the size of his appendage. It was brown and unamended at its end, unlike my own circumcised pink pointer, which immediately shriveled with respect as the garden hose loudly poured out its steamy contents with a sound like water spattering in hot grease.

Later I learned that any car Dale auctioned off would be titled as if old man Lynch were the seller. When I begged my parents for a car, my dad directed we would go to Dale and pick one out.

"Make sure we have the title too," he said to Dale.

My first car was a brown-and-gray 1952 Dodge that had seen better days. When it started, which was rare in cold or wet weather, it rumbled its way on groans and creaks as much as gas.

Lynch was the name of the seller on the title of my car. By putting old man Lynch's name on the title, the King wrecking yard eliminated the business tax when it sold me the auto. The company's books never listed the repossessed cars in its inventory, and the Kings never paid taxes on the sales proceeds when it auctioned them off.

I stole from the junkyard once—a rusted, age-stained steering wheel and shaft that was decoupled from its chassis like a severed hand. Actually it was Bobby Raskin, one of Harry's Hebrew Scholars, who spotted the wheel in the wrecking yard.

"It's just sitting there useless," he argued. "We'd be able to build our own soapbox with a steering wheel."

Although he was two years older than I was, Bobby was small, wild, and agitated, always scheming to accomplish a portentous project that would demonstrate his genius. Bobby was the one who read that the national Soap Box Derby winner would win a full scholarship to the university of his choice. At eleven he was already thinking about college.

We needed the wheel. I knew of all the car parts that mattered, the steering wheel was the most important. Turning the wheel was the way you steered the vehicle. Without a steering wheel, even a soapbox racer wouldn't work.

We broke into the junkyard late at night. The steering wheel on its shaft lay like an old skeleton in the shadows by the rear access road along the fence. Bobby and I snuck to the edge of the yard off the alley. We had seen a wide space in the loose slats of the wooden fence, wide enough for our skinny bodies, wide enough for the wheel. We pushed past the fence slats and crawled on all fours across the dirt and gravel for the short distance.

A light shone over the door to the junkyard office, but the inside lights had been extinguished. The junkyard was strewn with ravaged hulks painted gray by shadows and covered with dust, but the moon seemed to reflect off the shaft of the steering wheel. We picked it up, Bobby on the wheel end, I on the greasy shaft. The unit was cold and heavy—too heavy to heft it up, as we had hoped. We dropped it with a crunch on the gravel. On the way down, the shaft grazed my leg, marking my pants with a telltale trail of grease.

As we dragged the wheel to the fence, I could see how hard the dream would be to carry out. The wheel assembly weighed a ton. The shaft left a furrow of dirt on the ground leading to the fence. Bobby shoved the steering wheel end through the fence, splintering one slat with a crack.

The sound set off the barking of one neighbor's dog. Then another started to howl. The lights went on in old man Lynch's kitchen, and we abandoned the awkward load with a thud in the unmowed grass by the fence, fleeing, greasy and breathless, the three blocks to Parkland, where our two families lived.

Bobby and I parted under a streetlight on the corner, swearing we would say nothing about our break-in, and that if caught, under no circumstances would we acknowledge we were in this together.

Once my dad saw the grease, he guessed the worst right away. "You'd better come clean quick on this."

I immediately confessed, saying it had been Bobby's idea. I felt guilty telling him about the wheel and especially that Bobby was the ringleader.

As my father wheeled me down the stairs to the front door, there were Mr. Raskin and Bobby coming up our porch steps toward us in the same formation.

Bobby's dad was stooped and prematurely gray, with a bald spot on the back of his head. He taught math at the Bethell Vocational Institute, formed in the '20s by the five lumber mills, of which Skarbell's was the only remainder. His glasses hung from a string of rubber bands tied together, and he had a plastic pocket protector in the breast pocket of his white shirt.

"Leon," Mr. Raskin said with slow sorrow, "your son is getting my Bobby into something over his head."

"Your Bobby? It was his idea," my dad said. "Your boy's older; he should know better."

"What are you talking about?" Mr. Raskin was incensed. "Your kid swiped a piece of hardware from the Kings, and Bobby was taking it back."

I gasped when I heard that Bobby had betrayed me as fast as I had sold him down the river. I could say nothing. Dad took silence as my admission of guilt. He was so ashamed, he could not look at me, and as he led me over to Harry's early the next day, he still was not talking to me all that much.

Harry met us at the front door in his rumpled robe and slippers. "What do you have to say for yourself?"

I looked down. The only thing I could see was Harry's purple-and-white leg sticking out of his ratty plaid robe and his feet hidden in lumpy leather slippers. Harry's toes were crooked and bent, almost deformed. Huge bunions pushed out the slippers' sides.

"*We* never steal from one another," Harry said in a low, heavy voice. "Never."

My dad said nothing, but by his silence it was clear that even a steering wheel could be important. I owed a higher duty to the MOTs whether I liked them or not or whether they cared for me. By taking the wheel, I had broken a deeper duty than "thou shall not steal." I had broken the additional phrase: "especially from Jews."

Even in my shame, I could not help but wonder, at the age of nine, as I stared at Harry's crooked toes, barely disguised by his slippers, whether Harry would have been as concerned about my conduct if the King junkyard had not belonged to his family but had been the property of a member of the Snoline Country Club. I knew better than to ask. It would have set off a riot with my father. But I believed I already had a modest glimpse of the answer.

CHAPTER 5

The Glove Hunts for the Big Fish

* * *

DEIRDRE RUSHES INTO MY OFFICE and dramatically shuts the door. She has seen too many movies. Her hair is pulled back by a crimson headband, leaving her forehead taut and a bush rising behind her skull. I surmise this arrangement avoids a wash, rinse, and set.

"You didn't come by this morning. I was disappointed." Deirdre's voice is light, but her Maryland burr does not disguise a bit of a pout.

"Just distracted," I say, forcing a smile. Then I say to myself, Think like Ritchie. "Last night was great." My words carry all of the impact of last year's Hallmark card. She is waiting for more. I remain silent.

Deirdre's face wrinkles. Anger lines I had missed before. She shakes her head as she retreats without another word, leaving the door open. Her heels clicking down the hall is like an epithet. I think she read my paced words with silence as both a joke and an insult.

My aching head and the lingering scent of Deirdre's perfume has distracted me from the pink note blinking at me in the pile Hulda has left on my desk. It is a phone note from someone I do not know.

"Harold Nagle. Will call back after five."

No number left for me to return. This strikes me as odd, but I am new at this business of getting calls at my office from anyone but my friends.

And Aaron Sugarman has warned me about signing up new clients. The afternoon following the Cook trial celebration, Aaron chose the moment to yet again lecture me about office protocol.

"Now, Hirsch, you are aware that associates don't open files, right? You need to get an adult to authorize engagement with a new client."

Sugarman puffs up his voice with artificial authority when he speaks. I suspect practicing with a star like Lynn Reilly has had a diminishing effect on too many occasions. So when addressing me or other staff, he always employs a patronizing tone. As if I could not figure out that I have to seek approval from the senior partners before using the bathroom.

And it seems an odd time for Sugarman to be delivering what feels like a warning, but I know that with Aaron, there is always a backstory.

United States v. Bastion: a case name whispered by lawyers and staff with titters.

* * *

I had asked Alfred Gibbons about what happened in *Bastion*. He pulled me away, grinning with wild glee.

"It was Aaron's blunder of blunders."

I could see Alfred's teeth, prematurely yellow from smoking, as he smiled.

"Paul Bastion, a big-time Chicago executive in a publicly traded company, was investigated by the SEC for years and then indicted for insider trading by the DC grand jury. Lynn was Bastion's attorney.

"In the meantime an SEC employee named Sally Quesnell was being fired in a complicated administrative hearing. Some lawyer called Aaron Sugarman, who had published this esoteric article in the *Harvard Law Review* about due process rights of civil servants when he was a student. Aaron agreed to cocounsel with Sally's lawyer, who was trying to help her keep her job."

"Why would Aaron take this on?" I was incredulous.

"Why? Let me tell you why. Aaron couldn't attract a client if his life depended on it. The broomstick in his ass keeps showing. Anybody who meets him runs the other way. To say he needs Lynn Reilly is an understatement. So when some local yokel called Aaron with an article from the *Harvard Law Review* that Aaron wrote, he was positively slobbering to get at the matter."

Alfred looked around as if he were about to deliver the nation's nuclear secrets to the Russians.

"And this is the funny part. The SEC decided not to fire the lady before Aaron did a blessed thing in the case. The firm billed her maybe five hundred dollars, but there it was, an invoice in the firm records before the case went dead."

Alfred's eyes danced as he related the story. His dislike of Aaron is almost pathological.

"And Aaron never mentioned a word to Lynn about it, but Sally was still working at the SEC office when the case heated up against Bastion. It turned out Sally's boss was heading the Bastion investigation, and when the US attorney got the SEC witness list for the case, there was Sally Quesnell, whose job involved monitoring some market data the SEC used in its insider trading investigations. Naturally they turned her into a witness when they found out Reilly and Sugarman were her attorneys.

Alfred lit a cigarette and blew out a lungful of smoke.

"They hate Lynn Reilly in the US attorney's office. Must have made them crazy happy to hear that Sally was a Reilly and Sugarman client. I would have given my front teeth to have been in the office after Earl Silbert, the US attorney, the boss himself, called Lynn about the motion to disqualify him as counsel, and Lynn pulled in Sugarman. I bet there are still parts of Sugarman's anatomy scattered under Reilly's couch."

* * *

Lynn Reilly had made it clear he wanted to represent only "big fish." And around the office, Watergate drove the big-fish speculation every day. It had become a lawyers' cottage industry in DC to represent targets and witnesses subpoenaed to appear before Chief Judge Sirica's grand jury, and so far Reilly and Sugarman had no Watergate client.

Earlier that month, late in the day, Lynn had called us in for a meeting in our little lunchroom, its round table covered with cold Coke cans. Meetings were infrequent, so this felt important. Lynn popped a can top and sipped as he plopped down in a chair. We all followed suit.

"We haven't been asked to represent any targets in the grand jury investigation yet," he said. "Just a few nibbles, but as things go, I would be surprised if there aren't some indictments by June."

"Maybe we'll land Nixon," Alfred Gibbon said. Everybody laughed. The boss man, an inveterate and unrepentant Democrat, grinned at the prospect of the president being charged as a criminal.

"Maybe so," he said. "Maybe. But in the meantime, I want to know personally about any calls dealing with the Watergate burglary."

"Yes," Aaron Sugarman interrupted. "Only partners take in new clients. Period."

The interruption clearly irritated Lynn. I suspected that *Bastion* still stuck in his skin like a barbed fishhook, and he did not have to be reminded of it by the man who'd flung his line at him.

"No problem," I blurted. I have no idea why I spoke that day. No one in the Watergate picture would be hunting me out.

* * *

But on the other hand, Mr. Nagle seems to be. I am at my desk a few minutes before five o'clock, waiting for the phone but pretending to proofread a memo for Aaron Sugarman on suppression of fingerprint testimony. At five the phone jangles.

"Hullo, Mr. Hirsch. Harold Nagle here." I hear the accent of a Virginia resident. It's amazing: after six years in the District of Columbia, I can tell the twang of a West Virginia native from the drawl of a true Virginian and the muddled argot of a Baltimore terrapin. All three states on top of one another and each group of citizens with their own unique vocal sounds.

"What can I do for you, Mr. Nagle?"

"I've been interviewed by the FBI, Mr. Hirsch, and I'm a little bit concerned about what I told 'em."

"What's the case about?" There's no immediate answer to my question.

"Mr. Hirsch, I'd rather not talk on the phone. Can we meet somewhere?"

"Sure. Anytime. Our office is in Dupont Circle. I can be here after hours if that works."

"That's not going to work, Mr. Hirsch."

"Why can't we meet at my office?"

"I know it sounds ridiculous, but I think I'm being followed."

"By whom?" My voice is barely civil. This sounds like a nut who has read too many mysteries.

Another delay on Nagle's part.

"I work for the Committee for the Re-election of the President, President Nixon. The media calls us CREEP, which is bad enough. But now Mr. McCord's statements in court are making us all nervous, Mr. Hirsch."

James McCord, one of the Watergate burglars, had announced in open court that the CREEP had given him money for his defense. He did this because Judge Sirica was about to throw the book at him and the other burglars in the sentencing following their pleas of guilty of breaking into the Democratic Party headquarters.

I try again to test whether the caller is sane or just an agitated crackpot who's gotten the Reilly and Sugarman phone number.

"Talking to a lawyer is hardly a sin, Mr. Nagle." My voice sounds immature and reproachful.

"Well, Mr. Hirsch, I'm over fifty years old, and I've never thought to need a lawyer, so this is a new one for me too. But I'm pretty sure there are lots trying to figure out who's been talking to those newspaper reporters. And believe me, I'm not one of them. But that doesn't stop my boss from asking me every day what I do at lunch, where I pick up the bus, and so on and so forth."

My face flushes. This is within the warning circle boss man called out.

"Where do you live, Mr. Nagle?"

"That really doesn't matter. I prefer actually to stay away from home."

"What do you have in mind as a meeting location, then?"

"Tomorrow during morning rush hour, seven or so, at the White Castle, up on Connecticut Avenue at Thirty-Fourth."

"I think I should bring Mr. Reilly, my senior partner," I say. I have fibbed already, describing Lynn as my partner. There's silence on the other side of the phone. It is as if I can almost see Nagle shaking his head.

"I think that's a bad idea, Mr. Hirsch."

"Why not talk to Mr. Reilly?" I ask.

"'Cause you're not splashy like Mr. Reilly, not well known. Not that I don't think you know your way around," he says almost apologetically. "I just want this to be low-key. I read what you did for Reverend Cook."

I mumble agreement. It may be nothing, I think. A cab ride before work. Nobody will miss me in the office. No need to be dramatic until you know what Mr. Nagle wants.

After putting the phone down, I start to call Charlie Hogan, then think better of it. Who knows what watercooler gossip there is inside the US attorney's offices? Just listen to Mr. Nagle, I think. Just listen.

The early morning traffic on Connecticut Avenue flowing down toward the Treasury Department and the White House produces a deafening roar, even on the 14 bus going north, the opposite direction of the rush-hour traffic. I am lucky to find a seat sitting parallel to the aisle; the standing man to my right and the woman to my left are both fighting to keep their feet at each stop and start.

I carry my cordovan briefcase with brass locks that open with a pop when I push the floating button snaps. The case was a graduation gift from Auntie Riva. I wear a beige London Fog raincoat and carry a cheap black collapsible umbrella. It is threatening to pour.

The White Castle at Thirty-Fourth and Connecticut is a chain fast-food joint that has seen better times. It is in an aging retail swath built before World War II. Behind the Formica food counter is a lone worker, a slim lad with a paper version of a military overseas cap atop his head and terrible sloping shoulders that read disappointment.

I buy a cup of coffee so strong it smells as if it were extracted from the embers of a chicory fire and take a seat by a side window, looking for Mr. Nagle. At a booth across from me sit a couple in their fifties, each bundled up against the rain and cold, he sitting on the inside, she sitting next to him by the aisle. The two of them are smoking away, filling an ebony Bakelite ashtray with contrasting gray detritus. The lady is portly, her coat bright red. She gives me the once-over, gets up, wraps her coat tightly around her throat, and leaves without a word to her companion.

The man is bespectacled, short, and rotund. His hat brim is pulled down over his eyes. He stubs his cigarette in the Bakelite tray, sidles out of the booth, and, after looking around Peter Lorre style, waddles toward me.

"Are you Mr. Hirsch?" the man says, glancing past me and out the window. He has weathered, bulging cheeks balanced by deep lines. His face reminds me of Harry King's. Like Harry, I think, this man is in his midfifties. That's how Nagle described himself.

"I am. Mr. Nagle?"

He nods.

"My wife's getting our car. It's a reddish four-door Mercury. Just get in the back. I'll be along. The three of us can talk somewhere else." He sits back at his table and gropes out another cigarette, which he ignites with an iridescent-green Bic lighter.

This is odd, I think for a moment and then nod OK to the arrangement. Outside the White Castle door, a dirty wine-red Mercury sits by the curb. No one is behind the wheel. I hesitate like a character in a spy novel, briefcase, trench coat, and all. I open the rear door and enter the backseat.

Mr. Nagle is a step behind me. As I shut the door, he jumps in the front seat—a bit more nimbly than I would have expected—steps on the gas, and scoots north on Connecticut Avenue. After three blocks Nagle switches to the left lane and makes a legal U-turn so we are heading back toward our White Castle starting point, but only for one block. Without signaling we make a right turn off the main thoroughfare and pull into a neighborhood of row houses.

Nagle says nothing as he drives. I choose to let this meeting play out in silence as well, although my sense of foolishness has been triggered by the twists and turns Nagle is putting us through.

After one mile we are in Takoma Park on the DC/Maryland border. Alongside a small neighborhood park festooned with a swing set, a child's self-propelled merry-go-round, and a pathway meandering through barren trees, Nagle pulls the Mercury over to the side and turns off the engine.

"Let's go for a walk. There's an umbrella in the back. Could you hand it to me, please?" Nagle's voice is thick with exertion, as if we have been running a footrace rather than driving in an urban area at sauntering speed.

The park is empty save for two dogs chasing about as if it were summertime and not a cold, damp March day. We stroll about with our umbrellas open. I feel out of place wearing my raincoat and carrying a briefcase in this neighborhood of row houses.

Nagle coughs a phlegmy rumble. He covers his mouth with his fist, then pulls out his cigarette pack, Old Gold filters. He offers one to me, but I wave him off. I must be a bit impatient, because he launches into his story as he lights up again.

"I'm sorry for the wild-goose chase, Mr. Hirsch, but I'm pretty sure it's necessary."

"What's your excuse for not being at work, Mr. Nagle?"

"Good question, Mr. Hirsch. I knew you were a sharp one." He nods his approval through a cloud of smoke. "Doctor's appointment. That's why the wife is out too, if they check on her." Mr. Nagle looks thoughtful. He extracts a handkerchief from the folds of his overcoat and blows his nose.

"My appointment is in forty minutes back on Connecticut Avenue," he says. "I'll meet her there."

Nagle leads us to a wet bench under a dripping tree, its bare branches showing few spring buds. "Let's take a seat, Mr. Hirsch."

We sit on the wet park bench, open umbrellas conspiratorially bumping each other. I feel the water somehow seeping through my gathered raincoat. Mr. Nagle hands me a Watergate grand jury subpoena *duces tecum* asking for all accounting records in his possession. A relatively ordinary legal document, but somehow the paper carries a greater weight. I have read too many Watergate stories in the news. I sense that someone is watching us even though we are in rural Maryland, miles away from DC.

"I was served at home," he says. I sense there is a primness in this man. He seems to be on the edge of indignation, as if the subpoena power should not reach people of his propriety and responsibility.

"They served me at home," he says a second time. "The neighbors saw it happen." His statement is in response to a question he wasn't asked.

"Have you told your boss yet, Mr. Nagle?"

"I'm a nobody, Mr. Hirsch. I want this to go away. If I tell my boss, I'll be fired. That's the way the office has handled this investigation. They debrief you to see if you have anything in your possession and then let you go. They don't care about loyalty down the chain to the staff, only up the chain to the campaign."

"So who is your boss?" The entire country knows the cast of characters from the *Washington Post* coverage, and, like everybody, I am more than a little curious. "Do you work for Mr. Stans, the committee chair?" The president's former commerce secretary had resigned from the government, along with the attorney general, to run the presidential reelection campaign.

Nagle laughs in a dry, unamused way.

"Believe me, Mr. Hirsch, we never see anybody that far up. There's a team of accountants and one junior lawyer. We're in an office out there in Virginia. We just track the dollars collected by the campaign. Dollars in. Dollars out." He makes a looping motion with his hands to demonstrate the simplicity of it all.

"So why do any of you need a lawyer if that's all you do?" There's a pause. I can hear the rain suddenly plink on my plastic umbrella.

"I have a schedule that has the names of all the major donors. Not a big deal. But who the funds are paid out to—that's another story. We have also tracked how the money is disbursed. At the beginning of the campaign, we thought the accountings would absolve the staff from dipping into the campaign funds. The truth is I don't know who the persons are who have gotten money. I can just account for it by names on the disbursement sheet."

I am astounded by his naiveté.

"Mr. Nagle," I exclaim, "it's in the paper every day. The whole country has been asking if the money was used to pay for the burglars, their fees before the break-in, and the cost of their lawyers afterward in the criminal case. Surely you are aware of that." I must look disbelieving.

Nagle ignores my question. "The thing is, Mr. Hirsch, nobody knew that Mr. Stans would be so good at collecting so much money in cash and personal checks. They were literally sorted in piles on a mail room table until they were deposited into the safe, not a bank account. Some distributions would come right out of our safe instead from the deposited funds. Oh sure, there was a depository for the checks as well after a time because we simply had too many. But the cash Mr. Stans collected that's the problem. There's a lot of cash, let me tell you."

"What do you want me to do?" I ask.

"I want you to contact the US attorney's office for me and arrange for this to be kept a secret. I don't want to tell my boss, Hugh Sloan, or anybody else. We were promised—I was promised my old job back in the Commerce Department, a career position, after the election. The pay here is pretty good, believe me, but not worth losing my seniority and retirement. If I couldn't go back, I wouldn't have taken a leave from my old job in the first place. I could lose my chance to go back if they know about this."

Nagle swings himself around and looks me in the eye, although he doesn't seem that agitated.

"I don't have much more time this morning, Mr. Hirsch. I'm not a hardened person. I just want to get this over with. Will you help me?"

Mr. Nagle, Lynn Reilly would say, is no big fish. I would need to tell my boss, and he, in all likelihood, would give Nagle the boot. On the other hand, Nagle is *my* fish, and suddenly that matters.

As Nagle and I are speaking, the specter of my own office occurs to me. Perhaps Mr. Nagle's subpoena is the right case to get me underway on my own. I feel my face flushing with anticipation. I'll be just fine, I think, if I leave the firm and start out on my own.

But first I need to talk fees with Nagle. In the office Aaron Sugarman negotiates the fee arrangements with new clients. At the end of each new client interview with Lynn, he asks Hulda to see if Aaron is "available for a consult." Lynn announces that Sugarman, not he, settles "the business matters with our new clients."

Lynn then disappears, and I'll be called to bring in the form fee document for the client to sign, which I witness. Each time, the new clients say they couldn't care less about the costs. Just get it over with.

Sugarman leered at me after my first client meeting, daring me to think him crass.

"Always tell the client there are other lawyers who might charge less," he said. "We don't want any price point chippers for clients."

Actually I was contemptuous. The clients weren't coming for Aaron Sugarman. We both knew that. The draw was Lynn Reilly.

"So how much is it gonna be?" Nagle sounds frightened as he asks the question. It is as if he has become more terrified of the fee than of the subpoena itself.

"Fifty thousand dollars," I say, pulling a number out of the air. Nagle gasps. Looking at him through the rain-inflected air, it seems my number has caused his skin to take on a greenish tinge.

"I knew this might be a problem." Nagle sighs and then drags on his cigarette. "The most I can get my hands on is thirty grand cash. That's it. Max." The rain patters on his umbrella.

I sigh. This is not as easy as I hoped.

"I may be able to accept a check for thirty as a down payment," I say, "but without knowing any more of your role in the case or the amount of time it will take, I'll have to insist on the full fee. What I will do is put a ceiling of ten thousand dollars to scope out the case and hold the rest in my trust account. Then, when we know the government's appetite for your testimony, we can adjust the fee based on what they expect you to do for them in exchange for secrecy."

Nagle wilts. "I figgered the money could be a problem," he repeats. "I just don't see why it should be so much."

"Until you and I know what the government wants and what you will be expected to do with our help, I can't guarantee that our fees won't eat up more than the fifty thousand."

I observed this discussion before with keen interest. In a complicated criminal case, the payment of the upfront fee was typically followed by a secured interest in the client's home or business real property to guarantee future hourly fees. This was the only way to keep an attorney from being mired in a case and suddenly finding he is working for free.

"Lemme think about it," Nagle says, as if to himself. "I'll take you to the bus line, if you don't mind. I have to get over to my doctor's office."

Back at Reilly and Sugarman, I tell no one about my meeting with Nagle. Needless to say this leaves me uneasy, but at the same time I also regret that I set the fee so high I may have chased Nagle away. I harbor a sad sense that my chance to strike out on my own, my only opportunity, is over. The amount of the fee was too high, dammit, I think.

Then, at four thirty, the phone rings. It is Nagle.

"The wife and I agree to thirty grand in cash, and then we can see where it goes. We got our own home, Mr. Hirsch. It's not the Taj Mahal, but it's free and clear, if it turns out that you need more."

I hear *cash*, and a rumble in my brain starts up.

"Bring a check, Mr. Nagle. A cashier's check would be fine."

"I'll come by your office tonight, Mr. Hirsch, but it'll have to be after nine. I'm an early-to-bed, early-to-rise type. So then the lights are out in the house, and no one will be the wiser when I sneak out. The wife will be home to answer the phone and can always say I'm asleep."

Nagle has thought of everything. I agree to meet him at the building entrance at nine thirty.

* * *

I usher Nagle into my cubicle. He is smoking as usual and carries a bulging manila folder with a fat rubber band squishing the rim like the top of a porkpie hat. He looks at my small space approvingly.

"It's cozy, isn't it? But a nice private office all the same. You oughta see what we have to work in. It's open space, a pit, and the machines are clattering all the time, I tell you."

Nagle gives me a look that's almost crafty.

"Nobody followed me, believe me." As he tries to hand the crushed folder to me, his face flushes with relief. I am terrified. My hands stay at my sides.

"I asked for a check, Mr. Nagle."

"I'm not going to leave any footprints, Mr. Hirsch. I'm not buying any cashier's checks or writing one on my account. My boss will find out, believe me."

The mantra from the beginning of law school is commonsense: do not take cash in criminal matters. It is carved in stone. Cash traced back to stolen property can cost your bar membership and possibly get you charged with theft.

On the other hand, I'm reminded of what my father said: currency—cold, hard cash—can always be your friend. That from a jeweler who knew something about finance.

I think hard. A brass plate reading "LAW OFFICE OF NATHAN HIRSCH AND ASSOCIATES" swings into my mind. Cash would make it easier to set myself up in practice.

"OK, Mr. Nagle." I try to be casual, but eagerness is creeping into my voice. "I'll take cash from you, but before I touch it, you sign an affidavit and receipt that says these funds are yours and not taken from other sources. Agreed?"

"How do I know that what I sign won't get me into trouble?"

"You don't sign it, I get into trouble." I feel my hands by my sides involuntarily opening and closing.

Nagle hesitates, then nods. "OK, I'll sign. But go ahead and count it."

I empty the contents onto my table and stack the rubber-banded stacks. There are thirty piles of hundred-dollar bills, each wrapped with a paper inscribed with "$1,000." The bills are slightly warm, and they crinkle. They smell of ink and tobacco, the smell of my new career opening in front of me, blooming like a flower on a hot day.

"Thirty grand," I say. "OK, then." My voice cracks. I try to rein in my excitement but find myself repeating my earlier statement to Nagle.

"Ten grand will be the maximum I will bill until you approve of the plan. Twenty will be in the trust account until you say otherwise." This is no small deal. Every so often the paper carries a story of a lawyer who went to jail for stealing a client's trust monies.

I rush into Hulda's office and use her automatic typing machine to print out a receipt that indicates the money belongs to the Nagles. Nagle reads it.

"Where's it say that my twenty's in the trust account?"

I add the line at the bottom and put my initials on it. Nagle signs the paper modified by my handwritten note.

"Gimme a copy. It's getting late." He follows me to the copier like a pointer dog, takes out the copy, and folds it carefully, as if it were a card from a lover.

"Let's talk tomorrow," he says, a smoke between his lips, "about how you're gonna get this subpoena quashed." Nagle leaves this directive hanging in the air as he flies out the door, the receipt copy folded in his pocket.

For a moment I wonder how the term *quash* has come to a layman but give it no more than a thought. Now that Nagle has fled, I can go home and collapse, but I remain in my office. I feel my face flushed hot with opportunity, totally aroused at the possibility of my own office.

I wheel my chair back and stare at the clock. It is 11:00 p.m. I review where I stand. I've received a retainer from Nagle, packets of C-notes wadded into a manila folder. It is my choice to walk out of Reilly and Sugarman tomorrow and order that brass plate with my name on it.

I have a client.

CHAPTER 6

Shira Loeb

* * *

OVER AND OVER TONIGHT, I try to call Shira in her office to get her attention and to tell her of my plan. When she answers the phone, it is after midnight, yet her voice is completely alert. I marvel at her focus.

"I apologize," she says, her voice genuine with regret. "It's impossible for me to see the road clear until next Saturday." Shira talks to me as if I have reached her during normal work hours about a date.

I race to get my story out before she loses interest.

"A client just retained me—minutes ago, actually," I blurt against the retreating tide of Shira's attention. "Just a working stiff, but he's been served with a grand jury subpoena. Watergate—"

Shira interrupts me. "We can't discuss this. You and I, we have an agreement that we will not discuss our work. For all we know, this could be a matter before the court of appeals. So not another word."

Shira has always felt free to lecture me on legal ethics in a relentless way, without brooking any dissent. Tonight I push back.

"We don't have to talk about the specifics, but it's important enough to push me out to practice on my own. This case could let me do it now. I want to look for office space. I want to be ready. Before I tell Lynn Reilly."

I find that I am panting. I have said it out loud to another human: I'm going to practice on my own. In DC. My own office.

Shira is silent at first then tiptoes away with patronizing words. "I'm not able to talk about it tonight. I know it feels like I'm putting you off and that this is big to you." I can see her pushing an errant lock of hair off her face. "But at this moment, I am just overwhelmed with work."

"What about lunch in two days?" I press. "Surely lunch is not an unreasonable time to stop working. For most at least."

"I'll try," she promises, but her voice is wan, and I may not get that lunch or her advice before I have to talk to Lynn.

But this is Shira Loeb, court of appeals law clerk, Judge David Sheldon's go-to assistant, a prestigious, hard-fought-for one-year appointment, one step below the clerkship in the Supreme Court that Shira covets more than life itself.

Shira has persistently warned that I should keep her free from any taint about my work. She is not about to divulge the cases her judge has assigned to her. And with Watergate dominating the attention of the nation, who could tell what would find its way from its grand jury to the court of appeals?

Shira makes sense. Everything she says makes sense. We could affect our jobs with simple disclosures, by carelessly violating our oaths of confidentiality with pillow talk. Judges make their decisions in secret, whether at trial or the appellate level. The code of silence by all who work in the judicial system is ironclad.

I sigh as I hang up the phone. No question about Shira's priorities. She is a passionate, driven lawyer, and my life, just like the life of her former husband, at best rates a second-place finish.

* * *

I have been attracted to Shira Loeb from her first appearance at the law center as a second-year transfer student. Shira's smile turns down like an inverted half-moon, exposing her front teeth, small ivories on a pale creature with black hair outlining her rounded face, her curved swan's neck and bent shoulders weighed down by the gravitational pull of the legal tomes she would stack about her in the law center's oaken library.

Shira's black glasses frames were too heavy by far. They held her glowing, unblinking eyes prisoner in a reflective gallery on which the pages of the cases were reprinted upside down on the lenses, leaving a shadow on her pallid cheeks. I would swear, if called to testify, that Shira wore the same simple sleeved dress every day, a one-piece mini, tight around her torso and her willowy waist.

I furtively watched on more than one occasion Shira's knees conducting business together, bare to midthigh and usually ruddy, chilled almost. Shira never wears nylons, even in winter; she is allergic.

Shira's face is that of an immigrant—a Lower East Side tilt to her head, high cheeks, and a bony nose—but younger than twenty-four, her age when she matriculated at the law center. I had been rapt in my observation of her from the moment she and I began classes together, alert to the possibility of femininity. But Shira was always oblivious to my glimpses, unfailing in her focus, reading, and scribbling her legalisms on every scrap within her grasp.

I could see in class that Shira's notes on each case were voluminous. Her ink-tipped fingers and bitten nails held stubby pencils; she used spares as bookmarks. They stuck out of her three-hole binder, each pointing to a special page or footnote. Altogether that stuffed binder, thick as a hero sandwich, was a sorcerer's book of incantations, alchemy, and spells.

As the law center's professors and students would blurt and jerk out their words of law from uncertain jaws, Shira would shuffle through her concoction of pages, books, and pencils, scribbling away, utterly independent of the awkward, sometimes fruitless search around her by other hapless students for some seamless unity of legal theories. Shira clearly pursued the law on her own terms and without the necessity of engagement with any other human.

I had no idea where Shira lived. She seemed to precede me to the library regardless of my arrival, and I am an early riser. Did she walk on dark and dangerous DC streets, or did she secretly dwell like an acolyte in the stacks, bedding down on some aging purple velvet pillows piled upon the benches? I could see Shira stretching out silently for a brief rest, then rising again in response to the tidal pull of her law books, her moon face casting about for the volumes and tomes yet unread.

Whenever our professors questioned Shira, there was an unspoken acknowledgment of her depth, an awareness that this person was capable of seeing to the end of a legal trail that, by their design, they had strewn with confusion and pitted with digression and delay.

But it was not Shira's fate to rise and strike at false bait. In each course she wove tales of the case law, regulations, and statutes in a flat, high-pitched voice, scratchy as if from little use. Her sorcerer's notebook, that occult mess, had compiled in summary fashion the breadth of the chapters undergoing scrutiny. There were also a host of commentators whom she named as if they were confidants she had just left to attend this class session.

Shira's performance in class left the professors and students speechless. Suddenly she would become the scholar, usually the role of the man at the teacher's lectern. Those teachers frequently would ask Shira with genuinely inquiring voices to unravel the nuances of particular legal themes. Her answers invariably presupposed issues and theories that no student in our classes had yet conceived or pursued. Shira simply was spinning at the speed of legal light while the rest of us mere mortals trudged on foot, cold and without hope, through jurisprudential snowdrifts. I was stunned and smitten by her.

I found I could not leave Shira alone in the vast law-center library, even when I felt the fading daylight no longer enter my eyes. I hoped that as I sat there, she would see me and find me to be as dedicated as she, my tie loosened, hoping my beard had grown during the day, darkening my face with wisdom.

I brought extra legal pads with me to the library and made a great show of scattering them about, as Shira did, writing on my carefully piled and opened (but unread) cases, "Do not disturb. N. Hirsch." Thus they looked just like the unarranged arrangements of books, papers, and coffee cups Shira left nearby. I hoped my mountainous stack would call out to hers, and she might come by, curious about my search. But Shira never paid me the least attention. She was magnetically drawn to her place in the library after each lecture or class, to that mound of legal lore in her own self-proclaimed corner.

When Shira was absent, I, the mimic, would sneak into her sometimes still warm chair, noting in my imagination where her hip bones had rubbed its wooden sides. Shira's aroma was not perfume or oil; rather it was basic, tea-like; almost, but not quite, like fresh loam.

I would sit there hoping my maleness might suffuse the varnish with a lingering allure, a waft that would draw her attention toward me and my cosmetic student trappings. I hoped I might fool Shira into believing there was a commonality in our pursuits. But it was no use. The efforts I made went unobserved, unheard, and unsmelled.

So one day I simply asked Shira to take a coffee break.

"Do you ever stop?" I said, not waiting for an answer. "What about a bad cup of coffee?"

Shira stopped and looked around, as if driving a vehicle into an intersection. She oriented her glasses up toward my face and focused, and, to my pleasure, she smiled in that upside-down way and dropped her shoulders, as if unyoking herself from her legal cart.

"I can use a break," she admitted, and we walked to the lounge next door, where there was an excuse for a coffee machine on the wall.

It was desperately cold in DC in the winter, yet Shira wore a tatty blue unlined raincoat over a rubber or plastic raincoat bearing a hood on the back and no lining. I involuntarily shivered inside my woolen overcoat listening to Shira's fabrics rasping against each other as she moved like a rain-slickered fisherman.

Up close in the light of day, I could see Shira's humanity, smelled that peculiar breath of hers and its blend of peanut butter and drifts of cola. Shira seemed damp even in the cold, her pale forehead covered with flattened hair, lank and somewhat greasy. I saw her to be like a messianic rabbinical student—hallowed and otherworldly.

I watched her drink the coffee I had poured for her in a paper cup, her fingers small about the steaming drink. We made small talk, she slow to answer questions but warming to the conversation.

Her law life had begun with her admission to law school, a dream since childhood. Shira's ex-husband, Professor Herbert Loeb, had been the impetus to move to DC, having brought Shira from a little upstate New York college. He was a cultural aide in the Nixon White House.

"We're divorced now," she said. "That's that."

Shira asked me about the Northwest. "I've never been there, only San Francisco," she said. Her father and mother were professors, her mother an early development psychologist, her father an economist, but she did not want to talk about them, only the interrelationship between economic theory and corporate law. Talking law with Shira made me nervous and restless, made my tongue feel thick and unresponsive.

"I'm coffeed out," I said, stretching. "Now, do you stay here all night?"

"No," she said. "I live on the Hill."

"Me too. Want to take the bus up there now?"

"I park in the alley," she said. "It gives me a jump on the day." She hesitated, then gestured to the door. "Want a ride home? It is a misery out there."

Her car was a silver-gray Porsche ragtop. My face must have shone with astonishment even in the cold rain.

"My inheritance," she said. "My father died of a heart attack."

"I'm sorry," I mumbled. But it was my opening. "I lost my dad last year." I bobbed my head in plaintive sadness. Then out of my mouth popped a joke whose timing couldn't have been worse. "He would have done anything to get away from my mom."

Shira didn't stir. I couldn't tell whether she had even heard me.

"My mother couldn't take the loneliness," Shira said "She died six months ago."

"Had she been ill?" I asked. Shira didn't answer right away. The delay let me hear the musical evenness of the motor and the whip of the windshield wipers.

Shira pushed her hands against the steering wheel to control the car even though it was not yet moving.

"She killed herself. Hanged herself. I suspect she wanted the pain of choking to death. It's not easy to hang yourself, you know." The rain smacking the ragtop filled the car with sorrow. "And I bought this car with my inheritance." She turned toward me, and for the first time I saw her manifest perplexity.

"They didn't know how to live," she said. "I plan to teach myself." She let the wheel go as her obvious failure to live to date occurred to her. I remained silent. Shira was her own judge and jury.

"Well," she added, "at some point, anyway, I'll start."

I was without words as we drove the short distance from the law center to the Hill. What part of her obsession with full-time study was mourning? Shifting in the seat, instead of glove-leather aroma I smelled cold tea and bread crusts. It was as if someone had eaten meals in this car, but it was too dark to spot the stale bits I suspected were on the floor.

I gave Shira directions to my apartment and changed the subject.

"The project in corporations, the joint presentation, do you want to team up?" I asked.

She shook her head no. "I haven't thought about it at all. I may have to put it off a bit."

"You probably want someone working on the *Law Review*, right?"

"That doesn't matter." She had shut off the car. "I think we have different styles, that's all. I'm not much fun, and so there."

"Perfect," I said brightly. "This project isn't much fun. But I will be motivated. What about it?"

"OK, I guess." It was hardly an enthusiastic start, but it was enough. I had what I wanted. Shira was now my partner.

* * *

From that day forward, for three years, we have spoken regularly. Shira is never the person commencing the contact. Always I seek her out, pull her away from the library, her papers, and her ongoing lunar-like explorations of the law.

Neither of us, before my collision with Deidre, has had anyone else of the opposite sex in our lives or, for that matter, anyone at all. Up to now, our orphan status may be the heart of what bound us.

While Shira and I live together, our lovemaking is infrequent, abrupt, and tentative. And certainly conducted without any declarations of permanence or even momentary importance. Again I'm the aggressor, and she is the one liking the attention. Shira resists less and less, acquiescing in my effort to extract her mind from her academics. I imagine I oddly offer an anesthesia, an amalgam of sex, an unguent of attention, good humor, and moments of inspiration that surprise both of us.

When lovemaking is over, Shira smiles that upside-down smile, pulls soiled clothes over her still warm and sometimes damp body, and returns to the law. It is clear she has no intention of abandoning her primary ambition. Perhaps she is being wisely defensive, somehow recognizing some different ambition in me.

CHAPTER 7

The Big Fish Is Just Bait

* * *

I DON'T HEAR FROM HAROLD Nagle the next day. In thrall to my dreams of independence, I barely notice Hulda step into my room. Her eyes are bull red, her forehead furrowed.

"Sonny boy," she bellows, "you been using my autotype machine." A statement.

"Oh yes, I needed it last night for a memo." Actually I printed out Nagle's receipt for the thirty thousand and forgot to erase it. I pray Hulda did not open the file as she eyes me as if I were a car thief.

"You ask permission before touching my stuff. You got that?" There is a murderous glint in her eyes.

I back way off. "Sorry," I murmur, then smile my most winning grin. "Where were you when I needed you?"

Hulda looks at me long, and then she turns and walks away.

My hands are wet. Inside my file desk, I have the Nagle folder. It is bearing down on me like a boulder tumbling down an arroyo under the force of a flash flood. I hear the rumbling all day rolling toward me.

I consider filling out a trust account receipt card from the bookkeeping department just to cover my bets. Then I stop.

I haven't actually accepted Nagle as a firm client. I have no authority to do so. I weigh whether the funds are better parked where they are until I decide what I want to do. Or maybe I'd better fill out the trust account form and leave it in my desk as a security blanket.

I saunter over to the bookkeeper's desk, where the business forms are kept. I know that in there somewhere a folder holds a bar association–approved ledger that allows law firms to account for any cash receipts.

I wheel about to return to my cubicle, clutching the trust account receipt ledger, only to see Aaron Sugarman bearing down on me.

"Where's my suppression motion?" he says, eyeing me as if I were somehow stained.

I try to placate Aaron, if that is possible. "I didn't know you needed it today. You'll have it by this afternoon, I promise." I nod with sincerity. Aaron always makes me feel uncomfortable. His style of rational, arrogant parsing of the law drains my natural exuberance. I have always felt Lynn is a kindred spirit—another performer, albeit a Roman Catholic one—who is not inclined to judge me. He seems to like everybody; he reserves his critical skills for the one or two moments when conflict pays off. On all other occasions, he is charming, polite, and almost shy.

Aaron, on the other hand, trusts no one and looks suspiciously at each pleading we get from the government's attorney. Without much analysis or urging, he predictably smells a rat.

"They're pulling strings on this one," Aaron has said a dozen times if once. "Somebody got to the judge." And when hysterical he yowls like a hound, "It's a setup, a goddamn setup."

In three years Aaron has never given me a compliment or a nod, even after the Cook verdict. It is as if he, the Dartmouth and Harvard Law grad, remains so unacknowledged in his field that he is left pained by the success of others. Being Lynn Reilly's bridesmaid must be a constant suggestion that he possesses less than stellar skills.

I see that Aaron will always be lurking in Lynn Reilly's jurisprudential shadow. His bullying, unhappy presence in this moment of choice for me is the final straw.

Nagle can be the ticket to my own practice. No more hand in the glove. The engagement fee from Nagle would never see the Reilly and Sugarman trust account. I drop the trust account form in the wastebasket.

As I release the slight paper, a breeze, a shudder, a shapeless presence moves past me. I hear the shuffle of many feet moving with uncertainty, as if someone is present and unhappy. I look around to see only the well-lit and empty hallway. I hurry back to my office to finish editing Aaron's suppression motion that I have, for the most part, composed and drafted. But the draft motion is the last thing on my mind.

The next morning I walk into Aaron's office, intending to deliver my memo. Hulda is standing next to Aaron; the two stop and look at me the way startled deer stare at an onrushing car. Then Hulda walks out without a word to me.

"Here's that suppression motion," I say, but Aaron waves me off.

"Do you have something to tell me?" he says, his words more of an accusation than a question.

I feel the flush of red in my face and try to struggle into control. "Well, there is something I'm unsure about in the motion."

"No," Aaron says, standing tall in his imperious way. "Something else. Hulda's got a receipt for client funds on her machine, something about thirty grand. Have you taken on a new client?" He looks incredulously at me, at the specter of my violation of an ironclad rule.

Before I can answer, Hulda is back at the door, no more the overweight Southern country girl. She is now the low-toned professional.

"Aaron, we've been served by the government with some strange papers. Lynn and you better look at this quick." Hulda does not take her eyes off me.

I feel a flash of dizziness, nausea. I fear I may throw up.

"You just plant yourself," Aaron says. "Sit tight, and don't move. Something smells like day-old garbage." He rushes from the room.

I can tell that Lynn's door is ajar, because the babble of voices comes up the hallway to me. Then Aaron runs back in.

"Hirsch, you get over to Lynn's. You got some explaining to do."

Trembling, I walk into Lynn's office and face a grim jury. Hulda and Aaron stand glaring at me. On the wall there is a painting of a courtroom scene, an impaneled jury listening to counsel's argument. Lynn sits behind his desk.

Some other presences have filled the room as well, an ethereal keening sound accompanied by unseen footsteps. I feel the heat from eyes staring out from the draperies and behind the couch. I am being judged by more souls than I can see.

Aaron leads off heavily, his hands by his sides, opening and closing. "No room for crap today. We think you've been holding out on us."

My heart, filled with fear, wants to leap from my chest.

"Nathan." Lynn interrupts Sugarman's wrath with his hand and starts out slow and easy, just the way I have seen him begin in court. No accusations, just the facts we can all agree on. "We have been served with some mean-looking pleadings by the Watergate grand jury regarding a Mr. Harold Nagle. Do you have any reason to know why?"

"Do you, Mr. Hirsch?" Sugarman asks.

I can feel the jurors in the wall-mounted picture leaning forward, listening with intent. The ballet has begun. My soul sinks.

I tell all. Lynn never raises his voice. It seems the US attorney's office has subpoenaed him personally to testify regarding the receipt of $30,000 from the Committee for the Re-election of the President. They have also subpoenaed any records regarding the legal representation of a Mr. Harold Nagle or his retention of Reilly and Sugarman as his counsel.

"Where is the money, Nathan?" Lynn's inquiry is gentle, like a nurse questioning a patient about discomfort.

"It's in my office," I blurt. Someone in the jury gasps.

"Why don't you retrieve it now? I think that would be a good idea."

I stumble back down the hall and with wet hands open my lower desk drawer. A part of me wants the money and the porkpie-hat file folder to be gone. But there it is, wedged in tightly and not conspicuous.

As I walk into Lynn's office, Aaron says to me, "You better hand it over."

But again Lynn raises his hand to Aaron in polite objection. "No, I don't think so. Not yet." Then he asks me softly, "Did you ask Mr. Nagle how he raised the thirty thousand?"

"Yes and no," I mutter through shaking lips. "He said he had it on hand."

"Did you just believe him, Nathan? That's enough money to buy a pretty decent house around these parts. Now, why on earth would he be sitting on that much money?"

I stammer that no, I hadn't thought about this, but yes, in retrospect, it was a blunder on my part.

Aaron snorts, half to himself. "That's an understatement."

It's my death sentence.

I hedge in response. "I agreed to be Mr. Nagle's lawyer—that is, *we*. I mean *I* would represent him." I have butchered the pronouns. I try to lay off onto Nagle my efforts at secrecy, but Lynn will have none of it.

"Nathan"—Lynn is so gentle, so clear—"Mr. Nagle is a setup. He's not a real witness for the government. This whole sorry episode was designed to keep us out of the Watergate case. And I think it almost may have worked."

Lynn rises for the first time. "Have a seat, Nathan, until we return. Oh, and that folder," he says as an afterthought. "You hang on to it."

I realize I am trying to hand off the porkpie-hat folder. I hold it out in front of me like a soiled garment. There's no mercy in Lynn's eyes for me. Unblinking, they never leave my face until my own sense of shame forces my eyes down to the ground. It's the only way I can temporarily pull the shades over this searingly painful episode.

Harold Nagle was the bait in a trap deliberately set to embarrass and disqualify Reilly and Sugarman, and in particular my boss, Lynn, from representing prospective defendants before the Watergate grand jury. When Harold Nagle retained me, he was attempting to retain our entire firm.

I was forewarned. Charlie Hogan had all but spelled out the resentment in his office, the US attorney's office, directed at Lynn Reilly's success, and I had ignored the warning. I was the one who set the hook into my boss. Perhaps it all dated back to the Moore case. Who knows?

My own jury knows I was warned as well. Around the room, behind the desk and its credenza, behind the mirror and the worktable, their disapproval has become obvious in the unaccountable shaking of the windows and drapes, the flickering of the lights.

Lynn Reilly returns alone.

"When were you going to tell us about the thirty thousand cash, Nathan? You know, real criminals, drug dealers, thieves, rapists, murderers, and their accomplices may walk every day through this office. You know that. How did you think you were properly taking the client's funds into trust by not telling any of us?" His questions are rhetorical, fatal, and final.

"Maybe I should resign," I say.

"Not quite yet, Nathan. I am going to have you execute an affidavit first. It's going to relate the truth. After your engagement by Mr. Nagle, you intended to form your own office. That's the truth, isn't it? That's the reason you didn't come to me in the first place, isn't it?" Lynn's voice is soft and certain. Even as I am filled with discomfort and self-loathing, I realize that on the ultimate questions of fact before a jury, he is the best.

"Well," I say, "I'd be less than honest if I said you were wrong."

Lynn slides his chair back and sits upright. I realize he has closed the distance between us as he nails me to my fate.

"That's backing into it, Nathan. Your affidavit in that tone could make you the subject of inquiry."

I pale at the thought of testifying. "You mean before the grand jury?"

"Oh no. Don't give that another thought. The US attorney's not a bit interested in you, only this office. Notice you weren't mentioned once in their pleadings? Once your affidavit is filed, the whole matter will disappear.

"But be clear about this." Lynn raised his delicate fingers again, that brilliant step pointing the attention of any observer to what was to follow. "You will be free to set up that practice you were intending all along. Absent that admission of your intention to depart, Nathan, you've violated the attorney-trust rules, not only of the bar, but of this office. But because you don't have an office and a trust account of your own, you haven't technically violated the bar-association rules by failing to deposit the cash. Now, Reilly and Sugarman has one. So if you intended Nagle to engage our firm you would have deposited the funds as required by the bar. Therefore you simply were waiting to give me notice of your departure and the opening of your own accounts. Am I right, Nathan? Be careful in your response. The wrong answer, and you'll never practice law again."

Lynn rose from his chair.

"Good-bye, Nathan. Oh, don't get up yet. Mr. Sugarman and you can work out the details." At the door he turns back toward me one more time. "I recall you took the bar in Washington State, didn't you?"

I nod. My thickly clotted throat can issue no sound.

"Well, if I were you, I'd be planning my new office there and not here. Between the US attorney's office and this one here, I don't think you have many friends in the District of Columbia. And I suspect you are going to need some."

My former boss carefully and deliberately closes the door, as if to shut the lid on a coffin after the funeral and before interment of the body.

I would never see Lynn Reilly again.

Hulda appears in the doorway and, without looking at me, spreads three documents on the desktop and walks out. She has left my affidavit, an acknowledgment of the return of the funds from me to Harold Nagle, and finally my letter of resignation indicating I intend to pursue my professional career "elsewhere."

Aaron Sugarman gives me my warnings, as if paradoxically he has become a cop, the very type of person he detests.

"You're free to review the documents with a lawyer of your choice, Hirsch," he says. His words carry all the scorn he can muster.

"Not necessary," I croak.

"Good," he says. "A new start, then, Hirsch." He lays a folder on the desk. "Here's the contents of your desk. Saves you the time of cleaning it out yourself and facing the other folks while you're doing it."

Aaron turns away, as if he is trying to remember something.

"Oh, there's one other memento for you." He throws a sign on top of my pile of stationery, paper clips, and pens. It's plastic, not brass. "NATHAN HIRSCH, ATTORNEY" is etched through the faux walnut finish, exposing the white laminate underneath. It's the sign that used to be mounted to the left of my office door.

"Maybe you'll get a chance to use it somewhere else," he says. I can't tell whether his face has a grimace of irony or if he is smiling at me with ill-concealed disgust.

I sit in a taxi, not watching where it is taking me, thinking about the verdict that had been rendered. I cost Lynn by making him look foolish and careless, undermined by a trusted associate. With horror I imagine him as he enters the courthouse, the place where he has made his reputation. Now he will be the subject of false cluckings and words of empty pity from lawyers, clerks, and judges alike, but behind his back in that competitive, almost predatory courthouse there will be snickering and, worse, expressions of contempt.

I know that any number of Lynn's clients, more than I care to think about, can easily put me, or parts of me, in a bag and throw it in the Potomac River. All it would take is one phone call. I stop the cabbie, throw some bills at him, jump from the taxi, and run to a nearby phone booth outside a building entrance to call Shira. It has begun to rain, and I am quickly drenched, leaving me feeling slimy and unclean.

"I need to talk to you this minute," I say. There must be a tone of desperation in my voice, because Shira consents to meet me in the court's law library, and I head off to the federal court of appeals, oblivious to the downpour.

CHAPTER 8

Shira Loeb Throws Nathan Out

* * *

I MUST LOOK CLOWNISHLY WET to the clerk at the front desk at the court of appeals law library, where Shira said she would meet me. My shoes squeak with water as I walk down the solemn marble entryway. I am shaking like a leaf in a hurricane.

Shira appears, her reddened arms wrapped about her like protective armor.

"The judge has a habit of stopping in my office. Let's go to an alcove inside." She gestures to the clerk at the checkout desk, who is watching us with too much interest.

Shira gestures at me. "It's fine," she says to the clerk, but my dripping clothes defeat Shira's attempted smile of assurance. The clerk never stops staring.

I am accompanied by a moaning sound only I seem to hear. Looking for the source leaves my face in a perpetual state of panic.

When we are deep in the library stacks, without speaking, I abjectly extract and hand her my resignation letter and the copy of the affidavit I have signed. Shira's face turns white as she reads. It is as if she has seen a mutilation occur in her presence. She drops my document on the floor, where it soaks in some of the water leaking from my shoes.

Being open with Shira is my only chance. I tell her of my meetings with Harold Nagle, but she does not listen or look at me. She just strides aimlessly about, her arms still wrapped around her body, cocooning herself, as if it were she, and not I, who is doomed. I try to continue, but Shira has had enough.

"If I disclose this to Judge Sheldon, I'm damaged goods," she whispers to no one. Her tone reflects that her distance from me is now both emotional and physical. "You and I never discussed this matter," she finally says. "None of this conversation ever took place." She stoops to pick up the wet affidavit as if it is detritus and shoves it into my coat pocket.

"Take that…that *thing* out of here with you." It's a final order she has decreed. Her concern is not for me. To be with me would be to end her crafted reality of near-infallible, inexhaustible genius. In her eyes I am a leper.

"Give me a minute," I plead. Shira vigorously shakes her head, her eyes now shut.

"You have infected yourself, Nathan," she declares. "I won't let you infect me. I intend to behave as if we were never introduced, and believe me, I have that ability."

I think about Shira ignoring her former husband and their brief marriage, and I begin shivering, partly from the rain and partly from the shock of her words.

"Are you saying you have no feelings for me?" I implore her to look at me.

Shira ignores the question as she continues to walk about. "I am not judging you, Nathan, but it is as if you have learned nothing, nothing at all."

She stops for a minute as she searches for the right words.

"This is a frightening time. The White House is full of people who are both powerful and frightened—a bad combination. Among other things they are shaking the entire DC judiciary from the Supreme Court down. Watergate is all the judges talk about. All these politicians stand to gain and lose a great deal. They will use you and me to get what they want. I'm vulnerable in this courthouse. Judge Sheldon is already circulating my name as a candidate for a clerkship in the Supreme Court. You've known from the beginning this is what I want. So I am entitled to some protection. And you are a walking time bomb."

Shira's downturned mouth is not smiling. She is grim with anxiety. "Do not call me. Do not write me. Save me from being rude to you." She backs away, turns, and is gone.

Shira has swept me out with a broom, pushing me from the library down to the exit door and back into the rain. I cannot blame her. If I looked clearly at my status in the District of Columbia, as Shira has and as Lynn Reilly advised me to do, I would push me away with a flourish.

As I walk back to my car, I think about the trip Shira and I took after graduation. We flew to Bermuda together on a late bargain-basement flight. A two-day break at a cheap hotel. Shira agreed to go if she could bring with her on the plane the galley proofs of her latest article for publication, and I relented.

I hate flying over water. I fear that sinking stomach as the plane shudders out of control, plunging into the sea. For some reason flying over land doesn't bother me. But at thirty-five thousand feet, I think about the light that coats the ice-cold waves below. I know there are deep submarine valleys holding shipwrecked hulls, once tortured by a destructive sea, that now lie undisturbed on the bottom.

I immediately began dealing cards on the food tray to distract myself. Shira ignored the card hand I placed in front of her.

"I've got to work." She stared through her glasses at the pages in her lap, each one reflecting on a different lens.

"A quick refresher on gin rummy sharpens the mind," I said. The plane's bumps through the night caused me to look anxiously out the small window. There would be a small comfort if I could see the moon.

Then I confessed to Shira, "The cards take my mind off of the water down there. Do me a favor—a couple of hands of gin rummy. Then I'll leave you alone, and you can work."

Shira's moon face sized up her cards and the down card that she took like a pro. In two draws she laid down gin, her mouth drawn and impatient. I knew I was up against the wall; she was losing interest.

"OK, let's gamble," I said. "You can be beaten."

"Not a chance," she scoffed.

"Want to bet or just rest on your laurels?"

"You'll lose big," she promised.

"OK," I said. "Winner gets first sex at the place of their choice." I adored placing my face on Shira's stomach, her fine hairs tickling my cheeks. She smelled alive in those few moments, like ferns in the fall whose fronds drip down to the sod after a rainstorm.

"This is a setup," Shira said.

"No, I want to win."

"Actually you can't lose," Shira noted, "given your point of view." She pretended annoyance, but I knew it pleased her to be the object of my attention. "My brother warned me against strip poker," she said.

"You can stay fully dressed if that's what gets you to deal."

"Give it your best," she said as she snapped and shuffled the deck, then she began to slip the cards out.

From that night and for the rest of the trip, the galley proofs remained in Shira's briefcase.

* * *

Did I fool myself that Shira cared for me, that her emotional attachment to me would outweigh my obvious sins and the collateral threat to her career? Ruefully I conclude that if I were her, brilliant and ethereal, I would discard me in a minute as a reckless and unnecessary appendage.

I leave the courthouse and begin to walk down toward the junction of Pennsylvania and Constitution Avenues, an incredibly seedy part of DC. I am walking aimlessly, trying to think of one person to whom I can talk about this openly. One name occurs: Uncle Harry King in Bethell. What would Uncle Harry do?

Days ago I crowed long distance to Harry about my self-proclaimed brilliance in the Cook case. Now I call on him again, somehow appropriately for the shame I feel, from a run-down Pennsylvania Avenue bar that has a pay phone on the wall next to the men's room. I am sweating as I search for phone change. I have only one quarter.

I am going to have Harry breathing fire, because I am forced to call collect. When the operator places the call and he accepts, I heave, shake, weep, and proceed to spill my guts to him, detailing the whole sorry mess.

Harry calms me down. "OK, OK. Congratulations. It's time you come home. I'll find something for you, but first call your Auntie Riva, and tell her you're gonna need a place to stay for a while. Then hit the road. You got a long trip ahead."

Following Harry's direction, I call Auntie Riva at Fulton Jewelry, the Bethell family business, which, since my dad's death, is exclusively her domain.

With humility and water dripping out of me, I ask to stay with her temporarily. My auntie, unmarried, has always been in my corner.

"Well, let's think about this," she says, barely masking her real pleasure at the prospect of my return. "You'll want your privacy, and I'm keeping mine. Maybe the basement room would work for the time being."

What are my options? Pearl, my demented mother, haunted by the ghosts of my brother and my dad, has filled the home I grew up in with three Scottish terriers and their random droppings. The house has become all but a hospital for her. My mother's permanent caretaker, Carla Prism, lives there too, keeping Pearl's depression medicated and feeding all of the occupants. Carla is the only person who can tolerate the filth of the three dogs my mother insists on keeping about her indoors.

Pearl rarely leaves her bedroom, and the house has gone to the dogs in every respect, the furniture covered with hair and stains, the carpet marred by the dogs' frequent accidental discharges, and the windows smeared with dog snot. The three Scotties stand in tandem, noses against the glass, raffishly snapping, jabbering, and leaping about at anything and everything that passes the front of the house. Living in that place would be worse than torture.

On the other hand, I have no money and no job; any self-respecting landlord would say no thanks to a tenant like me, and some not so politely. I would also have to parry the onset of predictable and embarrassing questions regarding why I have returned to Bethell and chosen not to stay with my family.

I agreed to take the basement.

My despair lets Harry make all my decisions. I follow his command to immediately cross the country and return to Bethell. The lease remains with Shira. I need only to throw my clothes into an old suitcase, call an airport transport, and launch myself toward the state of Washington with a standby ticket to Seattle.

On a gray March afternoon, a Greyhound bus deposits me in Bethell, the town still sitting as I last saw it, unchanged and uninteresting, on the shoreline of Puget Sound. I step off the bus into the tiny terminal next to Palmer's Drugstore on Lansing Street and trudge the familiar six blocks to the ancestral home of the Hirsch family, now owned by Auntie Riva.

I must be a sight, standing on Auntie Riva's front porch: unshaven, my back bent from a stuffed suitcase, rain-soaked pants, my cuffs bagged about muddy shoes. I have no umbrella, and the perpetual Bethell drizzle I fled with relief is again driven into my nooks and crannies, chilling me into seeking my family.

Auntie Riva inherited the huge old place from my grandparents, and she is more than happy to let me stay there. The house stands on Parkland Avenue, less than two blocks from Fulton Street and the family's jewelry store. The house is a three-story museum in which Auntie Riva rattles around alone, dusting the old paintings and furniture bought almost a century ago and vacuuming to death the dark oriental rugs of equal antiquity. The house probably looks as it did in 1911, when Zayde Albert, my grandfather, had the place built.

The basement I would occupy was a root cellar, utterly empty and unused. Zayde Albert had converted it into a handyman's one-room dwelling. The entrance is in the back of the house, down lichen-covered cement stairs. As a kid I believed it was the home of the bogeyman and avoided the entry like the plague.

Though there is a stairway to the basement inside the house, Riva leaves it bolted shut—sad for me, because the cellar entryway possesses a drain grate leading to the storm sewer that always seems to be filled with mildew, moss, and drain water. Once I step across the puddle and shut the basement door, the world left behind, I am left to wonder, damp, underground, and bewildered, how I have fallen so low and how my plan to be rid of Bethell and my family has been thwarted.

Book 2
Bethell, Washington

* * *

CHAPTER 9

People of the Book

* * *

I STAY UNDERGROUND THE FIRST days in Bethell. In my basement bedroom, I question the wisdom of getting up. Sapped, I have no muscles. Like a child with no will, I ask Riva for permission to open the refrigerator, to use the television, or to wash my bedsheets. Only my beard grows independently.

I rarely leave the house, because I have no confidence I will make it back without permanent damage. When I do traipse to the Piggly Wiggly grocery, the soggy March cold pulls at my soul, the ground gripping at my feet with a sloppy suction, as if I were walking across the tidal mud of the Snoline River estuary at ebb.

Auntie Riva asks no questions but calls down to me periodically. "The coffee is on. Do you want lunch? What would you like for dinner?"

I have no opinion. Her rhythm is about food. I suspect she believes a woman to be behind the ache in my steps.

I consider going over to my parents' house and announcing to my mother that I am back in Bethell, but feel unready for what I might find there. Auntie Riva, as a welcoming gesture, has unbolted the stairwell door, but she insists I wear only my socks upstairs, no shoes. No tracking from the basement, please.

My aunt doesn't appear anywhere. I move room to room on the first floor of this house that I am told my grandpa built, calling my auntie's name to no answer.

In the wallpapered parlor, the light from the gray outdoors illuminates a vision of the past: damask-covered tables and divans, leaded windows. And there is the fireplace, fronted by a tarnished-brass spark screen and surrounded by a terra-cotta mantel. The hearth opening is big enough for a small child to walk into. Though there is no fire, the closed flue has left a smoky, damp scent in the room.

Cedar and fir moldings trim every doorway. With stained boxed ceiling beams, baseboard moldings, window sashes, and mullions, the room is a forest palace in which my stocking feet are an intrusion, evidenced by a complaining squeak in the quartersawn oak floorboards.

I find the light switch. It is the button style of the '20s, never replaced. The ceiling hosts no chandelier. There is only lamplight from two fixtures perching on fabric-shrouded tables. They throw a yellow glow onto the floor through their aged silk shades.

I am in an ancient museum of brocade and satin. Brown shadows drift down from the burnished fir onto the oriental carpet and its pattern of purple, soft pinks, and faded black. The room's memories, if there are any, remain utterly silent. Human familiarity is missing. The walls do not shake with the past chatter or the laughter that would make a place feel lived in, sounds you might expect to seep into the walls over generations and echo back across time.

I slide my hand across the tobacco-colored oaken top of the Philco radio console, a single dial in its center with a cat's-eye gauge. I twirl the power knob back and forth and find it useless; there is no catch anymore, no snap of power. I remember the slight punting sound the console made when it worked and recall the cat's eye slowly going from dark to glowing vivid green. I used to strain to see a face, a picture in the lighted gauge while I listened to the raspy sounds of faraway stations. In my childhood I hoped the green eye would blossom into a screen, like the television in my home, and erase the boredom I experienced in this undisruptable house. Alas, the green eye always remained visionless, with only transitory flickers when its power source waxed and waned.

The order in this parlor is cosmetic, the message: ready for inspection. Its faded sheer white curtains reflect gentility I suspect Bubbe would want to show if a gentile neighbor came by, as if Bubbe, with her thick Eastern European accent, ever had a klatch of non-MOT matrons drinking tea in this room.

Yet it is in the living room where the Hirsches' photo portraits rest, each encased in polished brass with velvet backings, frames I'm sure came right out of the inventory at Fulton Jewelry. Riva has positioned all the pictures of the tribe on a sideboard, the dead included among the few living.

In the center sits Zayde Albert in his lounging coat and fez-like sleeping cap, familiar but foreign. And my dad, Leon, next to him, dashing in his vintage World War II army uniform and wavy hair. Bubbe, whom I knew only in blind senility, has pulled herself erect like a plump proper dowager, full bosomed and, as a widow, suitably grim.

There is a shot of my brother, Ritchie, throwing a pitch. He is in the windup, left leg up, ready to kick, a shadow from the bill of his cap crossing his intense, unsmiling face. I suspect the photo is from the Totem High School newspaper.

To one side of Zayde Albert is a young Auntie Riva wearing a middy, her shoulders sloped. Perhaps this is her graduation picture. Riva is the only one not looking out, instead glancing dreamily away, the young woman yearning for her beau.

And yes, I am perched there as well, perhaps seven years old, wearing an out-of-date plaid sport coat over a sweater emblazoned with the face of the Lone Ranger. I judge myself even in those days to be incredibly eager and too ambitious.

There is no picture of Pearl alone, just the wedding photo of my parents surrounded by a host of her kin, the Levys, all posed outside in the garden, the day both impossibly sunny and at the same time frozen in black and white. I pick up the wedding photo, warm it with my hands, and ruminate on the improbability that these two people married and had me as a child in this place. While they called Bethell home, it feels utterly different to me.

* * *

Growing up, my family seemed like an unexplorable anatomical zone, like my back, or inside my ears—parts I could not see even if I strained. The mysteries of the Hirsches' origin, the nature of our reputation, of our accomplishment, even heroism, filled my childhood curiosity and imagination. My appetite was insatiable for Hirsch and Levy family stories, snapshots, portraits, letters, and documents.

I repeatedly studied my nose to test it as a replica of my Zayde Albert's. I would tug at my slightly curling hair to see if it would bounce back like my dad's or lift my hair to see if it receded like my uncle Bob Levy's. With no cousins in sight, I pestered my dad and my uncle when he and his wife, Aunt Sally, visited. I pestered Auntie Riva to the point of irritation.

Pearl was no aid. Like a cipher she simply answered my questions with questions. "Why should that be important to you?" was her constant retort. She did not profess ignorance. Instead she explicitly challenged my right to know. It never deterred me.

Auntie Riva was another story. She loved to curl up on the couch and regale me with stories about the Hirsches' arrival in Bethell.

"Before Grandpa Albert married Bubbe, who was sometimes called Sarah, sometimes Sasha—who knows what her real name was?—he took root in Bethell in the 1880s, just before the Alaskan gold rush. How he got across Canada, I don't know, but he came from Eastern Europe an orphan who soaked up the American continent and its energy, poetry, and greed all at once. He made his own pudding of life. Nobody, no set of rules, no one else's opinions, no gods, and no bullets would deter him from exploring what life was all about. A pioneer. And he picked this spot because he could see the salmon jumping in the estuary. If they could be so ecstatic, so could he.

"Now, Seattle was the primary US port of embarkation to the gold fields in the Klondike, but up and down Puget Sound, mills bustled to supply timber to build stores that sold the miners supplies and provisions to get to the frozen North. And in anticipation of successful gold strikes, towns like Bethell readied their streets to reward the returning gold miners with fine hotels, fine homes, fine furnishings, and fine jewelry.

"They say that during the rush, Skarbell's in Bethell and the other mills on the Snoline River ran all day and all night, slicing up half of the timber in the Cascade Mountain foothills and shipping it to Seattle, a day and a half away by boat. A Bethell vessel laden with freshly milled beams could sell its contents instantly to build new homes, new piers, and railroad trestles. What trees didn't get cut in the gold rush were harvested after the great Seattle fire. Here they even cut up the grove."

Auntie Riva's voice sounded incensed.

"What was the grove?" I asked.

"They say it was a forest of giant trees near the harbor that were arranged like a round sanctuary. Something to see, I suspect, though there are no pictures—just the story."

"When the first settlers, a religious bunch, stood below the mighty branches, they must have felt as if it were holy spot, kind of like a church, you know. So they named the town Bethell Firs. House of God in the trees. Actually, I kind of like that name, although believe me, there could have been cleverer ways to say it."

Auntie Riva became contemptuous. "When the grove became too valuable, too easy to cut and slice up and sell as timber, the lumberjacks clear-cut the entire grove. One minute it's like a holy place, the next minute it's a stack of boards for sale.

"Anyway, the city fathers, including your grandpa, renamed the town Bethell in the absence of the grove. What an embarrassment."

Why Zayde Albert thought Bethell was a better opportunity than Seattle is hard to understand. I wanted to believe that with his pioneering spirit, he could have been a founding father regardless of where he chose to pound in his claimer's stakes. Choosing Bethell might have been bullheadedness or foolishness, but my dad gave me a clue.

"Your grandpa liked to say it was better to hit it big in a small place than be a tiny pea in someone else's stewpot."

Uncle Harry put it another way. "They lived by hook and by crook in the old days. When you rob another man—or kill him so he can't steal from you—it's better not to be in a county where your picture is featured in the post office with the words *wanted* and *bounty* underneath."

Where Zayde Albert came up with his early money was murky. He rose quickly in lumberjack land. The family myth was that he started in a tent, then moved to the back of the general store as a jeweler and watch repairer, and then opened the street-front store on muddy Fulton Street. While others built with cheap lumber, Zayde Albert had bricks sent up from Tacoma for the Hirsch Building, with enough left over to build the family home in Parkland.

Then there was the vault at Fulton Jewelry, a story all in itself. Grandpa Albert had an idea that with all the gold ingots and cash he imagined would flow to Bethell from Alaska, he could sell storage, as if Fulton Jewelry were a bank.

Auntie Riva told me the vault arrived by ship, was unloaded by a boom at the mill dock, and was carried on timber rollers like a Roman siege machine up to the storefront, which was literally torn open to permit the vault's installation. Bethell's newspaper then and now, the *Daily Herald*,_announced the event on the front page, with a photo of the vault wrapped with bunting ribbon bearing a painted message that read:

"THE SAFEST SAFE IN THE WORLD—FULTON JEWELRY'S VAULT."

Standing ten feet high, a steel box bolted and riveted together, the vault still dominates the back of Fulton Jewelry. It is entered through a seven-foot door that is one foot thick, painted glistening ebony, and trimmed in shimmering gold.

The *Daily Herald*'s picture of the vault is prominently displayed to this day under glass in the Fulton Jewelry foyer. It features Zayde Albert in a waistcoat and string tie, holding his hat as if he were about to hurl it spinning in the air, a hurrah of success springing from his lips. He wears high boots by virtue of either style or necessity, to offset Bethell's persistent inclement weather and dirt streets that were transformed into pits and ruts of mud by logging wagons.

On the wall next to the counter, my grandpa stares out of a framed portrait, the same as at home, a bearded young man with piercing eyes, a Semitic Svengali wearing a silk lounging jacket and a velvet sleeping fez, the outfit oozing luxury and respectability.

Alas, the safe-deposit business was a fantasy. No gold bullion flowed to Bethell. The vault proved to be Zayde Albert's folly, a busted dream that became in time a storage room for baskets, wrappers, boxes, cleansers, and even the vacuum cleaner, all deadly dust catchers.

My dad, Leon, became the baron of the vault, making its desktop his office, an open checkbook lying there.

I never knew Zayde Albert. He died in 1944, before I was born. Bubbe survived him. Short, bulbous, and blinded by glaucoma, she had, I was told, a memory of one grandson. That was Ritchie, not me. By the time I popped into the world at Everett General hospital, she could distinguish only light from dark.

Auntie Riva said Grandpa Albert had gone "wife shopping" in Vancouver, British Columbia, after launching his store and our future in Bethell. Before he married Bubbe, he had already anchored his public reputation by serving as a Snoline school district board member and then Bethell's mayor, a ceremonial post.

"For the rest of his life, he was called Mr. Mayor," Auntie Riva proudly announced to me.

Bubbe apparently was a homebody who raised two kids and buried a third, my vanished Aunt Leah, a sad sepia shadow confined to a photo, who perished from Spanish flu when she was a teenager.

I would like to believe my performance genes come from Zayde Albert, whose father's name—Natan—I bear. My adventurous Zayde, fez wearing, string tie clad, boot legged, his chest puffed out like a peacock—that is who I imagined I would like to be like.

On the other hand, Auntie Riva never held my mother's kin, the Levys, in high repute. The Levys were Iowa scrap-metal dealers known to Bethell's King family, our own junkyard operators. Pearl was introduced to Leon in Minneapolis through Zolly King on a business junket. Even to me as a child, the circumstance seemed more commercial than romantic.

Pearl was the only daughter of Isaac and Minnie, my Levy grandparents. I never knew them or my uncle, Jake Levy, who I am told still runs the very successful family business in Davenport, on the Mississippi River. There seems to have been such disquiet between Pearl and almost all of the Iowa Levys that none showed for my bar mitzvah. Pearl was wounded to the quick.

"Your uncle Jake just wrote me off," she said about her Iowa brother, "like I was a heap of metal sold off to a slag smelter."

The exception to the Levys' abandonment was my uncle, Bob Levy, the family black sheep who ran off to California and married outside the tribe. Bob redeemed himself by becoming rich. After World War II, he built vast neighborhoods in the Bay Area, from San Mateo to San Raphael. Uncle Bob frequently traveled up from San Francisco to visit and, I suspect, to check up on the way the Hirsches were treating his little sister. He was a tall, bald, robust, and good-natured outdoorsman who wore sideburns long before they came in style.

"If I can't grow 'em on top, why not on the sides?" he would chortle.

His wife, Aunt Sally, had the energy of a marmot and a high nasal voice that sounded like a dentist's power drill. Bob and Sally would swoop in by Cadillac, insist on dinner in Seattle, and then drive us back afterward to Bethell, with Ritchie and me asleep in the back corners, my dad, Leon, cramped between our outstretched legs, and Bob and Pearl talking nonstop the whole trip.

Sally would turn our kitchen upside down and inside out, incessantly baking, stewing, roasting, canning, and pickling away at full speed, so that on their departure she left behind a wildly overstocked larder. Aunt Sally always behaved as if she were on family probation and needed to prove her Levy-Hirsch worthiness.

"Nobody will ever say we didn't earn our keep," Sally would gaily holler as she sailed out to the Cadillac for the trip back to the City by the Bay.

Auntie Riva relentlessly talked behind Pearl's back.

"Your mother was a disappointment to the Levys because she was unable to find a suitable husband between Chicago, Omaha, Milwaukee, and Minneapolis," Auntie Riva said, enjoying a recitation of her sister-in-law's fruitless searches for a mate, "and then she was unloaded on the Hirsches."

Aunt Riva discussed my mother as a commodity, intimating the Hirsch family were sold goods whose manufacture suffered from shoddy workmanship. Despite my difficult relationship with Pearl, sometimes Auntie Riva went too far. I felt her behavior was unfair to my mother, who had no local allies in Bethell to spring to her defense.

Once I shut down Auntie Riva's repetition of her claims and attacks on Mom by asking her a simple question: "If there's no Pearl, then there is no me either, or Ritchie, right? Are you unhappy with us too?"

"Well, your brother was adopted, which is one way to get a baby. Your mother was barren," Auntie Riva said primly, as if she, a spinster, dripped with fertility. Then she looked at me and qualified her answer. "Before you, of course."

The problem was that after all of the talk about Pearl, I became alarmed as well. Was I adopted, a mysterious process that meant I could not claim, as Zayde Albert's progeny, all of his imagined characteristics? When I needed real help, I went to Uncle Harry while I was studying for my bar mitzvah under his tutelage.

"Auntie Riva says Ritchie was adopted," I said.

"So what's it to you?"

"So I must be adopted too." I approached this slowly, half afraid Harry would refuse to talk about this subject, which would confirm for me that my suspicions were well founded.

"Why do you think that?" Harry said. "Look, it's one of the greatest things I ever done for your folks. And it was a long time before you came along. They wanted a baby. Who gets married and doesn't want kids? But who knows why, nothing happened.

"So things were tough up the Snoline River. The Depression left people melting snow for drinking water and eating boiled salal roots 'cause they had no moola for food. And this one family had a new baby, and they wanted something better for the kid. No, don't ask me who they are, because I wouldn't tell you even if they were around, which they ain't. The war pretty much shook the unemployed outa here, either to the army or down to Seattle to build boats and planes. So that's why your brother's adopted."

"So I must be adopted too."

Harry stopped puffing and stared at me. "You ever look in the mirror, kiddo? You don't think you and your old man aren't ringers? Look, you were born during the war, while your dad was overseas. But before he shipped out, he and your mom spent his last leave together at Iron Springs over on the Olympic Peninsula."

Harry lit a cigar and filled the room with the tropical scent of a burning pyre of palm fronds. His voice was buoyed up with smoke.

"The truth is, Nathan, that strange things happen to a man and a woman who figger they may never see each other again. Men were dying all the time then. Between the Nazis and the Russians, our people, Jews all over Europe, were being slaughtered by the millions. Who knows what went through your parents' minds about the future on that leave?

"But I'll tell you one thing. I promised Leon, your pa, that I would look after Pearl, no matter what or when. So did Auntie Riva. Those two women were in the jewelry store every day, trying to make ends meet by selling paper party gifts and decorations. Believe me, nobody was buying jewelry during the war. I saw Pearl day to day, and lo and behold, she started getting bigger and bigger. I grew up on a farm, so I knew a thing or two about women. Don't think I'm an ignoramus, because I'm smart enough to stay single."

Harry exhaled his cigar smoke.

"The truth is, I saw you grow inside your mom, was there the day you popped into this world. Well, you didn't exactly pop out. Your mom was in labor for two days. But there you were, just like you are today, bellowing at the top of your voice, howling for attention. 'Look at me. Look at me.' That's what you been saying ever since.

"Yes sir, you are Zayde Albert's boy, all right. All Hirsch, and I'd tell that to every Levy I ever see if they had the nerve to ask. For better or worse, you are a Hirsch."

* * *

Every Sunday morning Ritchie and I were grounded, no chance to see our friends.

"Sunday is *their* day," my mom said, and she made us stay put in the house. It left me wondering what day was our day.

It always seemed funny to me as a little kid that there were all these churches for all of our neighbors but no place the Hirsches could call their church, no place to get together on Sunday mornings with the other Jewish families I knew about. Why was it that in a world that made churchgoing so central to everyone and everything about us, we would choose to live where there was no comforting Jewish church spire, its bells chiming out a Sunday welcome? It made no sense to me at all.

I asked my mom about having a Jewish church, a place in Parkland where we could go on Sunday.

She shook her head. "We don't have churches."

I looked at her quizzically. Such questions were too much for her; I knew that. She arched her back.

"We are, after all, the people of the book," she said.

"What book?" I asked.

"The Old Testament," she said and then added weakly, "and all the other books too."

"Do we have libraries instead of churches?" I asked. "Can't we just go to the library on Sunday to read our books when everybody else is in church?"

That was when Mom called for Dad, who told me to clean my room, clean up the basement playroom, or mow the lawn. Otherwise I would have to stay in Sunday afternoon as well.

Because by noon, when church was over, Bethell would be back to normal, and in good weather we would be off to spend the day in Todd Park and its huge sports fields and playgrounds.

"We're all readers in the Levy family," my mom maintained. Books abounded in our house. We had the *Encyclopedia Britannia*, the *World Book*, and the *Great Books.* Magazines like *Theatre Arts*, *Harper's*, *The Atlantic*, and *The New Yorker* lay strewn across the blood-crimson mahogany coffee table in the living room.

Hardbound books arrived monthly in the mail from the Book of the Month Club or the Literary Guild. Paperbacks were surreptitiously passed among Pearl's secret society of women who shared books and lies equally. I loved the women's choices and inhaled them all with great relish. I could hear the bodice ripping going on between the pages even when I was ten years old.

I saw the outside world from the vantage point of Pearl's books, literally over the top, slouched in my favorite chair, an old wingback dragged over from Bubbe Hirsch's living room when Dad moved her into Bethell's nursing home. The old wingback now wearily slumps in the spare room of Pearl's house where Carla Prism lives. That chair had body dents that warmed instantly when I huddled in its seat and draped my legs over its arms, which were uselessly protected by ancient yellowing doilies.

Sitting there with my book in my lap, I could always smell the leftover cookie crumbs that had slipped into crushed amber piles under the seat pad, where the fabric was still tightly tucked into the frame. Plopping down raised an aroma of cardamom, anise, and cinnamon. When I reached for my book that had slipped down the crevices of the seat cushion, my hands always came up coated with cookie bits.

Sometimes, long after the lights were dictatorially shut off, I read with a flashlight on the page. Whichever book I was reading at the moment would cause a periscope to pop up, and I could peer beyond Bethell, my family, the neighborhood, and my school. With my eyes just above the top of the book cover, I smelled its glued backing and the metallic odor of ink, felt the chemical crinkle of its paper pages, and heard the smooth snap of the glossy liners. One page in and I could look up, and there would be dreams floating up from and above the words.

The characters emerging from the pages of novels had uncanny physical resemblances to the residents of the town of Bethell and Snoline County and the members of my family. The Erdmann girls, who lived down the street, resembled the tempestuous Southern beauties of *Gone with the Wind*, and Butch Strohmeyer was a ringer for Ashley Wilkes. My brother, Ritchie, was the dashing Danny of *Battle Cry*, in which our dad had the role of first sergeant. And the skeptics always looked like Uncle Harry King.

"So the Levys read literature," my dad would snort, "and the Hirsches read newspapers." While he had no use for the Levys except for his brother-in-law, Bob, my dad's means of speaking to my mom in general was to bait her into a squabble. The threat that would emerge from their protracted skirmishes—which I could not remember beginning and which never seemed to end—was always the same. The engagement would stop when Pearl, sniffling with frustration and rage, would say, "I'm moving to my brother Bob's in California."

"Fine," Leon would holler back. "Send me a postcard. Ritchie stays."

Ritchie, my older brother, read nothing except *Sports Illustrated*. He had a dream to play ball. Or maybe being the ballplayer was not just Ritchie's dream. His athletic success was Dad's as well; anyone could see that. From the earliest times, Ritchie, five years my senior, would be in the backyard or out in the street with Dad throwing baseballs, sometimes loopers or wide throws or grounders, Ritchie whipping the ball back sidearm.

When Ritchie pitched his sliders, fastballs, sinkers, and sometimes curveballs—everybody said Ritchie had a curveball at eight—our dad would be in a crouch, Yogi Berra style, yelling for effect, "Batta, batta, batta, batta, batta," as if someone actually stood in the batter's box about to swing at those strikes Ritchie threw, which I could barely see.

For the most part my dad, tanked up with so much ambition for Ritchie's pitching career, left me and my books alone. And that was not a bad thing.

Believe me, I had lots of applause. My bleachers were plenty full. My biggest cheerleader was Auntie Riva, who, with a high opinion of herself and a low view of manhood, had been left high, dry, and unmarried. For Riva the tide of marital bliss perpetually ebbed. She could note any new suitor's faults and could predict the oncoming storm of their manifestation, thus keeping her anchored in Spinster Bay.

At some point, by mutual accord, the suitors and she agreed to quit trying. Riva worked when she felt like it at the jewelry store and sometimes at the charity shop run for the Snoline County Foster Children's Home. She argued with my dad, spoke with barely concealed contempt to my mother, ignored Ritchie, and doted on me.

And I discovered music through Ritchie. As a little kid, I had snuck up behind my older brother as he practiced. When I played "Chopsticks," Pearl decided our neighborhood piano teacher, Auntie Mae Galitzer, should give me lessons.

Ritchie, the great athlete, was simply a clumsy piano player, his fingers suddenly splayed fat and slow. For him the piano was a cold machine in winter, balky and turgid, and in hot summer slippery and dangerously elastic. With a self-effacing grin, he quickly gave up, walking away from the piano that sat in our living room.

But my dimpled pudgers, rounded and soft, floated music off the keys the first time I touched the ivories. I unleashed one-handed melodies in a week; two-handed pieces came quickly. Every music teacher I would have for the rest of my Bethell days loved me. I had found a home.

When Pearl wasn't around, I learned another trick. I used my vocabulary, memory, and mimicry to do show tunes even when the specifics of the lyrics were beyond me. Pearl played her Decca seventy-eight records all the time. I heard Bing Crosby sing "Rock-a-Bye Your Baby with a Dixie Melody" when I should have been practicing. I heard it a million times.

Doodling on the piano, I cobbled the melody into chords. As Pearl walked through the door, she found me shouting out the lyrics, picking both the tune and words. Seeing my mother, I stopped.

She said, "No, play!" Then, "No, hold it." Her heels clattered down the hallway to the kitchen, followed by the clicking whirl of the phone.

"Dot," I heard Pearl yelling into the receiver, "you gotta come over here quick...No, nobody's dead."

Then a second ring. "Bernice, I want you to hear something...No, not on the phone. Come over right now."

Suddenly I had an audience—the entire book club, smoking their lipstick-stained cigarettes.

"Girls," Pearl declared, "pull up a chair. OK, Nathan, play away."

"A million baby kisses I'm gonna deliva
When I get back to that Swanee Riva
Rock-a-bye, my rock-a-bye baby, with a Dixie melody."

I had no idea what *Dixie* and *Swanee* referred to. I just bawled out the breaks and then gapped slowly on the refrain, just like the record. The women all joined me on the last line, then clapped, whooped, and shrieked in the cigarette-smoke-filled air.

"All he needs is a straw hat and a bow tie." Dot put her arm around me. "Move over, Eddie Cantor. Here's Nathan Hirsch."

Entertainment had become my territory.

* * *

I put down the picture of my parents' wedding and return to the present. Somebody once told me a mark of a good photo portrait is that the subject always appears to follow the observer, the subject's eyes seeming to penetrate through skin and bone. At this moment it is not easy for me to look at the faces of my family. Their eyes not only shadow me; they judge me as well. And, I must admit, rightly so.

CHAPTER 10

Just a Huddled Spot on the Road

* * *

UNCLE HARRY IS AFTER ME, and I try to avoid him. Not possible. I hear the phone ring, and Auntie Riva calls down to my dugout, "It's Harry."

"It's time to get moving," he says.

"I have been in retreat from my former life for only three days," I answer and try a joke. "Isn't the Jewish period of mourning a week?"

"But you're not *geshtorbin*—dead. You're alive. I'll see you at eleven today at Steve's." His voice is a command.

I know Steve's all too well. It is a hash house installed in a '30s railroad car, a rounded-aluminum, art-deco-style diner. In my childhood my dad brought me to Steve's, with its red-and-white linoleum counter and its matching floor tiles scarred by cigarette butts and punctured with holes from hundreds of hard-nailed shoes. The counter seats, round and rotating, were chrome-trimmed crimson Naugahyde. The diner smelled like cigarettes, hamburger grease, mustard, bacon fat, and coffee. I loved to turn the seats left to right and, when my dad wasn't looking, swirl all the way around.

Dad told me Steve Haskoll, who was a high-school friend, had been a navy noncom in World War II, a Seabee, and knew how to put things together that were useless to everyone else. After the war all the vets had helped Steve haul an old rail diner up from the train yard on A Street to an empty lot on Oakland Avenue. There he dropped it onto a pile of bricks that were so unevenly set even I, who couldn't pound a nail into a board, saw that the railcar was in dangerous retreat from level.

Foundation askew or not, Steve filled the diner's insides with a red-hot double stove and two sizzling fat fryers just behind the counter. His customers must not have feared fire or explosion, because no one could miss the exposed electric wires stapled up the wall, the live ends wrapped with gray duct tape right over the stoves. At least the aluminum exterior gleamed as if it were pretending to be the fuselage of a Boeing airplane.

* * *

As I walk to Steve's, the northwest weather wraps around me. I spontaneously lean into the intermittent gusts coming off Puget Sound as I make my way around puddles and across wet grass. Bethell has always seemed to me bent a little forward into the wind and the outer world. No proud flags fly upright around here, with the exception of the banner above the high-school football bleachers (the Totems' football team finished three and five for the year in '72.)

Even the American flag at the county courthouse has been mounted to swing laterally above the entryway. Only the smokestack at the Skarbell Mill has the courage to stick its neck straight up.

What is most disheartening in the cold is that nothing has changed in the years since I left for college. Did I ever call Bethell my home? As my footsteps slurp in the water, I feel as if I am standing still, a degrading stasis beyond boredom, beyond wasted time.

Yet I have no other place or people to turn to.

My path to Steve's crosses Fulton Street, where Zayde Albert built the Hirsch Building. Lansing Avenue to the north is really the main business strip of Bethell. Fulton is closer to the neighborhoods and thus is more of a buffer. Unlike Fulton Street, Lansing has pavements of cement and not asphalt. Stripes for angle-in parking have been painted in white, and believe me, there are no meters.

It occurs to me that the MOTs have their shops on Fulton Street—Fulton Jewelry and the Galitzers' two men's stores. Do Jews do business on Lansing Avenue? I promise to raise the question with Auntie Riva, the repository of all of the town's stories. She will have an opinion.

To me all Bethell's business buildings on both Lansing and Fulton Streets have a snaggled look. Like a mouthful of broken teeth. There is no rhyme or reason as to how each business street was composed. Some structures are one story, others two, but never more than three. The oldest are faced with dark brick, the newer ones with wood paneling from Skarbell's, and a few are coated with sagging, cracked stucco. Between stores, vacant lots gape, empty spots from where a rotten tooth has been extracted. The uneven silhouetted lineup appears to be in an earthquake zone, a few staggering survivors of the Big One.

I move down Lansing to where it runs into Oakland Avenue, which doubles as Highway 90 as it ambles north straight through town. The Lansing-Oakland intersection has Bethell's only traffic light. That is where Steve's Diner sits.

Sitting in one of Steve's booths, I face Harry's stony stare across a green Formica table.

"Look," I say, my hands open. "You were right. I should not have let my Washington bar membership go inactive."

"I didn't say anything." Harry sucks on his unlit cigar with a look of contentment on his face. I can see he is thinking, I told you so.

Harry has blue eyes and stares at me in a kind way, but I'm sure his mind is filled with book, chapter, and verse on my behavior. I find I cannot look away from him. After all, I want his judgment, even if it scalds my face with its wrathful blast. There is a part of Harry that has certainty like the tide. He seems as steady as a force of nature.

Harry says nothing. He waits for me to speak. My eyes rove about the diner. Sometime in the '60s, when I was in law school, Steve redecorated the place with avocado-green kitchen carpeting overlaid by mustard-yellow blocks and circles and edged in black. He replaced the old counter seats with fancy ones with backrests.

But the ceiling inside the diner is still cream-color military surplus latex paint, grimed up from twenty years of fry oil, cigarette smoke, and steam. And the stale smell of dried turkey gravy still seeps up and through the Formica whenever a hot plate or cup is set upon it.

"I was never going to practice here," I finally say.

Harry looks philosophical. "You know, Nathan, that's why they put a back door on a house—just in case there's a fire in the front hall. Like you got right now." This moment of wisdom causes Harry to reward himself by lighting his cigar.

"I thought you said you were cutting down by just leaving it in your mouth."

"I'm celebrating your return, *boychick*."

Like all the carpetbagger lawyers in Washington, DC, I took the bar exam in my home state. It was cheaper, and all lawyers could practice in DC if they were admitted to practice back home. But I was penny wise and pound foolish. After getting admitted to the DC bar and going to work at Reilly and Sugarman, I deactivated my membership in Washington to save on annual dues.

Now I have become a supplicant. I need the permission of the state board of governors to practice in this Washington. And I fear they will want to know what I have been up to in the other Washington. The thought of answering *why* questions makes me cringe.

Harry puts his bulging briefcase on the table and tries to open it. The lock goes turgid. After he pops it with his fist, the lock opens halfheartedly. Harry's hands search inside for papers, but his eyes stay on my face. He fishes out a couple of pages and throws them across the table at me.

It is the paperwork to reactivate my Washington State bar membership. Even before I reached Bethell, Uncle Harry had already obtained the forms from the bar office in Seattle. He is on my side, I think. What would I do without Uncle Harry?

I read over and over the critical questions and Harry's proposed answers:

Reason for activating membership? Change of residence to and intention to practice in the state of Washington.

Are there disciplinary proceedings against you? No.

"What about my resignation from Reilly and Sugarman?" I ask.

"Do you see any questions about your old job?" Harry squints hard as he asks me.

"None," I admit.

"So don't be a volunteer and tell something what nobody wants to know about anyway. Just sign your name, and send it in."

That is what I do—sign my name—while holding my breath and biting my tongue. What I am not telling Harry is that as soon as the bar allows me in again, I plan to go to the big city, Seattle. I can find a job there. I know it.

"Why did you sign without reading page two?" Harry looks exasperated.

"You said sign, so I did."

"Now I say read everything before you sign anything. I thought they taught you something at that fancy law school."

On page three, under current employment, the form says I'm clerking under the supervision of Harry King, bar number 375.

"What's this about?" I ask.

"You gotta do something, so I made a deal with the justice court here. Judge Kirkus is gonna use you under my supervision as a county public defender. Since I take those cases once in a while when they ask, now they are going to do me a favor. They are going to let you appear in court instead of me. Because I'm watching you, you see. I'm on the line. Better not upset my breakfast, buddy boy."

I am speechless. Harry is my safety net catching me before I have hit the ground. A public defender. That is more than I ever hoped to get.

I try to talk, but Harry waves me off.

"Don't make a big deal out of this. It's not. Look, justice court is the lowest court on the totem pole, not like your big fancy federal courthouse."

"What can I say? I don't know how to thank you."

"Wait till you show up a coupla times, then we'll see. Now remember, you ain't a volunteer, but your pay may be enough to get you a six-pack a week. So don't get too thrilled." Harry points his cigar at me. "I'll level with you. It's a job no one else wants. It pays nickels and dimes. But it's still a start and makes you look like you are able to do something. At least until we get the paper game over and we're done with the bar."

"Uncle Harry," I blurt, "you are a lifesaver. I could give you a kiss."

Harry grimaces. "Great to know it. So don't complain later." He sits back in his seat. "Where's a fresh cup of coffee, Steve?" This is his way of saying our business is done for now. I straighten up. I am back in Bethell for a while, and I have something to keep me busy.

Harry and I enter the Snoline County justice court, which occupies the former Owens Chrysler dealership showroom on Oakland Avenue. Under the neon light fixtures that previously illuminated Plymouth Valiants and Dodge Darts, we find the backroom office of the presiding judge, Vern Kirkus. Harry and Kirkus shake hands across the judge's desk, but the judge extends no such courtesy to me.

"I knew your dad," he says, looking down as he sinks into his office chair. "King here says you're not gonna embarrass any of us. Is that so?"

I feel like a child. The lawyer who obtained the acquittal of Reverend Cook in federal court less than four months ago has disappeared.

"No, sir," I answer like a novitiate.

"I sure hope so." The judge sighs. I struggle to make eye contact with him, but it's no use; he won't look my way. I sense there is a missing ingredient to this introduction. The judge is accepting me against his will. There must be some obligation he owes Harry.

Judge Kirkus is a portly man, garbed in a white short-sleeve shirt with a clip-on black tie. It appears he is suffering an outbreak of psoriasis about the elbows. Kirkus does not look happy. I try again.

"Thank you, Judge," I say, "and I do look forward to appearing before you in court."

For the first time the judge looks directly at me. "Look, Hirsch. I got one main job here. Those persons arrested by the Snoline cops who are broke, you know what we call 'em?"

"You mean indigent, Your Honor?"

"You betcha," he says. "I mean indigent. Thank you for that." There is no kindness in his courtesy. "Now, those persons, whatever you call 'em, they're gonna have legal counsel as required by law when they come before me. That's me, the law." Kirkus's face is flushed, as if he has been in a losing argument.

"Now, Hirsch, I'm willing to let you stand in for Harry King. So when you are in court, I'm gonna see Mr. King. I won't see you. Do you think you're gonna remember that?" I heard the term *stand in*. It sounds to me like another way of saying *hand in the glove*.

I start to answer, but a surprisingly mellow Harry overrides me as he hands the judge a cigar from his pocket. "Here, try one of these Cubans."

The judge reads the label with a look of curiosity, then grunts, peels off the wrapper, and puts the cigar in his mouth as Harry hands him his lighter. The judge pops it open, sticks the end of the cigar into the flame, and inhales. The cigar's tip burns bright red.

"This is gonna work real well for you, Judge," Harry says, retracting the lighter. "I think you will be surprised how good Nathan here is as a lawyer."

"Surprised, huh?" Kirkus retorts as he blows smoke in my direction. "The last thing I want is surprises."

* * *

Harry was right. My justice court work, the arraignment calendar, my sole assignment, would be absolutely humiliating to any real lawyer. I show up each day on the linoleum floor of the justice court. I read the names off the list of those broke and lawyerless persons the sheriff's only deputy, Earl Strunk, arrested the day before. I advise each defendant the same way: plead not guilty. Thereafter, Judge Kirkus releases the defendant without bail and warns him to show up for his next court hearing on time, and the person, so charged, goes on his way. My job is over.

Dishwashing in a restaurant must be more difficult and rewarding.

"Don't complain, Nathan," Uncle Harry says, chewing on an unlit cigar. "You're damn lucky I could get Kirkus to give you those appointments."

Harry may be right. Without a bar card, I am lucky to have any work at all. I should demonstrate my gratitude on my hands and knees, kissing the hem of Judge Kirkus's polyester robe.

The defender arrangement with Snoline County is rustic. There is no office. The regular defenders are supposedly private practitioners. There are two: Fred Parker and I. Both of us have practice impediments. In Fred's case no one will hire him. In my case Judge Kirkus treats Uncle Harry, and not me, as the lawyer responsible to the court. Harry is a member of the bar, and I appear only by virtue of his sponsorship. Even though the judge assigns the calendars to me, ostensibly Harry is my boss.

On paper Fred and Harry are on the top of a mythical court appointment list that includes Snoline County's twenty-two lawyers. In fact all of the justice court appointments go to Fred Parker and me. There is a reason for this. The county pays only fifteen dollars an hour to defenders of the indigent and limits the number of hours per case we can bill.

This canard, that private lawyers are taking indigent clients in the ordinary course of their private practices, lets the county commissioners meet their constitutional duty to provide indigents with criminal defenses, but with no defender offices or staff to support, the county saves a bundle.

My codefender, Fred Parker—known as Midnight Fred—is not good professional company. Everybody at Steve's Diner, the courthouse hangout, laughs about his ascent to the bar. Appointed assistant clerk in the Snoline County office by his father-in-law, the duly elected county clerk, Fred found himself each day behind a service window with no line. Fred was like a teller in a bank that had no depositors.

But Fred surprised everyone. In his spare time, he became a lawyer by reading the law Lincoln style—that is, by studying with Clay Denton, a Bethell lawyer. It was widely believed that Midnight earned Clay's allegiance, and his nickname, by stamping certain pleadings for him after Clay had missed filing deadlines. Long after the clerk's office doors were locked shut, Fred stamped Clay's delinquent papers as "timely filed" although the deadlines fixed by law had passed.

Clay returned the favor by certifying that Midnight Fred could sit for the three-day bar examination. After Midnight took the test unsuccessfully three times, in 1971 the state bar examiners grading the test went soft on their passing standards. And Midnight, like a boat previously stuck on a sand spit, was rescued by a high tide and floated over the bar. But the name Midnight stuck.

While no person in his right mind in Snoline County would hire Midnight, even he refused to perform the arraignments on the justice court calendar. That was why Uncle Harry was able to persuade Judge Kirkus to use me as a stand-in.

I attend the justice court arraignment calendar twice a week whether or not there are any pending charges. However, Harry is the one paid and then only fifteen dollars per actual arraignment. On days when no charges have been filed, I earn Harry nothing.

A tape recorder could easily perform Snoline court arraignments. My momentary clients are charged with petty theft, shoplifting, drunken driving, assault, and public disorder, usually arising from Saturday night bar brawls. Many seem suspended in some state between adolescence and adulthood. Ultimately, all of them will plead guilty. Living as they have since childhood in Snoline County—and most of them in Bethell proper—they regularly reappear on the calendar when the judge orders it and silently accept the modest penalties he metes out to them.

In work clothes, wearing the typical blue-and-gray quilted northwest parkas, some appear washed out and slightly bent in the presence of the judge. With hair lank and eyes resigned, they receive their deferred sentences, accompanied by orders to make restitution for their petty thefts, shoplifting, and modest pilfering. Shame registers on some. Most display a dry-lipped desire to get it over with. They seem to know that the remodeled auto showroom, with its ersatz-oak judge's bench and low-pile beige carpet, holds a power over their lives. They are onto the fact that the judicial trimmings signal a place of no choices.

Despite his disregard for me, I am forced to admit Judge Kirkus enforces the law with a very practical and judicious eye. The fact is most of the charged loggers, millworkers, farmhands, and gill-netter fishermen are the sole sources of support for wives, ex-wives, and children. In all probability Kirkus has enforced any particular defendant's divorce decree, ordered him to pay child support, and garnished his wages. Undoubtedly Kirkus goes to church with some of his defendants and their families. Bethell is a small community.

Twice a week at 8:30 a.m., I am stuck in the tiny dealership-turned-courthouse and on call the rest of the time. In between, with nothing to do, I drink government-issue coffee with the judge's bailiff, Delta Snell, and occasionally gossip with Scott Pelky, the county prosecutor's only deputy. Periodically Butch Strohmeyer from the *Daily Herald* is desperate enough for a story to come to the justice court. He and I talk about the weather as if we were a couple of farmers from Ohio, the risk of a freeze the dominating subject in both our minds.

Paradoxically, no one has ever asked why I am back in Bethell. Al Zilstra, the elected Snoline County prosecutor, who rarely shows up on the calendar, nicknamed me Perfessor or Da Man because I went to school in the East. Scott Pelky, less generously but for the same reason, refers to me as Hotshot.

Unlike the legend of Midnight Fred, whose legal adventure is common knowledge, most of the local bars tend to mind their own business. I have found that each of the lawyers in Bethell has personal reasons for practicing in Snoline County. Uncle Harry is the only one who knows my secrets.

In the few weeks since Kirkus agreed to let me do the arraignments in his court as Harry's stand-in, I have become accustomed to recognizing people with whom I grew up as they are arraigned in the justice court.

One day I call the calendar, and on it is John LaFrance. When he sat across the aisle from me in Mr. Oakley's history class at Jefferson Junior High, he was Johnny LaFrance, with toxic breath. Scrunched down to avoid being seen, Johnny made spit wads all day, stored the damp gobs in his desk, and flicked them behind the teacher's back. If I volunteered to work at the blackboard, Johnny would stick his feet into the aisle and trip me.

But here is John before the court, charged with indecent liberties with a fourteen-year-old girl. As he stands next to me, his junior-high classmate, now his appointed lawyer, both of us give shy glances of recognition—looks of "can you believe we're here?"—and both of us suppress the tendency to make small talk. The coincidence overshadows for a moment that Johnny has been busted. But only for a moment. What connects us is a charge of indecent liberties in the backseat of his car with a disrobed teenager. It's not a junior-high class reunion.

A bigger surprise is Joanne Crenshaw, charged with possession of cocaine. When she was a petite brunette study-hall clerk at Totem High School, I watched her typing up hall passes. I could not quite get up the nerve to ask Joanne out on a date, but we talked back then of college and the dream of leaving Snoline County behind.

Joanne married Doug Heidecker in the summer of 1962, a little too quickly, it now seems. And when she appears in court, she is a mother of two, divorced, working at Bartleson Mortgage and Title Company, and about to receive a deferred sentence.

I call the calendar and recognized Joanne's face. "Good to see you, Joanne," I blurt.

She stares at me, disbelieving that I am not mocking her, and then acknowl edges the greeting with a nod of surrender. Joanne is not a criminal type, and as we stand before the court, the two of us share a common discomfort. I am not sure which is the greater humiliation for Joanne: the admission of guilt or seeing me here, my participation reminding her of those plans and dreams she revealed in the Totem High School lunchroom.

* * *

I am reminded through my daily discourse with Bethell's store clerks and gas-pump jockeys and even Arlene Thornberry, the countergirl at Steve's Diner, that I treated many locals as unimportant when I intended to permanently depart Bethell. Many seem to have long memories.

Herman Millkin the barber: "Home to visit the mother, eh?"

"Not quite," I say. "I'll be around for a while."

"Thought you were gone for good." Herman's trimmer hums like a mosquito around my ear as he clips my neck hair. "Isn't DC where you live now?"

"Used to live."

"Light sideburns?" Herman asks. "Or the kind of hairdo you brought in here? That's how they cut it back there for the politicians, isn't it?"

I stop in to Uncle Si Galitzer's Union Wear shop next to the jewelry store, hoping to find a white shirt in my size. Uncle Si, a lifetime friend of my late father and my whole family, quickly sizes me up.

"Sorry, Nathan," Si says, his palms turned up. "Nothing of your high-end East Coast style. Maybe Brooks Brothers has some kind of mail order service for you." This from one of my family's friends.

The same kinds of comments about how I look or dress or talk are repeated at Ambrose's Mobil gas station, the Piggly Wiggly grocery, Dave Handleman's Hardware, even Steve's Diner across from the courthouse, where I have tagged after Dad or Uncle Harry my entire life.

The faces I knew are polite enough and their interest understandable. Each has small-town curiosity as to why I am suddenly walking among them on a daily basis when, despite being a son and grandson of longtime Bethell denizens, I disappeared almost a decade ago. I know this question would occur to me if the shoe were on the other foot. Since the truth is too painful for me to tell, I remain separate from all who might ask and who might, as a common courtesy, be entitled to the answer.

With my humble job, my vanity has vanished. My shirts are often unironed, and my lucky court tie's maroon silk is enriched with gravy from Steve's. My shoes, purchased when I worked for Lynn Reilly, when I still believed I had a reputation to maintain, are unshined. At Steve's Diner I look little different from the salesmen at Cobler Toyota on the opposite corner of Oakland Avenue from the justice court.

* * *

Last Monday morning I simply oversleep. Judge Kirkus had already taken the bench when I stumble in out of the Bethell rain with no excuse for my tardiness. I leave my raincoat on and run up to the bench. The judge was steaming.

"Welcome, Hirsch. Glad you could join us."

"Sorry, Your Honor," I mumble.

"No, no. Not at all. Take off your coat and stay awhile. Perhaps we could read the calendar, with your permission."

Delta Snell glares at me through her oversize glasses as she handed me the short calendar; then she calls the first and only case.

The only matter that morning is the misdemeanor charges against Terrence Bags, a cadaverous mill hand who regularly appeared on the petty crime calendar, usually for public drunkenness. This time Terrence was arrested lugging about a tire carcass that turned out to have been lifted from a pyramid of sale tires stacked near the driveway at Cobler Toyota.

"Look, Judge," Terrence pleads. "The tire, it's my spare. It's from my pickup." His clothes are stiffened with dirt, and his sagging spine seemed supported by the rigidity of the fabric.

"What pickup, Terrence?" the judge says.

"What pickup?" Terrence repeats with a look of confusion. "OK. You got me right there. OK, no pickup. No spare." Terrence draws himself up as if to take a blow. "OK. Guilty. Guilty as charged."

The judge holds up his hand like a traffic cop. "Hold it a minute, Terrence. Just pipe down. The charge hasn't been read yet. No guilty pleas."

"But guilty is what I am," Terrence says. "Guilty."

"Hirsch," Judge Kirkus asks, "have you read the charges yet? Ready to counsel your client?"

Delta impatiently points at the paperwork she had handed me, and I quickly scanned it, but not fast enough to cut off Terrence.

"Don't matter, Judge," Terrence says. "I did it, whatever it says."

Judge Kirkus points his hammer at me. "You see, Hirsch, this is what comes of the defender not being on time. Justice is delayed, and that won't happen again, not in this courtroom, sir, where everybody has counsel before they're charged and before they plead one way or the other. You understand?"

"Sorry, Judge," I repeat. "I do understand. I'll review the charges with my client."

"No need," says Terrence. "Guilty it is, all right."

"That's it; that's it." Kirkus rises from his chair. "Nobody's gonna violate the rules of guilty pleas in my courtroom. I refuse to accept any plea until—Mr. Hirsch, you take Mr. Bags here and counsel him privately on the charge. Officer, take the prisoner to the back room. You got it, Mr. Hirsch?"

"Yes, sir," I say. Thus the three of us—Terrence Bags, the deputy from the Bethell jail, and I—traipsed to the back of the courtroom.

I started reading the charges to Terrence, but he couldn't have cared less.

"Never mind," he says. "The cops got fresh rolls and coffee at the lockup. I'm hungry now. Real hungry. The quicker I say guilty, the sooner I get my breakfast. Plus, I could use a bathroom break."

"Then Terrence," I say, "keep your mouth shut until I tell you to speak, and we'll all get out of here."

"OK," he says, "I can do that." But as soon as we reappeared at the front of the courtroom, Terrence forgot his assignment of silence and piped up again. "Still guilty, Judge."

Kirkus just shakes his head. "Hirsch, you are on the edge of contempt. One more time late with your raincoat on when this calendar is read and Terrence Bags is gonna have company in the jailhouse, you understand?"

What could I say? Each time Terrence spoke, I was the one punished, the judge's indictments indirect and profoundly unfair. Like Terrence, I felt like pleading guilty to end it. There was nowhere I could turn to avoid judgment.

"Won't happen again, Judge," I grovel. Delta Snell harrumphs as she stamped a set of documents on her desk.

The judge turned his glare away from me. "Now, Terrence, I take it you're happy. Do you plead guilty as charged?"

"Yes, sir, I do."

As Terrence pronounces, "I do," he moves closer to me, as if the two of us were about to be married. As he steps forward, an intestinal rumble, deep and distinctive, uncontested by any other sound in the room, was loosened and erupted. It was as if Terrence had sprung a leak of animal vapors. An earthy scent rises into my nostrils. Delta wrinkles her nose. The judge recoils.

"Sorry," Terrence says. "No excuse. Missed my morning constitutional."

Kirkus looks afflicted. He pronounces justice in haste. "Then guilty it is, and now back to jail for the day. And turn on the damned fan."

As Delta waves a newspaper in front of her face to defeat the invasion of Terrence's aroma, the judge stands as if to flee the room and the penetrating exhaust from Terrence but gives one parting shot aimed at me.

"I don't think Mr. King would be too happy with you today, Hirsch." Kirkus stares at me as if I were responsible for the smell in his courtroom.

Then, as Delta chokes out, "Court adjourned," Judge Kirkus finishes his retreat to his back room, where, in the building's past incarnation, sweaty car salesmen had cut legions of used-car deals.

Delta hit the wall switch with the heel of her hand, the ceiling fan whirrs, and the scent of Terrence is yanked out to the street. With court adjourned, Terrence seems pleased. The hunger etched on his face suddenly vanishes and is replaced by a look of anticipation, perhaps complemented by relief following his gaseous expulsion. I feel like looking about for a rock under which I could hide. Perhaps I should have stayed in bed.

CHAPTER 11

Nathan Reads that Si Galitzer Is Dead

* * *

On Monday, April 13, 1973, the northwest sky is clear enough that at seven thirty in the morning, I foolishly leave my raincoat behind in the basement and risk that my four-block walk from Parkland to the justice court will be dry. But I fail to take the temperature into account, and I am blowing on my hands for warmth by the time I arrive at Steve's Diner, hoping for a cup of coffee with Uncle Harry King before I have to show up at eight thirty in the justice court, where, after my failure to be on time for the Terrence Bags hearing, I firmly have lodged my foot in the judicial bucket.

My watch says five minutes to eight. I have only a minute, but I still want a cup of coffee to get my blood moving again, plus seeing Uncle Harry is always reassuring. But as I enter Steve's, Harry is nowhere in sight. His usual booth in the rear of the diner is empty.

I decide to wait for him and grab a used *Daily Herald* out of a rough stack in a peach crate by the diner's entry. Steve's regulars are in the habit of snatching discarded *Daily Heralds* from the pile and, after perusing the recent news, returning the papers to the crate.

There is a high-backed swivel chair at the counter next to Bert Ambrose, who works in his father's Mobil gas station across from the courthouse. I nod to Bert, slip into the swivel seat, and order a coffee from Arlene, Steve's waitress.

Steve's home-baked cinnamon rolls are parked under a clear plastic cake bin on the counter. I help myself with a paper napkin, start to eat the roll as if I own the place, prop up the half-rolled, half-folded *Daily Herald* on the aluminum menu holder front of my coffee cup, and read as I check out each person coming into Steve's. I don't want to miss spotting Harry.

In the days when my father took me to Steve's as a kid, I could smell Harry's cigar as soon as I pushed open the diner's door. Harry would be installed in the back booth with his intense, unblinking ice-blue eyes staring out of his hound-dog wrinkled face, scrutinizing each person who was entering or departing.

It seemed to me at the time that a parade passed by Harry's table, as if it were a Fourth of July reviewing stand. Deputy sheriffs and state patrol officers on break, lawyers with business in the court across Oakland Avenue, contractors, local tradesmen, farmers, and millworkers wearing hard hats and jeans—they all stopped by, shook hands with Harry, and sometimes bent over to whisper jokes in his ear.

I took it in as they all paid their respects at his table, as if Harry were a potentate. The highest compliment was when Steve, smelling like French fries, would drop into the booth draped in his dirty apron, push back his stained white chef's cap, and chin with Harry over a smoke.

For that matter my father and Uncle Si Galitzer had been Steve's Diner's daily regulars as well. In the summers when I worked for my dad at Fulton Jewelry, I would walk with him to Steve's at exactly ten o'clock, and Uncle Si would saunter in exactly ten minutes later. Except for Uncle Harry, the all-male breakfast crowd had left, and Leon and Si would join Harry for a cup of Steve's coffee in big fist-size mugs. Sometimes Dad would smoke a morning Lucky Strike, a habit left over from his army days.

Then, on the stroke of ten thirty, Si and Leon would get up, leaving Harry, fling their jackets over their shoulders, and head back out to Fulton Street, my father to his store in the Hirsch Building and Si two doors down the street, to Bethell Union Wear and his inventory of workingmen's garb. I would scramble after them, behind by a step or two, trying to set my strut to their martial rhythm and pace.

Though Uncle Harry's table is still sitting empty, I note to myself that none of Steve's patrons dare occupy Harry's green Naugahyde throne while he is elsewhere. It's as if his arrival is imminent, and any temporary occupant will be branded a rude interloper, ripe for ejection.

For me it's no different. It would be an act of heresy to slide across the guest side of Harry's booth and wait for him there. Until Uncle Harry gets to Steve's, I stay planted on my counter stool, scouring the *Daily Herald* and trying to get the silence of the bar association off my mind.

It has been over a month since, with Harry's help, I requested that the bar activate my membership. A part of me wants to phone Seattle and rattle the bar's cage by reminding someone that while the board of governors dawdles, my life remains in limbo. I am also aware that Uncle Harry would poke fun at my impatience and repeat that old moldy chestnut that patience is a virtue.

With the folded *Daily Herald* in hand, I halfheartedly scrutinize the lead articles. Only once since I stumbled back to Bethell, when longing overcame my sense of awkward shame, did I buy a *Washington Post*. I read it for only a minute before drifting into a state of despondency. Each page brought Shira Loeb to my mind, and I had to fight the urge to call her on the spot. During the past four months, when my self-control failed I rang Shira's number at work. She hung up as soon she heard my self-pitying voice. Indeed, my raw animal whine had shocked even me. I swore I would never call her again like that, yet I have called repeatedly, with no different result. Shira is done with me.

Still, I have drafted letter after unsent letter to Shira, trying to explain myself. Each version seems less honest than the previous draft. They now form a sloppy pile on my basement desk. If I send any of them, in all likelihood Shira will simply throw the envelopes in the garbage unopened and unread.

It is less than twenty-six minutes before I must hotfoot it across Oakland Avenue to the justice court. I skip through the *Daily Herald*'s AP reprints on Watergate and the Saudi oil embargo. I pass the first-page report about the convening of the first Snoline County grand jury in over fifty years, in the courthouse on Lansing. These stories should grab my attention, but they do not. Instead I am drawn to another front-page story, one with a picture. Bethell's big Monday morning story is the selection of Eileen Narver as the 1973 Blossom Festival queen.

The *Daily Herald*'s photographer snapped a photo of Eileen holding a flower bouquet as she was hastily draped with the queen's sash from last year. I am drawn to Eileen's fetching pastoral smile, straight blond hair, and long figure, a kind of Lauren-Hutton-in-last-year's-prom-dress look. But Eileen's giant eyes are a long way from Shira's. Strange as it may seem, I miss Shira's wan figure, piercing owl-like stare behind goblet-size lenses, ink-stained fingers, nails nibbled to the quick, and lank black hair and that perpetual wafting aroma of a scholar's midnight fuel: peanut butter and coffee.

I wonder about Eileen Narver's midnight smell, and I find myself sighing out loud. Embarrassed, I look around to see if anyone notices my sounds, but the only person nearby paying any attention is Arlene, pouring refills into coffee mugs up and down the counter.

"You're so bent, Nathan, that you missed a real story." Arlene points at the corner of my *Daily Herald* with her pot. "Check it out."

"You mean the Watergate stuff?"

"Nathan, get your mind out of the clouds, and look at what's in front of your nose."

> LOCAL BUSINESSMAN FOUND DEAD IN STORE
>
> The body of Raphael Seymour (Si) Galitzer, a single man living at 185 Sagstad Drive on Route 20 in Snoline County, was discovered by a janitor Sunday morning in his clothing store, Bethell Union Wear, on Fulton Street. The sheriff's office has announced that the store's cash register was open, and the deceased's body was found on the floor behind the counter. There is no reported cause of death or the recovery of any weapon.

I read the first paragraph of the story over and over again, my heart's fibrillation jumbling the words on the page. I cannot accept the contents. Suddenly I realize why Uncle Harry is not at Steve's this morning. He must have found out about Uncle Si.

I force myself to read the article's background on Uncle Si, but it just reiterates what I already know.

> Bethell Union Wear, founded by the deceased's late father, Morris M. Galitzer, in the Alaskan gold rush era, has been in business on Fulton

> Street for over sixty years, during which time two generations of the Galitzer family have served the community. Mr. Galitzer was currently on the board of the Downtown Businessmen's Association. A past chair of the Bethell Blossom Day parade, he also was a member of Toastmasters and the Fraternal Order of the Elks.

"Uncle Si was not that old to drop dead," I say out loud. The shock of the story causes me to forget I am talking to myself. Nobody but Bert Ambrose even looks up.

"Hard to believe about Mr. Galitzer," he says, "but I'll tell ya. A killer broke in there and did it. I can smell it." Bert's Adam's apple bobs with each word.

"Bert," Arlene says, "you been beaned once too often."

"There's nothing about a killer," I say. In fact it's amazing how little information the story contains. Uncle Si's store on Fulton, where the break-in took place, sits only two blocks from the old rail tracks in the dying core of Bethell. Vagrants now hang out in the alleys off Fulton Street. Some have been my clients on past Monday morning arraignments.

Maybe Bert is right. Perhaps one of the vagrants murdered Uncle Si, but it's hard to believe. In Bethell, perched on the shores of Puget Sound, people die of cancer, heart attacks, strokes, and just plain old age. Or periodically they die in ragged traffic accidents on a Saturday night or, tragically, when a hunting weapon accidentally discharges or a farm tractor unexpectedly flips on its side. Suspicious deaths never happened. The pace of Bethell life does not raise the level of emotion to the point of pent-up discharge, the reckless excitement necessary for murderous violence. In Bethell, people expire by natural causes or by mistake.

Surely the county sheriff has more information: the time of Uncle Si's death, fingerprints, any scraps of clothes, fibers, or hairs that might have been left after a scuffle. I assume the *Daily Herald* story would repeat any information about what the sheriff has found that suggests foul play. But the story contains nothing.

While I pore over the article again and again, Bert Ambrose, the expert, rambles on.

"Murdered in his own store," he says. "I remember when James Stanger's brains were blown out at the Smokey Point Shell station. They never could get the blood stains outa the wooden floor." Bert is smiling—or maybe his look is simply a grimace.

"Happens in gas stations all the time," he says. "Anything's possible these days."

Ambrose Mobil has been all but shut down by the oil embargo. Even when they are able to get a delivery, gas prices are up to a prohibitive two dollars a gallon.

My face is hot. I can feel the color. I look around with some discomfort, as if someone is watching how I respond to the news of Uncle Si's death, as if someone is looking for some show of emotion, some sign of shock, grief, or loss. I am uncertain. How should I feel? How am I expected to behave? Where is Uncle Harry?

I glance at Arlene to see if she notices my unwinding, but she has moved to the back counter and is pouring water into the coffeemaker. No one else has stopped talking; no one is looking my way. Oblivious to my presence, Arlene now is moving down the counter again, refilling coffee cups. She sways and bounces, leaving Bert alone to chew his toast, his jaw moving slowly from side to side like a camel's, as if he has no intention to ever leave the diner.

I fight an urge to call Auntie Riva and tell her Uncle Si is dead, but I want to talk to Uncle Harry first. Alas, he is nowhere in sight.

Si is not a true uncle to me. His living relatives whom I know are his brother, Frank Galitzer; his sister-in-law, Mae, whom I call Auntie Mae; and their kids—the twins, Ralph and Roger; and their older, simpleminded brother, Victor. Frank's business, Frank's Western Emporium, sits directly across Fulton Street from Uncle Si's store. The two Galitzer brothers are combative and hostile. To my knowledge they have not spoken for years.

My father and Uncle Si were thrown together daily, as their businesses sat on the same side of the street. Their fathers were old-time friends. I am told my Zayde Albert and the Galitzer brothers' dad, Morris Galitzer, were proud fishermen, and Morris declared himself a onetime lumberjack. His affiliation with workers was how he began Bethell Union Wear. All the work clothing, each set of gloves, the rain slickers, the carpenters' belts, and the work brogans Si carried at the family store bore labels reading "Made in the USA."

Not every MOT approved that Uncle Si and his father were eager and vocal union supporters. When I was in junior high school, the workers at Skarbell's, Bethell's only major employer, went on strike. Morris and Uncle Si walked on the picket line with the millworkers.

Tensions ran high in town. Somebody set a fire in the garage of Herb Escola, the union representative, and the sheriff called up the posse, a group of bloated crew-cut farmers who armed themselves with shotguns and hunting rifles. Talk was ugly.

I remember sitting with my dad and Uncle Harry at Steve's when the subject of Uncle Si's support of the strike came up.

"Not smart. Not smart." Harry waved his donut. "You didn't need to picket to be on the side of workers. Just give 'em credit at the store. Si and Morris think they got to be out there walking around on the picket line. Dumb. Real dumb."

My dad was unimpressed as well. He had been in the Quartermaster Corps in the Pacific. Si's avoidance of military service stuck in my dad's craw.

"Easy to pick up a sign and strut in circles for an hour," Dad said. "Harder to pick up a rifle."

Farmers had been exempt from the military draft in 1942. Apparently Si had claimed he was farming at Rivers End, the Galitzers' large spread out on Route 20. Then, when the war was over, he gave up farming and went back to Bethell Union Wear. Uncle Si never put on a uniform.

Si's brother, Frank, couldn't have cared less about unions or uniforms. He opened Frank's Western Emporium across Fulton Street after Morris died, and his store was full of nonunion inventory, cowboy hats, cotton shirts, blue jeans, and cowboy boots, which by the '60s were manufactured in Asia.

That the Galitzer brothers didn't speak was almost as interesting as the fact that they really didn't compete. A mill hand might buy work brogans from Si and a cowboy shirt from Frank and not think for a minute that the two brothers despised each other.

Uncle Si even played a role, albeit a small one, in what I thought would be my permanent escape from Bethell. Twelve years ago, during the 1962 Blossom Festival, the Bethell Business Association awarded me a college scholarship.

They called it the Bethell Scholar of the Year Award. As those awards went, it was not a huge sum—$500—but the title that went with it, Bethell Scholar of the Year, struck me as worth its weight in gold.

I was preening backstage in the Totem High School auditorium, trying to catch the eye of Cheryl Connelly, the 1962 Blossom Day queen, whom I saw dodging around the curtains, looking for the *Daily Herald* photographer. My head was full of the fantasy of finding Cheryl alone and bare breasted, and I was startled by a hand grabbing my shoulder, jarring me as if it were Cheryl's dad, who had been able to read my brain and the naked fantasy of his daughter that filled it.

I jumped and blushed, but it was only Uncle Si, wearing an open-collar sport shirt and a flashy sport coat, with a little American flag pinned to his lapel and a purple ribbon declaring him to be on the Blossom Day committee.

Si gripped my hand roughly and tightly, jerking with a frightening enthusiasm bordering on epilepsy.

"You're the first, you know," he said, the salesman pumping the hand of a customer. "The first of us to get this award. No matter what he doesn't say, your dad is proud too. We're all proud. Damned proud."

My teeth were chattering from the action of Si's pumping arms. I would mount the dais with the Blossom Day queen, and later, possibly, having wowed Cheryl with my brains, I would get the chance to envelop the queen in the back of my car. I wanted my arm back, but Si wouldn't quit.

"Just because your old man talked about your brother all the time, forget it. I know about brothers, believe me. So Ritchie hit home runs, so he's a marine. So what? You can hold your head just as high. You hit a grand slam here. Outa the park. You made us all look good."

Comparing me and Ritchie, then on duty in Southeast Asia, did not seem right. To include my father and his feelings about either Ritchie or me in this conversation went too far. Uncle Si didn't know a thing about us, but everybody in Bethell knew he and his younger brother, Frank, didn't speak.

And it had annoyed me that Uncle Si would suggest I had received this award in some representative capacity, that I had some responsibility for the Bethell MOTs, when all I desired was to be on the dais with Cheryl Connelly and to somehow escort her to the Blossom Festival dance. If I could worm myself into that opportunity and then find some dark corner of the world alone with Cheryl, I would be in heaven. Representing others—Mom, Dad, Ritchie, Si, and all the MOTs—was not on my mind.

* * *

Now Si is dead. I make two calls from Steve's phone booth. Carla Prism is at my mother's home and answers the phone.

As I tell Carla about Uncle Si, she gasps.

"Oh my God," she says. "Pearl's gonna freak. Just freak."

"Make sure you hide today's *Daily Herald*. I'll come over after court and tell my mother what I can find out. But just ditch the paper, OK?"

Then I call Auntie Riva.

"I heard" is all she says. The line goes silent, and I step into the breach.

"I guess you and Uncle Si are old friends." How awkward that sounded: the present tense and Uncle Si dead.

"Don't you, of all people, worry about me." Riva's voice is shaking. "Something terrible is happening. I can feel it. Things come in pairs. You mark my words."

"What do you mean?"

"Too many of us dead. Your dad. Your brother. Now Si."

I can hear her racing breath through the phone, and then she begins to weep. Is she frightened at the prospect of being alone? Or does she foresee some kind of menace, some kind of retribution for Uncle Si's acts of the past?

It is eight twenty. I promise Auntie Riva that I will call back after court. The calendar will be read by Delta Snell at nine. I remember I've left my copy of the *Daily Herald* on the counter. I go back, grab the folded front section, place it back in the peach box, and depart.

The April morning mist is lifting. I practice breathing in and out, as if to a slow mental metronome. I jaywalk across wet Oakland Avenue, avoiding the puddles, and cross the asphalt parking lot to the low-slung former auto showroom now occupied by the court.

As I step inside the building, my watch reports it is eight twenty-five. Plenty early. Judge Kirkus will not be reading me the riot act this morning. One more time I turn around and glance back outside toward the parking lot, half expecting to see Uncle Harry, having arrived late to Steve's, following me across Oakland Avenue. But there is no Uncle Harry.

I turn left toward the courtroom door, and there Judge Kirkus stands, waiting for me.

"You got quite a client this morning," he says. "They've got Si Galitzer's killer. Now, get into my office."

CHAPTER 12

Wally Richmond Is Nathan's Client

* * *

JUDGE KIRKUS IS IN HIS shirtsleeves, short ones at that. On the bench his robed bulkiness makes him formidable. Now, standing with his exposed white arms, he looks hopeless and short. "I want to talk to you inside."

We walk into his low-ceilinged office, separated from the public chamber by sheets of walnut-veneer plywood straight from the Skarbell Mill. The plywood walls are thin, and Kirkus whispers. Outside, I can hear the rumbling of voices and shifting of feet in the courtroom.

"No time to get somebody else. Believe me, I've tried already. You're gonna have to represent the prisoner." Kirkus starts the conversation in the middle. He has always been uncomfortable with me, eyeing me as if I were trouble, a time bomb.

"What prisoner? What case?"

"You know the Richmonds? Not that it makes any difference. They booked Wally Richmond for breaking into Si Galitzer's. He's dead, you know."

"Are you saying Wally Richmond killed Uncle Si?"

Kirkus looks around, as if he is being watched.

"You and I, we aren't having this conversation," he whispers. "I couldn't tell you if I did know. But if you'd check the calendar once in a while, you'd have a better idea what's going on around here."

I start to say that before I got to the courtroom, Kirkus called me into his office. Then I stop.

"Can't you get anybody else?" I ask. "Si Galitzer has been my uncle my whole life."

"I thought of that, but the prosecutor, in all his glory, wants to arraign him now. Tried to call George Miffler to take the plea, but he's gone fishing."

George Miffler, a lawyer in Everett, often tangled with the local prosecutor. Two big fish in a small pond.

I must look shocked. If I call the dead man "Uncle Si," how can I represent his possible killer?

Kirkus seems to read my mind. He holds up his hands in a gesture of helplessness.

"There's no choice here," he says. "We don't have time to get somebody else. Just do your job, I'll do mine, and it's over quickly. I'll give you fifteen minutes to meet with Richmond. Then we'll do the calendar."

The judge pats the pocket of his coat hanging on the chair, looking for his pack of cigarettes. Finding nothing, he pulls at the desk drawer for reserves and yanks it off the stays. The contents clatter to the floor and scurry into cracks.

"Shit," he says and laughs ruefully. "This tells you what a mess we're in for. We're stuck with each other today, Hirsch, no doubt about that."

* * *

Wally Richmond is no stranger to me. We grew up together in Bethell and went to grade school together. He was kind of a tough guy, although we got along reasonably enough.

The Richmonds were a Catholic family, but not all of them enrolled at Saint Augustine, the parochial school where most of Bethell's Catholic kids went. Wally and two of his five sisters were at Shaw Elementary at the same time as me.

I remember Wally as one of those kids with a warning track around him and cold eyes. Throughout junior high and his sophomore year at Totem High School, Wally was always skulking around with a gang of greasers wearing jeans and engineer boots. Common sense dictated I stay away from him, although there was little opportunity for a collision. I was taking algebra and history while Wally was assigned to industrial shop and auto repair.

But I do remember that in second grade, Wally mimicked Alvin Guthman, who didn't know any better and rode his bike to school with training wheels—a no-brainer target for gibes and jests.

"Alvin the kike, he's got a four-wheel bike," Wally chanted in front of Shaw Elementary until the principal, Mr. Sunvold, swooped down in his shiny brown suit and bow tie and whacked Wally on the head, saying, "We don't talk that way."

At dinner I asked my parents what a kike was. Ritchie, wise at twelve, five years older than me, snickered across the table as he forked down mashed potatoes.

"Who said that?" my dad Leon demanded.

"Wally Richmond," I said.

"I told you it would happen," Mom complained.

"Never mind those Richmonds," Dad said. "The kid's just trying to get your goat."

"They're uncivilized," my mom Pearl muttered. "All those children, boys and girls sharing one bathroom in that tiny house. As if God wanted them to have all those children."

Whatever *kike* meant, I could sense my dad assumed that when Wally called Alvin Guthman one, he was talking about me as well. Why else would my goat be involved? But I also felt secure in my family's implicit contempt of the Richmonds. It did not matter what Wally called Alvin Guthman or, for that matter, the Hirsches.

We were above the Richmonds in my parents' minds, and that was how I saw Wally. He dropped out of school and out of my sight when he turned sixteen. I heard he went to work at the Skarbell Mill and married Lennie Nyquist, a girl who was also at Shaw Elementary. Lennie was a cute one with a quick smile. Lennie always made me feel I was physically retarded, for she had started to be a woman in sixth grade, the first to wear V-neck sweaters and flats with no socks.

I remember gaping at Lennie as she necked publicly after school in sixth grade with Henry Fowler, but by seventh grade she had moved up, making out with a gang of bigger boys behind the gym at lunch, taking turns, and getting lower to the ground on each round.

Lennie picked out Wally in high school. I would bet she was Wally's first.

* * *

The sheriff has put Wally in the little custodial holding room between the courtroom and the men's room. The holding room has two doors. One leads down the hallway to the door in back, where the deputies and state patrol officers park their squad cars. One door leads to Kirkus's courtroom.

I know the tall deputy sheriff, Earl Strunk, who stands outside the door to the holding room.

"Counselor," he says to me with a meanspirited grin, "it's old home week today." Earl touches his curled fingers to his forehead while straightening the middle one beyond the others and smiling broadly. "I'm sure Wally's happy he got you in his corner. Prosecutor will probably just cave in, drop the charges, and let Richmond out at the thought of you being his lawyer and all."

I knew Earl as a football player at Totem High. He was two years older than me and younger than Ritchie. A Mill Town kid, supposedly two college scholarships were waiting for him as soon as he clutched his Totem sheepskin.

Then, one spring night when Earl was out with his buddies, drinking shots of rye whiskey and Colt 45 chasers, he took on a tree at two in the morning, an alder sapling planted in the divider off the new public dock at the waterfront. The story was that Earl bet he could knock it down with a single bull charge, just the way he bowled over offensive linemen on his way to clobbering every quarterback in the league, but instead he ripped up his right knee. The severed ligaments never completely healed.

"What did Richmond do?" I ask Earl.

"Oh, nothing. Just burglarized Si Galitzer's store and murdered the old geezer. Nothing big." Earl leers, watching me for a reaction. Here in Bethell the old loyalties are barely below the surface, and there is not a person in town who's unaware of where those loyalties stem from.

Earl's hair is thinning, and he has developed a paunch from sitting around all day at the lockup, but he is still an imposing figure, and I choose to ignore his ribbing.

"You holding the PR file?" I ask. "What about a preview?" A police report comes over to the court and is handed over to the defense at the arraignment. A look at the PR file won't make a difference with Wally's arraignment, but it will give me something to report to Auntie Riva later.

Earl stops his silly grinning for a minute and then shrugs.

"Why not?" He does not want me thinking he is a bad guy.

The report file is brief. A witness named Evelyn Doornik was going home from work and saw a male running with a bag down the alley behind Si's Fulton Street store. Her statement said she saw the suspect jump into a car, a blue 1967 Camaro with license plate number BYF 674. Probably Wally's plates. Wally had been arrested three times before, all juvenile cases of theft and breaking and entering.

The report goes on to disclose that the investigating officer found the alley door to Union Wear ajar, the cash till open and empty, and a dead older male with a severe head wound lying on the floor.

Earl looks at me as if something has just occurred to him.

"Isn't Galitzer a relative of yours or something?"

I don't answer, but Earl and I are clearly thinking on the same track.

"Thanks for the peek." I hand the PR file back and point at the door. "Now, let's see the dangerous prisoner."

Earl turns the key. I step in, and he locks the door behind me.

Wally sits there behind a metal table, his chair tilted back against the wall. He is wearing his slicked-back hair tucked around his ears. Wally is spare, short, and dressed like a hood from the '50s, with low-slung blue jeans and a plaid shirt, collar up, open at the neck, sleeves rolled up. I note a little arrow tattoo on the back of his hand.

At thirty-two Wally's face is seamless, but his dark unshaven cheeks give off a soiled look, and his canines are crooked. Wally drums his fingers on the tabletop. The tips are stained auburn from too many smokes.

"Hey, Wally" is all I can say. I wonder if I am looking at Uncle Si's killer. Wally seems too small in stature, too light in energy to muster the flash, the explosion to kill someone.

On the other hand, I had stood in front of Judge Kirkus listening to criminal charges against John La France and Joanne Crenshaw, individuals I grew up with, ran into at the Triple X Root Beer, parked alongside at the Paramount Drive-In movie theater, danced next to in the Totem High School gym. Really, Wally is no different.

I just stand by the door, silent for a while. Wally's eyes never leave me.

"Why you here?" he asks.

"I guess I'm your court-appointed lawyer—for now, anyway," I mutter. I still lean up against the door, trying to appear relaxed. It is not the way I feel. I am threatened by the lock and the extra thickness of the door, so heavy that the conversation, at least in this one room, appears to be private.

"Well, lawyer," Wally finally says, "what're my chances of getting out of here?" His voice seems thickened with cigarette smoke and phlegm. His eyes are full of boredom and sad experience.

"Not good, Wally," I say. "They think you killed Si Galitzer."

Wally studies my face for the joke and then sets the chair flat on the floor.

"Then what about some takeout? A burger and some fries." He leans back again, chair against the wall. "You're bullshitting me."

"Si's body was found yesterday morning," I say. "It's in the paper. I saw the PR file. They say there's a witness. Saw you behind Bethell Union Wear. Si's store. Says you had a bag and were running."

"Not me." Wally tucks his hands behind his head, his eyes closed. He begins to rock the chair back and forth with a soft creak. There is nervous energy in his rocking.

Lynn Reilly taught me to give facts to accused clients one at a time and not to ask questions. He said if you ask for answers, then you're the prosecutor. "Let them make the decisions," he advised. "You're just their lawyer. They're going to do the time."

Still, the client is entitled to know what evidence is in the hands of the state, and I go on.

"The witness says you got into a blue Camaro and drove off."

"Not my blue Camaro."

"So," I say. "So, you still with Lennie?"

"Sorta," Wally says. "She's stayin' at home with her mom, actually. That way the kids are with their gramma while we work."

I need to pin down Wally's ties to Bethell. Nobody charged with a serious crime gets out on bail unless he has a local home, a family, and a job. It is better if the family is intact. *Significant ties to the community* is the term of art. People with significant ties to the community don't run; they show up in court and on time.

On the other hand, a big case in a small town may change the rules. I expect the prosecutor will ask for—no, he'll pound the table and insist on—a considerable bond if the case involves Si's death.

"Should I call Lennie?" I ask. "It would help to have a spouse in the courtroom. Even better if she's got the kids with her. We can ask to put off the hearing until she can get here."

Wally shakes his head. "She'd want to check you out, to see if you're still single. Figure you're looking for a date. Ask if you're getting any these days." Wally grins, but his eyes are rueful and sad.

I wonder what my face is showing. First Arlene over at Steve's and now Wally, both thinking the same thing. I sigh.

"The PR says you have three priors. One petty theft and two breaking and entering, all juvenile, two dismissed, one plea of guilty."

"I had nothin' to do with killin' Si Galitzer. Maybe he fell down or somethin'."

I was mentally rehearsing the call to Lennie. Wally's charged with the murder of Si Galitzer. Bond is $50,000. Wally told me to call.

Wally reaches for a cigarette. His hands are scratched, the skin rough, unlike the skin of his face. He takes a deep drag on his smoke. I see his hands shake.

"Now, you're not my permanent lawyer, right? Not the one who tries my case for me. No offense, but you ain't asked me one question, Nate."

I am taken aback by Wally's critical assessment of me, his assumption that I have no idea what I am doing. I shouldn't be surprised. A person like Wally—one of life's perennial losers, who has been in one petty disaster after another—can see through me and conclude I'm not good enough to get him out of his current trouble. How can I say he is wrong?

It is painful, too close, to hear the suggestion that even Wally can see he will do better with someone else. I feel like a marked man. Stained top to bottom. A man bearing a sign that says "Don't trust me."

"Right, no offense taken," I say. That is a lie, of course, but I must press on. "You are absolutely right, Wally. I haven't asked you anything. That's up to your real lawyer. I guess you're going to plead not guilty?"

"Damn straight." Wally swells a little with pride at his words, as if to say his plea would be enough to end the whole matter, as if his body's physical truth was all it took to put a stop to this ugly business. "You'll see," he says. "I didn't touch a hair on the old man's head. Ever."

I shrug. Not guilty. That's all the stained lawyer needs for the arraignment, all a defender on the arraignment calendar needs to get his job done. No need to know anything else. Besides, Wally is basically right. There is not a thing I can do for him. Get the plea over with, I think, then call Auntie Riva.

"OK," I say. "We'd better go." I knock on the door, and Earl opens up.

"Butts out, Wally," he says. "I gotta cuff ya now. Sorry 'bout that."

Earl reaches behind his back and takes from his belt a set of nickel bracelets, opening the big metal jaws. Wally puts his wrists in between them with resigned experience, and Earl snaps the cuffs shut. We form a single file, with me in the lead.

I am thinking about Wally's opinion of me and feeling fatally oppressed, ignoring that we are about to enter a courtroom, ignoring that I need to gather myself up for the important job of protecting my client. As I push open the door to the courtroom, a flash from a flashbulb blinds me, and an unidentifiable voice cries out from behind the burst of light.

"Wally, did you do it?"

CHAPTER 13

Wally Richmond's Arraignment

* * *

BUTCH STROHMEYER, THE OWNER OF the *Daily Herald*, has his notebook out. "Hey, Wally," he hollers across the courtroom, "give me a quote."

Earl, the deputy sheriff, has taken the cuffs off Wally, who is rubbing his wrists and looking about for someone to banter with. I would bet Earl has given Butch the PR file that he also disclosed to me.

I push Wally through the gate in the rail to counsel's table and away from Butch and his photographer.

"Grab a seat," I say, pulling a chair out and nodding toward the newspaper man. "And stay away from Mr. Friendly."

"I got nothing to do with it," Wally shouts back to Butch before I can stop him. I just shrug and sit down uselessly next to Wally.

The justice court teems with action. Two part-time deputy sheriffs sit with steaming coffee mugs, chatting up a storm with their boss, Sheriff Cal Iffert. The state and county squad cars outside of the building have attracted curious onlookers. Steve, in his food-stained apron, his head capless, has crossed the street. Chain-smoking Herman Milliken, the barber next door to Steve's, has hobbled over in his white smock to see what is happening.

The bailiff, Delta Snell, rambles about, filling dusty water jugs. She sets up an extra chair at the prosecutor's table in front of the judge's bench.

Through the parking-lot entrance, Al Zilstra, Snoline County's elected prosecuting attorney, strolls in. I have rarely seen Zilstra in this court. The elected prosecutor tries what few felony cases there are in the superior court, located in the county courthouse two blocks away, but spends most of his time politicking with the county commissioners. By law the prosecutor is their lawyer on all matters, the biggest item of which was building and maintaining the county road system.

Zilstra's razor-cut hair is so slick, it reflects light. His sideburns look tacked on. Zilstra is stiff and righteous, a local Republican politician in the Nixon mold, all frowns and concern. He seems ready for a battle.

The prosecutor is jawing away with his deputy, Scott Pelky, who is assigned to Judge Kirkus in the justice court and prosecutes the county's modest criminal matters. Pelky is the prosecutor I see on the justice court calendar. A naturally large fellow, he has too much time on his hands and appears to spend much of it eating.

Butch Strohmeyer saunters over to Zilstra, followed by a teenage boy with a camera and wearing a dirty blue parka. The boy is probably the *Daily Herald*'s photographer. The kid's face has erupted with acne. He looks infectious.

"So, Al," Butch says, his pen scratching on his pad, "what's the charge?"

Zilstra pauses as if his pronouncement was to be of high drama.

"Felony murder in the second degree and burglary. We're, ah, saying that Si Galitzer's death occurred in the course of a break-in." Zilstra looks at the pimple-faced photographer. He has buttoned the front of his suit coat in a lopsided fashion: top button, middle hole. Pelky is trying to warn his boss about the bad pose, but Zilstra is off to the races.

Harry told me all about Zilstra and warned me to stay away from him.

"The county commissioners gave him the job when he was nothing more than a deputy city attorney in Everett doing traffic court. Nobody here but Midnight Fred applied for the job, and of course nobody wanted Fred. So we ended up with Zilstra, who ran unopposed once, got elected, and now thinks he's goddamn Scoop Jackson."

I listen to Zilstra as he recites the charges to Butch. I was not given the courtesy of a copy of the criminal information. I feel almost invisible. And why should it be otherwise? I am simply Leon Hirsch's kid, who left town for a decade and then suddenly popped up in the justice court. It is not unreasonable that the elected prosecutor has not a clue about me. Why should he care one whit?

"What's a felony murder?" Butch asks.

Pelky steps up now, all nervous energy. He crowds in, as if his boss is about to say the wrong thing.

"When someone is killed during an intentional felony," he lectures, pointing toward the ceiling, "the state is not obligated to prove that the murder was intentional, just that the death occurred during an intentional felony, in this case the burglary."

Zilstra clears his throat and butts back in. I note he has adjusted his coat, and all of the buttons are now straightened.

"For instance," Zilstra says, "it coulda been a heart attack when Si tried to stop the burglar. Heart attack in the middle of the whole thing, and it's still a felony murder if the victim died trying to stop the burglar. All we have to prove is that death was connected to the break-in."

"Al, are you saying Si Galitzer wasn't murdered?" Butch has stopped writing.

Pelky interrupts his boss again. "That's not it at all. We didn't say what this defendant did or didn't do. We'll prove it all at trial."

Pelky is pushing against Zilstra's arm, and the prosecutor looks outraged. I have concluded that the felony murder charge is Pelky's brainchild, and he is going to protect it even if he has to step on his boss's toes.

The two prosecutors are behaving like Tweedledee and Tweedledum, utterly irritated with each other. I see that the pimple-faced photographer is smiling, as if he has never seen anything so funny as the two public lawyers punching and pushing at each other to get their story out to the *Daily Herald*.

It strikes me as comedic as well. After listening to the two of them, Butch Strohmeyer has no idea what constitutes a felony murder. Undoubtedly they will get their act together before Judge Kirkus takes the bench.

Pelky tries to cover his bulk by wearing a three-piece suit. He dons the same suit every day, and it is shiny in the seat and pilled in the elbows where they have rubbed on desks and tabletops.

Harry has told me Pelky has his eye on Kirkus's justice of the peace job.

"The guy circulates the damnedest rumors," Harry mused over coffee one day. "Says Kirkus is soft on crime, whatever in hell that means. Soft on crime." Harry snorted in contempt. "Zilstra just wants a yes-man in the job so he doesn't look stupid when he brings some crazy-ass charge that won't hold up in court."

The justice court tests the prosecutor's criminal charges for probable cause. Undoubtedly Zilstra would rather have his own man in the post than Judge Kirkus, who has been around decades longer than the relatively new prosecutor.

The photographer with the acne is zooming in on Wally, who looks straight at the camera, as if he is posing for the class picture.

"I got nothing to hide," he says as the bulb flashes.

"Shut up." I'm barking at Wally, a little hysterical myself, angry because I am stuck in public at the side of someone who might have killed Uncle Si. My involvement is clearly a blunder. But I can't believe that Wally can remain so cool, so unaware that the fuss in the courtroom is focused on locking him up and throwing away the key.

I take a deep breath and walk back over to the two prosecutors, who appear to be making up.

"What about a copy of the charges?" I ask.

"Soon enough, Perfessor," Zilstra says without a glance toward me as he shuts the file in his briefcase. The prosecutor can discuss the charges with the press but cannot give me a copy of the written charges. So I decide to get my two cents in to the *Daily Herald* as well.

"The deal is, Butch," I say, "felony murder is a sad excuse for a scary murder charge when the prosecutor can't find evidence of an intent to kill. They trot it out when the evidence file is empty and the witness list has no names on it. Did I get that right, Scott?"

I don't know why I have popped off like that. As I finish I feel a tapping on my shoulder and turn around to see Uncle Harry King. He looks apoplectic.

"Come over here a minute," he hisses and pulls me aside. Uncle Harry puts his big hands on my shoulders. His face is flushed and angry. "What in the hell are you in this for? And shooting off your mouth too?"

"I had no choice," I say. "Kirkus met me at the door and claimed he couldn't get anybody else to do the hearing."

"That don't mean you should stand up there when somebody who's like your family is involved."

"I couldn't get myself off the hook," I repeat. I am shamefaced. Harry is saying out loud what I have been feeling since walking into Kirkus's courtroom.

"I gotta say, kiddo—you specialize in being where you don't belong, that's all. Jesus." Harry waves his hand in disgust, a fly-swatting motion, a get-away-from-me gesture, as black-robed Judge Kirkus comes out of his room, climbs the short stairs to his seat on the bench, and stands above us. A skittering noise fills the courtroom as everybody attempts to find a seat.

"All rise," Delta Snell cries out. "Order in the court."

Harry has retreated to the back of the courtroom but is still within eyeshot. I stand next to Wally as the prosecutor approaches the bench in front of Judge Kirkus.

"What do you have for me?" the judge asks.

Zilstra clears his throat and introduces himself for the record. "The county and the state are presenting an information against Wallace Edgar Richmond, charging him with two counts. Count one is murder in the second degree of Raphael Seymour Galitzer on April 11, 1973, in Bethell, Washington. Count two is burglary on the same night and arising out of the same acts alleged in count one. I am handing defense counsel the charges and ask that the defense acknowledge receipt and waive formal reading of the charges."

In Bethell the prosecutors issue criminal charges in pleadings, called *informations*. Convening a grand jury to charge crimes is too expensive a proposition for rural Snoline County.

At this point Zilstra turns to me, holding a bundle out of which sticks a long sheaf of red-lined papers. This is the charge the prosecutor has prepared. I take the bundle and begin looking at what I have been handed. It includes copies of the sheriff's documents relating to the case, a list of witnesses, and an index of evidence in the sheriff's department property room.

I quickly scan the named witnesses. Exclusive of Evelyn Doornik, it consists of the two members of the sheriff's department who inspected the scene of Uncle Si's death, interviewed Mrs. Doornik, and arrested Wally. The only other witness is Dr. Parker Taylor, who apparently performed the autopsy on Uncle Si. His pathology report describing the body is missing.

I move to the bench, acknowledge receipt of the charges, and waive their formal reading. "Mr. Richmond enters a plea of not guilty to all the counts," I say. I speak as fast as I can, glancing over my shoulder at Uncle Harry in the back of the courtroom. That should do it, I think. Now get to a phone, and finish the call with Auntie Riva.

"Judge," Zilstra pipes up, "one more thing. I request that bond of two hundred fifty thousand dollars be set on this matter." A ripple of noise passes through the courtroom.

I am dumbstruck. "Are you kidding?"

Zilstra pays me no attention; he stares straight up at Judge Kirkus.

"Your Honor," Zilstra says, "this was a crime of violence, and given the defendant's previous record and the seriousness of the charges, a lesser bond would be imprudent."

I am stunned. To buy a bond, the family of a defendant must pay a bail bondsman a cash premium, usually 10 percent of the bond amount. Wally has no money. No bond will be issued without further collateral, usually the family home. The bond, when filed in court, will allow the prisoner to be released pending trial. If he fails to show in court, the collateral will be forfeited.

In all my cases before Judge Kirkus, I saw him set reasonable bonds. If the defendant was local, married, and employed, he required no bond in minor matters, no more than $5,000 in serious nonviolent felonies, and $10,000 for vehicular homicides, drunken brawls, or domestic attacks. The judge knew that as a practical matter, persons criminally charged in Bethell were not about to go anywhere. Nobody had enough money to run away. No one in Bethell could acquire a $250,000 bond. If Kirkus agreed with the prosecutor, Wally surely would remain in jail until trial.

I shuffle the pile of papers I was handed to find the missing coroner's report. I cannot spot it.

"Your Honor," I say, "I'm going to need a minute to check out the records delivered to me today before I respond."

Kirkus seems troubled. "Al, explain to me why a bond of this amount is necessary."

Zilstra's face is a mask of grim rectitude. "We found the defendant packing for flight, Your Honor. The rear seat of his car was full of his clothes. Out there in plain sight."

I turn to Wally.

"My turn to do the laundry," he whispers and grins. Wally is incredible. Ice water must run through him, I think. A pack of dogs hounding him, and he's telling me jokes.

"Hey, look," he whispers, seeing the panic in my face, "Lennie threw me out last week. I been livin' out of the back of my car. That's all. If they thought the backseat's bad, they shoulda seen the trunk." Wally seems to enjoy this whole episode.

I look at the evidence list. The items must have come from the back seat of Wally's car: a loose spare tire, extra oil cans, old *Playboys*, soiled jeans and shirts, underwear, and socks to boot. I relate Wally's story to Justice Kirkus with some editing.

Scott Pelky jumps to his feet. He looks as if he is about to burst.

"You see, Your Honor?" he says. "They admit it. No family. No job. The defendant's a flight risk."

Zilstra looks annoyed. This is like the press interview. Pelky simply cannot control himself.

Justice Kirkus is staring at the back of the court. I turn to see what has caught the judge's eye, but all I see is Uncle Harry sitting near the door, slumped down a bit, his orange tie now undone. I can swear he's nodding his head from side to side, like a slow fan.

Kirkus turns to me. "What's Dr. Taylor's report got to say, Hirsch? Just hand it up to me."

I paw through the stack of documents, but the coroner's report clearly is not in it.

"Your Honor, I can't find Dr. Taylor's report in here."

"What about that, Al?" Kirkus asks. "Where's Dr. Taylor's report?"

"Your Honor," Pelky stammers, "the written report is not finished, but—"

I jump in. "If this charge is anything more than a burglary, there should be a coroner's report before the court detailing how the death occurred. There's not one iota of evidence of violent conduct by my client before the court."

"The defendant was on the run," Pelky cries. "Doesn't that mean anything? Are you going to let a dangerous man like Richmond loose on the streets?"

Pelky is blustering at full speed, waving his hands in the air as he speaks. He has moved from behind the counsel table to the front of the bench, elbowing past his boss. Zilstra looks livid.

I cut in on Pelky's diatribe. "Your Honor, the prosecutors want it both ways. They file the case as a technical murder, no proof that Wally touched the deceased, no proof of the cause of death. But they want you to treat this as a case of premeditated murder, even though the prosecutor admits the case they intend to prove excludes premeditated violence by the defendant. This bond request is excessive."

Pelky is hot. "Counsel doesn't know what he is talking about, Judge. Before I was interrupted, I was about to tell the court that these charges may be amended as soon as the coroner's report is completed."

"Then we should come back and set bond when the charges and the facts are before the court," I retort.

Zilstra is speechless and silent, one hand in his pocket, a finger picking at his ear. Unprepared for this problem, he now finds himself preempted as the case starts going badly. He probably is second-guessing why he came to the justice court in the first place. Undoubtedly the prosecutor thought he would get a nice Tuesday-morning headline, and now he is being embarrassed.

"Where's the evidence of violence, Mr. Prosecutor?" Judge Kirkus asks. "Either of you on the state's side here, just chime right in on this." He is clearly sensing Zilstra's discomfort.

"There's plenty of violence here," Pelky repeats without much conviction. "We feel this charge is timely, and to protect the people, we are here." The pudgy prosecutor trails off a little. It's clear Pelky has lost confidence in his position.

Again Kirkus looks to the back of the courtroom, where Harry is seated. "Ten thousand," Kirkus says. "That's enough. Come back, Mr. Prosecutor, if your coroner's report supports a new charge. Plea of not guilty accepted. Now, is there any other business?"

"It's too damn low," Pelky says. The deputy prosecutor is facing his boss, but his voice, a rude growl, can be heard everywhere. Everyone knows that the two prosecutors are planning Pelky's run at Judge Kirkus's seat.

Suddenly Pelky points at the judge. "If this defendant takes off, this court will have been on notice." Zilstra has Pelky by the arm now. Pelky has gone over the line.

"Your Honor," Zilstra begins, but the judge interrupts, his face mottled in anger.

"Mr. Prosecutor, I've been real patient here. You bring me the case, so where's your proof of violence? Nobody says one word about seeing Mr. Richmond do anything to the dead man. Now, Mr. Prosecutor, you better have your ducks lined up before asking this court to make findings of fact on violence." He slams his gavel hard enough to drive a spike into the bench.

"Court in recess," Delta Snell bawls.

The room explodes in conversation as Kirkus stalks off the bench to his chambers. The hearing has deteriorated into a preview of an election battle to come in November. Wally's case has drifted into second place in importance.

"We're not done with your boy, hotshot," Pelky shoots back as he follows Zilstra out the back door. He has put his boss in an embarrassing position and will undoubtedly pay for it as soon as the two prosecutors retreat to their office in the county courthouse.

I feel fiery; I immediately deem myself critical to Wally's low bond. I am the crafty mouthpiece who pulled his client's chestnuts out of the fire. I float to the rail and lean toward Butch Strohmeyer on the other side.

"Need a quote?" I say. I'm like Al Zilstra. I want what I think about the case to be run in the *Daily Herald* too.

"I think can figure it out, Nate," Butch says dryly. He has remained impassive through the morning's events, his face placid, calm. Whatever turmoil the decline in the *Daily Herald* might mean for others, it does not shake that confidence Butch always seems to possess.

Only the pimply photographer grins back at me, or perhaps at the whole scene. He has probably been rooting for Wally the whole time.

Wally grabs me, trying to shake my hand. It is a clumsy act, the handcuffs binding his wrists together, but he grips my arm first and then, with enthusiasm, the ends of my fingers. I pull back. I want to catch Uncle Harry before he leaves the courtroom.

"Let's go," Earl, the deputy sheriff, says to Wally, taking his arm to lead him back to the jail. Earl looks at me and says, "See you next round, slugger." I detect a little less sarcasm in his voice.

Uncle Harry is outside the courtroom, lighting his cigar. I need to tell him I was just doing my job, but I also want some praise. I hope he is suitably impressed with the job I performed. But as I rush up to him, his face is full of foreboding, the face of a man who has just witnessed a home on fire or a tragic traffic accident.

"I got to see a guy about something," he says, as if dismissing me. "Let's talk later, maybe this afternoon, unless you got something better to do. And if I were you, I'd get over to Auntie Riva's to talk about this whole deal about your uncle, or you might not be so welcome living in her basement no more. Might move you out to the doghouse."

Harry quickly blends into the small crowd milling their way out of the courtroom. I am undaunted by his dismissiveness and still hungry for someone to rehash the details of Wally's hearing. I find a small man in a trench coat smiling at me. He is holding a coffee mug.

"Nice job," he says approvingly. "These local prosecutors are really clowns, pathetic. Hey, my name is Jerry Dwyer. You got a minute?"

Dwyer looks to be in his midthirties, slight balding, but self-confident and professional. His glasses frames are air force issue, the raincoat Burberry, his shoes English. He has a funny half smile, as if he is hiding something in his mouth.

"I'm Nate Hirsch. I haven't seen you around. You practice law in these parts?"

Again Dwyer gives me the half smile. "Naw. I'm up here on official business with Mr. Zilstra, your prosecutor, and he dragged me along to this hearing. Probably wishes he hadn't. I'm in the attorney general's office in Olympia. I just happened to be in the courthouse this morning on my way for a meeting in Bellingham."

Dwyer swings around and encircles my arm with his. He is creating an intimacy between us, as if he is about to ask a very personal question. "You know the guy you were talking to a minute ago?"

"You mean Uncle Harry."

"He's your uncle?" Dwyer looks surprised.

"Not officially. An old family friend and my parents' lawyer."

"Ahhh. Listen, I understand you're the new guy on the block in the county courthouse."

"In one sense," I acknowledge.

"I know this sounds strange, but from time to time I need somebody to help out the attorney general up here. I like the way you handle yourself and would consider it an honor if you'd give me a call to discuss this and that. Maybe give you an assignment from the AG."

I am flattered. Dwyer has seen me for ten minutes and is opening the state government to me as a potential client. I decide not to tell him my limited status. Harry's admonition to call Aunt Riva reoccurs.

"I'd be glad to, but right now I've got to make a family call. Call me if I can help."

"Hey, I understand," he says. "Don't think twice about running off. But hold on to this, will you?" He grips my right hand with his. In it is a business card. Then with a wave he is gone.

I turn to look for the closest phone booth, but then I decide the strange tale of today's courtroom would be better delivered to Auntie Riva in person.

CHAPTER 14

Harry Hires Nathan

* * *

I GIRD MYSELF AS I wait for Harry to pick me up outside Auntie Riva's home. A day after Wally Richmond's arraignment, I still feel uneasy, almost dizzy, anticipating that Harry will still be angry with me. Worse, he was contemptuous of my inability to dodge what—if I am honest with myself—was an utter conflict.

Yes, I felt out of place representing someone as a client who might have injured a relative in any way. Wally Richmond could be in that category. The break-in at Uncle Si's store is clearly on his plate. But Judge Kirkus left me no choice. So what could I have done? A poor job? I was duty bound to represent Wally as best I could.

Yet I know that Harry is going to assert, even in the face of my legalisms, that there are some lines that, in the name of familial allegiance, should not be crossed. I fear that Harry will not let me off the hook, and there will be an unpleasant collision between us.

At the same time, I am certain Harry will know the details of how Uncle Si died. Hope against hope, he will reveal proof Wally had nothing to do with Si's death, and the prosecutors were way off base even suggesting Wally as Si's killer. At least being with Harry will give me some breathing space from Auntie Riva.

* * *

After Wally's arraignment I all but raced through the puddles and across damp lawns to Auntie Riva's home, but she had already left for the jewelry store. I knew that was where she had gone. Since my dad's death five years ago, she has taken on the task of opening Fulton Jewelry each weekday morning. Nothing stops her from carrying out her mission.

"The day this store closes, you might as well shut down Bethell," Auntie Riva likes to say. "Like your grandpa, like your dad. I'm holding up the pole at our corner of the tent."

I retraced my steps from the justice court, this time stopping at Fulton Street and making a right turn, heading west to the Hirsch Building. As I trudged beneath the sodden sky, I rehearsed the complex message I would deliver to Auntie Riva about Si's death, the lack of information on the cause of death, the hearing, and finally my compulsory representation of Wally Richmond. I practiced over and over a false statement that would exculpate me: "The judge doesn't think Wally did it." The smell of fireplace smoke trapped in the Bethell air by the overcast filled my nostrils.

The doorbell at Fulton Jewelry is an electronic gong, a bogus Asian sound announcing a customer has entered. Auntie Riva was polishing the front glass counter. Her hands traced agitated circles hard enough to dissolve all but the thickest crystal. The polishing seemed to let tension escape her body. Her face was lined, and wisps of hair flew out and away from her face, as if what remained of her hope was abandoning her. My clothes reeked from dampness, and bits of mud fell from my shoes.

"You're tracking in water, for goodness' sake. Where've you been?"

"I went to the house. Thought I might catch you there." Even my voice sounded soggy.

"What did you expect me to do, sit in my living room and moan? I'm not the undertaker, and I'm not blood. Life's got to go on." My auntie seemed to speak to the polished glass.

I started to tell her about the arraignment, but Auntie Riva shut her eyes, stopped the compulsive rubbing of the glass, and held up her hand.

"Enough already with your craziness. I can't listen to your *mishegas*—craziness—today." In Riva's impatience she jumped to the conclusion that I was about to complain about my assignment in Judge Kirkus's court, a theme I had unfortunately overdone with her.

"I was there in the courtroom. They think maybe there was a murder." I did not mention my role.

Riva looked at me. "So what happened?"

"The fact is that nobody knows. They charged Wally Richmond with breaking into and robbing Union Wear. But nobody in court had one clue how Uncle Si died."

"You know, I really don't want to hear any more," Auntie Riva said. I looked at her red-rimmed eyes, the rigid posture, the black dress. Whatever my role in Richmond's defense, Auntie Riva couldn't have cared less.

"I'm sorry," I said.

Riva seemed shuttered against the storm, her little store filled with light dulled by the clouds over the bay. She looked past me, out into the faraway light.

"The truth is I'm not sure I can go to that cemetery again so soon. I called up your Auntie Mae, but she had no idea when they were going to get to bury him. Strange for the relatives not to know." She looked at me, forlorn and drawn. "Give me a hug, Nathan. I need somebody to hold me up."

I walked around the counter and held my thin little auntie in my arms. She shivered a bit but made no sound. I gave her cheek a peck. It felt hot and dry.

Though Uncle Si had been a resigned bachelor, I knew that when I was a kid he would accompany Auntie Riva to the MOT Canasta parties that my parents hosted.

Uncle Si had been a chronic smoker, as were the other card players. Once a week the chain-smoking bunch would gather at our house just to play cards and drink Seagram's VO Canadian and soda or, worse, sticky-sweet Tom Collins cocktails in lipstick-marked glasses from which I periodically would sneak a taste when no one was looking.

Those card parties were like cloud tournaments. After the tables were set up in our living room, with ashtrays at each, the players would light up and fill the trays with cancer sticks, their embers sending smoke signals to God only knows whom. Worse yet, cigar smoke would erupt from Uncle Harry, who never appeared in public without a smoldering Cuban Corona in his mouth, the dry tip of which he periodically would ignite with his Shriners flip-top lighter.

Uncle Si always would join in the smoking. Spare and balding, wearing a sport coat, an open-collar shirt, and two-tone shoes, he puffed away on unfiltered Lucky Strikes through teeth that were as yellow as a mongrel's canines. Si attempted to comb over his bald spot, but in these card contests, where winning seemed to matter big time, his bare pate would puddle up with dew.

The card games were intense. The men always played to win; the women played to be good partners. Everybody bet heavily, not only on their own hands but also on the hands of players at other tables. Pearl recorded the bets were on a little blackboard that she would set on a spare folding chair after the first round of drinks.

"Exacta time," Pearl would announce, her voice tinkling like doorbell chimes, and everybody would lay down their bets, a penny or a nickel a point. If Uncle Si was playing, which was more likely than not, then his brother, Uncle Frank, and Frank's wife, Auntie Mae, would be nowhere in sight. On nights when Uncle Si was missing, Uncle Frank and Auntie Mae would be there as if they had been invited to all the events at our family home.

When Uncle Si would bring Auntie Riva, her personality changed. "Call him 'Uncle Si,' Nathan. We're all just like family here," she used to say. As a teenager I had assumed her unmarried status made Auntie Riva sexless and prematurely drained of carnal lust. Most of the time, she was serious, cryptic, and critical, but around Uncle Si, my thin-lipped, slender aunt acted flip and light-headed. When Uncle Si squired her to Canasta, she became silly. She flirted with the married men and told off-color jokes.

"Not around Nathan, please," Pearl would say to her sister-in-law in a cold, austere tone. But Auntie Riva would hold her cigarette for Uncle Si to light and would cup her hand over his to steady the flame.

I could imagine that on the way home after one of the canasta parties, Uncle Si slipped into Grandpa Albert's old house and had his balding way with Auntie Riva. It had been mirthful configuring the scene: Uncle Si, knotted in his half-on, half-off polyester clothes, trying to woo Auntie Riva, the gray-haired virgin of fifty-six, in her layers of bodice-shaping foundation underwear topped by a satin nightgown and a vampy robe trimmed in pink fluff balls.

While I had no idea whether their congress had in fact been consummated, it had amused me to pretend I was the invisible voyeur observing them engaged in clumsy foreplay, two frumpy fifty-somethings locked into a juicily Victorian view of sex, trying to keep the room totally dark, struggling at once to both disrobe and yet remain dressed so as to reveal as little of the devastation I imagined smoking, careless diets, and the passage of time had done to their flesh.

* * *

"Maybe it was stupid for me to come here," Auntie Riva finally says as we stand together beside the store's plate-glass window display. Then she releases herself from my arms and looks around as if we're being scrutinized by a crowd. "Suddenly it seems a bit disrespectful. Let's close up." She slowly walks to the front door and flips over the "CLOSED" sign, as if that piece of plastic now will guard Fulton Jewelry.

"Slam the safe door shut, will you, Nathan? Can you walk home with me?"

"Sure," I say, thinking that it is Harry who is probably arranging to get Si's body released.

A block away from Auntie Riva's home, I can see Harry driving up in his garish olive-green Buick, with its brown-vinyl roof. He waves me in.

"Where to?" I clamber through the passenger door.

"Just get in, will you? You'll see soon enough. I got my hands full."

Once I'm in, We roar off.

Harry's driving drove me nuts. He possessed two speeds. When Harry was talking, he made the car crawl, ignoring the open road ahead, or as he approached any stop sign. But when Harry was focused and impatient, he pushed the gas pedal through the floor and tore through school zones and around law-abiding drivers, relying on his sheriff's posse card to rescue him from reckless-driving tickets.

Today it's the crawl. The Buick hiccups and shakes.

"Where are we off to?" I repeat.

"Rivers End. Gonna meet your uncle Frank and get some keys. Meantime, did you make peace with your auntie?"

I nod yes. "She wants to know when the funeral is going to be."

"In a coupla days. I gotta round up some folks first." The Buick cranks and rambles along as Harry talks. "Frank Galitzer says he's washed his hands of the whole matter because McPhee wouldn't let him in Si's store."

Curt McPhee, Si's handyman for as long as I can remember, works at both Union Wear in town and out at Rivers End, the Galitzers' farm.

Harry shakes his head. "Now Frank won't lift a finger. His own brother dead, and he says he's done as soon as he gives me the keys at the house, which he says he's gonna do out there so I can see he ain't stolen nothing."

Normally the prescriptive period before Jewish burial is typically one day. That has long been exceeded. Like most persons who die while medically unattended, Uncle Si's body was autopsied on Sunday night, April 10, and now, three days later, he still lies in the county hospital morgue.

Harry's unlit cigar is tucked in the wet corner of his mouth. His tie hangs loosely, the same orange tie he wore yesterday morning in court. His jacket is halfway zipped against the weather; he looks like a Maytag repairman. He has not yet said a word about what I did in court.

"I'm gonna need some help here," Harry says. "I have in mind you helping me."

"With the burial?"

"No. Something else." Harry lights his cigar stub and takes a puff. "Richmond's hired George Miffler for his trial, assuming there is one. And you ain't involved anymore, so it seems."

"I wasn't asked," I admit.

Less than half a day after Wally's arraignment, on the eight-thirty calendar in Kirkus's court, Earl Strunk, the deputy sheriff, showed up with a new prisoner and his old insufferable look.

"Easy come and easy go, Slugger," Earl said to me. "A real attorney came and got Richmond out." He told me that at two in the afternoon, Lennie Richmond had shown up with George Miffler, the defense lawyer Judge Kirkus had attempted to contact as Wally's counsel in the first place. Miffler had posted a bail bond.

"Ten grand. Cash collateral," Earl said. "Impressive. Maybe Wally got more offa the old man than we knew. Anyway, move over, Nate. Miffler is da man now."

"So," I say to Harry, "my conflict is over."

"I know all about it," he says. He is oversteering the Buick, and the car weaves like a drunk.

"If you know all about it, then do you know what happened to Uncle Si?"

"Why should I know more than you, the lawyer?" Harry grunts. He is still upset with me.

"How could I say no to Kirkus?" I defend myself. "He doesn't like me anyway. And now I'm not involved, OK? I just thought you might have talked to someone, heard something."

"No more than you. And enough with this Richmond crap. We have our own problems," Harry says. "I need a lawyer. You."

"What are you talking about?"

"Si's will, Nathan. The last will and testament. I wrote it, and I'm the executor. Gonna need some help running the show. Frank's gonna raise a fuss over Rivers End. It turned out that it was a big deal to get him to cough up the keys to the place that he's kept all this time."

"How did you do it?"

"Told him folks would say he stole stuff if he didn't give me the pass to the castle." Harry goes further. "Then he says to me he will walk through the place with me. 'And to hell with you, Harry,' Frank says to me. 'You can see for yourself nothing is missing.'" Harry harrumphs as he drives.

I marvel at his cleverness. He has outmaneuvered Frank, who seems to want nothing less than the family's homeplace.

"Amazing," I say. The Galitzers didn't even speak, wouldn't show up in the same room at the same time. Spit on the ground if you mentioned the other's name. "So Harry, how did you know Frank had a key in the first place?"

"He grew up out there, Mr. Smart Guy. How do you think Frank snuck in when it was too late without his pa seeing how loaded he was?" Harry grows contemplative. "Frank's gonna want to know who gets the spread. Wants to know about Union Wear. That's why we're really getting together. Also, I might need a witness."

My family talked all the time about the decades-old squabble between Si and Frank Galitzer.

"Simple," my dad had said. "It comes down to Uncle Si getting Rivers End and your Uncle Frank getting the shaft."

Sitting in the crook of the Snoline River northeast of Bethell, almost twenty miles upriver on County Route 20, the Galitzers' spread is a 160-acre Garden of Eden. They called it Rivers End Ranch and built a gate at the entry junction with Route 20. The gate is a grand one; two twenty-foot-high spars stand guard at the driveway. Lashed at the top with nautical ropes is a twenty-foot beam of weathered cedar that is at least two feet thick. Suspended by more nautical rope from the beam is a green signboard on which the name "Rivers End" is announced in carbon-black script.

The character of the Rivers End acreage is as diffuse as any in the county, from accreted bottomland along the Snoline River, where the spring runoff from the Cascades leaps the banks and dumps new soil on the side, to timbered uplands of cedar and fir surrounding a paradise of meadow, pasture, and pond. From the top of a knoll rules a proud two-story greenhouse skirted with a veranda like an apron on a dowager. Surrounded by clumps of cedar and hemlock courtiers, the house posture contrasts to the slumping sun-faded wooden barn and stable off to the east.

This is where Uncle Si lived with his father, Morris. I was taught to call him Grandpa Morris. The entire Hirsch family spent many summer weekend days at Rivers End. My brother and I picnicked, frolicked, chased Grandpa Morris's horses, threw rocks at the squirrels, trapped pond frogs in old fruit jars, and counted the flies on the snot-nosed old Guernsey cows the Galitzers kept in the straw-filled gray stable.

Uncle Harry told me Grandpa Morris initially favored Frank because he was married and had sons. His three boys were the twins, Roger and Ralph, and Victor, the oldest, who was dark like his father and already possessed a mustache like a chocolate milk shadow. They said Victor was "simple," so his name never was shortened. Victor was always called Victor to keep him from becoming confused.

Mae Galitzer was always Auntie Mae and my childhood piano teacher. Her blue eyes would dance whenever her fingers moved across the ivories. As she accompanied pop pieces, she would sing with a scratchy voice that was easy to listen to and always stayed on key. Her white grand piano floated on a carpet of snowy fur claimed to be taken from a polar bear. I had to take my shoes off whenever I had a piano lesson at Auntie Mae's.

My fingers seemed to naturally like the piano keys. They became rhythmic and flexible, the way Ritchie's hands behaved with the myriad of footballs, basketballs, and baseballs that were piled in his room like cannon ammunition.

Frank Galitzer rarely came into the living room when Auntie Mae was giving me lessons. I saw him as dark faced and worrisome. There was no day when I called him anything but Mr. Galitzer.

Grandpa Morris and his sons, Si and Frank, initially worked together in Union Wear. Grandpa Morris began the business by selling Bethell workingmen their heavy-duty, serious gear for dangerous work. There were thick hobnail brogues for the slick log-rolling floor of the Skarbell Mill; belts and straps; saw and hatchet holsters; tree scaling and gaffing equipment; canvas vests and leggings; storm jackets; and rawhide gloves—the lifeblood of loggers, millworkers, pole climbers, choppers, and chain whippers, all hung from racks on the Union Wear walls.

All the products sold there possessed the union bug: MADE IN THE USA, AFL/CIO. Union had been a religion for Grandpa Morris, a self-confessed socialist who claimed he could remember the 1904 revolt in Minsk, Russia. Whether it was true or not, he created a merchandise market that brought farmers and laborers alike to buy the specialty items that town-born boys like me never even thought of donning. The garb protected his leather-hard customers against elements I had never experienced.

Grandpa Morris died when I was ten. I remember the funeral. The entire millworkers' union membership turned out at the Jewish cemetery outside Seattle. I'm told the will reading was anticlimactic because Rivers End, the family home and farm in the silt-rich curve of the Snoline River flood plain, already had been deeded by Grandpa Morris to Uncle Si years earlier, behind Frank's back.

* * *

"So," I ask Harry as we drive east through the Snoline Valley on Route 20, "did that split up the business?"

"Jesus," Harry says, "you ask a lot of questions. The answer is no. While Morris was alive, the brothers got into a squabble over whether Union Wear should carry only union-embossed products. Frank thought they paid too much for the goods and wanted a change. Si refused to go along. I had to settle the dispute."

Harry brakes violently on a corner of the winding road and resumes his recitation. "Duff's Tavern across the street from Union Wear had gone broke. I got the rest of the lease in the bankruptcy and turned it over to Frank, with a loan against Morris's line of credit at the bank, so long as Frank would move out of Union Wear.

"Frank always wanted to put his name on his own store, and that's how he started across Fulton Street. Didn't cost him a cent, and he had business from the get-go without borrowing a dime. Pretty good deal, if I say so myself." Harry floored the gas pedal, and the car burst forward in approval of his brilliance.

"You know, Nathan, you might learn something from your old uncle Harry. I represented the whole Galitzer clan, even after the family war broke out and Si and Frank no longer spoke. Even after I got Frank the lease of Duff's, Si still told everybody I belonged to him; 'My brother thinks he can even take my lawyer away from me,' says Si. 'Well, he's damn wrong. Harry's my lawyer first. I'm older. Maybe Frank can tamper with the business, but he can't tamper with my lawyer.'"

Harry puffs his cigar. "Now, that's good advertising. Two clients fighting in public over who gets you to be their mouthpiece. So enough of this. You, Mr. Big-Time DC Lawyer, are gonna read your uncle Si's will. It's in the briefcase in back. Grab it, will you? I'm not taking my hands off the wheel."

This was typical of Harry: half contempt, half snare. He could suck me in every time. I pop open his beaten-up briefcase and extract a triple-folded pile of paper with "LAST WILL AND TESTAMENT OF RAPHAEL SEYMOUR GALITZER" on the cover. It naturally uncurls in my hand, an invitation to read a dead man's directions.

The wrinkled pages are red-lined on the edge, the paper softened with extra cotton fiber. The last page is signed by Uncle Si with a flourish, as if he were signing the Declaration of Independence, his embellished moniker followed by the more sedate witnesses'. As I read the contents, my eyebrows involuntarily twitch. "I am unmarried. My family includes my daughter, Sadie

Miriam Galitzer, also known as Sadie Miriam Welger, born November seventeenth, 1944."

"How come I didn't know about Si's having a daughter?"

Harry doesn't move his eyes from the windshield. "Live and learn, big shot."

* * *

Frank is waiting at Rivers End when we arrive there. His dark face turns quizzically toward me.

"Hello, Nathan," he says. "And what's this got to do with you?"

Harry speaks from deep in his throat. "He's my lawyer, Yankel, you hick. He's going to watch out for me. Besides, around you I'm going to need a witness and a bodyguard."

Frank appraises Harry with a look of stubbornness. "Harry, you never done business with him before. So how come now all of a sudden you need a lawyer when you're one yourself?"

"I'm getting too old. Besides, handling you takes two people."

Frank shrugs. "Suit yourself. Are we gonna be able to keep Rivers End in the family is all I care about."

"Absolutely," Harry says. "That won't change a bit. A Galitzer is gonna own this place forever." Harry shoots me a look with "shut up" all over it.

We walk over to the barn. Frank eyes the shiny classic pickup parked there. It is a '52 Chevy, all tricked out, a toy Morris purchased when he was dying of cancer. Si kept it shipshape but never took it out of the garage after his father's death.

Harry spots Frank's glance. "Could ya use an extra car?"

Frank tries to take his eyes off the pickup, but they are magnetically drawn to the teal green and beige paint job. "I suppose so," he says, slow and unconvincing. "Mae or one of the boys can use it."

"I assume you already been inside the house?" Harry suggests.

"For a while."

They shuffle along together, Harry kicking dirt with his foot, Frank stuffing his hands in his back pockets. Neither speaks. It is a silent duet, and I have become invisible.

"Why don't you come out here with Mae tomorrow?" Harry finally says. "Take the Chevy, then. Maybe check out some of your ma's things, inside, you know, stuff that Mae might want or such."

I begin to whisper to Harry, "What's the will say?" But he whacks my ribs with his big paw before I can get my concern out of my mouth. The palm of Harry's hand feels like the flat of a shovel, and I lose my breath.

"Sounds OK with me," Frank says after a while. His tone has softened from the harshness with which he greeted me. I can see that Harry has correctly sized him up. It is the family home, and, after all, the will obviously must have left it and the contents to Frank as the surviving brother.

Harry steers Frank back to the Buick in which we arrived.

"Lemme get my papers out of the back," Harry says, then straights up as if seized with a brilliant thought. He pulls a bottle of Canadian VO out of the trunk.

"Tell you what," he says, "let's go inside and have a quick one. Talking about all this has made me thirsty."

"I could use one too," Frank admits, and we traipse into the house together. As we look for three glasses, I think, I should have kept quiet, and my ribs would not have been bent.

There will be no mention of Si's daughter today.

* * *

After Frank goes home, we drive back to Steve's and assume our usual stations in Harry's booth. He opens the briefcase and pulls out Si's will.

"Harry, I thought Uncle Si's only relatives were Frank, the twins, and Victor."

"See," Harry says, "Si got married during the war. Then divorced. Gotta kid too. Daughter. Never had much to do with her. Si didn't leave much money anyway. But what he's got, his daughter oughta get. Not Frank. Anyway, that's what I need ya for."

"I can't get over Si having a daughter," I say.

Harry fills in the blanks. "She's your age. Her mom, Trudy, came from a bulb-farm family up by the north fork of the Snoline. Poor folk, simple. She was the pretty one, if you like the dirt-under-the-fingernails type. They say Trudy went to jail for something, theft maybe, down in Everett. Si bailed her out."

Undoubtedly with Harry's help, I think.

"Trudy's divorced now. That makes twice, probably enough for her. She's down in San Mateo, outside of San Fran. I called her. She won't be no problem. She sells Tupperware, Welcome Wagon, something like that. Changed her name to Hemphill. Sounds like a Limey cigarette. That's why you don't know anything about anything. So now are you gonna be my lawyer like I asked?"

I don't answer Harry directly. Since he always likes me to be in the dark, I have decided to give him some information he doesn't have.

"I made a call," I say. "One of my law school friends, Les Grim. He's settled in Seattle and wants to talk to me about practicing together. So I may not be here long. Besides, an estate—it's not anything I know about."

"That doesn't matter." Harry reignites his cigar before the osmotic movement of moisture from the cigar's chewed-on end to the tip makes combustion impossible. "I need you to run interference for me. Frank has got to be kept at bay. He's my client too, ya know."

I am silent for a minute and then address Wally Richmond's arraignment. "You never said what a good job I did in court before Kirkus."

"Good job!" Harry almost swallows his cigar. "I couldn't believe you didn't have enough sense to get outta the way." He looks at me with renewed contempt. "Don'tcha know which side you're on in this deal?" He throws his hands up in a gesture of surprise. "What would your mom think if ya were the lawyer for Uncle Si's killer?"

"You say Wally's a killer," I answer. "He didn't look like one to me."

"What kind of *schmendrick,* idiot, are you? One good motion in court, and you know how the world turns." Harry's face looks as if he's about to remind me about Washington, DC. I can tell. Then he gets down to brass tacks, his eyelids low and unexcited, his tone flat and down to earth.

"Besides, you already know that Lennie, Wally's broad, paid the fee to Miffler up front and in full."

"And how do you know so much before I do?" I ask.

"Mine to know, yours to find out." Harry looks at me, his cheeks the only movement. When the cigar smoke and smell have formed a cocoon of confidence about us, he answers. "'Cause I loaned the money to his broad. Did the bond too."

I am speechless. Harry is all over the defense of the man charged with killing Uncle Si. He pushes me one way because the rules of loyalty say so, but then he moves in the opposite direction, somehow exempting himself from that same rule.

"You put up the bond? You? Then what's the difference if I was involved?"

Harry looks at me with exasperation. "What I did is business. And don't think there isn't a difference."

"And so," I say, feeling the color of my face rising to crimson, "why'd you tell Uncle Frank he is getting Rivers End?"

"I didn't. You got wax in your ears. All I said is it would be in the family. So what do you think a daughter is—chopped liver?"

As Harry looks at me across the table, I realize he has started to grow sideburns. They trickle toward his jowls like rivulets of dirty snow. His hair on top is tree-limb dark by comparison.

He has an answer for everything. "I want you to be my lawyer. There's enough to keep us both busy, and you can use something to do. No reason to bring in a stranger." For the moment he sounds uncharacteristically vulnerable. It is hard for me to say no to him. I feel magnetically tugged to be of help.

"I don't have an office."

Harry shifts again in front of me; his old resilience has returned. "You know what?" He opens his hands in despair. "Never mind. Too much trouble. You just head down to Seattle." Then he looks at me with his clear eyes. "But what will you do until the bar catches up with you?"

Harry is right. I am better off taking my time here. I should wait in my hometown until the bar gives me my license to practice. I acquiesce slowly.

"I guess I can help for a while," I answer. "I should hear from the bar before making any new plans. I'm not going anywhere this month for sure."

Harry gives me a look I've seen before at Steve's Diner. It is the look of my father checking out who is watching the conversations across Steve's Formica table. Harry's low rumble of a voice aims at me.

"We been here before, you and I, haven't we?" he reflects, his arms folded and his face close to the tabletop, the reflected green neon on his intense face, revealing a heat of expression that draws listeners in close. I'm in the presence of conspiratorial secrets and the forestalling of disclosure. This is how Harry looked at me after my dad died.

"You can just work out at Rivers End," he says. "That's where everything will be anyway. We'll just set you up there for the time being. Let's get Si buried, and then we'll find a little working space out at the farm. And don't worry. You'll get paid for what you do. You'll be able to help yourself too. A buck in your pocket when you leave this place won't be so bad. If you want out later, that'll be OK, too...after a bit."

Harry pulls out a check from the folds of his Maytag repairman's jacket and from his breast pocket plucks a ballpoint. I can see the check says "Bethell Savings Bank." Harry scrawls on it with the pen.

"This will get you started," he states. Harry signs right-handed and thrusts the instrument across the table to me. The check is made out for $5,000. I feel like I might swallow my tongue.

What the hell? I think. Harry does everything for a purpose. As if my decisions are so good. I take the check from him and fold it back, as if it is a bird and I need to collapse its wings so it will not fly away.

"What will I need to do?" I ask.

"Maybe take the will, smart guy. And get a bunch of forms down at the stationery store. That's it. You got the dough. Use it. Christ, it's like a blind person I got on my hands here. You file the damn thing, the will, file it with the Snoline court clerk, send a copy to Si's daughter, to Frank, to his kids, the whole shebang. Send it to anybody named Galitzer. Run an ad in the *Daily Herald* with all the vital statistics about Si's death. So that anybody Si owes money to can send their bills to me. Oh, and put in an obit too. Butch Strohmeyer will be glad that you give him some business in the *Daily Herald*. Then, when everybody with an outstanding bill is paid off, I give the rest of Si's money and property to the daughter. She's the heir, as I told you. This isn't exactly rocket science."

I say nothing. I can't quite believe Harry. There is more to Si's affairs than he is saying by a long shot. But the $5,000 bird in my wallet is beginning to chirp. I do not want it to take flight, for I am earthbound, stuck in Bethell, and I can use the money.

I say to myself that it's just a short delay in the process, my next destination in life. A brief, uneventful delay. I look at Harry.

"So?" he asks.

"So," I say. "All right, Uncle Harry."

Harry laughs. "My God, I got a lawyer. Hey, Steve, give my lawyer here a refill. So, Nathan, use my address at the office at the Varney Building for the estate." He stops and then thinks for a moment. "No, maybe not there. Have them send the mail to you out at Si's place."

As Harry is talking away, I notice the overhead light behind me in the diner darken, and I half turn to see whether there has been a short. But it is the bulky body of Sheriff Clarence "Cal" Iffert blocking the light as he lumbers toward Harry's booth.

Cal Iffert was elected ten years ago after a decade of being the deputy to Sheriff Stan Hagberg. Iffert was a transplanted tar heel whose hardscrabble family lived up in the cascade foothills, where they logged cedar for the shake mills. He had been an MP in World War II, worked in the office of the state patrol, and parlayed that background into Stan's two-man sheriff's office.

The county commissioners were fond of Iffert. He kept their children out of jail when they were caught driving drunk. Iffert's sense of mission was clear. He hid the problems of the county from the public big shots, and they rewarded him with Stan's sheriff's star in 1963, ten years ago.

"I didn't know they let you in here, Cal," Harry says, his face filled with mock horror. "This place is getting too run-down for me." Harry's voice echoes a false ruefulness. Then he points toward me. "Hey, you know Nathan Hirsch, Leon's son? He's my lawyer now, so watch out what you say."

Cal laughs in a mean-spirited growl. The sheriff's little head, huge gut, and slovenly green uniform give him the look of an aging gas station oil jockey.

"Hell yeah, I know this guy," Iffert says. "Watched him get that murderer Richmond a ticket outta jail the other day."

Iffert puts his big hand on my head, as if I am his pet dog, as if he is actually kidding about Wally's arraignment. But he gives my head a menacing shove.

"A nice kid, real nice," he rumbles. I take it his words mean exactly the opposite.

* * *

When I was fourteen, my dad made me work on Saturdays at the jewelry store. I swept the sidewalk, washed the outside of the plate glass windows with a sponge and squeegee, and vacuumed the inside carpets. Then he would pay me my five-dollar weekly allowance and release me for the day.

I remember a slimmer version of then deputy sheriff Iffert coming into the store one fall Saturday. He was red in the face as he greeted my dad. In those days he wore a patrolman's cap and carried a nightstick.

"Hola, Speedy Gonzales," my dad said. "*Cómo estás?*"

"*Muy bien, gracias, amigo*," Iffert said, and they both laughed. Iffert and Dad were in VFW together. Dad told me they had a standing joke about robbing the Snoline National Bank and running off to Mexico. That was where the Spanish came in.

I saw my dad, Leon, pull out a bottle of Crown Royal whiskey from under the counter and pour two shots, which he and the sheriff clicked and then downed in swishing gulps. Then they slipped together into the back vault, where Dad had his office. When Iffert came back out that Saturday, I saw him slipping an envelope with currency into his pocket. He saw me watching and patted me on the head.

"He's getting sideburns, Leon," he yelled back at my dad, turning to me in mock seriousness. "Keep your hands off the chicks, you little butt hustler." He laughed as he disappeared down Fulton Street.

My dad shouted after him, "*Adiós, amigo*." He turned to me.

"What's he come here for?" I asked my dad.

"That's what the sheriff's office does," Dad said. "They are on the lookout for stolen property. I make loans to people in the back here. Like your grandpa before me. Loans people don't want to let anybody know about. It's called pawning."

He pulled me to him as if what he was about to say was a secret. "People who want to quietly borrow some dough, they leave their diamonds and gold with me, stuff, in exchange for a cash loan. When they pay me back, I give 'em the stuff back. But once in a while, the things they pawn with me turn out to be stolen. So the deputies check my pawn records to look for stolen property."

I didn't understand. "Don't you make them prove the pawned stuff is theirs?"

Dad looked at me. "That's the law's job. It's none of my business where folks get their things. I'm not a cop."

"Did the deputy find something stolen?" I asked. "He took something in an envelope." I knew there was money in the envelope. I wanted Dad to confide in me the purpose of giving Iffert the cash, but he simply looked away and waved me off.

"That's none of your business either," he said brusquely. "And you're done for the day. Now scram."

* * *

I get out of the booth to make room for the sheriff, who has to stuff his girth between the tabletop and the seat back. His face reddens in the effort.

"Steve," Harry shouts, "keep the java coming. Need another cup here for John Law."

I start to sit down, but Harry waves his hand at me, as if to brush away a fly, the same way my dad used to dismiss me.

"Get lost, Nathan," he says without as much as a glance my way. "Make yourself scarce."

CHAPTER 15

Miriam Shows Up at Si's Funeral

* * *

AUNTIE RIVA HOLLERS DOWN THE basement stairs, "Harry's on the phone."

I lumber up to the hallway spot where the phone cord comes out of the wall. Riva has cocked her hip as she holds the phone, feigning irritation at being its abused human cradle.

Harry's voice is full of phlegm. He pants into the phone. "They released your Uncle Si's body."

"Is there any news from the coroner on the cause of death?" I ask.

Not a thing," he rasps. "Now listen. Forget about that. I called the *Chevra Kedisha* in Seattle, the Jewish burial association. They'll pick your Uncle Si up this afternoon, and we can bury him *manãna*.

I hear the snap of Harry's lighter and the gasp of inhaled smoke.

"So what do you want me to do?" I ask.

"Do?" he says in mock surprise. "Show up. Bring your ma. Act nice. Wear black. Jesus, do I have to tell you to shave too? I got stuff to do, for Chrissake." That is Harry signing off. The phone clicks.

I go upstairs and relate Harry's plan to Auntie Riva. She is reading a *Ladies' Home Journal* in the living room with her reading glasses hanging on her nose, the handles attached to a strand of amber beads that wraps around her neck. The light reflects off Riva's lenses the dominant purple and violet dyes from the floor's oriental carpets, the colors a reflection of style in the twenties.

"Do you feel up to calling Pearl?" I ask. "She might want us to take her."

It feels natural to use *Pearl* to designate my mother. *Mother.* I stopped thinking of her that way long ago. She has been ill for so long, beginning before my dad died. Thinking of her as Pearl lets me do what I need to do for her and leaves no residue of feeling, since I no longer believe I have any for her.

I am sure there were times when Pearl drew me to her with a maternal scent and temperature, but those experiences would last for mere moments. By my adolescence, her eyes saw me as a stranger, and possibly a dangerous one. For no reason her voice would change in the middle of a conversation, as if I were new to her.

"Are you eleven yet?" she once asked me, as if her own child's birth was foreign to her. My father's chosen response to her was permanent and total deafness. I suppose I learned to behave similarly.

Harry has always been kind to Pearl in a gallant and gentle way, mindful of his formal role as her trustee under my father's will and as her legal guardian, for which I am most thankful. Actually I suspect Harry's consideration for her may also come from some guilt. Riva reminds him repeatedly that the Kings introduced young Leon Hirsch to a single Pearl Levy with all of her flaws miraculously hidden.

Riva slips off the reading glasses, and the purple glow disappears. "Pearl can let Carla drive her. But it's your business. She's your mother, not mine."

It is clear to all that Auntie Riva and Pearl despise each other. To my best recollection, Auntie Riva has never opened her home—which is actually her parents' home, the family home she inherited when Bubbe Hirsch died—to her sister-in-law. This has always struck me as odd. I hung about there throughout my life with Bubbe Hirsch and my auntie. So had my dad. But not with Pearl.

Riva sighs. "The funeral will be hard for me too."

I sigh too. The drama does not belong to Riva alone. It is mine as well. "This is a fight I don't want," I say. "I think we should take her."

Auntie Riva puts on her reading glasses and picks up the magazine in a gesture that seems to accept my words as final. While she doesn't agree, she doesn't say no either.

Pearl insists we drive to the cemetery in her mustard-colored Buick Roadmaster with its dated fabric top.

"My husband picked it out, and I will drive it forever," she declares, as if Leon had not been my father as well as her spouse.

Notwithstanding her devotion to driving the Roadmaster, Pearl leaves it to others to chauffeur her in it. Thus she is perfectly comfortable to stand by the rear right door until I—always the gentleman—hold it open for her, and she climbs in. Carla Prism also slips into the back, behind the driver's seat, and Riva sits in the passenger seat up front. Nobody has asked me to drive, but the driver's seat is empty.

The Buick is a mile long and glides across the lanes at each turn. Inside, the ride is as soft as a feather pillow. It is just as well that we have taken it. The Jewish cemetery is an hour's ride away on the outskirts of Seattle, and given the questionable affection between the passengers, more room, not less, is better.

No one speaks a word as we drive through Everett and down the highway. My mind keeps reverting to Uncle Si. Because his body has been released, I know that the coroner has ruled on the cause of death. His report has been given to the prosecutor. Harry's ear to the railroad track would have heard any rumbling if a definitive cause of death had been determined. I want to believe that Wally has been cleared.

A part of me believes if Harry knew more, he would have taken me into his confidence, but a part of me is unsettled and believes that Harry could be holding out on me. I resolve to push him to get the story out of him.

The weather has been uneven. Black clouds cover the sun as we pass through Everett to the north of Seattle. Just off Highway 90, near the King County border, the rain starts. I steer to the turnoff leading to the *Chevra Kedisha* Cemetery.

I know this turnoff too well. My father and my brother are buried here in fresh graves, my grandparents, Bubbe and Zayde Hirsch, in an older sunken part.

Between the beats of the windshield wipers, it occurs to me that my future home could also be in this graveyard, somewhere in its cold ground. *Chevra Kedisha* literally means "sacred fellowship." Auntie Riva will want me to help her find Bubbe's and Zayde's graves among the strictly arranged rows with their similar granite markers.

The curve of the ground in the cemetery's old section gives the gravestones the look of neat row houses. I was seven years old when I went there the first time, after Bubbe Hirsch's death. As Ritchie and my folks navigated ahead to her burial site, I trod with uncertainty. Where should I place my feet? Was there etiquette to walking on the dead people beneath the soft sod? Were they offended by my careless footsteps?

We buried Ritchie there ten years ago in the new section, with its flat stones and brass plates. It was wet and cold, and I still remember sinking down in wet ground. It was as if the earth were grasping at my legs. As we left I could barely keep up with the others; the sucking on my soles was like quicksand restraining my departure.

When my dad died, he was buried next to Bubbe and Zayde Albert in the old section. I feared that my feet would again be mired in the remorseless turf. Following my father's casket and his pallbearers carrying it to the grave, I tried my best to navigate on the slim cement ridge at the foot of the grave sites, but it was no use. My fear of losing my balance became a reality. I slipped into the soggy ground, and with each step I had to fight against a force that seemed to pull simultaneously at my feet and my soul.

I have dreamed over and over of Ritchie's funeral and my father's—terrible dreams, fearing that some presence dwelling in the place where my family was interred longed for me to be under the ground there as well.

* * *

The rabbi who will conduct Si's funeral is a short, slight fellow Harry hired. Harry tells me the rabbi is a newcomer to Seattle and is making a living by presiding when burial services are needed for people with no ties to Seattle's synagogues.

In the small stucco chapel with its rounded roof, I realize I am the only pallbearer who is bareheaded. The rabbi silently hands me a skullcap. Curt McPhee, Si's handyman, has left his balding head uncovered, with a look of uncertainty. Which custom should he follow? His own tradition of doffing your hat to show respect, or donning it as he sees the Bethell MOTs he knows doing?

With huge-knuckled hands, he nervously works the brim of his hat, the same one he wears whether working at Rivers End, the Galitzer farm, or Si Galitzer's Union Wear doing odd jobs.

Uncle Harry's brother, Dale, looks uncomfortable in his tie and coat. The Kings stand on the pallbearers' side of the grave with Oscar Asher, Morris Guthman, Harvey Raskin, and me. On the opposite side of the grave, Claire Asher, Dot Raskin, and Ilsa Guthman separate my mother from Auntie Riva. Behind the rabbi, at the head of the grave, Frank and Auntie Mae Galitzer huddle under an umbrella.

Frank and Mae's son, Victor, holds his mother's hand. Victor has partially shaved his face, leaving a lopsided mustache. His unkempt hair has caused his skullcap to drift off to the side of his head. Victor smiles at everybody who looks at him, sensing this funeral is like a picnic or a lawn party.

I take roll of the MOTs. In one way or another, each family is represented, yet none of my peers are there. Save Victor, no one of my age has remained in Bethell. Bobby and Danny Raskin are in graduate schools in the East. Hannah and Arlene Asher live in Seattle. Alvin and Robert Guthman, whose solemn parents survived the Holocaust, are married and live in Portland. Roger and Ralph Galitzer, who should be here, since Si is their true uncle, are caravanning about the United States, following the Grateful Dead, selling batik T-shirts and dope-smoking paraphernalia during the band's concerts.

Behind Harry stands a woman I can't recall seeing before. She looks to be approximately my age. Her red hair and freckled complexion remind me of my brother. She has a smirk on her face, a measure of smugness just short of contempt.

A bearded fellow stands next to the redhead and leans toward her, as if they are together. Both are in blue jeans and heavy Indian-style outer garments of black and white wool. Incredibly, as cold and wet as it is, they are wearing sandals, their bare feet like those of traveling minstrels who suddenly arrived from a different climate. They whisper, point, and giggle during the ceremony, as if they were visiting a zoo and are amused by the antics of the caged animals.

The rabbi is the only one who speaks at the grave site. He jarringly refers to Uncle Si as "Seymour." I can hear the hum of cars speeding nearby on Highway

90, the same hum that filled my ears the day we buried my father. That day the hum grew to a roar, louder than the presiding rabbi, eclipsing his admonishment to me as the surviving man of the family to begin reciting the *Kaddish*, the mourner's prayer. I remained still and mute until Uncle Harry elbowed me, took the edge of my copy of the prayer the rabbi had handed me, and, with his free arm around my back, began the age-old Hebrew recitation, urging me along with him.

Today the little rabbi chants the prayer of memory, first in Hebrew and immediately following in English, his voice both melodic and nasal. I remember at Ritchie's funeral stifling a cry at the thought that Ritchie's powers had been stilled so unjustly. I asked myself whether my brother was somehow better off dead than if he had survived the war in Southeast Asia with a blown-up body, crippled for life. I found no answer that day, either in prayer or in the faces of my parents, their eyes ravaged by despair and grief. If they had hope that Ritchie was in a better place, they did not reveal it to me. It was one of the few times I wanted to comfort Pearl and not criticize her.

And here they are today, the two adversaries, Leon and Ritchie, buried in the same cemetery. And I stand wondering if they would both be here without my betrayal of my brother.

* * *

We lower Si's wooden coffin into the ground following the directions from the groundskeeper. Two neighborhood kids lean on the cyclone fence outside the cemetery, their fingers laced about the plastic-covered wire, watching the parade of people dropping symbolic mounds of earth into the grave. Each shovelful seems to explode as it strikes the wooden coffin with a dull thud.

As the last mourner sticks the shovel into the shrinking dirt pile, the rabbi gestures to the pallbearers to return. Each of us works up a sweat filling Si's grave just before a soft rain shower begins to puddle the remaining dirt mound into mud.

Harry moves about the cemetery holding his umbrella in one hand and shaking hands with the other. The rabbi, unknown to us before the burial, silently scurries out of our lives to the parking lot, to avoid being drenched. I watch the redhead and her sandaled companion climb into an old Volkswagen van that starts up with a burst of blue exhaust smoke and the rat-tat-tat of a handful of small firecrackers. The van heads off in the direction of Seattle. The other mourners straggle to their cars and head in the opposite direction, to Bethell.

"Who was the redheaded girl and the guy?" I ask Harry, pointing to the departing VW bus.

"You looking for a date at a funeral, *kocker*, hotshot? It's Si's daughter. She's been up here in Seattle at some hippie commune hangout. When I talked to her mom, I told her where the funeral was. So there you are."

Pearl takes my arm. "I want to go to our place," she says, impervious to the rain that is matting her hair. I think by *our place*, she means the section where my brother, my father, and his parents lay next to each other. I know there is a plot for Pearl there too.

I grip her by the elbow and guide her along the cement ridge that serves as a narrow sidewalk, retracing our past steps as best as I can, to the cemetery's old section, with Carla a step behind. I look about, feeling lost in the mist, not sure of my bearings, until I see my grandparents' upright rose-colored granite memorial with the name Hirsch carved on top. Next to it I see a marker in brass. That's my father's resting place. Nearby in the new section, the row has a military-white upright memorial. A flag is stationed in the ground next to the marker. It is Ritchie's grave. The sod bulges as if his energy in death has forced the ground to accommodate space for his spirit to move, even in this place of perpetual rest.

I point and say to Pearl, "there," and we stand together in silence.

"They made me go to that horrid hospital room to see your father in that awful way," Pearl says. "The bodies are naked there, you know, no respect."

"I know," I say.

Suddenly her face opens up in bewilderment. "I wonder if there's a powder room nearby," she says to me, as if I am an usher. I see that Pearl no longer knows who I am.

I wave to Carla to join us. She puts her arms around Pearl and guides her back to the chapel. The place is empty. I can see Auntie Riva in the Buick staring straight ahead. All of the Galitzer family members and their friends have taken their leave and are driving back to Bethell. Harry is hosting a *shiva*, a wake, at his house in Bethell, and all will be gathering there, away from the rain, the dead, and Seattle.

* * *

Leaving Harry's, I drive the Buick to Pearl's and park it in the garage. Carla helps her exit the car. Pearl has been utterly silent on the drive. I move to kiss her on her cheek, but she makes no gesture of recognition, and Carla steers her into the house. I realize Pearl is lost, whether to grief or to madness I cannot tell. The fact is her dogs have a higher likelihood of drawing her back to reality than I do.

Riva and I walk back to the Hirsch family home two blocks away. Si's daughter, the redhead, keeps popping into my mind. The notion that someone grew up in Bethell unknown to me, a person my age and a child of my family's intimates, was a bafflement.

"So tell me about Si's daughter," I start.

Riva has always been my confidante. She would never claim the privilege of silence with me. "During the war the men were all gone," she says. "Si Galitzer had flat feet and claimed he was a farmer. Either way, they didn't take him. And with no men around, he had his way with the young women. There were a bunch of farm girls living in Snoline County, doing many of the jobs the men did when they were home. Especially in the mills. We needed lumber more than ever."

Riva adjusts her gait as we walk. The air is full of fresh pollen and sea air. Skarbell's Mill must not be cutting logs, because I detect no scent of sawdust.

"They were quite a remarkable group of hicks," Riva says. "Some couldn't read, if you can believe it. Milk girls really, from the dairy farms and lumber camps. Many of them were put up by the mills at the rooming houses over on Front Street. On the weekends they would get all tarted up. Fancy hairdos, silk stockings with seams—something you have never seen, young man. High heels and long cigarettes. They hung out at the Harbor Café. Man traps. A step away from streetwalkers. Here and there one would get her a husband and a baby a few months later. I imagine that's how Si met Trudy."

"Did they marry?" I ask.

"So Si claimed, but they never socialized. Si was living out at the farm with his dad, Morris, and Trudy moved in with them. After the baby was born, the same year as you, Trudy moved out. Si would never talk about the arrangement. He worked in Morris's store and kept to himself. Although he was your father's friend, I didn't see much of him then. Until later." Riva adds this last phrase to retain some credibility with me, although she looks away just as she says the two words.

"Did you see the redhead at the funeral?" I ask. "About my age?"

"You mean Miss Woodstock of 1973 and her sockless friend?" Riva snorts. "I can't believe those Seattle people couldn't find better caretakers for the cemetery than those two."

"The redhead was not a caretaker," I say. "Harry told me she is Si's daughter."

Riva stops dead in her tracks, oblivious to the storm clouds threatening again. Her face moves from shock to grim knowledge tinged with anger.

"I can see that." Her head bobs with comprehension. "Of course. That little backwoods money-grubber, Trudy, has sent her baby agent to pick the man's bones. Nathan, do you have anything to do anymore with this...this whole business of your Uncle Si's death?"

Riva scrutinizes my face for perfidy. I feel my skin redden. I haven't told her about Harry's employment of me or of the $5,000 I accepted.

"I've promised to help Harry," I say. "That's all. He's handling the estate."

Riva's face is severe, and her voice is low and telling. "You get in between Frank Galitzer and Rivers End, and you will be made into mincemeat. You listen to me, Nathan. If your father were alive, he would tell you to stay far, far away from the Galitzers' business. As far as you can get. There are shades and shades with that family, and you don't know the first thing about it. Are you listening to me, Nathan? Are you?"

CHAPTER 16

Nate Meets Katie

* * *

AFTER THE FUNERAL I TRY to refocus on Harry's instructions regarding Si's estate, but my mind keeps spinning. Couldn't Wally have asked me to continue being his lawyer? He didn't know my bar status.

I itched to defend Wally. There was no murder case against him in the files I saw, and he was much too cool at the arraignment hearing, way too amused that anyone could give him that much credit for doing anything violent.

And who had killed Uncle Si? What did the autopsy report as the cause of death? By now the Bethell rumor mill and the *Daily Herald* would have spun back some hints if Wally had been responsible. Lennie Richmond's girlfriends would have gossiped at the grocery. The tongues would have wagged at Steve's or, loosened by a few beers, flapped away at the Harbor Café's Elbow Room. But there hasn't been a sound from the courthouse, not an echo from the streets.

And Harry? He is an enigma, as silent as the sphinx on the subject.

* * *

After I find the probate forms at Little's stationery store, the repository of all of Harry's favorite documents, I fill in the blanks using my Smith Corona. Harry King, as executor, is not the most interesting question to be answered. Is the death certificate filed for public record? Yes or no? Does Harry have it?

Harry delivers the death certificate to me at Steve's, but only after I ask for it. Issued by the county public health department, the textured paper of Si's death certificate has the fiber and feel of a dollar bill. The coroner's official seal imbues the paper with permanent rock-like authority, like the engraving on a tombstone. It weighs heavy in my hand. It is a verdict signed by a judge, a final order.

> Deceased: Raphael Seymour Galitzer
> Age: 67
> Time of death: 11:00 p.m., April 13, 1973
> Cause of death: cranial contusion

In other words, a crushed skull. No other facts offered.

Harry shrugs away any questions from me. "Need my signature anywhere?" His answer is a question.

"As the executor," I ask, "aren't you entitled to a copy of the autopsy?"

"Haven't asked and don't intend to."

I pay the *Daily Herald* to publish successive notices of Uncle Si's death, as if everyone in Snoline County does not already know that Si is dead.

I also begin preparing an inventory of Uncle Si's assets. The executor files the inventory in the probate proceeding, a requirement that assures any creditors their pending bills will be paid.

In fact the notice in the *Daily Herald* causes Si's suppliers at Union Wear to come out of the woodwork like cockroaches. Those companies who have sold merchandise to Union Wear send me antiquated and unpaid invoices, some over five years old.

While it appears to me Si was a slower payer of his bills, none seem to be that large. I ask Harry to settle them when we meet at Steve's.

"Why should I have to keep track of them?" I ask. "They total less than fifteen hundred bucks. It's chicken feed."

Harry shakes his head. "In due time. All in due time. You don't have to rush this. What are they gonna do, sue a dead man on a fifty-buck bill?"

But I have learned a trick or two from Harry.

"What about your bill?" I deliberately prod him, then hand him a copy of a two-year-old statement for $250 made out on Harry's legal stationery. "It looks like when Si died, he was sitting on one of your bills, Uncle Harry. Something about a property foreclosure years ago?"

Harry looks at me malevolently. He shrugs. "Let's get that one paid." He heaves himself up from the table. "Gotta get going now. Best pay 'em all while we still got the cash. Make out the checks, and I'll sign 'em later."

Harry knows I played him on this one just to let him know how it feels. So he heaves a final shot across my bow.

"Any word from the bar?" He grimaces as if he just saw something gruesome. Then out the door Harry goes.

I didn't answer. Harry did not expect me to. Besides, he knows he would be the first to hear it from me.

Harry's reminder that I am not a member of the bar is just his way of cementing my dependence on his largess. "And don't forget it, Nathan" hangs silently in the coffee- and nicotine-scented air Harry left behind when he departed.

The fact is I have received no word from the Washington State bar. And if something is hanging up the decision to activate my membership, I have no way of telling.

I still cover the Monday arraignment calendar in justice court. Harry keeps me occupied with a myriad of tasks I must chase. Si's business, Union Wear, is in the tank. Harry has concluded the inventory must be liquidated and expects me to deal with the detritus of the dying business. Yet he refuses to discuss it with me.

"Don't bother me with details," Harry virtually shouts as he dramatically waves his right hand in front of his eyes. "That's why I paid you the big bucks." Harry always brings up the $5,000 retainer. I have to admit my acceptance of it keeps my attention, just as Harry knew it would.

* * *

Auntie Riva expects me to keep my quarters immaculate, but when I venture upstairs to retrieve her vacuum to neaten up, I can see it needs a new bag. The machine, a feeble, gutless Eureka, fails each time I fruitlessly attempt to sweep my meager space with it. Throw the switch and I am greeted with a purple cloud spewing cat hair, stale bits of potato chips, pieces of candy suckers, plain old dirt balls, and a stench that might exceed the aroma of postgame laundry in an NFL locker room.

"It's a piece of junk," I say to Auntie Riva as I return the vacuum cleaner to its closet exile upstairs. "Why not buy a new one?"

My aunt will have none of it. "It barely has been used since your grandma's death. It just sits. So get some new bags." She thrusts into my hand a piece of paper with the machine's number. "Take. Try Sears. Get a bunch."

In the Sears appliance section, I spot a saleswoman standing behind a counter. Her back is to me. She wears a gray Sears smock—a bag, a disguise, at best a uniform. I expect her to be a grim matron, perhaps equipped with a salesperson's false grin.

"Excuse me," I mutter, and she turns about. There is a comely woman hidden under that drab Sears wrapper. A plastic tag pinned to the smock says "Kate Martin."

She has magnetic green eyes. I cannot stop staring. I have seen those green eyes before.

* * *

In Washington, DC, I reveled in the fact that I was born new to each person I met. I carried no burden of grandparents, uncles, and aunts, no past deals, no past promises pledged or broken. When I met new people, I didn't know their brothers or sisters. I would not find myself waiting in line at the same stores as their cousins.

It is just the opposite in Bethell. Familiarity with neighbors' lives dominates conversations. All know everybody's details, from addresses to hair colors. We know what vehicles they drive. If a strange car parks on Parkland's leafy street in front of the Hirsch family home, Auntie Riva will believe she has cause to call the police. Living in a small place can give information overload.

As far back as I can remember, the neighborhood women, my mother's friends, shared every aspect of their lives. I could assume any statement I made, any school play in which I was involved, any episode I related to my parents, any grade I received on a test (good or bad), or even a new haircut would be reported for blocks around our Parkland address.

The good side of familiarity was that I didn't chain up my bicycle wherever I went. Who could steal it without being caught? The front door of our house was unlocked. Friends, family, and neighbors still knocked, and nobody, it seemed, wanted to break in. What would they do with whatever it was they stole?

My dad once told me of a theft. The Dahlgrens were buying a replacement set of their fancy silver that Mrs. Dahlgren had reported stolen. While the order was pending, into Dad's store came a farmer to pawn a set of silver.

"Couldn't remember his name if had to," my father stated. "The fellow just wanted nickels and dimes, beer and peanuts money, nothing close to the silver set's pawnshop value. The two of us, the farmer and I, we opened the silver chest and looked in at the same moment—no, we stared together at the label sewn to the satin lining. There it was in all its glory, blinking like a neon sign: "FULTON JEWELERS." We saw it at the same time."

"So what did you do?" I asked.

"I looked at that old farmer, and I closed the top. He reached over and picked the box up off the counter and walked out the door. Two days later Flora Dahlgren canceled her order for a new silver set. Her silver box was missing, not stolen. 'It showed up,' she said. I asked her to bring it in out of curiosity. That box had a chalk mark on the bottom, as had the farmer's. In the old days we used to keep track of inventory with chalk marks."

"Was it—" I asked.

"Yep," my dad said. "The same box. Says Missus Dahlgren to me, 'My housecleaner spotted the missing box under our bed. One serving spoon's gone, though. I can't remember where I put it."

My dad chortled. The housecleaner's husband was the farmer.

So there were no calls to the police, no words, no letters, no lawyers, no lawsuits. Mrs. Dahlgren just forgot about it. In Bethell we just know one another too well.

But seeing Katie Martin is different from seeing other Totem High School grads. She was Ritchie's girl. I knew her as Katie Milbert.

Katie was ahead of me at Totem High School. She graduated after my sophomore year. Ritchie ran away the next year, and thereafter, when I saw her coming, I scurried off to avoid like the plague her green eyes and their judgments. Now, over a decade later, it is hard to believe those same eyes, in a head cocked in disbelief, are taking me in.

"I was looking for some bags, vacuum-cleaner bags," I say, my voice around my knees.

Her eyes, resigned to Sears lighting, search my face. "You're Ritchie Hirsch's brother, aren't you? It's Nathan, isn't it?" Her voice is slow. It feels as if she is trying to paint my face from her past.

I nod my head up and down like a string-puppet. She sighs.

"Oh dear. It's years since I've seen any of you." Her tone is weary, not pleased, as if not seeing my family or me has been a blessing. Her hands hang limply at her sides. "The bunch of you could have left town for all I knew."

"Actually I did," I answer. I watch her as the flood of recognition flushes her face, standing there behind the counter in her shapeless Sears smock. She may have forgotten me, but I could never forget her.

Ritchie, who had all sorts of girls at his beck and call, was smitten by Katie. She was younger than most. In an era of teen pimples, Katie's face was perfect. "Katie, the queen of the fairies" Ritchie called her at fifteen. Not a princess, a queen. She looked that grown up. Back then I could not keep my eyes off her either.

At Totem High Katie's hair was dark and long. Sometimes she wore it in a sultry Veronica Lake style, sweeping across one eye. Sometimes she wore a ponytail like an eager bobby-soxer. Now her Katie Martin hair is short and frosted, a pixie cut, with ragged little designer bangs.

"I remember you too," I whisper, "only your name was Katie Milbert then, not Martin. Katie Milbert." My tongue fumbles, tripping in confusion over her similar names and their matching syllables. My face grows hot.

She crosses her arms and nods her head. "I'm Martin now. Not Milbert."

"So, your husband is from around here?"

"My husband was Bobby Martin. That is, he's my former husband." She stops for a moment. "You may have known him. He was about Ritchie's age.

Maybe a speck older. They lived out on River Road; the parents still do. Bobby and Ritchie played ball together."

I feel my face blanch at her pronunciation of my dead brother's name for the second time. I search her face to see if she intended to judge my reaction, but her face is impassive.

"I don't recall Bobby. His name doesn't ring a bell," I say. "Maybe I saw him play ball, but I can't be sure." I realize I am gaping at this new Katie who has replaced the teenage queen of the fairies, this woman in a Sears smock. My tongue seems bent.

"What do they call you?" she asks. "Nathan or Nate?"

"Either one. When I'm in trouble with my aunt, it's Nathan. The rest of the time, it's Nate."

"Is your mother still alive?" she asks. I nod. "I met her once, went into the jewelry shop in the Hirsch Building after I read that your dad died. I assume the woman behind the counter was your mom. She was way too harsh to me, and I left. If I handled Sears customers like that, I would be out of here in a minute."

"Not my mom." I laugh a little. "That's my aunt. My mom would never set foot in the store. As for Aunt Riva, actually, she's OK. Just seems a little starchy. She was trained to be a librarian, not a jeweler."

Katie spots a customer. The woman is looking impatiently at me, her eyes saying, "Do your courting on your own time." She can see I am in thrall.

Katie moves away from me. "All the same, you have to please the customers. I'll be back." As she rushes over to help, I hear the customer simply ask directions to the women's restroom. Thus I can understand and forgive her impatience.

As they talk I have a chance to gawk at Katie without looking foolish. Her body makes curves against the block-shaped smock as she moves about. Katie glides, actually, like an athlete. Then, smiling at the woman, she says, "No problem" in response to a thank-you and returns her attention to me.

I sense she is as hungry for information as I am. I try to separate myself from the rest of the Hirsches.

"I really didn't—that is, I don't—" I stumble about in mushed syntax. "I mean I haven't been home for years. Lived in the East."

The undercurrent of curiosity without judgment leaves Katie's mouth open. Her teeth seem a bit modified from school days. Then Katie had canines that overlapped in a charming, incomplete way. Now her teeth come straight from a fashion magazine.

Katie sees I am staring. "Got the teeth fixed. Didn't have to spend a dime. Sears has a great dental program. They paid the whole bill."

"I remember you with long hair," I say.

"The hair was too much trouble to get ready for work each day. Tiffany, my daughter, cried when I cut it off. We kept it, though. Maybe I'll have a fall made from it for myself." She laughs to the side, self-consciously. "There's probably enough for my mom and my daughter too. So then, what are you doing here?"

"Just working for the court as a public defender for a while," I stammer. "Nothing permanent."

"No, I mean why did you come to Sears?"

I blush at misunderstanding her question and blab the story of the old Eureka. "I need a vacuum bag. Really."

"Well, I'm the bag lady." Katie grins at her own joke. She also knows how the Sears smock makes her look.

I slowly search my pocket and retrieve the slip Riva gave me with the model number of the old Eureka. I take my time.

Katie. She is a woman now; the queen of the fairies has lines about her eyes and no baby fat on her cheeks. As she squeezes behind the counter to find my replacement bag, I watch her crouch down to search underneath the counter. She gathers her smock slightly above her knees to move about. It no longer conceals her indented hips and legs. They show the swells of parenthood and time, yet her silhouette still reminds me of a younger body.

I can remember seeing those legs, younger and thinner, wrapped naked about my brother. I hope she will not find the bags easily. Alas, she arises too soon, clutching my Eureka replacement product.

"This will do it," she says, eyebrows arching as she focuses on the price tag. "Not that bad, actually."

I reach for my wallet. "Why the name tag with Martin on it if you're divorced?"

"I never liked Milbert. My mom's remarried and doesn't use her old name. Besides, it rhymes with the name of a nut. I used to get teased all the time: 'Milbert the filbert.' Stupid, isn't it? Looking back like that."

"So where do you live?"

"Tiffany and I have a little two-bedroom house over in Mill Town. Close enough to Mom for babysitting. Far enough for privacy."

I pay for the Eureka bag in cash, and it is time to go. I want to linger, to say more. Katie's eyes seemed to glitter as we talked. Was it her memory of Ritchie, buried all those many years, that I rekindled, just as seeing her brought to my throat the little-boy shame of long ago? I had no idea if she knew my role in the undoing of her relationship with Ritchie.

I had caught Ritchie and Katie making love—throttling each other, really, from the standpoint of a thirteen-year-old voyeur standing in the half-light of an ajar door, the two of them partially exposed, as open, noisy, and boisterous in their antics as if they were Adam and Eve, the only humans in the world.

And in a fit of jealousy, I told my dad. I tattled on my brother, who, I believed, had always gotten everything he wanted. And I set off an explosion in my family that left us all burned and broken.

Maybe Katie doesn't know. She has said nothing to me, treating my appearance in Sears as a coincidence. Maybe I am making a bigger deal out of it than it was. Times have changed. Perhaps her episode with Ritchie was no more than an adolescent experiment. Maybe she didn't care.

Katie hands me my change. "There you go." She smiles. "And thanks for shopping at Sears. So then, Nate, why are you in Bethell?"

"It's a long story." I sigh. Perhaps too long. The thought of her legs, her sad eyes, the long questioning makes me want to see her again.

"You remind me of your brother," she says. Katie's face is sad and happy, caught simultaneously in the past and in the bright Sears light of the present.

"The way I look?" I say. I must look astonished. I feel as if I have misunderstood her.

"Not that way." Sadness and remembrance bump into each other on her face, each emotion trying to get ahead of the other.

"It's the way you tilt your head. That laugh. You both whinny like a foal, just about out of control. I can see the family connection."

Ritchie and me? I think. Now, that's astounding. I have always been sure, in my sense of inadequacy, that there was nothing about my super brother I could match in any way.

"I'd better get back to work," she says, but her voice is slow and reluctant, not dismissive. "Maybe I'll see you the next time your vacuum bag overflows, and you can tell me how the long story ended."

"What about before?" I venture. "I mean if you're not seeing anybody, we could have a beer or dinner. Maybe we could talk then. Not a date."

Katie hesitates, and in that moment I dive into a different place full of glass shards and mud. I speak low so others cannot hear. "You and I loved the same person." My voice repeats what I've been thinking from the first moment I saw Katie's green eyes.

"What a funny thing to say." Katie sighs. The melancholy in her eyes wrenches me. I have regret—for being in this town and for dragging this sad-eyed woman into long-buried attachments.

"What is there for us to talk about?" Katie says. "That was a long time ago." Her voice sounds bleak. "I don't know what good it would do to talk. I'm not about the past." She turns away, and I hear her shuffle the keys in her pocket, and then she turns back. "But it is nice that you remind me of a face and time. And a not-a-date is a compliment for an aging mother. Mostly it's married guys who are *really* interested. Lots of them."

"I can imagine," I say. "And how do you know I'm not married?"

"No ring. You needed a note telling you what bag to buy. You get used to noticing those things. Besides, you don't look housebroken." She smiles at me.

Those perfect teeth jolt me again, and to cover up, I try to be the quipster. "Well, you're hardly an aging mother. Maybe some other time."

"Yes," she said. "Perhaps we'll see each other again."

I read no invitation in the words, only the tension between the tedious reality of Sears and the sudden tidal rush of the past that has soaked my spirit.

And, I suspect, hers as well.

CHAPTER 17

Ritchie

* * *

KATIE'S APPEARANCE RUSHED RITCHIE BACK to me like the tide. "You remind me of your brother," she said. Looking at my curly headed softness, I have no clue why she said this. I am a puppet; he was a force of nature who surrounded each moment of my day as long as he lived.

* * *

Ritchie was angular, long in the muscle and as sinewy as a twisted steel cable. Ritchie's physicality emphasized his five-year seniority over me. I was the flea on his elephant, the remora fish around his maw. I was parasitic. Ritchie's tolerance for my clinging and squeezing was un-Hirsch-like. He was a sponge soaking up my veneration.

I could no more disregard Ritchie's presence than ignore the waters of the Snoline River or a windstorm in the forests of the Cascades. Ritchie carried me about as a tike, swung me upside down by my ankles, me chuckling in the safety and control of his great hands even then. He never dropped me except into soft landings: beds, couches, snowdrifts, and warm summer lakes.

I loved to trace the veined highways on Ritchie's hands where they circumscribed his knuckles and then headed up the peninsulas of his fingers like highways sweeping around a mountain and down to an adjacent shoreline. My little dimpled stubs were embryonic by comparison, but I never stopped expecting my appendages to blossom with veined machines of strength like Ritchie's. Doomed optimism.

Everyone in the Hirsch family but Ritchie talked. He acted. Kinetic, taller, a rush of red hair and freckles, shirt out, stretchable, and purposeful, Ritchie successfully bested gravity to snare a pass while playing any sport. He could snap a football across his body with dart-like accuracy. He could throw a basketball to a teammate the length of the court.

Ritchie had an infinite capacity for practice. He was patient, shooting jump shots by the hour at the loosely hinged metal hoop attached to our alley light pole, throwing baseballs from a bucket through a tire carcass hanging from the maple tree in our backyard, hurling the entire contents one at a time at the hole in the tire center. Sometimes my dad would push the tire so it was a moving target.

Ritchie was not sports specific; sometimes he would chuck a football at the tire or pick up a Frisbee and hurl it like a boomerang in one direction, knowing it would curve to the tree and through the tire as he intended. Hours would pass, and Ritchie would be tossing, collecting, lining up, and tossing again as the light in the alley cast a lemon glow on the tire's darkening shadow.

Practice was the main event with Ritchie. "A business," Dad would say, highly satisfied after a rebound and outlet pass. "He's taking care of business, after all," as if the Hirsch family business were winning basketball games and not selling the inventory at Fulton Jewelry.

My dad's admiration for Ritchie's skill was rich, enduring, and dominant. He wanted Ritchie's counsel on the course of the baseball season, the rise of Arnold Palmer, and the demise of Ben Hogan and Slammin' Sammy Snead. They put their heads together closely to consider the coming of Elgin Baylor. I remember Ritchie at sixteen, playing over the basket because he saw Oscar Robertson do the identical act on TV. He possessed perfect kinetic memory.

My parents, Leon and Pearl, and I—and even Auntie Riva—went to Bethell football games together to watch my kinetic brother in action. Even when he was a fourteen-year-old freshman, Ritchie was already playing varsity sports. We sat on cold bleachers next to rain-soaked football fields in league towns like Acme, Sedro Woolly, Oak Harbor, and Stanwood as Ritchie, covered with mud and as wet as a Labrador in duck season, ran and passed on offense and on defense angled in for tackle after tackle like a low-flying boomerang.

Ritchie's intensity was expressed through his body. He rarely spoke while competing. Even when sitting on the bench, he never left the game; he stayed in mentally because it was not a game to him. He focused eagle-like on the hunt, his eyes bloody cold.

While I saw the admiration for him in the eyes of game visitors and supporters as well, he never winked, smiled, or acknowledged them or, for that matter, our family huddled in those floodlit stadiums, wrapped in wet blankets, or in gym stands, thigh to thigh with total strangers and enveloped in the reek of sweaty tennis shoes and liniment.

Because of Ritchie the name Hirsch powered Totem high-school sports for as long as I remember. Despite his meager academics, Ritchie passed each class because teachers loved to watch him perform. He advanced from year to year regardless of his exam scores and, I suspect, because he was sweet and uncomplicated. Ritchie never rushed to the park after school. His classmates would never choose teams until he got there.

Ritchie's temperament was also his and his alone. My dad's bursts of anger were different. First he would became molten, then volcanic, but Ritchie went off like a thunderclap—*boom!*—and then it was over. He rarely was challenged at school, but when it happened he reacted with spontaneity to any adversary, his hand shooting out to grab arms and throat before his adversary could throw a punch or rush in for a tackle. Ritchie was no counterpuncher. He was cat quick, a frog shooting his tongue to grab a fly. And swallow.

Ritchie had rhythm and could dance. He would put Broadway show tunes on the Motorola in the living room and sweep Pearl into a waltz or a fox trot, or he would swing her to the musical colloquies of Duke Ellington and Billy Elkhorn. Ritchie's feet could talk our mother into bopping, with Little Richard braying and praying two-four time to the backbeat. Pearl whined and protested and loved it at the same time, her apron swirling. Then, after a while she would put that working garment aside, stripping down, as it were, for real dancing, even though her partner was her son. I never saw her dance with my dad.

Ritchie was warming up. Large for his age, he'd had girlfriends from twelve on. They liked being around his freckled grin and those big hands that offered to carry their books to class. They seemed to love his natural scent, somewhere between his sun-bleached madras cotton shirts and his pheromonic hair pomade. His girls liked the excuse to rest on his giant forearms. Mary Agee, Julie Ruger, Estelle Castellano. They all fell into line. I never tired of keeping my periscope on Ritchie, because I was convinced there were tricks to learn there.

Even blind Bubbe Hirsch in the old folks' home near the park lit up for Ritchie. She became incandescent in his presence on those days when my dad would bring us to her overheated room, which smelled like melted candy bars, disinfectant, used diapers, and the stagnant scent of an ancient bird's nest puddled by a rainstorm. A silent, darkened person in her blindness, she chattered for Ritchie as if she had a reservoir of stories preserved just for him. She had seen him before losing her sight. I, born after that sad event, was simply a name to her. I seemed to remind her only of what she could not see.

But Ritchie! She stroked him, pawed him, whispered little Germanisms in his ear. "*Liebchen*," she used to call him. She held his arm in her clawlike hand covered by thinning yellow skin with blue veins showing through the translucent tissue.

As I said, the old woman was blind before my birth. Her inquisitive hands touched me only infrequently. At first, I recall, she threw off a rosewater scent that traveled across my face. I pulled back once, frightened that blindness had an evil corrosive effect I might catch. It was as if there were a sight-dismembering disease that might strip me of the ability to read—my greatest fear.

For the most part, Bubbe ignored me even when my dad would say, "Ma, Nathan's here too." There was an unwillingness in her to look at me when she spoke unless she believed I was elsewhere. She would fix her unseeing eyes on me with no idea the person receiving her blind stare was the grandson in whom she had no interest.

She was mushroomlike. Her crepey clothes shifted with her, their sags giving in to nature, her humped back like that of a molting salmon, red in the wrong places. It was hard to hold her as an object of affection.

But Ritchie did. He snuggled her, sensing her response to him, and put his arm around her as she sighed contentedly, positively cooing. I felt with some jealousy that Ritchie was practicing again with his easy anticipation of Bubbe's zones of pleasure, not presuming—as I had—that on her they had all dried up in the arid droughts accompanying great age.

And Ritchie and Bubbe were buried in the same cemetery. I want to imagine a remaining current of warmth coursing between their graves. Now someone very alive has seen something of Ritchie in me, and I feel warm from it as well.

CHAPTER 18

Nathan and the Queen of the Fairies

* * *

IT IS THURSDAY NIGHT, TWO days after I saw Katie Martin at Sears and almost two weeks since Wally's arraignment. I abandon a viewing of *All in the Family* with Auntie Riva and instead remain in my room, drafting yet another letter to Shira Loeb. So far there have been many unsent, thus unanswered, their pages scattered about my bedroom desk like leaves in a windstorm.

After an hour I give up. I cannot face another failed effort. Instead I slip on my coat, raise the collar, and walk out in the cool evening of Parkland with its budding trees, in part as an attempt to refocus my thoughts from Shira to Katie. The coincidental meeting with her keeps coming to the front of my mind.

The absence of any similarity between the two women is remarkable. I remember Shira as pallid, almost anemic, in tone and color. By contrast Katie seems robust and athletic, hobbled only by the sadness I saw in her face.

I desperately want to complete one coherent letter to Shira, but the weather, while overcast, is neither rainy nor terribly windy and invites me outside. I set off on foot toward the harbor while I mentally organize the words to convey my feelings for Shira.

The smell of the sawmill saturates the atmosphere. The solid wood is ground into fine powder by the diamond-sharp blades. *Kerf* is the cut. A blower clears the dust left from the kerf off the cutting tables and spits it out of a funnel from the top of the mill into the air, after which it falls to the ground in a conical pile that looks like a sawdust dunce hat.

The dust from the kerf smells like mushrooms and fern stalks flavored with maple syrup and machine oil. Dense and earthy, its scent is carried in the air like a light sweat a constant on any day that Skarbell's cuts logs. At night the scent has no competition from the oily exhaust of loggers' rigs on their daily delivery and pickup treks though Bethell. It now falls on me in each layer of mist. I feel as if I inhale it with each breath.

It occurs to me that I am like kerf dust—left in Bethell. All of us here are like sawdust. The trees, they are chopped down and hewn into logs that are hauled off. But the ground-up kerf dust lies here, inert on the ground. The logs become boards, studs, beams, posts, and plywood. Logs travel elsewhere to be fashioned into houses and buildings. But the kerf dust piles up inertly in the mill's yard. It lies there, its smell a signal of uselessness and no future.

I walk up to the Harbor Café with my hands stuck in my coat. In the café's front window, a neon sign invites one and all to the Elbow Room, a little dark nook in the rear. Since my return to Bethell, I have been no stranger to the Elbow Room. I could sit at its little bar, its warm walls lined with fir planks and its sepia-tinted pictures of lumberjacks and giant trees. I could chin for a minute with Eddie Bach, the bartender, or whoever might be sitting next to me. Or I could nurse a bottle of my own at one of the four little round tables under the single dim ceiling light in the center of the room.

A sudden wet squall makes the thought of shelter attractive as I enter the café's door. Two men I don't know are hunkered at the bar, dressed in jeans, work shirts, and baseball caps. Their conversation seems constrained and almost conspiratorial. I ask Eddie for a Henry Weinhard's Dark on tap.

In the corner sits an unlit jukebox; the light overhead is extinguished. An eight-track sitting on the counter behind the bar is playing Bread's *The Guitar Man* out of hidden speakers.

Deputy Sheriff Earl Strunk is sitting alone at one little table, his leg with the bad knee sticking straight out. Behind him two women occupy the remaining table, their backs to the bar. They have their coats draped on their chairs, as if to create a curtain of privacy about them.

I walk over to Earl. "Hey, can I join you?"

"Sure, Counselor," he says, grinning. "Pull up a chair. I can always use some free legal advice."

I plop down and take a pull from my beer. "Not to talk shop, but what's the scuttlebutt on the prosecutor's refiling against Wally Richmond?"

He laughs. "You *are* out of it. Richmond pled guilty in superior court up in the county courthouse last Tuesday. Burglary two, that's it. He's lying low, still out on bail, and sentencing is next week. Al handled the plea himself. Pelky was nowhere in sight. And the state's OK with Wally serving two at Monroe on the sentence."

"So what about Si's killer?"

"What killer?" Earl holds his hand up to his face in mock surprise. "Apparently they don't have clue in Al's office, but it wasn't Wally, that's for sure."

"I'm not surprised," I say, trying to keep the smugness out of my voice. "You think there's any way to get a peek at the coroner's report?"

Earl looks at me sharply. "Fuck no. There's no case here. No one in the sheriff's office has seen it. And even if I saw it, which I haven't, I wouldn't tell you about it anyway, even if you were my mother."

"So is Emerson going to sentence Wally?" Snoline County shares a superior court judge with Skagit County in order to save money. Eric Emerson is the regular visiting judge. Unless he has a case to try, Judge Emerson is in the Snoline courthouse no more than two afternoons each month. Most legal matters in Snoline County are handled by the justice court.

"Emerson was not on it, didn't come in for it," Earl says with emphasis and swallows some beer. "Interesting that you ask. The word is they brought in a King County judge all the way from Seattle just to take the plea. That's a hell of a drive for a visiting judge who's gotta come back for a sentencing too. I mean, how often does that superior courtroom get used here? Usually it's one of the Island County or maybe Whatcom County judges who brings some business from his own turf with him at the same time. But no sir, this time it's gotta be King County."

"I don't get it," I say and sip.

"Me neither. The word is that Al was bundled up with the judge on something else, though, and he took the plea just 'cause he happened to be here." With that Earl sets down his bottle, lifts his bad leg into a cocked position, and pushes himself to his feet. "Gotta shove. By the way, the judge is one a yours, a guy name of Weinberg. Hell, you probably break bread with the man, or whatever you people do when you're in Seattle." Earl the wise guy winks at me. "Nice talkin', Counselor," he says and heads for the door.

The story Earl told me leaves my mind turning. Wally is not a murderer but now admits to breaking in. Harry probably knows Weinberg; and Harry, who had issued Wally's bond, will be released from that bond as soon as Judge Weinberg enters Wally's sentence. It gives me an excuse to talk to Harry about Wally.

The two women at the table behind me stand up to put on their coats. As they leave I see that one is Katie Martin. I wave and smile as she crosses the room. She returns the smile as one of the men drinking at the bar turns and blocks her path to the exit.

"Katie, honey." The drunk gestures grandly with the bonhomie of the intoxicated. "How 'bout goin' home with me?"

I stand up from my seat. The drunk, though plastered and weaving, is stockier than I am, and I am no fighter. But Katie said, "You remind me of Ritchie." Ritchie would do something.

"Is there any trouble here?" I ask. As the words leave my lips, I realize I sound like a cheap version of Sheriff Matt Dillon.

The drunk is leaning on his barstool. "Who the hell are you?"

Then I am on my back. Katie is kneeling next to me. Her hand holds a Kleenex to my nose. The drunk must have popped me. Katie's perfume blots out the kerf-dust scent tracked across the fir planks.

Eddie, the bartender, has come around to keep the peace. Katie looks up at the drunk.

"OK, Phil." Her voice is measured, sure of itself. "Just call Natalie for permission to bring me home, will you? Eddie, where's the phone? Phil wants to call his wife."

Phil's eyes dart from Eddie to Katie. Calling his wife was not what he could handle at that moment.

"Hey, Katie, I was just kidding around," he mutters. "Sorry." His voice trails off, and he plops onto his barstool, suddenly oblivious to the standing crowd.

"Sorry 'bout that," he says to me as I get up on my haunches. I wave up at the drunk, as if it's OK to be clipped by a sucker punch. No problem. But I'm not sure I'm ready to get up.

I feel Eddie lifting me to my feet, his strong hands under my armpits.

"Everything OK, Nate?" he says, patting me on the back.

"I think so." I'm able to stand, at least, I think.

"Nathan, why don't you come with us?" Katie says. "Grab your coat."

I follow her directions, throwing on my jacket and joining the two women at the café door. The chilly night quickly restores my wits and multiplies my embarrassment.

"We'd better drive you home," Katie suggests. "Nathan, this is Eileen, Eileen Gubrud. She works at Sears too."

Eileen is a matron in her late forties or early fifties and looks impatient to be going. I clamber into the back of Katie's Plymouth Valiant.

It is clear to me that Katie knew everybody in the little drama. Phil the drunk, Eddie the bartender. Nathan the useless rescuer. The Bethell axiom "everybody knows everybody" has been proven again.

Katie drives steadily to Eileen's. The older woman exits the car, and I move to the front seat. I start to direct Katie to Auntie Riva's house in Parkland.

"No directions necessary," she says tartly. "I know where that is. I wasn't being fresh when I told you that you reminded me of your brother."

I gently palpate my tender nose with the fingers of my right hand. There seem to be no loose pieces, just swelling.

"I have a feeling Ritchie would have been better at this than I was. Anyway, I was flattered by the comparison, even though it's hard for me to believe it. You're the first one ever to see any resemblance. So now that you protected me, couldn't I get you some fish and chips or a hamburger?"

Katie shakes her head. "Mom is watching Tiffany. The store was open late tonight, so she'll want to head home." Katie stops speaking as she pulls to a stop in front of Auntie Riva's.

"What about a break next week?" I propose. "We can try the Harbor Café again."

Even though Katie's face is drained from a long workday and her raincoat is plain and not at all fashionable, her green eyes and long eyelashes continue to have the appeal I felt at Sears. She catches me staring.

"Sorry," I say, "but I can't believe how you still look like you did so long ago."

"I don't feel like I felt so long ago," she says with a laugh. "You'd better let me go home quick, or I'll pass out."

"Then next Tuesday after work?" I persist. "My nose will have recovered by then."

Katie is silent, debating, I suspect, the merits of ever seeing me again. Then I win over doubt.

"Tuesday's a normal workday," she says. "No Thursday marathon. I'll walk over. Meet you there."

With that Katie drives into the night, a trail of smoky exhaust from her car exploding the sawdust smell still hanging in the air. I watch with the scent of her handkerchief about my face until her taillights fade away, and I wonder whether Ritchie would have given my invitation to Katie his approval.

* * *

We sit in the Harbor Café eating French dip sandwiches and drinking beer. Katie tells me about the divorce, motherhood, her new job, the absence of interesting men in Bethell, and the joy of exercise—specifically jogging, which she states is a substitute for sex. Her last statement makes my face redden.

Katie describes herself as Heinz 57 sauce: Swiss, German, Norwegian, and Dutch. Her parents were local, but everyone else scattered to the winds.

"After two years of Snoline JC," Katie says, "Bobby and I got married. Then four years as a flight attendant. Western Air. Remember 'Come Fly with Me'? Remember those little pillbox hats? That's me. Then Tiffany in '68."

"It's hard to believe you're a mother."

"I swear if the draft hadn't been out there, I wouldn't have Tiffany. My little sweetheart kept her daddy out of the army." Abruptly she shifts to me. "Did you go?"

"Nope. Deferred."

"Why?"

I choose my words carefully. "When Ritchie died over there in my junior year of college, I was taken off the 1-A draft list. Then Dad had the fatal heart attack before I lost my student deferment. No other available males to support my mother. That was my ticket to become an antiwar protester. There was nothing they could do to me then."

I withhold the details of my meager radical participation. Even though I was at the march on the Pentagon in 1967, I was just in pursuit of Shira, a vocal opponent of the Vietnam War. Katie would not be interested in hearing about Shira.

I change the subject. "So you were there in Seattle. Why come back?" I immediately regret the question. It invites her to ask me the same. But Katie plunges right in and gallops past my fears.

"Tiffany, I suppose. Otherwise I would be out of here." She laughs. "Grandma Edna, that's Bobby's mother, loves her only granddaughter and babysits all the time. And I wouldn't take Tiffany away from my mom, Phyllis. They adore each other. My mom is my best friend, and Daryl Miller, her new mate, is OK for an old grump.

"All this family makes working easier. Bobby left for California in '69, when Seattle was a bad place to find a job. I thought about going to Bellingham, but the Valiant broke down right at the Highway 90 turnoff to home, and Tiffany was hungry. I needed to work, and Sears here came through for me. So that was that." Katie looks at her watch. "I really need to head home now."

"Mind if I walk with you?" I ask.

Again there is that hesitation. "Isn't it out of your way?"

"Yep," I concede. "But if I can't pay you back after you broke up that vicious fight, what can a gentleman do?"

We cross over Fulton Street and head toward Mill Town. Katie draws her raincoat around her and shivers.

"I read about your dad's passing at the time," she says. "It was in the *Daily Herald*. I mean, I know there's the Hirsch Building. It's been there forever. And I told you about going to the jewelry store."

"My grandfather, Albert, was actually a mayor here," I say, "back in the gold rush era. He built the business with the profits from that era. I suspect he made a fortune selling nugget watchbands. I still have one—my father's."

"I want to see it."

"I keep it at home, actually."

"Well, invite me over to show it to me. I would love to meet your mother. Does she like children? I could bring Tiffany. We could have a picnic."

Explaining that my mom is all but crazy is impossible. "My mom was born allergic to the outdoors," I apologize. "We never boated, dug clams, or fished. She was a city girl. She used to say she only wanted to do things that required white gloves."

Katie goes blank, her handsomeness lost in embarrassment. "Maybe I'm pushing you too hard. It's no big thing, really."

"Not at all," I say. "Anyway, I live at my aunt's, not at home. It's complicated." I take a deep breath.

"What do you do for exercise around here?" Katie asks.

"Nothing, I'm ashamed to say."

"Ever try jogging? Next to dancing, it's the best exercise there is. Never seem to have the chance to dance anymore." Katie laughs and leans on my arm as if to say, "Don't take me seriously."

"I'm not exactly James Brown," I say, "but I'm willing to embarrass myself jogging, if that sounds good. I might even find some tennis shoes. Let's try jogging sometime."

"What about Saturday?" Katie is serious.

* * *

We jog together at her insistence. She is good at it, and she helps me, a beginner. We go out on Snoline County roads, starting on the edge of town.

When running, Katie seems to give little reflection to any subject or idea that flashes across her mind. They all rise simultaneously for review: the Sears new model vacuum cleaner, Tiffany's new tooth, her mother's mammogram, the smell of the mill, the latest season of *All in the Family* (Katie hates Meathead), her Plymouth Valiant, the fact that Bobby doesn't call Tiffany enough, the latest style of clothes in the fashion magazine she saw in the beauty shop, what I do at the justice court.

All this rushes from her like a creek's torrent at spring runoff from the high Cascades. Sometimes I attempt to jump into the current. Sometimes I simply stand on the bank. I never have mentioned Uncle Harry, Uncle Si, or his estate.

Katie loves the wolf whistles aimed at her from every passing car.

"They really are nice," she says, her chin a bit higher after each shrill sound trailing out of the latest pickup truck to come by. I find myself feeling proud too that I am running with someone who richly deserves to be whistled at. Katie dogs it so I appear to be her equal. Admittedly I was afraid she would see my weakness as a runner. I am no Ritchie. Now people whistle at my companion. I find it thrilling.

I persistently think about Ritchie as we run. I am alive and running with his girlfriend. My mind mulls this over. It is as if my huffing and puffing have conjured up a remembrance of his effortless skills, and she detects it there silently waiting for exploration.

"Ritchie was my star," I say. "I knew he was such a great athlete. All things considered, if he hadn't gone to Southeast Asia when he did, I bet he could have played baseball about anywhere in the country."

"I had a cousin who was a baseball player," Katie says as we huff up a hill. "Eric was his name, Eric Hagberg. The Danish side. We'd go down to Sultan, where his family lived, and watch his games when I was a little girl. I loved to cheer for him, and when he hit the ball I thought my heart would leap out of my chest."

"I loved to watch Ritchie too," I say. "He was five years older than me, but he always gave me his bats and balls and showed me how to do tricks. I could spin a ball on the end of a bat like him, but that was about it. I watched. He played."

We slow to a trot to preserve breath. Katie periodically looks at me while we run, checking to see if I am all right.

"I was engaged to Bobby when I heard he had died," she says. "I thought my life was about to open up. But somehow, hearing about Ritchie—that stopped me. My mom said to me, 'You can't control the world. You were just little kids. You have a new life. Take it. You don't have to forget the past, but don't live in it.'"

I think about Auntie Riva. Her life is in the past. I recall my feelings when Ritchie died.

"I was in the third year of college." I am barely running now. "I couldn't identify Laos or Vietnam on the map. My mom got letters from Ritchie maybe once every three months or so. Ritchie and Dad had a row before he went in the service, and they weren't talking or writing anymore. Ritchie had been all over the world. We really didn't think what he was doing was dangerous. It seems so stupid now, of course, but then, in 1963, we weren't at war, were we?

"Dad got a call from the local base in Seattle. There had been an accident, they said. Dad needed to call the commander to find out that Ritchie was dead. The VFW here gave Ritchie a full burial. It was a big deal to my dad. He put the flag from Ritchie's coffin in a trunk, my dad's trunk from World War II, with Ritchie's baseball gear and his military citations. The trunk is still at the house."

We stopped running and are standing on a little road out in the middle of unplowed fields.

"Funny," I say, "I haven't thought about it for a while. I didn't cry when Ritchie was buried. I honestly didn't believe he was in there, in that flag-draped coffin. Then later, when I was rummaging around in the basement one year while I was still in college, I found the trunk and opened it. I took out Ritchie's glove, slipped it over my hand, and pounded the ball into the palm for a while, just feeling my hand slide into the indentations where his big left hand had gone. His hands were a lot bigger than mine, and I could feel the looseness. That's when I knew he was dead, and I cried then—in the basement with the trunk open, all by myself."

Katie, in running togs, purple sweats, and a stocking cap, has tears in her eyes. She kisses me, hugs me hard, and holds on. There, I want to say, there, there. I want to comfort her about everything in her life. Something inside me locked up tight wants to be released, but I cannot speak of it for fear of destroying the fragile thread that is just beginning to weave Katie and me together.

We start to jog again, and suddenly I feel brave enough to try.

"My dad couldn't do anything for weeks after Ritchie's funeral. He sat in the living room all day, wouldn't go to the store, didn't want to eat meals. My Uncle Si and Uncle Harry took care of my dad. It's one of the reasons I'm helping Harry now that Si is dead. My Uncle Harry made me realize how important family and friends can be."

Katie stops on the word *Harry*, and I turn to see if she is hurt. Her nose is red, the breath coming out of her smoky. She looks at me hard, looking like Mrs. Oliver, my high-school English teacher, after catching me plagiarizing an article.

"Who is Harry?" she asks.

"Uncle Harry King, the lawyer. I'm not his nephew, really, but he's a close family friend, and I'm helping him with my uncle Si Galitzer's estate."

"Does that mean you work for Harry King?" Katie's face has changed; it's mottled, and her jaw is working with uncertainty. I sense my answer could have a consequence to Katie that I do not understand.

"Helping out, yes, for a while," I say, "but why…why is this upsetting you? Is there something wrong with that?"

Katie starts to run again, this time at her own high pace, not dogging it so I can keep with her. I race to catch up.

"Yes," she pants. "Yes there might be, Nathan." She looks as if she is talking to the fence posts on the roadside.

"Slow down," I say. "You're getting way ahead of me." I'm speaking to Katie's back, thumping along, wearing down. "What did I do?" My voice is that of a penitent child.

"It's what I'm doing that bothers me. You just woke me up." Katie's breathing is even but intense as she heads off with a burst of speed back toward Bethell. I trail behind. At the top of a rise, she delays a second and cries back over her shoulder, "I'm sorry, but I'm going to run by myself for a while."

"Wait a minute," I call out while trying to keep up with her, but it's no use. Katie will not stop. I watch her fly over the hill and then disappear around a bend in the road.

A few cars drive by as I run. Wild daffodils that tenaciously grip the road's gravel edge wave sadly as I pass. I lose energy and slow to a walk, my brain and body sapped by some gaffe I have unintentionally committed.

When I get back to the city limits, Katie is nowhere in sight. I do not know what I said or what I did. But it is clear that my association with Uncle Harry and my allegiance to him has unsettled Katie, and I have no idea why. I have come to a stop with her, at a barrier raised by my loyalty to Harry that renders me distressing to her. And though the reasons remain unknown to me, I am no fool. I have been here before.

I can tell that Katic, like Shira, believes certain barriers to be impassable.

CHAPTER 19

Si's Estate Includes Some Unusual Accounts

* * *

HARRY ASKED ME TO PICK up any of Uncle Si's checkbooks or business records I might find at Rivers End. Before Saturday, when Katie blew up in the middle of the run and took off, I planned to ask her if she would go with me. So, having nothing to do on Sunday, I borrow Auntie Riva's Lincoln and head out to the farm solo.

* * *

When I was a kid, no more than eight years old, the Galitzer place had a strange attraction. My parents frequently visited Si and Frank's father while the old man was dying of cancer, and they took Ritchie and me with them. Si and Frank were actually talking then, as if a truce had been called, the two of them taking care of their dad, waiting on him hand and foot. Pearl and Leon would sit in the living room with the dying man while Ritchie and I roamed the outdoors.

Ritchie would try to get me to play catch in the unmowed grass of the meadow. The stalks were brown, but underneath the stems stayed damp, and my eight-year-old legs and feet stuck in the thatch. It seemed to me I could never get to the balls Ritchie threw.

More important, I was drawn to the woods beyond, which were shaded and blue, whereas the meadow was wheaten. I wanted to sneak into the shrubs and trees to look for dead Indians and hunt bears and deer, none of which I had seen in my life. I knew the woods to be cool. In there I would be out of the itchy prickles of the grassy meadow.

When I retrieved one of Ritchie's hurled missiles, I would heave it as hard as my little arm would permit, past Ritchie's outstretched limbs into the brush on the edge of the clearing.

I would grovel and run after the ball. "Sorry. I'll get it," and I would head right into the tree line.

Once inside I would call out to Ritchie, "Berries!" Food Ritchie understood, and for a morsel he reluctantly would give up sports for the moment.

Whatever else we did on those trips, I stayed out of the house as much as possible. I hated looking at Morris Galitzer sitting in the living room, his skin as tan as tea-stained paper, with gray chalk marks for lips. He barely moved. The room was filled with rubber tubes, hot water bottles, Vaseline jars, towels, and a small metal clothes rack. It looked like the sick man lived there, not upstairs in his bedroom. The living-room smell was close, as if the activities of the house's only bathroom on the second landing had migrated downstairs, while outdoor air was excluded by tightly closed windows. It was dark in that room.

Pearl always let Ritchie and me eat our sandwiches outside on those visits. I remember sitting by the clotheslines, eating tomato, sardine, and butter sandwiches on thick slabs of home-baked white bread and drinking fresh lemonade. The smell of the dying man would periodically sneak out of the back door, but the drying sheets hanging from the metal wires billowed in the breeze like sails, the sheets smelling fresh like new snow in the sun, evaporating the staleness.

I thought lying on those sheets might alone cure Morris, and I told Ritchie, who laughed pieces of his sandwich out of his mouth.

"You can't cure cancer," he said.

"What exactly is it?" I asked.

Ritchie was honest in these situations. "I can't tell you exactly. It's like a rot, like rotten fruit. Once you get started, it just gets worse, then you're rotten all over and bingo, dead as a doornail."

I imagined a rotten apple fallen in the road from the orchard, crushed by a passing car, the fruit exploded all over the asphalt by the tires, the pulpy insides turned brown by the sun and air.

The Galitzer farm road looms around the bend. The sun has cracked through the rain clouds, and the road cuts a trough through the lime-green huckleberry and salal shrubs along the shoulder. I see ahead on the roadside a yellow Volkswagen bus, its rear-left side sagging toward the ground and a small red-haired person tugging on the flattened tire. It was the VW I saw at Si's funeral.

I roll down the window. "Need a hand?"

The redhead looks up with a girl's face. Or, more accurately, the face of a smallish woman with cheeks that look like the battleground of a freckle war. She wears a stained parka, a wool stocking cap, and bell-bottom jeans that have unraveled into muddy threads around worn out tennis shoes.

"Anything you can do," she says. "Motherfucking tire." The woman has a low hoarse voice and long frizzy hair that reminds me of Ritchie's—straw red—but coiled.

I get out of the car and take a look at the tire. The redhead's knuckles are bloody and scratched. She must have tried to slip the jack under the car.

"Man, what a bitch," she grumbles as she tugs upward on a tire wrench wrapped around a tire lug. The lug does not budge.

The sides of the faded yellow bus are covered with graffiti. A hand-rolled cigarette with a glowing tip puffs star-speckled smoke. A streaking orange comet arches across the side panel trailed by a purple tail. Plump naked buttocks straddle the gas tank cap. One could imagine the face of any attendant inserting the pump nozzle between those painted pink cheeks.

I turn my head to avoid inhaling the vapors from the open driver's door. The scent is an ugly blend of dog hair, orange peel, tobacco, body odor, and incense. There is no one else inside. It strikes me as impossible that one person could generate such a pungent aroma. It seems to ooze out of the van like spoiled milk.

I wrestle the jack underneath the van, crank the body up until the wheel rim is off the ground, then put all my weight on the tire wrench atop a wheel lug that first locks, then breaks free with a grunt. I loosen each lug one at a time.

I can hear the redhead inside the van. It sounds as if she is ripping open the panels in the back as she searches for the spare. Then she utters, "Shit. Jesus."

"Don't worry. It's all jacked up," I say.

"Won't do any good. Got no fuckin' spare. That prick sold me this pile of crap without a spare. What an asshole." She sits on the ledge of the van's open door, pushing her hair back in frustration. Her locks corkscrew in the air.

"I need a joint," she growls. Her jeans have a hole in the knee, patched with a piece of red bandanna. Her shirt is stitched out of an American flag. Even with her salty voice, she looks beaten about and vulnerable, like a dirty, winded bum.

It has begun to drizzle.

"I'll drive you to a station," I say. "Why don't we get out of the rain in my car?"

The girl squints at me. "Man, didn't I see you at that funeral up in Seattle?"

"You mean Si Galitzer's funeral?"

"Right."

I recall the VW van, but without the exotic graffiti on the sides, parked on the street at Si's funeral.

"You were with a guy who had a beard and wore sandals."

"That pretty much describes everybody I know." The redhead squints at me. "But yeah, for sure, that's Harvey, my old man, sorta." She points at the van, her hands on her hips. "He's the artiste."

As ridiculous as it sounds, and as wet and frustrated as she seems, she guffaws at the thought of the auto graffiti as art. Then she gets serious.

"I wish you were a grease monkey. Then maybe you could fix this shitbag of a car. First the motor stalls on me, then the tire pops."

"So where were you heading?"

"'Cause I'm supposed to be the dead guy's kid, so I've been told, I thought I'd check out the homestead." The words pop out quickly, like fizz from a shaken soda bottle. "So how come you were at the cemetery?"

"Just an old family friend. You're Sadie? Sadie Welger?"

"Miriam, OK? Or Amber, whatever you want. Only forget the Sadie shit. Believe me, nobody wants to be called Sadie. And anyway, what's it to you?"

That iced it. Uncle Si named Sadie Miriam Welger in his will. This was Si's daughter.

I explain to Miriam that I'm the lawyer for Si's executor, Harry King.

"My name's Nathan, Nathan Hirsch. Actually I was going out to the same place you're heading."

Miriam stares past me with indifference. "I don't care if you're Perry Mason. How're we gonna fix my tire?"

I think about trying my car's spare, but the notion that the Lincoln and the VW van use the same tires is ludicrous.

"I suggest we drive my car to the farm and use the phone there. I can get Floyd's to send out a tow truck. They can fix the tire or tow you back to town."

"I dunno." Miriam looks at me suspiciously, her crinkled locks like red spaghetti in the rain. "How do I know you aren't gonna try to get into my pants or somethin'?"

I breathe deeply, trying to think like Uncle Harry. Given who she is, I can't just tell her off. She's Si Galitzer's daughter.

"We, you and I, are not going to spend the afternoon at the old place. Besides, there's a caretaker out there. He'll protect you. We'll call Floyd's, I'll look around for a second, and we can meet Floyd as soon as he gets to the van. Unless you have a better idea." I feel my voice going up as I get wetter.

"Jeez, Louise, what got you so uptight, man? Your throttle jammed open or somethin'?" The whine from Miriam's throat is like a fingernail on a chalkboard.

"You can stay in the van," I answer. "I can call Floyd when I get there. Or we can check the place out now. I'll give you the house keys, and you can stay overnight if you want."

"Nah, probably too spooky. Just as soon stay in the van." Then her face brightens. "Maybe there's still grub in the fridge."

"It would be rotten by now," I say. "Anyway, the caretaker probably cleaned up the place. We can grab some food on the way back."

Miriam softens up. "I guess I want to see the place."

"Then let's go," I say in resignation. I feel exhausted just talking to this person who seems enveloped in chaos and agitation.

Miriam silently looks out the window as I drive. Then she speaks as if in a trance.

"I don't even know if he was my old man, you know. It's only my mom's word, and that's not been much good for anything."

"I don't know," I demur. "I mean, your name is in the will. Why would he do that if you weren't his child?"

"I mean, shit, he never, ever made one call to me." Miriam shakes her head, as if to clear out the cobwebs. "I can't remember my old lady saying a word about anyone named Seymour until she heard he was dead. Then she was all over me. Did you know the guy?"

I nod. "He was a friend of my dad. I really didn't know him all that well, but he used to take out my aunt, and they seemed pretty tight also."

"Hey, you and I coulda been relatives." She brightens up. "That's a good reason for you to stay on your side of the car seat."

The Galitzer farmhouse is the preserved past. The veranda that sweeps around the entirety of the structure invites a visitor to walk around and take in the view to the west, where the night sky in summer shines with the reflected Bethell township lights. In the back the meadow begins with the first step off the porch and stretches to the forested mountains to the east, which seem topped by licorice-black heavens. The sounds emanating out of the forest on the far side of the field, even in the rain, seem wild and untamed.

Curt McPhee still lives in a fire-red lean-to behind the barn. He comes out bareheaded as we drive in.

I roll down the window and wave.

"It's OK," I say. McPhee stares at me for a moment, his rage at the intrusion unconcealed. Then he sees Miriam, his eyebrows leap, and his lip rises in disgust.

I begin to explain who Miriam is, then I stop. I conclude there is more of a problem in the story than in saying nothing.

"Her car's stalled out on the 20. Is the phone still working?"

McPhee virtually spits his words at me. "What do you think?" He retreats to the barn, his few remaining hair strands flying about in the wind.

My key fits the front door, which creaks open. Inside, the old house smells of homemade cleaning soap brewed on a wood-burning stove. The linoleum floor by the door is scrubbed through to the cork backing, and the aroma of linseed oil wafts off the mahogany dining table. Yellowing crocheted doilies lie like spider webs over the worn fabric chairs in the sitting room; tan-striped wallpaper is stained around the windows, where wind has driven in the rain.

There in the corner sits an oaken rolltop desk, the top decorously pulled down over the writing surface, the way a doyenne might pull down her skirt hem to carefully cover her ankles.

Miriam and I walk up the creaking stairs to the bathroom at the second-floor landing. The room's odor announces an old male warren. A claw-foot tub rests in the corner next to a rust-stained commode and its Depression-era overhead tank. The floor about its base is bleached by urine.

In the two upstairs bedrooms, there is one rocking chair and two metal-spring beds stripped of sheets. The closets are empty of clothing. A ghost house. Miriam is silent as we return to the first floor.

I set about finding checkbooks and any related records, as Harry requested. In a closet I find an apple-scented fruit crate full of papers. I set it on the floor by the desk and raise the desktop, which rolls smoothly up and back, as if on ball bearings. The shallow top drawers hold junk: mail advertisements, pens, rubber bands, and monthly newspaper receipts.

A Parker Pen box rests on the side of the top drawer. Opening it, I see it is lined with yellowing white satin, like a tiny casket. The fabric bears gold-leaf calligraphy: "PRESENTED BY FULTON JEWELRY." The pen is of the Old Master series, with a mock-tortoiseshell casing and a gold tip, the kind my father carried at Fulton Jewelry probably beginning in the Depression. He sent me off to college with a similar one.

The desk has a nest of cubbyholes. One is labeled *G*, the label taped to the wood. I fish around in the cubbyhole and find two identical sawtooth keys. I suspect they are Si's safety-deposit keys.

This is not the first time I have looked for such keys. When my dad died, my search for his keys turned up nothing.

My dad possessed an old desk too, a giant surface of thick glass that covered a forest-green felt pad. The desk was pushed up against a metal wall of small mail slots, each cubbyhole numbered with white paint. The desk sat anchored to the inside of Fulton Jewelry's famous but useless steel walk-in vault, next to shelves stacked with empty jewelry trays and boxes of old business papers.

The thick door of the vault was painted black with gilded scrolling in the corners and was opened in the center by a brass knob and handle as round as a baseball bat. Dad left the vault door open most of the time. As a kid I was permitted to play with the store's canceled checks that were stored on the vault shelves. I pretended the green-colored checks were dollar bills. Inside the vault I always felt Rockefeller rich.

Also as a child, I imagined being accidentally locked in that vault. Though the door was rarely shut, I shivered deliciously at the possibility of finding myself pressing against the immovable steel from inside, shouting at the silent slabs of iron, slowly starving while the world blithely went about its business before finding my bones.

My dad did paperwork on the desk inside the vault, sitting on an old folding chair under a single bulb, sometimes just slouching down, reading the *Daily Herald* or some jewelry trade magazine, always drinking coffee.

Once as he sat there, I asked my dad about a way to unlock the safe from the inside. He seemed to misunderstand my question.

"There's nothing in here that's so valuable," he answered. "Theft's not a problem. The family jewels, now, that's another story. They are in here." He stuck his fingers into one of the cubbyholes just above the surface of the desk, fished around for minute, and pulled out a small paper envelope. Smiling, he shook out two keys. They were heavy nickel with sawtooth runes, a dull glint in the glare from the plain bulb.

My dad's eyes took on the focused stare of a searchlight.

"Safety deposit box keys. At our bank," he said. "Remember, you need both keys to get in." He carefully slid the keys back into the small envelope and laid it gently in its cubbyhole. The white number on the cubbyhole had been covered with a small white tab bearing the letter *H*. The tab was attached with clear tape. *H* for Hirsch, I guessed.

"What do you mean the family jewels?" I asked. "Money?" I couldn't have been older than fifteen.

Dad always talked to me sideways. A comment from me usually raised the object of importance to him. Then, like a glancing blow, Dad would pursue his own subject that my comment had triggered. I knew this pattern and began to slip by him and out of the vault, but he blocked my way.

"You just listen to me," he said. "Don't forget. The family jewels. If anything happens." Dad tapped the rolltop-desk glass with the ring on his fourth finger. The glass top clinked like ice in a highball.

"Watch out for the family jewels," Bobby Raskin had once yelled up to me as I'd stood on the high dive at the municipal pool, cupping his hands over his crotch in demonstration as I was about to jump feet first off the board. "Watch out for the family jewels."

Two keys to a drawer that held secrets I could only guess at now replaced my testicles as the family jewels. Yet they had disappeared, those two sawtooth keys, when I went to the store after Dad's funeral, the windows covered with black bunting; the inventory of watches, rings, and loose stones, usually in the polished glass display cases, now tucked away in the vault; the pawn book lying closed on the desktop.

I unlatched that black iron door and used all of my body to shove it open. I entered the vault to find the family jewels, those keys Dad had so carefully displayed that day many years before, but the slot marked with the scotch-taped *H* no longer yielded the little envelope, no longer held the keys.

I pointed a flashlight into each cubbyhole and pulled out all the contents: telephone and utility bills, invoices from wholesalers in Chicago and San Francisco, a letter from stationery suppliers, an old Longines calendar from the '40s, dozens of velvet-covered jewelry boxes that felt like cold furry mice when I blindly reached in and touched them.

Thirty-four cubbyholes and no safety deposit keys. No records of a box at the Bethell Commerce Bank.

"Maybe you misunderstood." Mr. Narver shook his head from side to side, his hair pomaded in place. "Just your mom and dad's joint box," he said. And Uncle Harry had stood there too, shrugging, for once having no information. Pearl wept; said, "Not now"; and waved her damp handkerchief. I asked Auntie Riva, who answered with a question.

"You have got to be kidding. The Hirsch males giving me keys to any part of that place?"

That chapter was never closed. The Hirsch family jewels, represented by two matching safety-deposit box keys. Wherever they were, they had disappeared.

* * *

Now I hold Si's keys. They look just like my dad's had looked. Or were they Si's all along? The two I held years earlier were also etched with numbers. I strain to remember them but cannot. So similar in heft, so familiar in shape.

I slip them in my pocket and resolve to find out whether they bear any relation to those missing from the jewelry store after Dad's death.

While I rummage through Si's desk, I can see Miriam from the corner of my eye, walking about, running her fingers across the photographs that hang on the Galitzer walls. Brown, black, and white visages from another time and place: women with lined faces wearing high-neck dresses, hair parted in the middle, the men bearded and wearing full-brimmed hats, children staring blankly at the camera.

The light reflecting off the glass illuminates Miriam's face. She looks like the faces in the frames, I think: hard, high cheekbones, her nose slightly hooking. It is as if her flesh, her hair, her chin, her teeth absorb the features of the people in the photos, transferring back to the sepia apparitions under the glass.

Miriam shakes as if she is shedding an invisible assailant. "Fuckin' Christ, I get weird vibes from these pics," she whispers. "This is why I couldn't stay out here. These might be my relatives for all I know. Creepy."

I say nothing as I wade through the papers and the dust in the bottom drawers of Si's desk. Then, at the bottom, there is a stack of formal checking account books, hard-ring binders of black plastic, each creaking like a rusty door when I spread open the top. Unsigned checks, some aqua, some tinted varying shades of blue gray. One at a time, I set them into the fruit crate.

The last checkbook binder is different. It is the full-sheet variety but bound by a strap with a clasp, which holds the binder shut. The style is not anything I have seen before.

I stop and press the back clasp button. It slides easily, and the checkbook pops open with a click. The account name is printed on the top of each check: "TERRITORIAL INVESTORS, A WASHINGTON PARTNERSHIP, SEYMOUR GALITZER, MANAGING PARTNER."

The checks are of the old-fashioned green stippled variety that tear off, leaving stubs behind in the book. The bank issuing the account is not the local Snoline Commerce Bank, where everyone does business with Harvey Narver. Uncle Si chose Seattle First National Bank, which has no branch in Bethell, to hold the funds of this partnership.

The Territorial Investors check stubs are old and curling, the bottom ones faded. I flip the stubs with my thumb, like a deck of cards. Only twenty checks have been written in twenty years. The first stub bears the date August 4, 1954.

All the blanks on the stubs appear to have been filled out by a single scrivener, the handwriting cramped and shaky. I try to recall the signature on Si's will; is it the same as the shaky check signature?

Picking up some of Si's old monthly bank statements bundled in their envelopes with rubber bands, I blow off the dust and look at Si's personally written checks that the bank processed, honored, and returned. The cramped shape of the signature's letters and the numbers written on the checks are identical to the writing on the Territorial Investors stubs.

I see that only a single check is written on the account each year at the end of March, and the listed payee is always the same: Haver Limited, a Limited Partnership. No explanation for the payments is entered on the stubs, but the check amounts grow dramatically and steadily throughout the '50s.

The first checks to Haver Limited began at $7,500; then, in 1962, they increased to $50,000. In 1967, six years before Si's death, the annual checks rose to a huge sum—$165,000 a year. Each year since, I see, Si wrote a check for $165,000 at the end of March to Haver Limited, including this year on March 31, three weeks before he died.

I riffle through the other books, trying to find the Territorial Investors deposit record, but see nothing but the infrequently used checkbook I took out of the desk drawer. I find Si's personal account at Snoline Commerce, the deposit book opened in 1965 and marked with the name Seymour Galitzer. The deposit amounts were written in on the stubs.

I cross-check the dates of Si's deposits with the Territorial Investors checks written to Haver Limited in 1972 and 1973. Within four days of Territorial Investors paying out $165,000 to Haver Limited, Si Galitzer deposited $41,250 into his personal account. An even 25 percent of each Territorial Investors check.

I paw the books in the box for Si's older personal checkbook records and find ten years' worth. In each year he deposited in his personal account at Commerce Bank one-quarter of the amount Territorial Investors paid out to Haver Limited.

I go through the pile on the desk one more time, but there is no Haver Limited account book. Whoever possessed that account book, it was not Uncle Si.

Si owned shares in both Haver Limited and Territorial Investors; that was obvious. He received money from them year in and year out. It is a puzzle to me why Si would transfer Territorial Investors money to a separate account only to automatically receive back 25 percent for deposit into his personal checking account.

I find a stack of files labeled "tax returns," Si's personal IRS returns. The signature page shows Si had no accountant. He did his tax work himself.

I look carefully through each year's tax return for entries showing Si's interest in Territorial Investors or Haver Limited partnerships. I find nothing. There is no evidence in Si's taxes that he was a partner.

Tax fraud, I think. Si's operation of Territorial Investors looks like money laundering, the age-old process of hiding the sources of cash by running the funds through a series of accounts. I recall from my law school years that money laundering was commonly employed for decades by crooks and scam artists everywhere, and then I stop. The partnerships are part of Si's estate. The rest is none of my business.

On the other hand, Harry would have to list and value the partnerships on Si's estate inventory if Si was a partner. As a part of valuing the partnerships as assets on the estate inventory, I might have to find out what the partnerships owned. Perhaps Harry already knew.

I pick up the Parker pen and shake it before scribbling on a scrap of paper. The tip skims smoothly across the paper like a boat on a wave of ink, leaving a flow of cobalt blue in its wake. The color of the writing on the Territorial Investors stub entries. The color of the writing on Si's personal checks. There is nothing sinister here, but I wish I could read the memory of that pen.

Miriam makes a noise behind me.

"Snooping?" she says as I jump in surprise at the sound. Her face brightens at her successful sneakiness, and she grins. "Gotcha thinkin' something dirty!" She cackles like an intoxicated chicken.

I cap the Parker pen, place it in the case shaped like a coffin, and hand it to her.

"Take care of this," I say. "It knows more about your old man than either of us ever will."

* * *

Floyd helps me silently with a loaner spare tire, but the VW won't fire up. He offers Miriam a ride back. "Unless you and the new squeeze got something else in mind." He winks as he wipes his hands on a rag. I do not want to dignify Floyd's gibe with an answer.

"I'm traveling in the limo, buddy," Miriam says to Floyd as she slaps the Lincoln's side. I can feel Auntie Riva wince. She would have a conniption if she knew Trudy Galitzer's daughter sat in her car.

I pay Floyd and promise Miriam I'll drop her off at his station.

"Keep both hands on the wheel, Perry Mason." Miriam leers at me as Floyd lifts up the VW's front axle with his tow truck and turns toward home, his paint-streaked automotive invalid trailing behind on its two rear wheels.

As I drive back to Bethell, I am not sure whether I should mention the safe deposit keys to Harry. *Perhaps not just yet*, I think. Not until I know they were in fact Si's and not the Hirsch family jewels.

CHAPTER 20

Two Women with Grandchildren

* * *

KATIE'S RECOIL FROM ME HAS extended the entire week, and I do not know how to interrupt it. In one sense her behavior is entirely too clear; I have disappointed her, but I can't figure what has triggered her antipathy, and that is utterly unsettling. A part of me says this rejection is so unacceptable, I must respond.

But there is more at the root of Katie's outburst. Harry committed some act unknown to me that resonates a revulsion in Katie so intense, it infects anyone associated with Harry. Her assumption is that however terrible Harry's conduct may have been, some unspoken level of loyalty will prevent me from seeing it her way. I think in Katie's mind, the Hirsches, the Galitzers—and the Kings, for that matter—will always come first for me. It makes her feel different.

I pore over the last few weeks for a clue. The notion that Bethell MOTs are a faction is on Katie's mind; that's certain.

Two weeks earlier, by chance, we had a beer late in the afternoon, after work. Sitting at the Elbow Room bar, Katie spotted me, waved, hesitated, and then walked over.

"Want to join me?" I asked.

"Well," Katie said, "I guess for a minute." There was that delay again, a nod, and then she slid onto the stool next to me, waving off the bartender.

"Funny," she said, "that you come here, of all places. I never ran into any of you all here or, for that matter, wherever I might be, and then in less than a month I see you again and again in this dive."

"So what do you mean by *you all*?" I asked.

"You know exactly what I mean," she said, turning red. "Don't try to make a big deal out of it."

"*You all* means all you Jews, doesn't it?" I tried to soften it up by smiling, but my cheek muscles were tense.

"No, it didn't mean that, and don't put words in my mouth. See you." Katie rose, and each set of eyes in the café watched as she strode by. I tended to be pleased when I saw others watching her. But that day I remained puzzled.

You all felt flung down as a roadblock to *you and me*.

Is Sadie Miriam Welger *you all*? As Uncle Si's daughter, she is inside the circle. But why? Based on what Harry told me, Si had been no more in Miriam's life than a name on a birth certificate. Miriam's estrangement from her dead father contrasted with her prominence in a will that Si and Harry had crafted with deliberate exclusion of Frank, Si's only brother.

I was a personal witness to the farm's importance to the Galitzer family. Whatever their differences, Frank Galitzer and his family, like Uncle Si, had remained in Snoline County and cared for their father, Grandpa Morris, out at the farm when the old man was riddled with cancer. Both men had sacrificed to keep and expand the holdings. The farm had a certain grandness to each member. The MOTs all thought well of the Galitzers for sharing its rolling meadows, pastures, and tree-studded forests. It's hard to believe that Miriam, a total stranger, is the intended owner of this vast place.

I ask myself over and over why Uncle Harry permitted Si to do this to Frank and his family. It is impossible for me to believe that Harry did not guide Uncle Si to exclude Frank from inheriting the family's most prized possession. I saw Harry mislead Frank about Si's will. Harry's words led Frank to believe the farm would be his.

I am confused. It seems to me that each generation of Bethell's MOTs worked hard to preserve their homes, their businesses, and their savings for the next generation. Riva lives in Zayde Albert's home. She runs Fulton Jewelry, as did my father.

Who owns them now that Zayde and Leon are dead seems irrelevant, as long as it is a Hirsch—either Pearl or Riva.

The junkyard still belongs in the King family. You can't tell whether Harry or Dale is the owner. To them it doesn't seem to matter.

I thought the Galitzer farm would be no different. Stay in Bethell. You are entitled to your family's possessions. It's your birthright. Uncle Si's will—drafted by Harry—seems to break a compact. It disrupts the order of things.

* * *

It is Sunday. The weather is clear, and I long for an invitation to go outside, but no one is asking.

I feel overcome with a need to talk to someone about my confusion over Miriam's inheritance of the Galitzers' farm. I can't mention this to Riva. But Katie already has no use for Harry. It occurs to me that this may be a chance to make up with her. Simultaneously I feel a fear that Katie has already ended our budding relationship, and I will no longer have the pleasure her spirit exuded when we ran together, along with the incidental bumps of hips, the touches on my arm, the scents of her heat and breath when she panted at the end of a run, the energy pouring from her. Grieving with her over Ritchie was intense and intimate.

My obsession with Shira did not turn on what we shared but on my fantasy. With Katie I feel a familiarity of time and place and a sense of good fortune. In her absence I am sad and acutely aware of our separation.

I conclude it is time to go to Katie's place, pound on the door, and talk it out. What can she say? "Get out?"

On the other hand, I can make a grander gesture. I can propose we take Tiffany and have an outing. The weather is great. Maybe a picnic at Todd Park. And I'll take Tiffany on the swing. In my lap.

As I head out of Riva's house, my step feels lighter. I believe I have persuaded myself that Katie and I will clear the air and return to where we were before. The walk to her house seems to take less than the twenty minutes I expected.

As I turn onto Second Street in Mill Town, where Katie's small home sits in the middle of the block, I see a white convertible. Katie and a good-looking man my age are striding together toward the passenger side. I gasp involuntarily as I recognize Butch Strohmeyer, the owner of the *Daily Herald*. He places his hand on Katie's back, as if to guide her to the door that he is holding open. I see Katie glance about for a second, then, not looking at me, she steps into the front passenger seat.

I freeze, standing in the middle of the street for a moment, the promise of Sunday's sunshine evaporating. A honk out of nowhere...The driver coming toward me is waving, as if he knows who I am, waking me from my paralysis. I have no idea who the driver is. I wave back.

The aftershock of seeing Butch Strohmeyer with Katie makes me wonder whether I have fabricated yet another relationship where none in fact exists. Katie has never mentioned Butch, but in a small world it's no wonder she would be the object of attention. I heard that often enough in the whistles and catcalls while we ran.

Then I ask myself, Who is taking care of Tiffany? Curious, I walk up to Katie's house and ring the bell. A woman dressed in jeans and a work shirt opens the door. She is a silvered version of Katie.

"Hello," she says. "What can I do for you?"

"I'm Nathan Hirsch," I say, "and I apologize for bothering you. Should have called first. Sorry to interrupt. I'm looking for Katie."

"No bother at all. I've heard all about you, Nathan. My daughter has filled me in on her new running bodyguard. Katie's not home. I'm her mother, Phyllis Miller. Don't look so disappointed. I'm the best you're going to get this afternoon."

Phyllis laughs just like her daughter. And I think she's laughing at me.

"It's nice to meet you Mrs. Miller," I say. "I might leave her a message." That sounds strange coming out of my mouth, but I have no other excuse for ringing the doorbell.

"Please, it's Phyllis." She has a kind voice. "And it's nice to meet you in the flesh. I knew your dad and did business there at the jewelry store. Katie has told me what a nice fellow you are. Why don't you come in? My granddaughter is asleep. There's a homemade pie in the fridge, and one piece has your name on it."

"That's kind of you, but it's not necessary. I just thought I could settle some things with Katie. I guess I just missed her, in more ways than one." I find myself rambling. I imagine my emotional underwear is showing. I must look like a saddened dog in a rainstorm.

"If you don't sit a minute, what am I gonna do with that pie?" Phyllis says. "Look. I heard about it a little. You two had a disagreement. That's why you're here, right? Maybe there's room to start making up now by eating some pie. Anyways"—she laughs—"talking to me will be better than talking to my daughter. I'm a better listener. She's the talker of us two."

I acquiesce and step into the living room. Tiffany wanders in, sleep dusted from a nap. I crouch down low and wave to her.

"Hi, Tiffany," I say. The little girl looks at me warily, grasping her grandma's leg like a sailor clinging to the ship's mast in a storm.

Hopeless, I think. Hopeless. She's the competition, and I will lose every time. I feel like a failure, lacking as I do the vocabulary to light up a baby's eyes.

Tiffany's thumb lodges in her mouth. Its placement looks permanent. There is a chapped spot on her cheek, red as a ripe raspberry patch, where her hand lay while she simultaneously sucked on her thumb and napped.

Tiffany reminds me of my obsessive childhood sucking on my left thumb, never my right. She and I, we have that in common. In my bed, my left index finger would spontaneously seek the vermilion of my lip, steadying the inserted thumb just as a glottal click would rise between my tongue and the roof of my mouth. A small seepage of saliva would wet the pillow under my cheek in a pleasurable way that, to this day, I cannot describe in words.

For a moment I envy Tiffany, her thumb. That thumb, the substitute for her mother's breast, is worth longing for. We share that too. At least you have the thumb, I think.

Phyllis lifts her granddaughter up into her arms. "Honey, let's get our guest some pie." The two wheel around toward the kitchen and return with a wedge of confection on a plate for me and in a dish for Tiffany. The peach pie, the color of summer poppies, smells warm and pungent.

"Katie made it," Phyllis says. "And this one loves it, don't you, darlin'?"

Tiffany attacks her dish with gusto. Half of her first bite makes it to her mouth. The other part drips dangerously toward the carpet. From nowhere Phyllis has whipped out a napkin and catches the wayward piece.

I marvel at her anticipation. "Nice catch."

"It's the nature of parenting. This sweetheart"—she pats her grandchild—this is a beauty."

Tiffany eats without acknowledging her grandma's adulation, her hands working her spoon into the pie like a tiny steam shovel.

"They come number one, you know," Phyllis says. "They stay on your radar screen at all times. Bobby never understood that."

"I'm not sure I know any better."

Phyllis shoots a look at me. "It's hard for you, isn't it? Never been around any little ones before, I bet."

"Not really. I was always the little one in my family."

Phyllis is not laughing. "Men. It never changes. You get big and strong. And you're the babies. You want Katie to think about you when her mind is on Tiffany. That's all she cares about night and day. Day in and day out. And believe me, you wouldn't want it any other way. The kind of woman who puts a man up on a pedestal, an imitation of Papa most likely, they're hard. Not one drop of the tenderness you want."

"My aunt Riva put my grandpa up there."

"I didn't say that. You did. And I do know your aunt; we grew up together. My bet would be she is the other kind, all right. I'm sure she loves you, but I wouldn't want to put my slippers under her bed if I were a man. It's the children who make women the softies that men need."

"So what did I do wrong?"

Phyllis puts her hand on my knee. "I'm not about to talk about that. Besides, you've made up already and don't even know it. You came here, after all, and ate some of that peach pie. Shows you care, doesn't it?"

I throw up my hands in mock surrender. "I'd like to confess, but I really didn't do anything. We were running out on River Road. I told her I'm helping my uncle Harry with Si Galitzer's estate, and all of a sudden I'm the bad guy."

"*Bad*'s not the word for you at all." Phyllis's face has become rigid, stony. "But I will give you some advice, since you asked for it. There's serious business going on here. This angel has to be raised right. You decide what you want at this house with my daughter. And be straight about it. Don't pretend to be after one thing when you want another. Think about that. I am not being a mother here. I am giving you advice, after all."

* * *

In the month since I published the notice of Si's death in the *Daily Herald*, the bills have trickled in and then ceased. However, the time to file claims has not run.

Another clock is also running. I still have no word from the bar.

Back at my basement lair, I read the paper for the third time and think about checking on Riva at the jewelry store. Then I remember she has headed off to go shopping at the Piggly Wiggly grocery. She promised to pick up some ice-cream bars to stock in the fridge for me out at Rivers End. Eskimo Pies. My favorite.

I hear the doorbell ring upstairs. A chime, actually, three modern notes. An elevator sound. I wait for two more chimes. They seem to grow insistent as I walk upstairs and open Riva's front door in my socks. A woman stands there in a billowing print dress, her purse held in front as a shield. Her gray hair parts in the middle and is bobby pinned on the side. Her face is not unpleasant; her eyes are blue and open. But lines from her nose curve past her mouth, arcing toward her chin. It is as if she is aging from inside out, her lips plain and lined. She is in her late fifties.

"Yes?" I ask.

"You must be the young Hirsch lawyer." Her words are unbending, an announcement. "You look like your father, whom I knew."

"I don't think know you, though."

"That's right, but I want to talk about Mr. Galitzer's estate. I saw the newspaper notice. Saw your name on it." She leans forward with some embarrassment. "There is some money owed."

"And you are?"

"Trask. My name is Lilly Trask."

I start to tell the woman she needs to file a claim. She shakes her head.

"I don't want any trouble," she says. "Just a few words." A gust of wind blows the woman's hair, and she reaches for the railing to steady herself. The metal wobbles. The wooden treads that support the rail creak. I look up the street for Auntie Riva's car. The little Evanson kid is on the sidewalk across the street riding his tricycle. Playing cards are clipped to the wheels with wooden clothes-pins. The rattle of his spokes against the cards flows up and down the street. It is the sound of a loose bearing.

"Mrs. Trask, what about meeting me tomorrow at Steve's Diner with the executor, Harry King? We can talk about your claim."

She vigorously shakes her head. "I don't want no one to know I'm here. Mostly not those Kings. That's why I came to you." Now the woman searches the street herself. "I would prefer that this meeting be private," she whispers.

"I'm not sure I'm the one to talk to. That's all."

"Just your help will do fine, I'm sure."

Her insistence on secrecy has both of us whispering. The breeze and the clatter of the Evanson kid's simulated motor are louder than our voices. A part of me wants to tell her to put it in writing, but her quiet insistence raises my curiosity. Territorial Investors. Haver Limited. Now this.

"Mr. Galitzer had a farm," I say. "Outside town on Route 20. We could talk there. Are you sure you don't need an attorney?"

"I don't want no lawyers involved," she says. "I don't need nobody on my side. I suppose out at his farm will be fine."

We agree to meet on Tuesday after my appearance in justice court.

* * *

Sitting in Si Galitzer's living room, Mrs. Trask wears the same dress. She is perched on the edge of the sofa, her back straight, unwilling to sit in deeply. It is as if she is a bird prepared to flee on a moment's notice.

"I hope you told no one about this," she begins. I shake my head.

"I don't live here anymore, Mr. Hirsch." Mrs. Trask speaks in a plain style, but her voice has a musical quality, lilting backcountry notes that float her sentence endings up in the air.

"We are in Alaska. The mister came down here with me. He's at the hotel in Everett if you want to check on me or anything." She smooths her dress over her legs as she talks, her hands insisting on neatness and propriety.

"In the old days," she begins. Then she stops herself and starts again. "Mr. Galitzer has some money of mine. Mr. King is the one who recommended I see Mr. Galitzer and your father. Do you think I could have some water?"

"Sure," I say. In the kitchen I find two coffee mugs and fill them at the sink. She seems older today, closer in age to Pearl and Riva.

I return to the living room and hand Mrs. Trask a mug. She takes a drink, thanks me, and continues.

"I can't talk to Mr. King. I went with him, went to Havana once. I can't remember when specifically, but in the years after the war. I just want my money from Mr. Galitzer's estate, that's all."

"Harry is Uncles Si's—Mr. Galitzer's—executor," I say. "Why not ask Harry directly?"

"Mr. King warned me off a long time ago," she says. "I come to you because your father, Leon, was always fair to me."

"How much money did you give to Uncle Si—Mr. Galitzer?" I ask.

"That's nice, the way you all call one another 'uncle.' Like family."

I hear that phrase *you all* again; Mrs. Trask sounds like Katie.

"Twenty thousand dollars is the amount," she says. "I don't think it's a lot, do you? And I am pretty sure you'll find a record."

"Do you have anything in writing, like a receipt that shows the amount?" I ask. "Perhaps a canceled check or a bank withdrawal?"

Mrs. Trask nods. "I earned it working, working for Mr. King. He was the one who…who—" Mrs. Trask stops again and looks for a word, then finds one. "Mr. King introduced me to Mr. Galitzer to invest with him. It was the only business I did with Mr. Galitzer, nothing else."

"What did you do?"

"I managed a trailer park for Mr. King. That's all I did." Mrs. Trask seems to stumble over this rather simple question. She has become agitated as she answers me. I decide to pass up the issue of what she did and return to the business transaction.

"What did Mr. King tell you about the investment with Mr. Galitzer?"

The question allows Mrs. Trask to recompose herself. "He said this was my opportunity to make some money. Mr. Galitzer would invest it for me but wouldn't take my money directly. Mr. King said to buy cashier checks. At Snoline Bank. There were to be ten of them, all made out to a company. That's what I did each week for ten weeks."

"The bank would have copies."

"You know, that Mr. Galitzer was a clever one, but I kept the copies." She hands me a stack of yellowed duplicates. There are ten cashier checks, each for $20,000. They are dated ten days apart, beginning on June 5, 1955, each made out to Territorial Investors. Two hundred thousand dollars.

I whistle in spite of myself. "That's a lot more than the twenty thousand dollars you're asking for, Mrs. Trask."

"All of the money came from Mr. King. My part was only twenty thousand. I earned that money, believe me."

"Who is Territorial Investors?"

"That's what Harry told me to do." I note Mr. King has disappeared, and Harry has surfaced in Mrs. Trask's dialogue. "Have the checks made up this way, Harry tells me. He said Si Galitzer knew about all the foreclosures on the Indian reservation, knew all the old Indian property titles, knew where all the bodies were buried."

I must look puzzled. "I don't have a clue what you're referring to, Mrs. Trask. What bodies?"

"Perhaps some more water." She hands me the mug with an uplifted face. She must have been pretty when she was young, I think. When her face stretches and her jawline suddenly emerges from the puffy flesh, she looks youthful for a moment, a snapshot of the past.

"You know old Mr. Galitzer figured out where Highway 90 was going to go. Everybody talked about it. And after World War II, he made a bundle when the state highway people bought it from him. That's how he could afford all the farms around this place. I imagine his son could figure out where the next highway would go too. I'm not a lawyer, but I know a little about foreclosures."

"I didn't know about any of this," I say. "And it's none of my business, but did you pay any taxes on this money?"

Mrs. Trask looks flustered. "Mr. King said he'd take care of my taxes like he did for all of my money. Now, I'm not claiming to be an owner of any of Mr. Galitzer's real estate. Don't want a share of the pie, just my money and a little interest. Do you have anything stronger than water?"

I retreat to the kitchen again and open the shelf where Harry stashed the Canadian VO less than two months before. I take the bottle and a Coke back into the living room. Mrs. Trask pours bourbon into the cup without any Coke.

"This will be fine," she says. First a sip, then a swallow. "I want no trouble with Harry or anybody else. I would like my money sent to Alaska. No trouble. There should be no problem." She puts her hand on my knee, a confessional gesture. "Besides, I understand Mr. Galitzer's got no family anyway."

"Not true," I say. "There's a daughter. An old marriage."

"I got a daughter too." She takes another drink, as if what is to come requires medicine first. "I gave her up during the war. The money's not for me. They say she's got kids. That makes me a grandmother. And I haven't seen my grandkids. I need the check."

Mrs. Trask is swaying a bit. She's getting tipsy, I think. She drains the remainder of the bourbon in the mug, a straight shot swallowed like a person who likes her liquor.

"Your father would understand," she says. "He was so smart. All of you Hirsches were smart. I knew Riva; we went to Eastwood Elementary together. I knew your grandma too. I used to wash her hair at Irma's. She told me I was pretty. I *was* pretty—too pretty, maybe. Riva probably doesn't remember me. I was so nice then, but I wanted to live on my own. Too sassy for my own good, I guess.

"Up in Seward I'm respected. The mister and I, we fish a little, for sport mostly, during the good weather, the steelhead runs and spring king salmon. The mister is a lot older than me. He used to be a milk farmer. Although we own the property in Alaska, he needs the warm weather. We winter in Sugar Beach in Hawaii." Mrs. Trask is on a roll, the bourbon in charge.

"Mr. Hirsch, I want the money so I can see to my daughter. Maybe if I come in there with the money for her kids' education, maybe a new house, it's all the same to me. Maybe she'll talk to me. The mister and I never had no kids."

"I can't do this without Harry King," I say. I think about having a conversation with Harry about Territorial Investors. I imagine saying to him, "Uncle Harry, what do we do with all this cash Si Galitzer put into the Territorial Investors' account?"

"You'll think of a way," she said. "You should have seen Harry King after the war. Was quite the local sport in Bethell. He bought this yellow Cadillac convertible. 'Let's go south,' he said, and we drove on down to California, right through the border at Tijuana down the Baja Peninsula. Drove for three days straight before we stopped on a deserted beach. We drank gin from a bottle, with the top down in the sun most of the way. Even in the rainstorms.

"Harry was a gentleman on the trip; don't get me wrong. He always gave me a gas station to do my business. And the other part what he wanted was complicated—maybe not for your generation, but different for me. He had this camera and wanted me in the buff, so to speak, on the sand, and I admit it—dumb as I was, I loved it. It actually made me feel free. I could stretch down there. Foolish, though, as it turned out.

"We bought some weed too. Harry spoke that Hispaniola stuff. We smoked and drove, and it felt like the night sky was a road, let me tell you. He never laid a hand on me, though. Was always a gentleman until I wanted the pictures back. Then he said, 'Tit for tat. I want you to do something too.' But even after that, he never called me a name, never called me a...a whore, though I used to tell myself that's not what I was. I just had to get the pictures back, and I did some favors. That's all."

She stops and begins again. "Dear me, I said too much, didn't I?"

A silence of judgment fills the room. I sense that presence of others watching what I am about to say or do. Their murmurs coincide with what I have heard. The very people I have been taught to respect have wrongfully used this woman and then discarded her.

I clear my throat, feeling hot and clammy. Mrs. Trask has receipts that support her veiled declaration that Harry and Si were somehow profiting from prostitution in Bethell. These activities poured assets into Si's estate, perhaps further. I dare not ask Mrs. Trask more questions. I fear the answers will lead closer to my father as well.

I have no authority but rightness to do what I am about to promise.

"I'll see you get your money, Mrs. Trask."

She sighs deeply. "Thank you, you're so kind. You sound like your father."

I turn pale at this statement, but Mrs. Trask does not seem to notice. "I believe you will do the right thing for me."

As she stands on the steps, Curt McPhee comes around the corner. I forgot about the caretaker. Lilly and Curt stare at each other, he uncomprehending, she anxious and upset. Glancing with disgust at me, McPhee turns back toward the barn. Each time he sees me out here, it's with a woman, I think. I resign myself to being the worst in McPhee's opinion.

"Oh dear," Lilly Trask says, "oh dear. I've been seen."

"That's Curt McPhee. Worked here forever. Would he know you?"

"Never seen him before, and that's the truth." Mrs. Trask has turned pale and is breathing hard. I offer her a lift.

"Not necessary," she says. "I'll be fine." She stumbles toward the car. The engine wheezes and refuses at first to start. Then, as if thinking better of it, it begins to stir. The car jerks and bumps as she turns the wheels for the gate and the highway beyond and drives off.

I trot across the gravel in the dark to my car. I would never forgive myself if she had an accident. I decide to trail her, just to be sure she makes it. And as I pilot down Route 20 toward Highway 90 and Everett, I feel as if I am being followed.

Lights strike my rearview mirror. Behind me, a car disappears into the shadows before reappearing like a smoky phantom magnetically drawn by me.

CHAPTER 21

Lilly Trask Reminds Nathan of Harry's Role after Leon's Death

* * * * *

I TRAIL LILLY TRASK DOWN Highway 90 back to her hotel in Everett, trying mentally to put the pieces together. Lilly told me that somehow she was a prostitute, and Harry paid her. And she invested some of it, at Harry's direction, with my dad and with Uncle Si.

Following Harry's orders she delivered Si Galitzer money at a time when he was buying property out on the Tamlips Reservation, which was being foreclosed. Some of the money was hers. It's clear she believed the property might be in the path of the interstate freeway turnoff to Highway 90. But nowhere in Si's records have I seen any paperwork showing he owned blocks of land other than the farm at Rivers End.

I feel hamstrung. I can't talk to Harry. But I promised Lilly Trask. I am surprising myself. Somehow now it matters what I promise.

It has started to rain. The car I sensed following me is nowhere in my rearview mirror. Lilly pulls off the highway in Everett and into the Best Western Motel on Hewitt Street. I drive past, turn in the lot of an adjacent gas station, and shut off the engine, on the lookout for any car tailing us. No one follows Lilly into the motel parking. It seems as if hours pass. I sit in the car without moving, my breath the only sound. The windows fog up.

I am certain no one has followed me to the motel. I open the door, walk across the parking lot to a lit phone booth, and call Katie's home. The phone rings three times, and I hold my breath. Then Katie answers.

"I know it's late," I say. I have to begin somewhere. "I need to talk to you."

"I heard you were here" is all she says. I sense she is being cautious, but she seems open.

"Phyllis gave me some good advice," I say. "I need you—that is, I need you to help me, to talk to me now. About lots of things. Us maybe in there too." I stop. Cars grind by on the highway. Their sounds echo in the phone booth, as if it is a stereo speaker. Katie is silent.

"Maybe you've got something else to do," I finally say to the void on the other end of the line.

"Not really," she says. Her reticence to speak is so unnatural, I feel unnerved. Perhaps I shouldn't bring her into this Galitzer mess. What is it to her? On the other hand, who else can I tell? Who else cares enough about me to listen?

"It's going to take a while to explain," I say. "It involves Si's estate, Harry King, my father, and somebody else I met today. What I found out. Things aren't as they seem."

"They never are," Katie says slowly, carefully. Her words are uncharacteristically few, but they give me such comfort I think I might weep.

"I'm coming over right now." I rush to the car and start the twenty-minute run north to Bethell. As I drive I feel the unanswered questions chilling the inside of the car. Lilly Trask's simple request for money carries with it the swirl of a corrupt world in Bethell that was staining three men I knew. I grip the wheel, thinking about the roles Harry, Si, and my father played in this woman's life. It was one thing for Trudy Welger to trap Si into marriage; it was another for three men like them to benefit from prostitution.

For the first time since I returned to Bethell, I have ceased seeing my own life as the centerpiece on the table. Harry has held out on me. He's the one who has a lock on the facts surrounding Si's life. And his death. Remarkable.

It is true as well about the death of my father, what I know and don't know. What Harry knows and hasn't told.

That day five years ago, Harry reached me by phone. His call let me know my dad had died from a sudden heart attack.

"Your dad is dead. No easy way to say it, but I'm sorry—for you and me both. Now you gotta be someone else. Get your butt to the airport. There's more shit hitting the fan than you can know. And call your mom. Tell her you're on the way."

Pearl was inconsolable. "I've lost my life," she wailed when all I had said was "Mom?" My tears dried up immediately. Her loss was going to be bigger than everybody else's.

I called Auntie Riva too. She was alert but drained.

"If you have to get a cab at Sea-Tac Airport, I'll pay for it. Nobody can come and pick you up. Your dad was a good brother, Nathan. Stay for a while at my place when you get here. I don't think I want to be alone."

"Right," I said. "OK, I'll do it."

"That's what you get for being old," she said. "They die around you, and the quiet of the night is too noisy after a while. You will stay for a while?"

"Yes," I lied.

There was a sigh on the other end of the phone. It was as if I could feel the Northwest rain, blue, gray, and soft on the roof of the Hirsch family home, Riva standing in the hallway outside the dining room, the receiver of the old wall-mounted phone in her hand.

"You are all I have," she finally said.

"I love you," I said, and I hung up.

I packed my law books in a bag. Why, I don't know. I had no doubt I would not touch them. I had no appetite for tangles of evidence, the prohibitions of criminal procedure, or the arabesques of income tax.

I sat on the synthetic seat covers of a 707 beside two strangers as the jet looped out of the storm-filled Maryland sky toward Seattle, dodging the unstable air, thunderstorms, cloudbursts, and tornadoes that dotted the Midwest in the late-summer heat.

The family jewels, I thought. Dad left the jewels in the safety deposit box. That was what he'd told me that day the two of us stood inside the vault in the back of Fulton Jewelry.

I had left a note for Shira, briefly explaining that my dad had died. I signed it "Nate." No "love, Nate," no "I will be thinking of you." Just "Nate."

Shira had a project. She was composing an article, a note on some new but bizarre and obscure Federal Trade Commission regulation. It would be published in the law school journal. Shira was on one of her marathon hurtles through the task, reading, absorbing, interpreting, digesting, ruminating, writing, rewriting, editing, thinking night and day. Her body odor had become pure, like tidal kelp. Submerged, she no longer breathed oxygen. Her face had taken on an alabaster sheen.

I wondered why Shira stayed with me at all. I was at best a mechanic, a processor of other lawyers' ideas. Shira, on the other hand, was birthing the law, a genesis in motion driven by conviction and purpose. I was a photo of a lawyer, Xerox quality at best.

The plane roared through the summer night toward Sea-Tac. Would they bury my dad before I got there? How did I feel? I tried to remember the days when he liked me. Not many, although there was a real respect when the law school acceptances began to roll in. The scholarships took him off the hook, I guessed. But I thought, That's not generous. That was cheap. My dad never bellyached about money—to me, anyway.

Was there a point where I had changed what my dad thought about me? I recalled the day I squealed on Ritchie to my dad, the words I chose to describe what I had seen Katie and Ritchie doing, detailing what I'd seen in those tangles of surplus military blankets in the garage storage room, that makeshift bed in Ritchie's hideaway right under the nose of everybody. It was astounding I was the only one who had seen the room where Ritchie secretly took his girlfriends. I told it all.

My father, in my memory, looked down at me. I was thirteen, skinny, little, wavering, insolent, my solemn eyes filled with false righteousness. There it was. Out in the open. I was just as good as Ritchie.

My father had peered over his glasses, his eyes glaring back as if I had been spying on him, as if he and not Ritchie had been in bed with Katie. As if I had wandered in on them wrapped together in the spray of pink flesh, wordless sounds and movement, moans without a mouth, a writhing snake. My dad had set down his paper slowly, his belly wrinkles rising with his breath through his white shirt. They looked like foothills below the Cascades. He sighed, looked at the ceiling, and walked to the door. Not looking at me.

"Nothing good happens to a snitch," he said, speaking to the door in front of him. Then he ordered me out. "Into your room and turn up the radio. Now."

The plane wobbled a bit. A woman in the seat next to me smoked a Tareyton, crossing and uncrossing her legs with the regularity of a metronome. She gasped when the plane dipped and dragged on the cigarette for safety. When the flight smoothed out, her breath relaxed, and smoke poured from her nose. I could see lights on the ground between the clouds, a landing path to the Pacific, even though we had barely crossed the continental divide.

My father's death would be a cramping moment in Bethell, a little place made smaller by one more grave. The Fulton Jewelry storefront would be covered with black bunting, as when Clinton Bloch had died and the windows of the Amusement Center, his little store in the Hirsch Building, were draped with Halloween-like décor, black drapes swept upward like a witch's smile.

Clinton Bloch had been only a wrinkled chain-smoking stranger. What about losing someone I might love? A word, maybe a longing to have Dad's thick hand rough up my hair or softly hug me before bed. Little gestures.

I wasn't sure my dad had ever wanted to touch my hair. Once he told me to keep a crew cut.

"The curly stuff makes you stand out, for Christ's sake. Makes you look like a foreigner."

I dreamed about the Bethell barber shop, the smell of lavender and spice, and the puffs of talcum powder for your neck, the scent of lubrication oil on the shears, the heat of the electric clippers on my neck, and the rhythmic snicker of the scissors in all three of the barber chairs at once, and I suddenly was asleep high over the Rockies, sailing toward a Jewish funeral in the rain forest.

The midnight runway at Sea-Tac Airport was soaked. Blue runway lights flickered off the nighttime puddles. The ground transport from the airport to Seattle was old territory. I turned up the collar on my navy surplus pea coat and slung my bag over my shoulder like a carbine rifle.

I thought about hitchhiking to the Seattle bus terminal but dismissed it as quickly as the thought had bubbled to the surface. I needed to catch the last run to Skagit, Whatcom, and Snoline Counties. The airport ground transport would stop in Seattle, right at Bob's Chili, across from the old dirty Greyhound depot on Eighth Avenue downtown. That was where I needed to be in less than an hour, or I would have to lay out Auntie Riva's dough to a cabbie just to get a homemade bed in the house my grandparents had given to her.

Only two persons clambered with me onto the Greyhound in Seattle to Bethell and parts north, a fat woman and her whiny kid, its gender indistinguishable late at night. The woman crooned, "Now there," a cookie produced from her cloaked stomach folds, the child instantly grasping the sweet with a careful grip, slowly eating with glum bites.

The driver with weary sideburns swung the bus door shut with a slam, knocking the ash off the cigarette dangling from his lips, and started the engine. The Greyhound ground its gears, and the engine rumble rose to blot out the sound outside as we rolled down Highway 90.

I thought more about Ritchie than about my dad. Everything would have been different if I had not told Leon. Ritchie would not have left home. He would not have entered the marines, wouldn't have been sent to Southeast Asia. I looked at my hands, my nails soiled a bit, the nails ragged.

Everything would have been different. These words tumbled about my head like the unmuffled engine until I fell asleep in the back of the bus, my bag under my head.

Auntie Riva was awake when I banged on her door, her eyes red rimmed. She kissed me but said little. The bed on the main floor, the old maid's room behind the kitchen, was made up with Bubbe's scratchy sheets and two old woolen blankets covered with a handmade quilt. After passing out on the plane and the bus, I found it hard to sleep. I kept seeing myself sitting there in the dining room as Bubbe's blind eyes searched me out when I yawned or squirmed.

The next morning Harry King was at the back door, his too-short topcoat darkened with rain, his hair plastered to his scalp. Riva had put a coffee cup in his hand by the time I was dressed.

Harry nodded at me. "Your mom's a wreck. Makes me glad I'm single." Harry slurped a little coffee with exaggerated lips, and before I could speak he slapped the cup back on the table. "Riva, we gotta go. We got some lawyers' business to take care of."

We scurried in the rain to Harry's car. He drove to King's Auto Parts.

"I kinda set up now in old man Lynch's house," he apologized.

"Uncle Harry, Mom, and Auntie Riva told me nothing on the phone. What happened to my dad?"

"You don't want to know, believe me." He stopped and looked at me hard. "I got your dad's stuff with me. We're gonna get some things done."

We ducked quickly into the ramshackle house used by the Kings as an office. Harry slammed his beaten-up briefcase on an old table as the tapping raindrops the roof seemed to signal the search for a leaky entry to drip on us. Harry pulled out a red-lined will document. It looked fresh.

"First, I never got your dad to sign a will. So here it is." Harry flipped through to the last page. There were two witness signatures, one Harry King, the other R. Seymour Galitzer. But the testator's line, with "Leon Abel Hirsch" typed clearly below, was blank. The witnesses had witnessed nothing. The document Harry was showing me was a forgery.

Harry pulled a real estate deed out of his pocket. It was signed "Leon A. Hirsch." He slipped a transparent vellum over the deed's signature line.

"There," he said. "Try it a bit."

"What are you talking about?" I protested.

"Try it," he insisted. "Nobody's gonna look that close. You're both left-handed. I want you to sign your old man's hand here. Rest of the stuff's taken care of. Don't worry."

The anxiety was building up behind me like water behind a dam.

"Look," he said, "this way your mom gets everything she's entitled to. There's a trust for her and no trouble with Riva. She'll be fine. Your grandpa Albert set up some accounts for Riva. The problem is without the will, your mom's out in the dark on all the Hirsch family stuff—the business, the home, all the savings from before the folks got married. There's a lot. Pearl don't share it with Riva without this. They'll scratch each other's eyes out. You know what I'm talking about. This way we're doing what your dad woulda wanted done."

I saw my days as a lawyer over before I started. "I can't do it, Harry. Auntie Riva would spot the difference in the signature immediately."

"Look here, Nathan. You are a hell of a mimic. You'll pull this one off too."

"And if I don't?"

I watched Harry's face for some doubt or hesitation. His blue eyes didn't blink. They were glacial. Then he sighed. "You shouldn't know, but God forgive me, you better know. He wasn't home. Your mom thinks there was a card game at the VFW. We're sworn to that one."

"What are you saying?" I felt Harry, the master puppeteer, pulling my strings.

He lit an old cigar sitting in the ashtray. A stray wrinkled stogy. He sucked at the lighter, bending the flame into the butt. Smoke billowed up. Harry waved the cigar in the air. "That's why I got to sit out here. Dale says he can't stand the smell of these goddamn things in the office."

Harry is going to conjure his next line from a puff of smoke, I thought.

"Maybe I oughta quit." He looked reflective.

"So where did he die?" I asked. We sat there in that makeshift office, the rain beating on the roof. Somewhere a leak plinked a musical note.

"Your dad, he had this friend, Harriet Sorensen. I don't think you knew her. Lived on the Sterling side of town, on the other side of the highway. Went to grade school together, your dad and Harriet. Actually with me too, all of us. Anyway, Harriet and your dad, they stayed friends all these years."

Harriet. I had this image of a woman with multiple chins and a curly bobbed permanent. Bad teeth. My chest constricted. The words thickened in my mouth and stuck behind my tongue.

"So?" I sounded shaky. I cleared my throat. "And what else was made up? Was there a heart attack? Or was there something else?" I sounded smart-ass, sarcastic, but I was knotted with doubt. I knew it was best if I knew none of the details, yet I had to know them all.

"No, nothing else, I swear." As he spoke Harry shook his head from side to side, like a lion tearing a piece of meat from a carcass. "It was a heart attack. He was at Harriet's house over on East Tenth Street in Sterling."

"Was Harriet married?" Why for the life of me was I asking this?

"Nope." Harry puffed clouds, but his eyes remained unblinking. He stared me down as he slowly answered. "Never did. Worked as a secretary at Saint Paul's Hospital all these years."

"Harry, I need to know the truth. Was Harriet my dad's girlfriend?"

"I wasn't there with a candle," he said," but he was naked when the medics got there, so it doesn't look good. But don't worry. The coroner's report won't say a word. I have that on a guarantee. Nobody wants any trouble here." Through the smoke he watched me, his eyes unblinking, cold.

The picture of my dad's rage at Ritchie so many years ago flared up in my mind. Even through the wall with my radio on loud, I had heard him screaming with scorn.

"Sleeping with some chippie?" my dad had cried. "With your talent? What the hell's wrong with you?" His voice had been laced with venom. As I heard the blast of his words, I vomited on the floor in my bedroom, choking on the vile act of betraying my brother. But my illness blocked me from hearing what was actually happening. Now it was clear to me. My dad, Leon, had been talking about himself and not Ritchie. He was talking about Harriet Sorensen.

"Give me the pen," I demanded, and Harry put out his cigar. I scratched away my anger at Leon A. Hirsch's deception by repeatedly writing his name. Make it better, I thought. Make it just like that scrawl on the old deed. I imitated my father's cursive in the same way I automatically imitated so many things he'd done when he was alive.

Harry, impervious to my emotions, observed, judged each effort, and encouraged me on.

"Good. That's better." Then he said, "OK, let's try it."

The paper was stiff. Typed underneath the line was "Leon A. Hirsch." The ink lubricated the tip of the pen, and I swung it onto the will. With each stroke I felt awash in dirty water, sinking toward the bottom. Then I was done. I read the lines on the last page. The document I had just forged named Harry as my mother's trustee.

Harry took my forgery up close to his face. "Looks like he did it, all right." He relit the cigar, as if the smoke would no longer interfere with our work. "This happens to be the best thing you ever did." He folded the will in half and blew some extra smoke on it, as if that layer of scent would somehow legitimize my forgery.

"Don't worry," he said. "The coroner's going to do the right thing. It's taken care of now." Harry lapsed into that polyglot mix of Yiddish and pig Latin that all of them—Bubbe, Riva, Leon, and Pearl—used to talk around the little ears of children.

"So utshay your aptray, *ferschtayes*? Get it? Your old man was at the VFW, that's all. Him, Si Galitzer, and me."

Harry got up and put his arm around me, his hand holding the cigar resting on my shoulder. "Your dad's looking down, smiling."

Harriet Sorensen couldn't leave my mind. "I thought we didn't believe in heaven."

Harry sighed. "You're just a wiseass. Can't help it." Then he grabbed me by both shoulders. "Remember one thing and one thing alone. You shit in your britches before one worda this comes outta you. 'Cause if it does, Pearl's screwed. So just keep your eyes on the ground, dammit."

"You keep saying the coroner is going to do the right thing. What do you mean?" I waddled out to the car. I wanted to get behind the wheel and honk the horn in alarm.

"The coroner's report has got the pickup where it happened at the VFW, that's all. Nothin' wrong, nothin' illegal. All the rest is just the way it should be."

* * *

Sitting in the darkened car outside Katie's house, I can still hear Harry's voice. And the coroner's report on Uncle Si? Harry would say it is just the way it should be too. All the details true except with some fundamental omission, some central lie. Harry is deep into all of us in Bethell. He understands what everybody wants so well.

CHAPTER 22

Nathan Tries to Get to the Bottom of the Break-in at Si's

* * *

EVEN AS I PULL THE Lincoln up to the front of Katie's Mill Town bungalow and turn off the motor, I can't stop stewing about Harry's role in Si's affairs and his death. Katie will ask me about it all, and I need to be prepared to answer.

I take a deep breath and summarize to myself what I know.

Si did his own tax returns, but they did not show Territorial Investors or the cash paid out by Haver Limited, as they should have. None of the records I found reveal what Uncle Si, as Territorial's managing partner, did to make so much money. And the records made no mention of any loans from outsiders, no mention of receiving money from Lilly Trask.

Harry has made me feel like a rubber band. Pull me one way to do a job and then pull me back from doing it right because I owe him. Well, he promised Lilly Trask too. And who knows what else he promised and to whom. Maybe he's made too many promises to me as well.

I finally get up the courage to leave the car and ring the doorbell. Katie is wearing sweatpants and a yellow T-shirt with "MAUI BOOGIE" printed in black over a huge green cannabis leaf. It is after eleven. She is barefoot.

"It's too late," I say. "Thanks for coming to the door. Tiffany's asleep?" I am hemming and hawing.

"She's not up."

"Well, I'll admit, I didn't really come to see your daughter."

Katie smiles in spite of the hour. "Mom told me you were out here last Sunday. She liked you right away, and believe me, that's rare. She can pick sins off a saint.

Anyway, she says I'm a jerk." Katie's eyes drop away from my face. Then she looks up. "I'm sorry for..." she mutters, searching for a word. "OK then, being a jerk."

"Stop it," I say. "Besides, it was a great excuse to get served peach pie." I can't believe I said that. I feel stupid.

We sit on her couch almost in the dark, leaning toward each other in the spot where I ate that peach pie, Katie's knee against mine.

"Let me tell you why I'm here in Bethell," I say, "and why Harry is involved. I'll start at the beginning."

I divulge the whole story, my shame in leaving Washington, DC, my anxiety as I wait for the bar to let me practice in Washington, the death of Uncle Si, Harry asking me to help with the estate, my discovery of the Territorial Investors and Haver Limited partnerships, and now my meeting with Lilly Trask. Katie does not interrupt.

I try to wind up my confession without whimpering. "Harry's helped me with the bar association, helped me get the job with the court, and hired me to handle the estate. Without him I have nobody else. But I don't like what I see." I stop talking. I am out of words that will let me off the hook.

A light from a passing car on the street throws a shadow on the curtain. It stops in front of the house, uncertain whether it has reached its destination. I hear it idling. Then it revs up and drives off into the night.

"In pretty deep with that Harry," Katie says. "Which is where it seems he likes folks to be." She looks at her watch. "Good grief, it's two in the morning. What about a cup of chamomile tea?"

I nod.

She goes into the kitchen and returns with two cups in hand. "Do you have to deal with him?"

"What choice do I have?"

"You sound like everybody else." Katie sighs. "Everybody around here knows that when you get into trouble, Harry King is the one who can help you out. Need a loan? Need to get out of jail? Need a favor from the police? Want to put a baby up for adoption? You name it. Lawyer King is the person."

Katie takes a swallow of tea. I can hear the trickling sound in her throat. "I don't know the details, but if a girl gets into trouble, he can get you to Seattle too, so you could…" Katie looks for the right words. "You could get fixed up. In a little town like this, that's a service as valuable as anything."

I notice that Katie's shoulders are hunched a little as she speaks about Harry and the dilemmas that have forced people to seek his help, as if she is curling up to ward off a blow.

I think about the car passing outside at two in the morning. It was just a car. I am getting daffy. I consider asking Katie if she was one of the girls who needed Harry, then dismiss the notion. What about Ritchie's adoption? Finding him had been one of those Harry King favors Katie was now describing.

This was never the way I wanted to see Harry. What did Riva or my parents know about Harry that they never told me and didn't want to know themselves? For that matter, what did Si know about Harry? Was it enough to get him killed?

As Katie and I sit, I recall out loud what Wally Richmond let slip that day in the holding cell before his arraignment.

"Before they charged Wally Richmond, he told me someone else was involved in the Union Wear break-in." It feels like a confession as I say it. "Maybe he might give me something. Or maybe his wife knows."

"I don't like this," Katie says. "There's something unhealthy for you in all this. You're too close to everyone involved. I think you need to get out of it now." She shivers unaccountably, the outdoor cold of the night seeping through the room.

"I have to get some sleep," she says. "It's almost time to get up." Yet she doesn't move her leg. I feel the tension in her thigh muscle as she presses her knee into me.

"Can I just rest on your couch for a couple of hours?" I ask. "I can clear out before Tiffany wakes up."

"Don't worry about my daughter. She'll sleep through a hurricane. Let's try something else," Katie says. Her voice is both sleepy and wide awake.

We sleep together for what is left of this May night in Katie's double bed, surrounded by pillows, me in my underwear, Katie in her sweatpants and T-shirt. We lie there hugging each other, not making love, just keeping warm. I doze and wake intermittently, dreamlessly, smelling Katie's hair, feeling her relax with sleep, her abdomen swelling then receding like the tide. Finally I sink into slumber, forgetting to worry whether Tiffany will find me in bed with her mother in the morning when the sun rises.

* * *

Lennie Richmond has that same dimple in her chin that I remember from kindergarten, but her blue eyes are rock hard, and the weeds are high around her wood-frame one-story house. She wears jeans and a sweatshirt. She won't open the screen door.

"And what do you want, Nathan?" Her skepticism could corrode the screen mesh.

"I thought Wally might talk to me," I venture.

"Why should he?" She looks at me with curiosity, the way one stares at a fly before swatting it. "I thought you're working for Harry King now. Maybe he could put in a good word for you." A baby waddles up to the door and sticks out his tongue, as if to taste the screen wire. Lennie pulls the child back by its diaper.

"You get back there, mister," she snaps. Mister plops on his rear, surprised. Then his face erupts in a wail of sorrow like a cloudburst.

"Look," I say, "nobody knows I'm here. I'm on my own, and believe me, it's better that way. You know I was Wally's attorney at his arraignment?"

Lennie nods her head. "So he told me." She is listening, that hard-as-steel look still in her eyes, but a part of her must be thinking there may be an opportunity in this for her.

I press on. "Something's not right about the night Wally went into Union Wear and found Si Galitzer dead. I don't believe for one minute that Wally had anything to do with it or that he just happened to be unlucky that night. I believe somebody put him up to go in there."

Lennie laughed like a crow. Unfunny. "So you say. And he had no reason to go in there and break open a cash register other than at that moment we were so flat broke we were eating unboiled macaroni."

Under the grimness Lennie is still pretty. When we were children, I used to stare with admiration at her drawings. Her small hands with the dirty nails could, with a paintbrush or with pastel chalk, draw beautiful pictures. Lennie possessed an artist's natural touch.

I look at her hands by her sides—adult hands, reddened and thin, the nails painted pink but chipped and broken.

"I can still see those pictures you made in school," I say. "When we were little kids, you used to be terrific." As soon as it leaves my lips, I realize how trivial, patronizing, and banal I sound. I am so obvious in what I want. And Lennie never wanted me. She cut down the Bethell boys like a scythe, and then Bethell's men. A female power mower who somehow never targeted me.

"Nice try, Nate. Your timing is a little dated, and I don't need your stale bull. Unless you can give me some cash and maybe a job, and throw in a babysitter too, I really don't have the time to chat about the old times and what a great artist I was. I get a little check from the county and some food stamps. It's not even close to breaking even. Wally's left us in a hole. Now, if you can get me some dough, maybe get Wally out of jail, then you get the Nobel Prize. Or some other prize." She leers at me through the screen.

"Tell Wally when you talk to him that I still want to help," I say. "You can reach me at my aunt Riva's if he says he'll meet me."

Lennie makes no answer, then deep inside her house a bump of a metal pail causes her to turn away. A baby's wail like a siren rises, followed by Lennie's epithet.

"Jesus, you keep outa that. You hear me? Jesus. Good-bye, Nate." Lennie slams her front door, and I retreat to my car.

The next day Riva calls down to me in the basement that there's a phone call. It's Lennie. As I answer, Riva stands there staring at me with all the disapproval she can muster. I cup my hand over the phone.

"I don't know why I'm doing this." Lennie's voice sounds as if she's calling from a foreign country. "Wally says he'll meet you. But guess what. It will have to be at his place in the Monroe Hilton. He's a little tied up now."

I don't know what to say. "This is important to me, Lennie. I'll try to help you. Really."

"Send me fifty bucks. If I don't get the money, Wally will forget about the whole thing. Make that a hundred."

"Is there anything else I can do for you?" I ask.

Lennie's answer drips with bile. "You know, Nate, if I could bank promises, I'd be rich. I'll be truthful with you. I told Wally he should stay away from all of you. Somehow you people seem to get the cream while the rest of us suck hind tit. But for whatever reason, Wally thinks you'll help us out. A fat chance, I told him."

I hear the refrain again—*all of you*. This is how Lennie sees it. I can't blame her. This miserable drama involving her husband seems to have cast Jews in every role: Si as victim; Harry as the financial rescuer; and now me, the snoop, with promises. And is it possible one of the MOTs is also the coconspirator who sent Wally into Si's store in the first place?

"You get the money today," I promise, "and if you need anything else, I'll try to help out." The last statement is a lie that just slips out. I have no idea how to get Lennie anything she wants besides money.

* * *

I sit across from a smoking Wally Richmond in the Monroe Reformatory common room. It is like any other government building—well lit, linoleum floor, beige walls, and gray Formica tabletops. Just the absence of windows gives the room away as a prison inner sanctum.

"So how are you doing here?" I solicit Wally's response with a false caring note. It's alarming how much guile I have been practicing. I seem to be copying Harry more and more as time goes by.

"It's not so bad here," he notes thoughtfully, almost professorially. He is sporting a new tattoo on the back of his right hand. It is a cloud with the word *Smack* written inside. Across the room a black inmate with a giant Afro and a cake-cutter comb sticking in it talks to a young woman holding a baby.

"I been in worse. You never saw the Green Hill Academy for juvies. You needed a razor to keep the guards offa you in the shower. I was in there twice."

I remind Wally of what he told me at the arraignment. "You said somebody else might have been in Si's that night."

"Hey, not might. Somebody was. The guy was on the floor, his head split open before I got there. I just screwed up by taking his dough."

"Why'd you happen to be there, Wally?"

"I ain't going there," he says. "Not going to talk about that. This is over in two years. Less with time off for good behavior. Don't want to be stuck to my bunk with a knife when I'm not looking."

"Wally, I don't want to be involved in anything any more than you. I just want to know about why you happened to be in there."

"How you gonna help out Lennie until I get outta here?"

I hesitate. "I gave her a hundred bucks on my way in to see you. Maybe I can help some more." Slowly I have let another false promise leak out.

"You should tell her to come and see me." He looks closely at my face. I suspect he is searching for some sign I am fooling around with his wife. He must be satisfied I'm not, because he shrugs and starts to talk.

"I was supposed to be looking for some files," Wally says. "Some papers. The old guy wasn't supposed to be there late at night. Actually, seeing him lying there scared the living shit outa me. I felt a little set up, you know, like I had been suckered in to being in the wrong place at the wrong time. But he's helped me out so far, so why should I think he was screwing me?"

"Did Harry King hire Miffler to make the deal for you with the prosecutor?"

Wally looks at me. I keep talking. Lynn Reilly's rule: keep trying on the facts like clothing until something fits.

"I know he got you the money for the case. He told me he loaned you the money."

"Loaned me hell." Wally snorts with derision. "He gave me the dough. Lennie knows it. So does Miffler." Wally stops. "I already talked too much."

"You were looking for papers with the name Territorial Investors on them, weren't you?"

"I ain't answering a goddamn thing about what I was looking for."

I bait another hook. "I'll be sending another check to Lennie if you help me figure this out. You don't have to tell me anything. I'll say a word, and if I'm wrong, say so. Otherwise say nothing, and we still have a deal, OK?"

Wally lights a cigarette, sucks in a cloud, and exhales in my face.

"Don't smoke, do ya?" he says. "I just want ya to feel what it's like to be barbecued."

I take a deep breath. "It was Harry who had you go in there, wasn't it?"

"Wrong. Wrong. Wrong." Wally is nearly shouting. The guard looks up. Wally realizes he is standing. He nods to the guard and then returns to his whisper. "You don't know nothin' about nothin'."

Nothin' about nothin'. I hear it, though. Even Harry's expressions have soaked into Wally.

"Then let me tell you something about something," I say. "I said Lennie would get some money, and I came through. Do your part."

Wally signals the guard and gets up, not looking at me.

"This is getting dull." Wally's eyes glance about the room. "You seem to be hell-bent on finding out what is other people's business. Sneaking around is not cool, and you know about sneaking around. That woman you run with, she used to be your brother's high-school heartthrob and all that, right?" Wally turns back, his face a wicked grin.

I am stunned. How would Wally, sitting here in the Monroe Reformatory, know about Katie and Ritchie? And for that matter, how did he know about Katie and me?

He looks at me with contempt. "It was Frank Galitzer, you dummy. He wanted me to look around that store. Si and Frank, those two didn't talk. Bad blood. Frank couldn't even set foot in the old family business, so he asked me to have a midnight look-see. Paid me a couple of bucks. Wanted a file that belonged to the old man, their dad. Store was his, after all, if you asked Frank. From his point of view. So it wasn't as if I didn't have the owner's permission, see."

"What did Frank have you looking for?"

"Something about where the roads go in the county. The old man was famous for making a fortune when Highway 90 was built after the war. Supposed to have dug up a whole bunch of public records from the '30s. A big secret. That's how he figured out where the highway was going, I guess. Frank wanted to find his father's papers on the highways. And anything else interesting too, I could take. That was to be my bonus. Nobody gave a rip whether I grabbed his brother's dough from the cashbox, believe me."

Wally gets up and walks away, saying over his shoulder, "More money for Lennie."

* * *

On my way back to Bethell, I try to separate the wheat from the chaff of Wally's story. I cannot believe that Frank would have been involved in his brother's death, but it was possible he urged Wally to look around for papers he wanted. For my entire life, my family—and all of the MOTs—lorded over the rest of Bethell in civility. They saw there a propensity toward violence that was unseemly—contemptible, actually. That was the way the MOTs talked. "Those people are like animals" was a regular statement from Leon or Pearl.

Uncle Frank was no animal. He wanted justice; his share of Morris's estate was the measure of his birthright. Si's death gave him nothing. I would wager Frank longed to gloat in his brother's face, not stand over his grave.

I remember Auntie Mae and Uncle Frank at Si's funeral. Uncle Frank's face like the granite grave markers, Auntie Mae, her eyes cast down, dismayed, not looking at any of the other families there, holding her son Victor's hand. It is impossible for me to accept that Frank had set Wally in motion.

And Wally's use of Harry's phrases sticks in my mind, his unwillingness to discuss Harry with me in any way. Wally is so in debt to Uncle Harry he would deflect me toward another suspect.

Impulsively I drive to the King junkyard where, at twilight, Harry is talking to his brother, Dale, at full speed as I bring the Lincoln to a halt. Harry laughs as I lumber out of the car.

"You look like thunder on the road in that old Lincoln. Dale, we gotta get Nathan something better to get around in. So where you been lately? I ain't seen you for a coupla days. Now you come tearing in here. What is it that can't wait?"

My head is full of questions The words *Territorial Investors* and *Haver Limited* bubble up. I say them out loud. No introduction. No verbs.

Uncle Harry eyeballs me the way a boxer might stare at an opponent before a match.

"That's a lot of questions," he says, although I have asked nothing. "For your sake you better write 'em down, because we're not going into that tonight. So let 'em stay questions until tomorrow."

Harry stops for a moment.

"I'm going to give you a little Bethell on-the-job training. You be at Steve's first thing in the morning, and we'll talk about all those things you've written down. And put on your traveling clothes. We're going places early mañana."

But in the sunny morning, Harry is in no hurry to leave Steve's. He is content to read the paper and puff away on his premier cigar of the day. When I try to raise the subject of the two accounts, he shuts me down. "Not here. Let's take a ride."

Harry's green Buick is parked outside. We drive with the windows open, the sun filtering through Harry's cigar smoke. The Buick has not weathered the winter well. The passenger door rattles. The engine grinds like a washing machine in the spin cycle on each bump.

Harry chews on an unlit cigar. Even with windows down, the tobacco smell and ashes reign. The Buick is heading out toward the Tamlips Reservation, where there are Douglas fir and madrona trees everywhere.

"I want ya to meet somebody," Harry responds when I ask where we're going.

"I didn't see any Territorial Investors tax returns," I say. I have to shout to be heard over the Buick's orchestra of noises.

Harry looks at me sharply, his new false teeth brilliant in his mouth like a car grille. I shiver at his stare for that short moment.

"I don't get it," Harry starts. "What are you doing with the *goyishe* gentile girls again? It's enough already. A little here and there, OK, but this is getting regular. You've been seen, Mister. Big-time." Harry sounds like my father. All knowing. I think of the car following me at Rivers End and the night at Katie's.

With a sinking feeling, I wonder if Harry got a call yesterday from Monroe Prison. Did Wally give him a report of my visit? I can just feel it in the air.

At the top of a rise, Harry pulls over. The road ahead is old Highway 90. Barely visible, it snakes in front of a rolling meadow, farm fences, and a tree line that marks the beginning of Carter Creek, which leads directly from the Tamlips Reservation into Puget Sound.

"Lemme say this, buddy boy. The new highway's gotta go somewhere. State and feds are going to pay for it. That's the system. So then, who's gonna figure out where? Answer is old man Galitzer. Si's dad had a nose for these things. Way back when, he picked up this piece of ground. Everybody else saw the res. He saw a turnpike."

We glide down the hill. A house lodges in a driveway, out of place like a desk in a road. Three broken-down cars and trucks sit outside, dusted like floured fillets before being dropped into a deep fryer. Harry pulls in and honks. A man in his thirties wearing jeans, an army-fatigue jacket, and a pigtail emerges from the front door. Behind him are dogs and a plump woman. Small children in the shadows. Big smiles all around.

"Long time no see, man," Pigtail says and holds out his left hand, which Harry grasps. I see a long sleeve on Pigtail's right side but no hand.

"Nathan, say hello to Henry Three Bears. Henry, this is Nathan Hirsch." Harry went slow on my last name. "We do business for what, twenty years now, Henry? Something like that. Nathan's helping out these days. I'm getting older, you know."

Again Henry extends his left hand, this time to me, and I take it. A dried salmon. Maybe his right hand is busted.

"You must be OK if you're with Harry," Henry says. "Leon was your kin?"

"My dad." I watch Henry's face.

"Saw your brother play ball. I was over there too." Henry fingers a patch on his fatigue. A Screaming Eagle. The 101st Airborne. I can see now that the right sleeve is pinned shut. A part of me wants to ask how Henry lost his hand.

"Henry takes care of this place," Harry says. "His family's been here now for what? Five years?"

"Since you got me outta the slammer, Harry."

"Didn't do a goddamn thing, Henry. Was your time, that's all."

"Yeah, and I believe in the tooth fairy." Henry turns back to me. "He's way too modest. So what's up, Harry?"

"Nathan and I are just walking around the place. Talking some."

"We gotta talk too," Henry says earnestly to Harry. "Me and Alice are about ready to spring back and pay you off."

Harry acts pleased. "Well, all right for you. Hats off." Harry points at Henry's wife, as if to orient me to a tourist site.

"His Alice runs the whole show at Skarbell's Lumber. Used to be in packaging and now is in the Skarbell front office. Best secretary you ever seen. Borrowing the money from the bank, Henry?"

"Nope. Better yet." Henry looks excited. "BIA gave us a deal. Home loans for the whole tribe. Money's due in soon."

"That's real good. Fine." Harry lights up his cigar. Smoke envelops all of us in a fog of mismatched words.

"It's always good to see you, Henry, and good luck with the home. Nathan and I, we'll just walk around now."

One dog follows us to the old fence. Inexplicably it begins to growl as we walk west down the pathway toward a pasture. I almost sense a warning in the dog's tone.

My curiosity is stronger than my common sense. "Why was Henry saying he and Alice are going to pay you off with a loan from the BIA?"

"Because I bailed him outta jail three times, and he jumped bail once. He gave me the title to the house so he could pay me for his bail money. Plus, there's the pack of losers he's been gambling with. I settled up with everybody and got the house in the process." Harry's words came out testy, but then he quieted down.

"Henry lost the hand in a car accident after the war. Likes to pretend it's a battle wound, but his unit never left Saigon. Always thinks the BIA is going to help with a home loan. Let him have his dreams. Meantime, nobody is fooling with this real estate."

I can't leave well enough alone. "How many houses did you get this way?"

"I didn't get any houses *this way*, wise guy. Go stick your nose in the county title records if you don't believe me." Harry stares out toward the horizon. "OK, so we hold a house or two, maybe fifteen, maybe twenty. What's it to you, anyway?"

Harry walks off, puffing on his cigar in a way that can only be pretend anger. Why does he want me here?

In the far meadow, I see eight trailers parked like an air squadron, with three cars and one truck in front. I see a woman come out of a trailer in a robe accompanied by a man. They embrace, and the man gets in the car and heads out toward Highway 90.

"Whose property is that?" I ask. "Also in the highway path?"

Harry doesn't answer. Instead he asks a question. "So where's this Miriam Welger staying?"

"In Seattle," I say. "I told her she could stay out at the Rivers End house, but she said it's too spooky. I thought about calling up Auntie Mae and Uncle Frank, but I'm not sure how they feel about Miriam and the inheritance and all."

Harry gasps at my words, then starts laughing, as if what I said is the funniest thing he has ever heard. The laughing turns into a phlegmy cough. I think he might pass out. Finally his voice recovers.

"How would you feel," he says, "if you got cut outta the Hirsch Building by some stranger you never laid eyes on? You'd shit a brick, I bet. That little girl ain't seen the end of Uncle Frank, and neither have we."

The wind blows a scent of the brackish waters of Carter Creek and the smell of fertilizer across the pasture. A single cow chews on grass at the far corner. Another pickup has pulled into the trailer squadron, and the driver is met by a woman. They walk into another trailer together.

"Uncle Harry," I say. "What's going on over there?"

"I wouldn't know," he says. "It's a trailer park. And you should mind your own business."

My blood turns cold. Lilly Trask told me she managed a trailer court for Harry that was a cover for prostitution. This is part of the property that is owned by Territorial Investors. And so is the operation going on there. I can feel it.

"Is this Territorial Investors account my business?" I ask. "What do we list on Si's estate inventory? The checkbook says the balance on the account at Si's death was a cold hundred and fifty thousand."

"That's good," Harry says. "Now there's no problem paying your bill."

"What's in the partnership, Harry?"

He looks out over the pasture, his eyes shining. "You got a hearing date with the bar association. They may call you to Seattle, even take your testimony. I got a copy of a letter to that effect, now that I'm your sponsor. Thanks to Mr. Hotshot Washington, DC—Mr. Lynn Reilly, Esquire. Says you took trust fund money from his firm. I think he makes you out to be a *goniff*, a thief. Wants 'em to take your pants down, Nathan. They may want your license." Harry puffs a cloud of Cuban cigar smoke.

My temperature falls to zero. My feet cannot feel the ground. The air smells like a witch's broth; a storm is brewing. I exhale and smell my own breath, a sour odor. There is no place to hide. Snoline County is no safer than Washington, DC. Why had I succumbed? Why had I come back?

"Now, you were asking me?" Harry breathes tobacco. For a moment I think I see a gleam of triumph in his eyes, but as I glance again, all that is left is a sagging concern on his jowls. Harry's head tilts like the head of a dog watching his master.

"Harry," I say. "I took a client but no money. I thought about leaving the Reilly firm. I was dumb, and I know it, but that's not wrong."

"The problem," Harry answers, "is you did it behind his back. You made him look stupid, careless. You made him angry, Nathan. I thought I told you long ago. Don't sneak around behind the backs of your friends. You can get hurt."

I look at Harry. Is he talking about my visit to Wally? What I told Katie last night? Does he know about my meeting with Lilly Trask? Am I being watched?

"Hey, listen to me," Harry says, his face brightening. "This whole thing with the bar will blow over. Don't worry a bit. I got all sorts of folks lined up who loved your pa. They'll put in a good word for you, and that'll matter. Don't worry about a thing."

Harry's face mirrors the same false jolliness, the same bogus fraternal pleasure with which he greeted Henry's announcement of a loan payoff from the BIA. Totally intended to mislead.

You can't fool a mimic, Harry, I think bitterly. I've learned how to copy feints as well as genuine praise.

As I take my leave from Harry, it occurs to me he has distracted me from the trailers and the activity there. He didn't want to talk about it, but I can figure it out. The trailers are being used by prostitutes.

And I should have realized that the first call Wally would make after I left Monroe was to Harry and not to Lennie. Harry knows what I have been thinking but have been unable to say out loud.

I think Uncle Harry killed Uncle Si. Harry can read me like a book, and he will destroy me if he must.

CHAPTER 23

Nathan Travels to Seattle to Try a Hat Trick

* * *

I STEER THE LINCOLN DOWN Highway 90 in a haphazard way, distracted by the three major tasks I have set for today in Seattle. Harry knows of only one.

I need to find Miriam. To my knowledge she has not set foot in Bethell since we traveled together to Rivers End. I have Harry's direction to find her in Seattle and get her to sign a power of attorney naming him as her attorney-in-fact.

"It'll help me deal with Frank," he told me as he tossed an unsigned form to me across the table at Steve's. I marvel that Harry has these printed forms sitting in boxes somewhere.

Harry's name is missing from Miriam's attorney-in-fact form. I have another candidate. Me. I intend to have Miriam name me instead of Harry as her choice.

And Harry has no idea I have also set a late-day meeting with Arthur Curtis, the bar-association lawyer assigned to my reactivation application. Curtis told me nothing over the phone, made no mention of the letter he sent to Harry, but agreed to meet with me. I want to know firsthand why my application has not been granted or denied.

But first I plan to go to the Seattle First National Bank and obtain, by hook or by crook, as many Territorial Investors and Haver Limited bank records as I can glean or wheedle from them. They may hold clues to the nature of the common business enterprises of the Galitzers, Hirsches, and Kings and maybe the other Jewish families in Bethell I have known my whole life.

I am about to put whatever is left of my legal career at risk as I stand in the foyer of the Seattle First National Bank. Without Harry's knowledge, direction, or permission, I intend to get the records of the Territorial Investors account Si opened here. Thus I must induce the bank personnel into believing I am acting with Harry's authority as his lawyer.

I have no choice. Harry has me over a barrel. Continue to aid and abet him, and I'm no better than he is, either his dupe or his confederate. But if I can get to the bottom of his enterprises, I might be able to revive my own status, if not in the eyes of the bar then perhaps in Katie's.

I have no illusions that Harry intends to help me leave Bethell and continue my career elsewhere, no more intention than he has to help Frank and Mae Galitzer or, for that matter, Henry Three Bears. The last person Harry is concerned about is Miriam Welger. Harry helps Harry.

The worst is I am driven by a curiosity both righteous and morbid. I want to know how the Galitzers, the Kings, and the Hirsches have become tarred with corruption in the course of their day-to-day lives. My dad received Haver Limited checks. My mother's bills are being paid by Harry, her trustee and guardian, from the same source.

Haver Limited washes cash from prostitution, payoffs, shady loans, and foreclosures. Harry has acknowledged secrets about the new highways to be built in Snoline County. My bet is the Galitzers, Kings, and Hirsches have used Territorial Investors as their cover-up in buying property within the proposed off-ramp from the highway. Today at the bank, I intend to confirm what I believe.

My disguise is trial-day finery: a charcoal-gray suit with a white handkerchief poking out of the breast pocket, a white dress shirt with button-down collar, and cordovan wing tip shoes. And, last but not least, an imitation Hermes silk tie interwoven with rich burgundy and gold notes, the kind of tie Lynn Reilly wore with ease and aplomb. No mimic with self-respect would own a real

Hermes. I look like the kind of legitimate customer on whom any bank would lavish loans and, I hope, reveal other people's bank records.

I push open the high revolving bank door and approach the reception desk. I smile at the receptionist.

"My name is Nathan Hirsch," I announce in character, wise, experienced, and professional, "and I'm here to see Mr. Stoen."

"Have a seat, Mr. Hirsch." Her face blossoms with a mile-wide smile that I return.

Stoen is thirtyish with long sideburns that signal *I'm trying to be stylish*. He reminds me of all of Richard Nixon's henchmen, who are being torn apart on TV these days by Sam Ervin's Senate Watergate Committee. Mr. Stoen could easily work for Dwight Chapin or Jeb Magruder. But who am I to criticize any of them? I am the Donald Segretti of Bethell, and today my first trick may be my last. My intent is to obtain bank records by deceit, a basis for over a dozen state and federal felonies.

"Thanks, Mr. Hirsch, for calling us. We would be glad to open a new account for you and our mutual client, Mr. King." Stoen has clearly been practicing his handshake. It is firm and warm.

"Well, I appreciate your help," I say. "You know confidentiality is important, and Bethell is so small. Mr. King thinks it is to the advantage of the Galitzer estate to do business in Seattle. The deposit of substantial funds and the sale of valuable local assets can spread rumors through a small town like wildfire."

Stoen nods at me. His eyes attempt to flash the experience that his baby face says he lacks.

"Mr. King is a longtime valued customer," he says, "and we are glad to meet you as well."

"I also want to open an account for myself," I say. "A small safety deposit box. Will that be a problem today?"

"Not at all," he says grandly. "I will get the forms and get you set up with keys right now.

"Keys?" I say with mock surprise. Si's two safety deposit keys are electric in my pocket. "Not just a single key?"

"No, sir." Stoen is all business. "We've got a two-key system here to protect our clients. One into the vault, one into the box." An attractive secretary gives Stoen a portfolio, from which he extracts a set of application forms. He places the forms in front of me. "Will you be using the vault today?"

"Yes." Now a small bit of sweat is gathering on my back. I jump in. "And I almost forgot. The monthly records I've requested during our phone conversation for the Territorial Investors and Haver Limited accounts?"

Stoen shrugs apologetically, a dog's gesture in front of his master. "Do you have written authority from Mr. King?"

I also shrug but imperiously, looking somewhat astounded. In fact I'm not at all surprised. But I push on as if I am shocked. "Mr. Stoen, these are partnership records of the deceased Mr. Galitzer." And then my big lie. "And as the attorney for the estate, I need them to marshal the estate assets."

"But you are not the executor, thus I'm afraid our bank's policy requires that Mr. King gives us a signature before we can copy them for you."

"In his capacity as executor?" I hang the question like Ritchie hanging a curveball. The question is aimed at finding out whether Harry controls the Haver account as a partner.

"Yes and no." Stoen reports like a second lieutenant speaking to the colonel. "Mr. King can sign as either a partner or individually as manager on the Haver Limited account. But I will need a court order regarding the Territorial Investors records—an order, I believe, from the probate court, yes?"

Strike three, Mr. Stoen. Now I know Si alone owned and controlled Territorial Investors, but Harry is both the manager and a partner of Haver Limited. And Haver is the recipient of the profits deposited from Territorial Investors as well as the paymaster to my family, to the Kings, and to Si Galitzer.

I try one more pitch. It is a subpoena I prepared with Harry's signature. This is a dangerous fastball. If I sign a subpoena without my bar license, I will never practice law in Washington. But Harry has let me feed him a number of blank documents to sign, and I have carefully copied his signature in executing this subpoena. My hands are wet, and I dig in my pocket for a Kleenex.

"I appreciate this, Mr. Stoen. That is why I prepared a subpoena for the bank. Please note Mr. King is the signatory."

Stoen examines the paper as if it has been scripted in Egyptian hieroglyphics and then coated with poison. He lays it on the desk.

"Would you like to speak to Mr. King?" I am bluffing, but I carry it off. "I have him available in Bethell." It is a half-truth that Harry is ready to talk with us by phone. Harry has no idea I am at the bank. He thinks that I have come to Seattle only to meet Miriam, and only then should I call him in Bethell.

Stoen frowns, punishing himself for being less than responsive. "I suspect I will need to run this by legal counsel, Mr. Hirsch. I can see why you are entitled to the records, but I'm not sure we can get them today."

"What about the account balances on the day Mr. Galitzer died?" I ask, as if it has suddenly occurred to me to raise that question. "That would be of assistance."

Mr. Stoen brightens. "I can give you the balances. No violations there." He shuffles off to check with his secretary, humming what sounds like a Beatles tune as he returns.

This break has given me time to practice my deep breathing. His secretary smiles at me as she delivers him a paper. I smile back and then realize my brow is sweating. I pat myself dry with my breast-pocket handkerchief.

"Hot in here," I say to no one.

Stoen reads the information to me, his master. "Today there is nothing in the Territorial Investors account, Mr. Hirsch."

"Which is the same as of the day of death?" I suggest.

"No. In April there was a hundred and fifty thousand. That was six months ago," he says. Mr. Stoen is like a pet at this point.

"And the Haver Limited account?" I lean forward to see for myself. There was nothing when Si died in April. But today there's $123,543.

"This is helpful, Mr. Stoen." I take back the subpoena lying in front of us. "Why don't I send this to your legal counsel directly? I'll copy you on it as well."

"Terrific," he says. Stoen is happy the court paper is no longer his problem.

Notwithstanding Stoen's persnickety standards about giving me bank statements, he has revealed that Harry became the sole person who could access both the Territorial Investors and Haver Limited funds once Si was dead.

Harry has controlled the two accounts from the day Uncle Si died. Harry can sign for everyone. In my family he is my dad's trustee and Pearl's guardian. He holds Uncle Frank's power of attorney, and now he is Si's executor. Harry needs nothing to withdraw the Territorial Investor funds and funnel them through Haver Limited to himself.

I can see why Harry did not want me inside his office. I might see all the files on my family, the records of the partnerships, and their bank accounts, and I would know about the funds Harry has the ability to take.

I almost forgot the safety deposit box. I brought Si's keys with me from Bethell, and now I have my own new set. My plan is risky. Possibly when I pretend to open my new box, I can also open Si's by swapping the keys.

I further inquire who will help me with my new box in the vault. Stoen forgot as well.

"Of course," he says. "Irene Pallino, the registrar in the vault, will explain our system to you."

In the vault Stoen introduces Mrs. Pallino, a matronly white-haired woman. I hold her hand in both of mine and tell her what a pleasure it is to meet her. I use every ingratiating move I have learned since childhood, when I practiced on my mother's coffee klatch.

Mrs. Pallino is beaming as I hand her Si's keys and not mine. Clearly she can trust me, which, of course, is her mistake. She leads me to a wall of slots and inserts both keys. The tumblers clank with a click on the first key. Mrs. Pallino retrieves what she believes is my new box and returns to her desk, giving me privacy. She cannot see me as I examine the contents of Si's box and not mine.

The show has begun.

The vault bell rings, and I jump, but its timing could not be better. Mrs. Pallino is distracted by another customer who has entered the vault.

Si's box is replete with legal documents, and I riffle through them quickly. What stands out is a will envelope labeled "R. SEYMOUR GALITZER." The letterhead on the envelope says clearly "LAW OFFICES OF HARRY KING."

I dig deeper and find another will envelope and retrieve it just as Mrs. Pallino begins to look for me. I grab the two wills and quickly shut the box, tuck the envelopes inside my coat, and drop the keys into my pants pocket.

Mrs. Pallino approaches me. She looks disturbed. "Mr. Hirsch, the key numbers you gave me when you signed in do not match the number of your new box."

"Of course," I say. "Wrong keys." I bring out the new ones and start to hand them to Mrs. Pallino. Then I stop. "I'm sorry for any confusion, but I mistakenly brought the wrong documents to store here. The correct ones are in my office. How late will you be open today if I retrieve them now?"

She stares for a moment. "Four thirty," she says to me, her eyes unsure what has happened, "but you must fill out a request for the other box when you return. For our records, you see."

"Of course." I thank her profusely and state I will be back shortly. I say good-bye and quickly leave the vault. I feel her eyes on my back as I leave. I want more time to review the other papers in Si's box, but I am lucky to be out of there without detection.

In the bank lobby, I stop long enough to open my briefcase and place the two wills inside. As I depart I can hear my heels clatter on the marble. I feel as if each step may set off an alarm. I believe I have committed a myriad of federal offenses today to determine that Harry controls the partnerships' monies, not to mention that I opened Si's deposit box without authority.

In the sunlight, the rush of traffic, and the urban street noise, I breathe more easily. I become invisible in the ebb and flow of downtown Seattle. The Lincoln sits in an adjacent parking garage, and I plop into the seat and open my briefcase.

There is a will I have never seen, signed by Uncle Si on February 16, 1967, witnessed by Curt McPhee and my dad. The executor and sole beneficiary is Frank Galitzer. Harry has notarized the signatures.

There is no mention of Miriam Welger.

I pull out a copy of the will Harry lavished on me as Uncle Si's. I brought a copy for the bank's benefit, establishing Harry's status as executor. That will is dated February 16, 1971—four years later, long after my dad's death.

Even though I have been working with this will since Uncle Si's death, this is the first time I have studied the signatures of the two witnesses.

On the top line, I make out of the scrawling "Henry T. Bears." The lower signature is Alice Bears. Her handwriting, unlike her husband's, is elaborate and clear. Their signatures are unnotarized. There is no certification from Harry attached to this 1971 version.

I am not at all surprised. I would bet Harry forged Si's signature and secured Henry and Alice to falsely witness after Si died. He probably told them the same cock-and-bull story about Si's daughter that he told me.

Harry knew that Si had the original will. Harry prepared it. Harry couldn't care less about its existence, I surmise, because he would have the opportunity to destroy the original if and when Si died. I suspect that Harry's ego did not allow that Si might not want Harry to know where he had hidden his will.

The fraud on Uncle Frank and his family is monstrous, and for that matter the deflation Miriam may experience is as well. Harry has transformed her from an outsider to a daughter with an inheritance. The real will makes her an outsider a mere few months after she learned of a dad whom previously she did not know.

I consider driving to the reservation and confronting Henry Three Bears and his wife, Alice, but that is a bad idea. If I do so, they'll run right to Harry.

I assume the other will to be Si's as well. I open the second envelope and gasp. The will inside purports to be the will of Leon A. Hirsch. It is the will Harry alleged my father had never signed.

I quickly recompose myself. My heart is beating like a drum.

Harry told me, "I never got your dad to sign a will." Those were his words to me five years ago, as he pressed me hard to forge my dad's name on a will that named Harry as both executor and trustee.

But my father's real will sits in my shaking hands. I run my fingers across my father's carefully calligraphic signature, dated 1956. The will named my auntie Riva as executor and left the entirety of the estate in trust, as you would expect, to his family. During Pearl's life the trust was to benefit all three of us: Pearl, Ritchie, and me. When Pearl died the estate would be divided between Ritchie and me.

The witnesses to my dad's will were Uncle Harry and Uncle Si. The two signed off in 1956, a decade before Harry had me forge a will that left Harry, and not Riva, running the Hirsch family show.

The family jewels, my dad had said, were the safety deposit keys. His words keep running through my mind. Then it hits me. Uncle Si and my dad used the same safety deposit box because neither trusted Harry. Si took the keys from the Fulton Jewelry vault after my dad suddenly died. Si's presence in the store would have been totally acceptable to Riva or Pearl. He was family, after all.

And Harry had been looking for those keys too. I simply found them first.

To me the pattern of Harry's perfidy is complete. The Territorial Investors partnership was designed as a cutout, a wall concealing the true real estate owner from the world. Harry used Si to hold the cutout company. But Harry, not Si, was the boss of Haver Limited, which served all the families as the paymaster.

Had this arrangement been going on for generations: Albert Hirsch before Leon and Riva, Zolly King before Harry and Dale, Morris Galitzer before Si and Frank? Were the monies paid into Territorial Investors always from ugly sources? Harry's contributions from his illegal businesses mixed with the monies my dad contributed—money from Harry's bail-bond schemes, earnings from prostitution, and the sales of Mill Town homes taken in foreclosure from millworkers who sinned a little on Saturday night and then were punished for the rest of their lives because they couldn't repay the loans Harry made to them to pay their bail-bond fees, court-imposed fines, and, incredibly, Harry's own fees. They gave up their homes and autos to repay the loans.

And who owns the homes? Who rents them back to the former owners? For that matter, who is Katie's landlord? I shudder to think it's Territorial Investors.

My stomach is churning. My family and the Galitzers all knew what Harry King was up to. They financed his illegal enterprises.

Now Harry has become the master of all. The wills, trusts, and powers of attorney he has doctored or forged have placed him in possession and control of the money and property belonging to all of the families, against their stated desires in legal documents to have someone else in charge.

I can see that in each instance, Harry's creation of bogus wills served to make him responsible to no one. In Si's and Leon's concocted wills, Harry is falsely elevated to trustee, executor, and guardian—thus the custodian of the

Territorial Investors real estate and the Haver Limited cash—disbursing money only when the need might otherwise create a problem for him.

I recall the lie Harry told Uncle Frank about the ownership of Rivers End: "A Galitzer is gonna own this place forever."

Harry did not hesitate to tell anyone what they wanted to hear when they wanted to hear it, regardless of its truth.

While Si was alive, he was in charge of the cash that came out of Territorial Investors. To protect himself Harry didn't want to distribute out of the Territorial account. That's why Lilly Trask carried checks to Si made out to Territorial Investors, even though she had no direct knowledge of the source of the funds. Harry never made the deposits. He avoided his fingerprints on the funds going into Territorial Investors because the money was dirty.

Blood is pounding in my ears. In April, when Si was found dead, something had happened that caused Harry to need money, and Si wouldn't release it to him. Possibly he had held Leon's true will over Harry's head. I suspect Uncle Si had found my dad's will when he took the box keys back from my dad's desk.

Or not. Perhaps Harry has no idea Si could have proved he is a criminal.

These conclusions increase my desire to have Miriam name me and not Harry as her power of attorney. I peel down a bit by taking off my tie and jacket. My shirt is wet with sweat. I have a trump card in my hand, and if necessary I can use it to block Harry's schemes.

Miriam's address is in Georgetown, on the outskirts of Seattle, just north of Boeing Field. It is an area with dilapidated houses that look as if they were built at the turn of the century. The neighborhood is riddled with junkyards, repair shops, cheap corner groceries, and sundry stores sitting among the patched single-story cottages that wilt and tilt toward one another.

I find her address: South 912 Lucille Street. I try to settle myself as I walk toward the porch. The path through the grass in front of me is muddy. A baby-buggy carcass lies on its side. At the top of the steps, a rolled-up rug partially blocks the doorway. The smells of curry, mold, and dampness waft over me as I stand there. A guitar is being played inside; the putative artist is struggling to do a blues riff with little success and repeating the effort like a cracked record whose needle can't get to the next groove.

At my knock an unshaven, long-haired young man wearing a sweatshirt opens the door. He is smoking a cigarette and blows the smoke my way, eyeballing me as if I am a cop.

"Miriam Welger around?" I ask.

The doorman shrugs and hoarsely calls back into the house.

I hear that rusty voice answer, "All right. All right. Jesus." I can tell it's Miriam. She walks out of the house with her hands protecting her squinting eyes, as if she never saw the sun before.

"Hey, Nathan." She eyes me up and down. "What's shakin'?" Standing there, Miriam looks like a grown-up Orphan Annie with her wild red hair and freckles. Not friendly. But not hostile either.

"I had an errand in town and thought I could save you a trip to Bethell."

Miriam puts her finger to her lips. "Shh," she says. "Cool it. Let's try a little place where we can talk. Nobody around here has to know about my stuff." Miriam tucks her arm into mine as we walk to the car. "Besides, I could groove on that monster Lincoln of yours."

We sit in a Boeing Field café whose hygiene makes Steve's Diner look pristine. I explain about the problem over the ownership of Rivers End with Uncle Frank.

"You can let your father's lawyer deal with Frank, or you can hire your own lawyer." I let this thought settle in. I suspect the last thing Miriam would consider would be hiring her own lawyer.

"Man," she says, "I just need some scratch. I mean, the home is cool and all, but if he wants it so bad, let him buy me out."

"That's not going to happen. Uncle Frank has no more dough than you. His wife, my auntie Mae, teaches piano to make ends meet."

"You keep up with this uncle-and-aunt stuff. You sure you're not my cousin? 'Cause you're kinda cute, but I don't know if I could get it on with a cousin and so forth." She laughs.

"Well, we're not cousins," I say. "I grew up with your family and your grandpa Morris. That's just the way we were taught to address our families' closest friends."

"So we're not cousins. Then no bar to groovin' together unless you got some squeeze who'd say no." She is plainly toying with me again. "Ever do a little grass?" She winks. "I gotta a little number on me, and we could go over to that park and do this joint together."

I hold up my hand. "Another time, Miriam. Now, Harry King...he's your father's lawyer. He wants you to sign a power of attorney naming him as your attorney-in-fact."

"What happens if I say no?" Her voice is both defiant and uncertain.

"Look, Miriam," I say, "there's going to be some trouble in the estate. There's going to be a dispute with your father's brother, your real uncle, Frank Galitzer. You're going to need some help, and you should think hard about getting an attorney."

"Once my mom got me a public defender on a speeding beef. But that's it. I got no way of doing it on my own or hiring somebody. That takes scratch. Besides, when I get some dough, I'm outta here. It's too cold. A coupla guys hanging at the house want to go to New Mexico, up by Taos. If I could get me some walking around money, I'd go with 'em."

"I have another thought," I suggest softly, as if I have thought up a solution this moment. "You could name me as your attorney-in-fact, and I can try to negotiate some funds for you right now. Anytime you want your own lawyer, I can help you hire one. That's what cousins are for." I flash the ultimate gag grin.

Miriam smirks but then gets serious. "Are you being real? Would you help me out?"

I settle down and nod in a sober and thoughtful way. It is one of my best dramatic moments. I am full of preposterously false paternalism.

"I'd be glad to help out—for a while at least. Let's find a bank around here and get you to fill out this power of attorney. You have to sign in front of a notary."

"Great," she says. Then her face brightens with her own brilliant idea. "Then can we smoke this joint?"

* * *

I am exhausted, full of trepidation from what I found, but there is still one more leg of my Seattle mission. I set a three-thirty meeting with Arthur Curtis in the bar office. Without bar approval I am stranded in Bethell.

My phone call with Arthur revealed trouble. "There are questions we can answer only in a face-to-face meeting," he intoned. It was a damning comment, as if the board of governors had already reached a conclusion regarding granting me the right to hang my shingle out in Washington State.

I find the bar office on sloping Madison Street, less than five blocks from Puget Sound. It's a rented space above a posh eating club, the kind that used to offer white men an elite and exclusive retreat from home. I know that such a world is now gone. Famous lawsuits in the mid-'60s threatened to take away liquor licenses from any club that discriminated based on race, religion, or gender.

While the shared building entrance floors creak with privilege and discretion, the elevator leading to the bar office upstairs is strictly government issue, as is the bar office, with beige walls and Formica desks. I can see the heads of staff members slightly above the low cubicle walls. Their heads bob up and down as if with the music of the clatter of telephones, typewriters, and printers.

A bespectacled man with a wispy mustache meets me, shakes my hand, and introduces himself as Arthur Curtis. He invites me into a conference room.

Arthur looks nervous. The file he carries is disturbing in its thickness. I pray it does not apply only to me as we sit on opposite sides of the conference room table.

"The coffee machine is busted," he says. "What about some water?"

I nod. I am too unsteeled to speak. Arthur rises to get water from a room next door.

I stare at the file and consider taking a peek, but Arthur reappears too soon. He has brought someone with him whom I recognize.

"Nathan," Arthur says, "this is Jerry Dwyer from the attorney general's office." Dwyer still has that one-sided smart-aleck smile on his face I remember from the day Wally Richmond was arraigned.

"Nate and I have met before," he says. "How are you doing, Nate, since the last time we met? You never called me back, did you, eh?" His question is self-answering. Dwyer doesn't offer me his hand. Instead he seizes the file in front of Arthur as if it's his. He opens it and combs through each page, apparently seeking a particular document. He doesn't look up as he talks.

"It's kinda like kismet, Nate, you asking for a meeting today with Arthur while he and I are also looking at some other lawyers. You recall last time we met? I asked you to let me know if you found anything odd in the justice court. Never heard from you. I was kinda disappointed."

"Actually I thought you said you would call me, Jerry, not the other way around," I falsely retort. My discomfort at being in this room at a disadvantage with Curtis and Dwyer must show.

"Whatever," Dwyer answers, still smiling as he flips page after page. He is wearing a three-piece suit of superb twill, unusual for a government employee. His silk tie and button-down shirt could be standard dress for the eating club downstairs.

Arthur speaks up. "Jerry is looking at some things that came up in our review of your activation application. We both have an interest in your answers."

Dwyer looks up at this comment. "So Nate, we've been looking into bad apples in law enforcement up your way. You probably read that between the lines last time we talked, right?"

"Not really," I say.

"Well, let me help you." I note sarcasm in Jerry's voice. "Here it is. We think Sheriff Iffert is a central character in a scheme involving bribes, prostitution, gambling, and shady government contracts. Actually, Nate, it's pretty slick for a backwater like Snoline County. Anyway the investigation leads us to one of his henchmen who, it turns out, is your sponsor, Harry King." Dwyer pauses for dramatic effect. I say nothing; I move no part of my body.

"Our sources tell us you now work for King daily on private business, even while you are supposed to be a justice court PD under his supervision with a limited license to practice law."

"Harry asked me to help him handle an estate for a close family friend," I answer. "I have no knowledge of his business with Iffert."

Dwyer's split face is still smiling on the left and deadly grim on the right. He has a gap between his front teeth that his lips unconsciously attempt to protect. Despite his thinning hair and aviator-style glasses, the gap leaves him appearing almost childlike.

"Well, I am glad you know who the sheriff is. Look, Nate, when this meeting is over, I expect you will not mention it to anyone, and perhaps your cooperation today will help the bar overlook your indiscretion in DC."

I am incredulous. Arthur Curtis has been silent, staring at the ceiling. He refuses to meet my eyes. In the corner of his mouth, he chews on one end of his droopy mustache.

Dwyer tugs on his shirt cuffs, pulling them down from his jacket sleeves. It seems to be almost a nervous habit until I see the cuffs are monogrammed with his initials. It seems to be his way of showing off.

"Arthur," I say to my bar-association host, "I didn't expect or deserve this kind of treatment. Whatever the government has on Uncle Harry or the sheriff has nothing to do with me."

"Uncle Harry, is it?" Dwyer is now laughing, openly mocking me. "Let me show you what your uncle wrote about his beloved nephew."

He extracts a manila folder from the big file and hands it to me. Inside is a letter addressed to the bar. The letter is from Harry.

> While I have supported Mr. Hirsch's application for active status in the bar, I feel obliged to share with you a suspicion that his departure from practice in Washington, DC, was not altogether voluntary. I also believe Mr. Hirsch may have handled client funds in violation of his firm's policies and possibly in violation of our Code of Professional Responsibility. While this information was not known to me until this

week, I felt it incumbent on me to write immediately to the bar before action is taken on Mr. Hirsch's application. I sincerely hope Mr. Hirsch can clarify these issues; however, I also feel this is within your area of inquiry and not mine.

Sincerely yours,
Harry King

The letter is dated June 12, 1973, the day after Harry and I traveled to the Tamlips Reservation, when I asked him about Territorial Investors and Haver Limited for the first time.

Harry's two-faced treatment of me has me stunned. He has all but forced the bar to contact Lynn Reilly, who will certainly not fabricate the facts surrounding my termination as his associate. A part of me wants to end the meeting and dash from the building. A part of me struggles to regain some control of my stomach and my breathing.

First I say to Arthur, "I need you to tell me whether my conversation here with Jerry Dwyer has any bearing on my bar application."

"Look at it this way, Nate," Arthur says. "We are looking at Harry King's license as well. Anything you can do to help from your unique vantage point as—" Arthur stops and gropes for a word. "As his *protégé*," he finally says.

Dwyer grins when he hears the term and looks mirthfully away. I sense he has a desire to use this as an avenue of attack on me.

Arthur continues, "Anything you add to the state's investigation could weigh on your behalf, in particular if Mr. King turns out to have violated the Professional Code of Ethics."

"Fair enough," Dwyer says, as if Arthur were speaking to him and not me. He attempts to regain control of the interview, ignoring Curtis.

"Nate, tell me if you ever sat in with Iffert and King."

"Everybody, including Iffert, would come by Harry's booth at a courthouse hangout."

"Steve's?"

"Yes, Steve's. But I have never heard the two talk business. Do you mind telling me what the connection is between them?"

"Sure, I can tell you that much. They go way back after the war. Iffert was a discharged MP who got into the state patrol. Alcohol led to his being fired, and Harry King and the locals in Snoline were looking for a new deputy sheriff. He has always been totally worthless as a lawman, but nobody seems to run against him. Now Iffert gets a regular check from some company called Haver Limited that was set up by Uncle Harry. Did I get it right? That's what you call him, right?" Dwyer leers at me. "And the bucks are for security services for the King junkyard. Now, that's a laugh."

"I know nothing about payments to Sheriff Iffert."

"OK," he says. "Meantime, Iffert has warmed up to his old buddies in Olympia who are now in the Highway Department. He told them the county needs advance notice for the new interstate highway linkup and turnoff near the Tamlips Res. Claimed the Planning Department required him to do a study for new stoplights, signs, speed zones, et cetera. But the Snoline Planning Department says that's bull. They say the opposite—that Iffert came to them and demanded that same info."

Dwyer closes the file.

"The fact is, your uncle is paying Iffert to give him advance notice of the interstate turnoff location and construction details. And Uncle Harry has been picking up property out on the reservation. He's been buying in bits and pieces. And guess what? Each piece is smack in the middle of the turnoff right of way. What a coincidence."

This is now the third person who has told me about Harry buying property. I would bet a search of the right-of-way buyer's title would show the name Territorial Investors.

"And Iffert's getting his reward through Haver Limited, not a paycheck from King's junkyard. I can smell a connection between Haver Limited and the property buyers." Dwyer is standing now, his knuckles on the table.

I know that Dwyer has been dealt the right cards. I also have picked up cards in this hand, but I need to play them carefully. Arthur is a witness to the meeting in the room. He can affect my status with the bar. If I look like I am reacting to Harry's betrayal, they will both deny me what I desperately want: my bar license and my departure from Bethell.

"Jerry," I say, "this is all news to me. I can sniff around in the estate office and find out something, I'm sure. You may be on to something. Haver Limited is partially owned by Si Galitzer's estate, and those records support the estate inventory."

I choose not to tell Curtis and Dwyer that my family is also a Haver Limited partner. It will only increase Curtis's suspicion that I am involved in the payoff scheme Dwyer is investigating. It will bury me.

I choose my words carefully. "I will see that you get what's in the estate records, but it will take me a day or two. I have no reason not to cooperate."

"That's an understatement," Dwyer adds dryly. "But I want more. I want copies of any documents that are publicly filed by Harry King where he has signed for other people. You know, powers of attorney, estate documents as an executor, trust documents as a trustee, that kind of paperwork. You get the picture. I don't want any private files, no privileged files. I want his handwriting where he has signed for others."

And that has been Harry's whole life, I think. What an irony it would be if Harry's alter ego documents, his pride and joy as a lawyer as long as I have known him, now may disclose his role as the sheriff's coschemer.

I make no mention of Territorial Investors. I make no mention of Harry's complicity in forging wills. I do not tell about Lilly Trask. But Miriam's power of attorney naming me as her attorney-in-fact is setting my coat pocket on fire. The documents inside my pocket and briefcase make me look like a Harry King clone.

"I'll check out the estate records I can find," I state flatly. "I don't have them all. Believe it or not, I've never been in Harry's office."

Jerry points at me. "Understand something, Nate. I'm after the sheriff. King is small potatoes, but I'd love to trap him into turning Iffert inside out. I can't subpoena a public official. That tips my hand. But if I get King, he can give me Iffert."

Jerry can't stop sneering, even when he is trying to persuade me to help him. "I'm looking for proof that King took money on false authority. If you give me that, I guarantee the investigation of your departure from DC will end, and you'll get your ticket to practice law. If you go to King and sell this investigation down the river"—the half smile again splits his face—"the loss of your license will be the least of your problems."

Dwyer extracts a calfskin wallet from his suit coat and flips a business card to me. My hands are shaking.

He smirks. "Maybe you lost the last one. Well, don't lose this. When you have what I want, you get in touch. And make it soon."

CHAPTER 24

Nathan Gets Advice from Katie

* * *

KATIE AND I WALK ACROSS the Todd Park lawn one late June day, across the baseball field Ritchie owned with his sweeping catches and towering slammers, past the cedar picnic tables and river-rock grills, over to the swings and teeter-totters. The sky is cloudy and uncertain; rain is unlikely, but so is a late-day burst of sun.

My tie hangs loose, and the grass clippings from the latest mowing coat my wing tips. I couldn't care less. I begged Katie to leave Tiffany with Phyllis for an hour, and she relented, throwing on a pair of running shoes and baggy gray sweats. Her hooded blue varsity sweater reveals the rise of her breasts underneath. It reads "WESTERN WASHINGTON."

The day has exploded into a kaleidoscope of consequences for me that I can't handle alone. Driving home I weighed going to Riva. What good will that do? I thought. She'll be offended that until today I have left her in the dark. Ultimately she'll treat this as more proof of my imbecilic lack of judgment.

And Harry? I'm a jailbird to even contemplate communicating with him until Dwyer and the state arrest the sheriff. Besides, Harry has used me all along. That is not going to change. I suspect he wanted the money moved to his control in Haver Limited because he is sensing the net over the sheriff is about to drop, and it could trap him as well.

Even now it is hard for me to see Harry in a rage, killing Si, but everything leads to Harry's calculated execution of him to gain control over the cash pool Si had stored in Territorial Investors. If Harry knows one-tenth of what I have found out in Seattle, his bags are packed already, however inconceivable it is to me that he could leave Bethell.

And Frank Galitzer, a person I have never been able to talk to even after traipsing weekly into his house for piano lessons over ten years, seems unsmart, too mired in the travails of a disabled son and betrayal by his now dead older brother. And Harry has him distracted. The forgery of Si's will leaving Rivers End to Miriam is simply a ploy to keep Frank from following the money from Haver Limited to Harry.

That leaves Katie. Whatever chance we may have, whether as lovers, as friends, or as expeditioners searching for a common life, turns on a feeling of trust. I believe I am willing to try, but I find it hard to see how she could trust me. That's what Phyllis was talking about. Katie has been disappointed twice, maybe more. And how can I, with this built-in set of alliances and beliefs that are tied up in my Jewish genes and lashed to my biological and communal family, be trusted with Tiffany? That is Katie's acid test. Phyllis told me that clear as a bell.

I plop down in a swing seat made of an old tire carcass. Katie does the same next to me.

"When I was a kid I loved to swing," I say. "I used to believe the higher I pumped, the farther I could see."

"That's funny," Katie says. "Me too. At night after the sunset, I would stand up while swinging away. When I stood on the seat and really got going, I could reach all the way up to the stars. I swear."

We push off a little, each of us guided by a small breeze and the memory of a common dream that we can untether somehow from the earth and reach a higher place of peace and beauty.

"If you sigh any deeper," Katie says, "I'm taking you to the hospital. Now, what's up?"

I tell her only of my second run-in with Jerry Dwyer and the connection between my application for reinstatement and the investigation of Iffert. I tell her about Harry's letter to the bar calling my application into question. I leave out the details about Seattle First Bank and that I obtained Miriam's power of attorney. Katie listens and swings. I watch her face for judgment, but she remains placid and serious, moving about without responding. Silence builds between us as the sky darkens.

When Katie finally speaks, it seems her voice is coming from a different place, a world she has chosen not be a part of.

"Everyone knows that Iffert and King are in cahoots," she says. "The trailer park is famous. The jokes about the girls there are circulated daily at the Harbor Café. 'That's where you'll end up' is what all the local mothers would threaten their daughters with before they went out on their weekend dates.

"Wake up, Nathan. You told me about Harry's bail scheme with the deputies as if this is operated under some blanket somewhere. Do you think this started with Cal Iffert? I don't. The Skarbells wouldn't want it any other way. Their workers get drunk on Saturday night and go back on the line on Monday. Who cares how it's done? That's how creatures like Iffert keep their jobs."

Katie shudders in disgust. She has stopped her small rhythmic swinging. Her left foot has dragged her still.

"What I find odd is that you're genuinely surprised by all of this." She looks at me with her head cocked. "It's as if you missed the train at the common sense station. For the last three months, since Si Galitzer was murdered, you've worked hand in glove with the one person who probably benefits the most from his death."

The hand in the glove. First Lynn Reilly, then Harry King.

I try to wiggle away from the truth. "I feel Uncle Harry held my family together when my dad died. How can I fault a man who got bagels and cream cheese for a bunch of little kids—not his kids, mind you—every Sunday, year in and year out, so they would feel special about being Jewish, even living as we do now, far from places where we might feel we belong?"

There. I've said it to Katie. Straight up and no frills. *We all*; we Jews. We are different. And unique. It's a pitch I have thrown to her as if she is a batter standing ready to swing. She does not miss, even in the dark.

"That makes it worse, not better." Katie speaks so fiercely to me, I am overjoyed. Her caring is manifested by her disappointment in someone important to her: me.

"The hard part," she states, "is that your family has been enriched by every bit of it. Oh, I can see this being like a protection plan. But you're like those fish around the mouth of a shark. Eating the leftovers. And for generations, that's what you've done. Why is it a surprise there's a bit for the sheriff, that the girls setting your mother's and grandmother's hair at Irma's earn a few bucks on their backs at the trailer park? Does that have something to do with being Jews? I doubt that."

Katie is haggard with truth telling. The pain is visible on her face. She has it pegged right. The compromise of sticking together in this small place means principles be damned. Maybe if Ritchie didn't die, maybe if my dad cared about me, maybe I would know what to do.

Katie pushes her swing over to mine, grabs my chain with her left hand, and places her right on my knee to hold me close by.

"I have something to tell you, something that is so deep within me I would like to believe it didn't happen. But it did. When Ritchie and I…" She stops for a moment, gathering momentum like a tidal surge. "You know, we made love those many years ago, I got pregnant. I was sixteen. I had an abortion in Seattle. Harry arranged it. For a fee, of course. Your dad paid it all. And life went on. I was too young."

The sun is trying to peek out from behind a cloud over the Olympics, but it is losing the battle against obscurity. Katie's voice is relentless, but her eyes are full of tears.

"This was before my life had even begun." She weeps as the words tumble from her memory. "Your brother just ran away. I had to make up my own mind when I was sixteen." I remember that handkerchief in my pocket and hand it to Katie. Her fingers touching mine vibrate with love. She blows her nose, wipes her eyes, and begins again.

"Then a week ago, Harry called me. He said if I didn't stop seeing you, he would tell you about the abortion. I tell you this now so you'll know who you've been dealing with your whole life."

Katie's face has lost its angles in grief. Her eyes are swollen and reddening. She has no more to give me this evening on the swings in Todd Park, no strength to stand and pump up to the stars. Just enough love in her to break my heart.

"Make it right this time," she whispers, getting off the swing. "Now take me home."

* * *

I call Jerry Dwyer the next day. I have in my possession every signed durable power of attorney, every will, and every bank document signed by my family, the Galitzers, and the Kings, all either notarized by Harry or naming Harry. It is impressive. Pearl's and Leon's wills, Riva's will, Si's will, and Frank's and Mae's wills. I even found the late Morris Galitzer's will. Each person named Harry at one time or another as the holder of the power of attorney. Harry's name and signature are everywhere.

I also have Harry's signature on copies of real property deeds from the county auditor's office on a myriad of property deals since Si's death. To avoid being seen seeking the public records at the county courthouse, I ask Phyllis to retrieve them for me. Harry, as managing partner of Territorial Investors, has been selling real estate and signing deeds.

These are the documents Jerry requested. In and of itself, the task is hardly a difficult one for an investigator. My sense is Jerry is a little lazy, but, more important, he wants the pleasure of having his bespoke English shoe on my chest. Only a small part of me resents the arrogance he manifests. I repeat to myself, "As long as I get what I want, why should I care that I'm dealing with a bully? This is my part of the deal."

To get Dwyer's assurance that I have done what he asked, I have prepared a letter thanking me for my cooperation and stating that the office of the attorney general does not stand in the way of the activation of my license to practice law in Washington. Read between the lines.

I call Dwyer and tell him he will have to meet with me to get the documents. "I'll be at the Everett courthouse tomorrow at three. I want you to review them with me and assure me you are satisfied that I have helped you out."

"Nate, you sound like you don't trust me." I can hear Jerry smirking over the phone. He delays for minute. "OK," he says, his chewing gum smacking in his mouth through the phone.

* * *

Dwyer gets out of a government-issue car in front of the Everett courthouse. I rush over before he enters the front door. My stuff is in a cheap file under my arm. Dwyer is wearing a blue blazer with a maize shirt and madras tie.

I am in charge here. I have what he wants.

"Don't you ever dress for the country?" I ask.

Dwyer is caught off guard by my remark, and for a moment he looks almost abashed. Then the armor reappears.

"So what do you have for me?" he asks sternly, his hand out.

"Before I give you this," I state, "there is more I have to say. One, I hadn't a clue before our meeting about Iffert, but the entire town and possibly the entire county does. My point is this: it's not me who's been talking about Iffert's activities. I intend to leave Bethell, not stick around. So if the sheriff knows you're on the lookout for him, don't knock on my door."

"OK," Jerry says. "Now that you have that off your chest, give me what you found."

"First this item," I say. I hand over my letter on top of the file. It reminds Dwyer of his promise made in front of Arthur Curtis.

Dwyer reads my letter. "Fine," he says after each line. "I'm good with this." He signs at the bottom, using the file as a portable table, but hesitates to give it back to me.

"Well, Nate, there is one more thing." His tone is softer now that the file I've brought him in exchange for his promises is in his hands. He seems embarrassed, almost apologetic. "A thing I'm afraid only you can do. We are aware that the word is out, and we're going to pick up the sheriff this afternoon. He'll be charged here in Everett, not in Bethell. A subpoena server has tried to get to King, and he's nowhere to be found."

He hands me a folder. "Your last job, Nate. You find King and serve this."

Jerry has handed me an investigative subpoena, returnable to an inquiry judge in the Everett superior court.

"Once you do this," he says, "I am out of your life. I don't need your testimony. All I want to know from you is that you stuck this in his hands. Then I put your letter in the mail."

They now want me to find Harry. My final break from him will be a personal act of betrayal, face-to-face. It is on the level of Brutus stabbing Caesar. My grievance with him, his deliberately destructive letter to the bar, will be matched paper for paper. An eye for an eye.

My fingers are stone, and I drop the subpoena folder. I stop and pick it up.

My life apart from Harry has begun.

CHAPTER 25

In Harry's Lair

* * *

JERRY DWYER'S SUBPOENA FOR UNCLE Harry hangs out of my back pocket. If I see Uncle Harry and serve him, I am off the hook, and my problems are over with the bar association. I can leave Bethell and be gone forever. Then it occurs to me that Katie has drifted from my future. And how will it feel, I think, to be alone again?

As I walk around the corner of Lansing Avenue, toward the courthouse entrance to the sheriff's office, three state patrol cars are blocking the street. A Washington State patrol trooper in a Smokey Bear hat has the cuffed Sheriff Iffert by the arm. The patrolman does not look friendly as he pushes Iffert's big body to the patrol car with the same irreverence he would any drunken driver on a Saturday night, cupping his hand over Iffert's crewcut and shoving his dome into the backseat.

In the moment he ducks to clear the doorframe, Iffert's belly hangs down like a pregnant woman's, his jaw slack and foolish. Earl Strunk, the sheriff's lame-legged deputy, stands there in front of the sheriff's office, favoring his bad knee, leaning hard on the post holding up the office door overhang, a look of bafflement on his face.

And Harry is next. They would never look for him at the Varney Building, the office he never uses. I run down Fulton, the street empty, the clip-clop of my steps the only sound. Across from Steve's Diner, the two-story brick building is as dark and empty as ever, its windows shuttered with weathered plywood, the front door barred, the streetlight in front an empty socket.

It is a quick sprint to the back alley. There are no cars behind the building. The tandem rear doors are built to swing in. I shove the first with no success, but the second opens a crack. I push in hard, and it opens into a barren, unfinished room with exposed studs on all walls. Swirls of dust surround each of my steps on the unfinished plank floor. Past the door are piles of newspapers, old tires, ancient tools, and an open doorway to a dark stairwell. Above the staircase a shaft of June afternoon light drops down through an old wire-mesh glass skylight.

At the top of the stairs is an open door; on the wall next to it a number two is painted in black over brown peeling paint. The stairs groan at my passage. This is the office Uncle Harry would never let me visit.

Pandemonium rules the room. Boxes are strewn open on the floor, a swivel chair lies on its side, and there's a smell of liquor mixed with cat urine. Rodent droppings. A lawyer's safe, black and dusty, sits in the corner, the door ajar. No Uncle Harry in sight.

I pull out the safe's top drawer. Wills stitched to parchment backings cascade out in no apparent order. They date back to the '30s.

Stuffed into a Florsheim shoebox are old black-and-white photos of Uncle Harry. In one he is wearing a two-toned short-sleeve sport shirt. He might be thirty-five years old, handsome, his hair lubricated and wavy. Harry is sitting on the bumper of a Caddy convertible, one leg bracing his haunch. He looks like a movie star about to leap into action.

There is one of Harry walking on a sunny, marquee-studded street. He is wearing sunglasses and that same two-toned sport shirt, but in this one he has a pretty girl on his arm. Her other bare arm is swinging. She is wearing a pleated summer skirt. She's what my dad would have called a real looker. A sign on a store behind them reads "*Se Vende*." Maybe they're in Mexico, maybe Cuba.

I pick up another photo. Harry is seated at a dining table posing with the same girl. She holds a cigarette, and the camera dutifully records the smoke winding its way upward.

I peer inside the safe. In the back a new white stationery box, totally out of place, catches my attention. It appears to contain unused envelopes, but they bulge. I extract the first envelope. Inside are ten bills, each one worth a thousand dollars. I have never seen a thousand-dollar bill. Each bears the engraved replica of Grover Cleveland.

There are ten envelopes absolutely identical in appearance. I shuffle through all ten. Each holds the same number of bills, each trim and crisp, as if starched and ironed. Stuffed inside a suitcase, they would be undetectable. One hundred thousand dollars. A fortune.

The sound of a car, it sounds like Harry's Buick, comes up the staircase from the alley; then it stops. It is as if the car is parked in the hallway. I look up, and Uncle Harry is in the doorframe. His hair is combed, and instead of his usual khaki coat he wears a gray suit, a white shirt, a black tie, and black polished shoes.

Harry's courtroom clothes, I think. He is dignified looking, almost a stranger. I grab the wad of stuffed envelopes.

"So you're adding breaking and entering to your repertoire, boychick," Harry says. He looks tired, though, not the usual ebullient Harry.

"No one is here to be fooled, Uncle Harry. You mucked up your room here, not me. You wanted to make it look like a break-in. I think you killed Uncle Si just to get control of Territorial Investors and the titles to all that real estate. He was the last obstacle."

I shift to the light to see him better. "You had Uncle Si's power of attorney so you could control Territorial Investors, but I think he was about to revoke it. I bet that's what the argument was about the night you killed him."

Harry can't speak, but his eyes have not blinked while I've talked. They continue to glare straight at me, black and intense, trying to intimidate me. Not this time, although I am shaking. It is the same adrenaline I felt in front of Reverend Cook's jury in closing argument. I have Lynn Reilly's absolute moment in me, the ballet of the courtroom.

When you know all the facts.

"You needed the money," I say, "because you got caught in the investigation of Sheriff Iffert. You needed to cover up your payoffs to that whole bunch in the sheriff's office, but there are too many folks involved. There were too many payoffs. And too many people knew about the hookers you and the sheriff kept out in the trailer park. Too many deputy sheriffs over the years got your kickbacks for tipping you off after they made a drunken-driving arrest. Too many deputies were on to the phony loans you arranged for your so-called clients when you bailed them out of jail."

Harry clears his throat. "First of all, give me that money, Nathan." He uses his angry, authoritative voice.

I pull back. "What are you going to do?" I challenge him. "Call the sheriff? Too late. My arrangement is with the attorney general's office. It's simple. You get served a subpoena with my help. That's all. Then you can't stop me from getting my bar license back. So go ahead, Uncle Harry. Use the phone. But who are you going to call?"

He looks astonished.

"Uncle Harry, I now know all about your shenanigans with my life. I've seen your letter to the bar association describing why Lynn Reilly fired me." I'm shouting now. "You wanted to hold what happened in DC over my head just in case I got wise to you and wouldn't go along with your schemes. But just when I think you've done every evil act possible, you hit rock bottom. You called up Katie Martin, your client when she was only sixteen years old, and you threatened that you would disclose she had an abortion. Ritchie's baby. So much for your notion of attorney-client privilege, Uncle Harry."

I rant on. "I bet you paid off Lilly Trask too. She's run off, you know. Or maybe she's dead too. I can't find her anywhere. So who do you kill next, Uncle Harry? Is it going to be me?"

I'm panting. I hold the envelope box high and away, as if it's a spear and I'm about to hurl it at Harry.

He purses his lips. "I need a smoke."

Carefully he sets up the overturned office chair and sits down. He reaches into his overcoat pocket and pulls out a Cuban. He twirls it in his fingers, rolling his lips about it, and then lights it, letting the smoke linger in front of his face. In spite of it all, I inhale the rich scent of Caribbean tobacco.

Harry crosses his legs and points the cigar my way. "You're just like me, you know. If I'd had a son, I would have wanted him to be just like you, Nathan. Adversity doesn't stop you. You use people to get what you want when you want it. And so what if they get hurt? They're all grown-ups. But this is a new high-water mark. Or maybe a low one. Who knows? Working against your Uncle Harry, against your family."

"Family?" I say with heat. "You, who forged Si's will? You, who lied that my dad had no will? All of it so you alone, Harry, could be in charge as everybody's everyman. But loyal? To no one but yourself. My family has got nothing to do with this."

As I'm talking I feel the presence of my dad and Ritchie as well. They have entered the room with the waning light of the day. Zolly King, Zayde Albert, and Grandpa Morris, all of their eyes are watching the two of us. I can feel them. And somewhere there is Uncle Si too. I hold out the envelopes toward Harry, the hard evidence of theft.

"Is this little stash for the family, Harry? No, sir. You're taking the partnership money, money that belongs to three other families, for yourself."

Our otherworldly visitors can see the money box too. Those visitors, they are my jury now. They are about to confirm the rightness of my accusations, the wrongness of Uncle Harry's conduct. I see interest on their faces, but no one speaks.

Harry waves the smoke away from his face. "If that's what you want to believe, it's OK. We got to go back a ways to make this all make sense to you, and I ain't got all day. But if I was you, I'd ask why your dad didn't get himself in big trouble with his girlfriend, Harriet. And why Si didn't get into big trouble over his daughter, Miriam. Why is it that Frank Galitzer never got caught with his pants down, so's Mae would have to live her life in this place with that embarrassment?"

Harry's eyes were solemn now, not frightened or amazed.

"You think about human nature, buddy boy, and who's left to make our little life here all acceptable. That's what I been doing, just as my dad—*alava sholem*, bless him—Grandpa Morris, and your grandpa Albert did before me.

"So you got all upset about the trailer park. Let me tell you—that business is not even worth the time and the money. It's what the sheriff does for the mill hands. It keeps them happy. They keep the sheriff happy. So we collect a little rent on property gonna turn into a freeway someday, just like Morris said it would. Just rent we collect. That's all. Sheriff is the operator, not me. Not Si either, by the way." Harry draws on the cigar, the smoke clouding the faces in the room listening to every word he utters.

"You want to know about Uncle Si?" Harry says. "OK. I'm not perfect, but here's what went wrong. First it's about Frank, not your old man or me or anybody else. Frank can't stop thinking about what happens to Victor someday when he and Mae are dead and the twins are gone. The twins got no brains between them, as you well know."

A light sweeps the alley and casts away shadows across the room. The ghosts of Bethell are all listening to Harry too. He has the rapt attention of three generations.

"So Frank says to me, 'Help me make a deal with Si. Let's make a deal,' he says. 'Can't my brother, who's got Rivers End and all that other property he's squirreled away, can't Si set up something for Victor?' Of course Frank don't know about Miriam, but Si's got a heart. Plus Victor's his nephew. It's kin after all."

Harry gets up and walks to the window. The ghosts part to let him by. It's dark outside now.

"You didn't tell anybody where you were going, did you, Nathan?"

I shook my head.

"You're sure of that?"

"I'm sure."

"We don't have much time." Harry turns to me. The cigar has gone out; the room has grown cold. The ghosts have brought with them the chill of judgment.

"See, Frank was careful not to go to Si directly," Harry says. "I did it for him and said, 'Si, where I'm coming from, there's enough money in the highway deal to make everybody happy. Let's help Mae and Victor. I'll throw in a little of it too. Hell, I got no kids.' So Si said, 'Send him over sometime. Let Mr. Union Buster who broke his father's heart come to me. Maybe I'll help, and maybe I won't.'"

Harry is lost in the past now. He sees the room filled with the generations before us, and he gestures to the wall away from me. They are his jury too. He needs to uncover a doubt for them as well.

"I mean, it was a bad moment," Harry recalls. "I almost lost all respect for Si right then. But I said nothing against him, nothing to set him off. I went at it another way. I said, 'You got that one daughter, OK, who you never saw, and why not help out? Do it for Morris, for God's sake. Victor's his grandson.' I pulled out all the stops. It was a symphony."

Harry has become his own audience, facing the wall, his bull-low voice bouncing over me from the corner to the places where the ghosts fill the room.

"I didn't get a no, but I didn't get a yes either. So I left it that Frank was to see him. Why not? I figured this would do it. I proposed a time, and it was at his place to make it easy. And that was the only reason too, by the way.

"That day—the day Si died—Si called me and told me to meet him at the store with Frank. He didn't want to meet Frank alone. But by the time I got there, Si was lying there in the dark, a piece of his head left on the counter and his wig fulla blood.

"This is where things get complicated," Harry says between puffs as he lights the cigar again. "I call Wally. I tell him to do a job for me. He owes me on an old bond, his house is in foreclosure, his wife is living with her mother, so I can help him big.

"I say, 'Wally, find me some real estate records in Si's tonight. File called Territorial Investors. Papers only. And leave the money in the cash drawer alone,' I say, but I know he can't stand to see the dough. So before I leave, I salt Si's till with fifteen hundred bucks, and of course when Wally breaks in and sees the body, he freaks out, but not enough to leave the cash behind. He takes the cash, and you know the rest."

"So now you say Frank killed his brother? How convenient for you."

"Was I there?" Harry holds his hands in a questioning pose. "You wanted to know how this thing unraveled—but see here, Mr. You Go and Figure It All Out. Frank will never tell, and it looked like it could have been an accident to me. Who knows what Cain and Abel really did to each other? Anyways, it's a store, for Christ's sake. There are zillions of fingerprints everywhere, no firearms. Who's gonna settle on one set of prints versus another? Plus Clyde McPhee goes in there and mucks the whole scene up anyway."

"Then why did you forge Si's will?" I ask. "You took the property away from Frank twice."

Harry is back at the window again. "So you figured that out too, did you?" His voice has real respect. "Look, this way nobody suspects Frank. He didn't get anything with his brother dead. Besides, either way, the girl gets at least half of the property, will or no will. Nobody's ever going to know. Cain and Abel repeats itself all over again." He shakes his head like a hound dog. The jurors do not stir.

My body is wet, and I am shivering with cold. It's dark, and the rain has begun. Si now stands in front of Grandpa Morris and Zayde Albert, who is in front of Bubbe Hirsch. He is nodding his head, as if to say it's basically all right. Their mouths open, and the cold has become unbearable. I cannot speak.

This group of friends, this *havera*, they kept one another together here in this little corner of the world, far from where their journeys had started. Somehow they knew what they should do. Would that they could tell me what I should do.

"So what's next?" Harry says. His breath is blue and illuminated.

"Where's Lilly Trask?"

"She's a decent person," Harry acknowledges, "just another one of those girls who got stuck on the farm and wanted something better. Well, she's got it. Her kid took her in. That's what money can do for you. They all changed their names and vamoosed. And believe me on this, nobody's ever going to find that one. They are dependent on nobody, but nobody, anymore. Not even a trace. Can't blame her a bit."

I've almost forgotten that Uncle Harry has taken advantage of me as well. "You left me high and dry. Writing the bar association. And then you threatened Katie for no reason at all. As if our family hasn't hurt her enough. That and that alone is reason for me to give you this." I take the subpoena out of my back pocket.

"But you're not Lilly Trask," he says. Harry is talking to the jury too, and the room is filled with nodding heads. "The only place you got to work is here. You turn on me, then everybody will know. Lawyering is about trust. Why should they trust a guy who doesn't have a clue about loyalty? They say love makes the world go round. I say no. It's trust. It's that the system makes you safe only if someone can teach you how it works, somebody to help you get on your feet, to reach the pedals, so to speak."

He holds out his hand, palm up.

"Go ahead. Gimme the damn thing if you want. Then you can tell everybody you served me. I'm leaving anyway, but remember this, boychick: they will turn on you whether I get this piece of crap or not. Here, give it to me."

Harry snatches the subpoena from my hand. He reads it for a minute and snorts as he recites the top to the jury. They are spellbound by his voice.

"Fail not to appear at your own peril." Harry mimics solemnity. "What a crock."

I stand helplessly. What should I do? What should I say? Harry's right about it all. In the end of days, no one really cares unless it's your family.

Harry breaks the silence. "Listen, you can tell them now that you've been a good boy." His voice has become soft, sympathetic. The faces in the room are cloudy, foreboding. "There's a good bottle under the file in the left desk drawer, and I need a drink. Grab it for me. My old bones won't let my knees bend."

I turn and open the drawer. A Crown Royal whiskey flask, my dad's favorite, and two shot glasses are lying next in the bottom. I hand the glasses to Harry, then the bottle. He pours one and hands it to me.

"Here," he says, "take a drink. It won't kill you."

I hesitate, then reach for the glass. After all, it is just Uncle Harry. My bar mitzvah tutor, my support for law school, my model.

I hear the moans from the jury as I take the glass from his hand. It is ice cold. I swallow the liquor. I can barely feel it in the back of my throat. I can't swear that he poured one for himself, but Uncle Harry's head goes back with a jolt, the shot glass on his thick lips. He looks like the Harry in those old pictures in the safe, taking life right down the gullet.

Immediately my head reels. I am too wired to be touching liquor. As I lean on the desk to steady myself, I hear a roar in my ears. Was the drink doctored, a Mickey? Has Harry set me up again?

I try to speak, but my lips are stone. I try to grasp Harry's escape money, just one more chance to prevent him from leaving, but the envelopes fall through my fingers to the floor. Harry sweeps them into his pocket as he moves to the doorway.

"You take care of Pearl now, Nathan. And Riva too. Maybe check in on Miriam out there at Rivers End." Harry's words float through the fog of the drug, and then he is gone.

The room goes black and cold, but Ritchie is holding me up, his smooth muscled arms around my waist and chest. I grasp him too in waves of gratitude and love. Here I am being held again in my big brother's huge hands and strong arms, warm again, my body feeling safe and alive. My dad, Leon, stands over me, watching. Zayde Albert and Bubbe Hirsch lean in to look at me, to let me know they're with me.

I hear Ritchie say, "He'll be fine." Then suddenly my family is gone. They have left me to make my own way in this cold and dirty room, in this, my brand-new world.

I hear the door below being pried open by a crowbar. I try to rise to my feet, but I can't tell which way is up, and my head crashes toward the floor. This second time no one catches me, and I travel into the void alone.

CHAPTER 26

The Chosen One

* * *

"THEY SAY EVERY MAN MUST need protection; they say every man must fall." I keep humming this Bob Dylan song as the verdant August 1974 day turns toward the end of summer, and September looms, gilding the alder leaves with red and gold. Nixon is gone now. I watched the whole sorry episode with some compassion for the president, even the maudlin, self-serving way he said good-bye, awash in self-pity. I have danced on the edge of that knife myself. I recognize the power of feeling sorry for yourself. It's a wonderful emotion.

Like Nixon, Uncle Harry King is gone as well. After a year there still is no trace of him, although Auntie Riva repeats a rumor that some travelers on a Jewish Federation mission from Seattle to Israel ran into Harry in Tel Aviv.

"They said he looked like a fish out of water with the Israelis." Auntie Riva laughs at the thought of Hebrew Harry. "All in all I still miss having Harry around." For a moment her perpetual frown has turned away, and her eyes sparkle with the mirth of the moment.

The funds from the sale of Territorial Investors' real property on the Tamlips Reservation have been impounded and placed in the hands of a court-appointed receiver. Some money belongs to Leon's trust, some to Uncle Frank and Auntie Mae, and some to Uncle Si's estate. The rest—the King share allocated to Uncle Harry and his brother, Dale—will probably be offset by the myriad of lawsuits that have been filed since his departure.

The lack of income from Territorial Investors won't matter to Pearl. There's enough for her from the Levy family settlement without worries for the rest of her life. Uncle Bob Levy has seen to it that she receives her checks from the family business she and he inherited. The Levys were right in the end. Their Iowa business makes Territorial Investors and Haver Limited profits look like peanuts.

Uncle Frank Galitzer is dying of cancer. Auntie Mae has all but told me so with her sad eyes. It is not possible to take care of him at Rivers End the way he and Uncle Si took care of their father when he lay dying of the disease. Instead Uncle Frank lies in the ICU in Everett General Hospital and could go at any time. I wonder if the story Uncle Harry told me was real and whether some force of justice is at work in decreeing Frank's terrible illness as retribution for fratricide.

Under Uncle Si's real will, Frank inherited more than enough to provide for Auntie Mae and Victor, unless someone were to kick over the can and proclaim Frank a murderer. It's no surprise, but the law doesn't let slayers inherit from their victims. However, no one has bothered to ask Wally Richmond about Uncle Si's death since his release from Monroe. Wally won't volunteer anything without a check.

The minute that Frank became too ill to work, his store, Frank's Western Emporium, that antiunion canker sore that had stuck in the throat of Morris Galitzer, was shut down, as was Uncle Si's Union Wear, its rival across the street. Strangely, the departure of the Galitzers' competing men's stores has left scars on Fulton Street. The Hirsch Building, occupied by Fulton Jewelry, was for a while the only building on the street with a retail business in it.

In the meantime I have found new tenants for the space behind Fulton Jewelry. It's a bunch of hippie-looking craftsmen working as a collective to manufacture mandolins and zithers. I was a little reluctant to do business with them, but one of the group whispered to me, "Don't let the clothes fool you." I took that admonition to heart and have been pleasantly surprised. They ship all over the world, and the rent adds a few shekels for the common good of the Hirsch family.

I also helped the next-door neighbors on Fulton Street lure a coffee shop with an espresso machine. They hung up a few paintings on the wall, and the next thing, the theretofore empty Fulton Street shops developed a small gallery-antiques-and-restaurant thing. On weekends the Seattleites come to Bethell to look for bargains and sip coffee. Maybe Bethell has a future as a tourist attraction.

As hard as it is to believe, both of the Galitzers, Miriam and Uncle Frank, asked me to finish Uncle Si's estate as soon as Harry disappeared. It's complicated. I have gone to Seattle and hired a first-rate accounting firm to compile a real inventory of Si's estate and liabilities. Taxes are due to the feds and to the state of Washington. They will take their toll. When it's all said and done, Miriam and Frank's family will split the proceeds from the sale of Rivers End.

Auntie Mae has opened her home and her heart to Miriam. "I feel like I found a daughter," Auntie Mae fondly says. It's called *kvelling* in Yiddish. Miriam absolutely laps up Auntie Mae's affection like a starving street cat.

It turns out the Galitzer twins and Miriam hit it off like brothers and sister. They all got loaded together on acid in midsummer out back by the meadow at Rivers End. The flower blossoms have been bursting out there in Technicolor ever since.

I am also helping out at Fulton Jewelry, basically to keep Auntie Riva company. She moans that the store is too much for her, but then in the next breath she declares, to my horror, that in honor of Zayde Albert she intends to keep the store open until its one hundredth anniversary—in 1991. That's seventeen years from now.

Uncle Si's death, Uncle Harry's departure, and Uncle Frank's illness have hastened Auntie Riva's natural gloom. She expresses her desire to write a memoir of the Hirsch family, some legacy that will somehow validate her singular life here. She is smoking a great deal.

I see my mother once a week. At first I brought in sandwiches from the Harbor Café, but in a strange burst of self-righteousness and renewed Jewish identity, she refuses to eat food that is not kosher. This, of course, is a first. As I was growing up, our refrigerator always had bacon and shellfish galore. But for Pearl this issue presents a theatrical moment, and with me as the audience, it is too rich. A real reversal for a former mimic.

With Harry gone, the case against Sheriff Iffert has gone cold for the want of a key witness, but the scandal has brought him down anyway. The county prosecutor, Al Zilstra, is also a victim. The commissioners deem that Al was asleep at the wheel, since the exposed corruption was running under his nose on the first floor of the county courthouse.

Zilstra's assistant, Scott Pelky, my tubby adversary in justice court, has gotten a promotion, although not the one he sought. The county commissioners have named him Al's replacement until a special election in September. The Democrats are licking their chops at the thought of running a candidate against Pelky, who has bulked up since his appointment, if that's possible.

My situation with the bar is not resolved yet. Dwyer has broken his promise to help me. He claims that he was relieved of his commitment because I had "tipped off" Uncle Harry. Arthur Curtis is noncommittal about the meeting we three had at the bar office in June 1973. The cloud over Harry and my role with him have supplanted the bar's interest in my departure from DC, and my license remains in limbo after a year and a half of inquiry into whether I had anything to do with the corruption in the Snoline County sheriff's office.

I hired a Seattle lawyer who negotiated a semihearing for me with a committee of the board of governors; that took place last week. After all this time, the event was more of an informal meeting. The three board members in attendance were kindly old geezers who suggested I had been, at worst, disingenuous when I returned to Washington. I thought my meeting went well, but you never know. I might be reinstated when the full board meets in September.

Katie and I stayed away from each other for a while after the sheriff was arrested and Uncle Harry disappeared. I suspected that some of the ghosts I'd seen in Uncle Harry's office were appearing in her life too, whenever she would think of my family and me.

Then, last November, Katie stopped in the store. She said Sears was sending her to check on my vacuum-cleaner bags as a part of their warranty program and asked if I would mind "demoing" the machine sometime for her.

In that moment I felt some hope that our relationship could renew and grow. When spring came around, I bought fancy running shoes with Katie's help. I resolved that I would actually improve myself by becoming a runner with some expert coaching, which she agreed to provide.

On sunny days I take Tiffany to Todd Park. I taught her to swing, which she loves. She now behaves as if I have given her the secret to the universe.

Katie and I are now up to having dinner together with Tiffany two and three times a week, and that wonderful five-year-old eats off my plate, as if I belong. She is no longer asking her mother why I have to stay overnight.

I have slowed myself down considerably since my days in DC, and my career as a mimic is behind me. I am not sure that Bethell will ever feel like home, but having Katie in my life brings another reality to me. It feels good to be in a family where what they call you doesn't matter as long as they call you to dinner. My appetite seems fine for what Katie is serving.

On Sunday nights I have Chinese food—an old Jewish tradition—with Katie, Tiffany, Riva, Phyllis, and her husband. It is my job on the day of rest to head south on Highway 90 to Everett and buy Chinese takeout. The honor afforded me for my service is first pick of the fortune cookies. My first foray into the cookie bag, with Katie and Tiffany looking on, revealed a fortune so remarkable that I mounted it in a shining chrome picture frame I took right out of Fulton Jewelry's inventory.

My fortune is inscribed on a tiny piece of low-rag-content paper, but it speaks volumes. I also realize that not only does it hold my fate, but it could be a quote from the Old Testament, a phrase as likely to be attributed to one of my biblical ancestors as to me:

"Among the lucky, you are the chosen one."

August 26, 1974